THE EXTINCTION CODE

Dean Crawford

ISBN: 1533067414
ISBN-13: 9781533067418
The right of Dean Crawford to be identified as author of this Work has
been asserted by him in accordance with sections 77 and 78 of the
Copyright, Designs and Patents Act 1988.

Dean Crawford

I

Varginha, Brazil

1996

'Move, and tell nobody where you're going!'

Corporal Rodrigo Martinez almost fell over himself as he dashed toward the truck parked nearby in the compound, one of several normally only used by engineers, not junior infantry soldiers. The Colonel had been precise in his instructions, adamant in fact, that Rodrigo should follow his orders to the letter, and there had been no mistaking in his cold tones the consequences of his failure to do so. *Be there on time, or you'll never see your family again.*

Rodrigo clambered into the truck and started the engine, the cab sweltering after a day spent stationary beneath a summer sun beating down from the hard blue sky above. Now, the sky was almost dark but for the last glow of sunset behind the hills, and the town to the south was a flickering constellation of lights against the darkness. The diesel engine belched a cloud of brown smoke as he crunched the vehicle into gear, the compound gates already opening as he accelerated forward and drove out of the Tres Coracoes Army base.

Rodrigo followed the road south as instructed, heading toward town and allowing nothing to block his route. The battered old truck rattled and thumped as Rodrigo drove, his rifle alongside him in the passenger seat. His police uniform was hot and uncomfortable but he was glad of the fresh breeze billowing in through the open cab windows. The smell of the wilderness gusted around him from the depths of the night, and it was then that he noticed the lights appearing in the sky.

Across the valley he could see a stream of lights descending the main road toward the outskirts of the city, heading it seemed toward the same location as he was. For a moment he thought that they were illuminated objects flying through the air until he recognized them as headlights, the occasional flare of a brake light visible as the vehicles braked while descending the steep hillside. Moments later, the radio was alive with chatter.

1

'*Lo has visto?* Have you seen it?'

'*No, donde esta?* Where is it?'

'*En la ciudad la gente tiene miedo.* In the city, the people are afraid.'

Rodrigo glanced at the radio, uncertain of what to make of the chatter as he descended the hillside and turned onto the beltway road that bypassed the city center and headed for the edge of the wild ground to the north–west. Ahead, he saw the other vehicles turn away from him, all heading in the same direction. Military Police, he identified their plates, streaming toward a location identical to his own.

Another voice on the radio channel.

'*De donde viene desde?* Where did it come from?'

The reply sent a cold chill down Rodrigo's spine.

'*Se bajo del cielo.* It came down from the sky.'

Suddenly the radio channel was cut off and Rodrigo could hear nothing but static. He twiddled the controls but nothing came through, the static hissing through the cab but the vehicles ahead of him still forging toward their target.

Rodrigo kept driving, pursued by the sense that something very odd was happening further up the road. He realized that he was gripping the wheel tightly, his knuckles showing white through his skin, and he chuckled at himself as he let his tension go and forced himself to relax as he drove. There was nothing to worry about, and whatever was driving the military police up the wall would likely turn out to be nothing more than a crashed airplane.

The thought that there could be injured survivors of an aircraft crash galvanized Rodrigo and he prepared himself for the worst. The region's harsh terrain and violent weather were often precursors to aviation accidents, and the horrific aftermath of such incidents haunted even the hardest of minds.

The convoy ahead of Rodrigo began to slow down, and he eased into line behind a four–ton truck loaded with soldiers. They peered out at him, faces hard, no smiles, no waves. Rodrigo kept his anxiety at bay, tried to ignore a clairvoyant concern nipping at the heels of his awareness as he saw the trucks being waved through a military cordon just ahead.

The armed guards at the makeshift cordon glanced at Rodrigo's identity card as he eased alongside them, and he saw one of the soldiers tick off his name against a list that he held in his hand. Rodrigo wondered how on earth he had been selected for what seemed like quite a major assignment as he was waved through the cordon and he followed the line of trucks down between ranks of trees toward an area that he knew to be mostly wasteland, scattered copses of trees around a lethargic stream that ran down from the hills.

The convoy suddenly split up before Rodrigo and formed a loose semi-circle of vehicles as the troops spilled out, their rifles held at the ready. They fanned out and away from their trucks, forming an imposing ring of soldiers as Rodrigo pulled up and killed the truck's engine. He climbed out of the cab and looked at the soldiers' faces; all of them were young, minor ranks and recruits. All of them were staring out toward him, their backs to whatever was in the center of the ring of trucks, apparently too cowed by their superiors into doing anything other than precisely what they were told.

'Maintain position!' a voice echoed faintly, the only officer that Rodrigo could see emerging from the ring of vehicles. 'Face outward and don't you dare look behind you or you'll spend the rest of your lives behind bars!'

The soldiers all yelled their compliance back at their Captain, and Rodrigo almost obeyed himself before he recalled that the Army man had no authority over him unless direct orders from the government said that he did. A tall man with a thick moustache and a back so straight it seemed he was on the verge of toppling over, directed his stern glare at Rodrigo.

'Martinez?'

It sounded more like an accusation than a request, and Rodrigo nodded. 'Yes sir.'

'With me,' the captain said.

Rodrigo noticed that although the officer wore the shoulder insignia of a captain, he could see no identification patches on his uniform. He hurried to keep pace as the officer directed him past the vehicles.

'Over there,' he ordered. 'You're on watch on the hillside. I've been advised that you're a model soldier, you were recommended. Ensure that you continue in that vein and stop anybody who tries to enter this area. Complete your duties and forget that you were ever here, understood?'

'Yes sir,' Rodrigo replied.

The captain turned away toward the nearby forest, and Rodrigo clambered up the hillside. As he climbed, so he saw a glow coming from within the forest nearby. It shimmered and flickered, one moment green, the next red, then blue and white, as though a kaleidoscope were passing across beams of light that pierced the misty forest gloom. Rodrigo flinched as a harsh whisper cut the silence.

'Don't look at it!'

Rodrigo turned to see a policeman standing on the hillside, beckoning him urgently over. 'They've already arrested two men for looking!'

Rodrigo hurried across to the young policeman, whose uniform bore the name Marco Eli Chereze.

'What's over there?' he asked.

'It came down an hour ago and I was close to the scene in my patrol car. That's why they kept me here on guard, because I'd already seen it.'

'Seen *what?*' Rodrigo asked in exasperation.

'The machine,' Marco replied, struggling for his words. 'That's all that I can call it.'

Rodrigo frowned in confusion and then a sharp crack echoed through the forest nearby and he flinched as he turned, one hand moving to the butt of the pistol in its holster at his side. Marco also turned, raised his rifle.

The faint glow from within the forest cast enough light through the foliage for Rodrigo to detect a hint of movement, as though something were huddling among the ferns and bushes nearby.

'You see that?' Rodrigo asked.

'Yes,' Marco replied, edging closer to it. 'It's probably a dog or something.'

Rodrigo followed him, one hand still on his pistol as they approached the bushes. Rodrigo was about to say something when Marco coughed and turned his head to one side in disgust, and then the smell hit Rodrigo too. An overpowering stench of ammonia soaked the air, sufficient that Rodrigo coughed also and his eyes blurred as he winced and turned away.

Marco covered his mouth with one forearm, the rifle held in one hand as he advanced. Rodrigo sensed danger and cried out, his voice taut.

'Don't go near it!'

The bushes shivered as whatever was within tried to escape as Marco came within a yard of the foliage.

'Come out whoever you are! We're police, and we're armed with...'

Marco's sentence was cut short by an inhuman screech, a terrifying, wretched cry that soared from the bushes across the hillside. Rodrigo felt his guts convulse as something leaped from the bushes, a thin yet muscular form with sinewy skin that shone in the faint light as it rushed at Marco, its small mouth agape and its huge eyes wide with rage.

Marco's rifle fired, the shot deafeningly loud in the darkness, and the creature's enraged cry was twisted sharply with agony as it swung for Marco. A long–fingered hand smashed across the young policeman's chest and hurled him backwards into the bushes as the creature rushed past them and vanished into the darkness.

Rodrigo stood in horror, paralyzed by what he had seen, his hand frozen in place on his pistol still lodged in its holster. His brain seemed to have gone into slow motion, processing and re–processing the terrible sight of that awful creature leaping from the darkness like a demon from his nightmares to...

Shouts alerted him and he heard men swarming up the hillside toward their position, search lights sweeping the forest as they rushed into the woods and saw Rodrigo standing rooted to the spot.

'Where is Chereze?!' the captain demanded as he stormed in among his men.

Rodrigo tried to reply but his voice would not work. Instead he simply pointed to the foliage nearby where Marco had fallen. The captain hurried across to see Marco hauling himself to his feet.

'Did you see it?!' the captain roared. 'Did it touch you?!'

Marco nodded. 'Here, it hit me, but it only knocked me over and...'

The captain turned away from Marco and spoke into his radio. Within minutes, the soldiers had surrounded them and doctors marched onto the hillside bearing a stretcher and a large tent of translucent plastic. Rodrigo stood and watched as they erected the tent and ordered Marco inside.

'But I'm fine,' Marco protested. 'Shouldn't we go after the...'

'Silence!' the captain roared. 'Put him in!'

Before Marco could react a doctor plunged a needle into his arm. Marco yelped in pain and staggered away from the medical team, but within moments his legs gave way beneath him and he collapsed onto the forest floor. Rodrigo watched as Marco was lifted onto a stretcher and into the tent, which was sealed behind him.

The captain turned and stalked toward Rodrigo.

'Did it touch you?' he demanded.

Rodrigo found that he could still not speak, so he shook his head slowly instead, his eyes fixed upon the tent into which Marco had vanished.

'Did you see it?'

Rodrigo swallowed, gathered his composure. 'No, it was just a shape, a figure in the darkness. What was it?'

The captain raised his chin and spoke clearly.

'It was a homeless man, a local, whom we believe to be armed and dangerous.'

Rodrigo's gaze moved across to the glowing lights in the forest. There, far away through the trees, he could just about discern the shape of something that was anything but an aircraft. He opened his mouth to speak, but the captain shifted position and blocked his view.

'You're dismissed, corporal,' he growled. 'You were not here. None of you were here. You have a sister, two brothers and a family of your own, yes?'

Rodrigo's attention snapped back to the captain, shocked that he would have such knowledge of his family. 'Yes?'

'If you love them, never speak of this again, understood?'

Rodrigo's eyes narrowed. 'Who are you, what regiment are you from?'

The captain took a pace closer to Rodrigo. '*Understood?*'

Rodrigo glanced at the soldiers surrounding them, and nodded once. 'Yes sir.'

'Escort this man away from the scene and ensure that he never, ever returns.'

Moments later Rodrigo was dragged down the mountainside by four men, a black sack over his head and sickening fear pulsing through his veins.

***

II

Hell Creek, Montana Badlands

2002

'It's out here somewhere.'

Doctor Aubrey Channing knew that he was in the right spot, if for nothing else than the sweltering heat of the sun hammering down into the barren valleys stretching before them. The brutal landscape had been carved by erosion through the ages, the tens of millions of years separating the upper mesas from the furnaces of the valley floors clearly visible as lines of horizontal strata etched by the endless procession of time into the living rock.

Channing crouched down onto one knee as he slid his rucksack from his back, and from within it he retrieved a hand written letter that he read again for the fiftieth time, the hairs on the back of his neck tingling as he did so. Individual lines leaped out at him, firing his determination as much now as when he had first read them a week before:

> *I can't bring myself to publicize what I have found...*
> *Nobody will believe me...*
> *It's located north–west of Jordan, Hell Creek.*
> *Do with it what you will...*
> *I want nothing to do with any of this.*

Channing checked a compass he had brought with him, set it down beside him on the rocks as he pinpointed their current location on the edge of Hell Creek's fearsome beauty using a map.

'You think that it's out here?'

The voice of Channing's companion, Rory Weisler, intruded upon the deep thoughts coursing through his mind. He nodded absent–mindedly. Weisler was a newspaper man instructed to bring the letter to Channing;

enthusiastic, talented and intelligent, he lacked the discipline of silence that was the hallmark of the true scientist. Interrupting a thought process was the academic equivalent of pointing a gun at your own mother.

'It's here,' Channing said as he plotted a course down into the shimmering waves of heat trembling out of a valley to their west that twisted like a wounded serpent through the bare rock. 'It's close.'

Channing stood, slung his rucksack across his shoulder and marched down the slope toward the valley floor. Weisler followed, never more than a few footsteps behind as they carefully negotiated the rock–strewn paths into the depths of Hell Creek.

The formation was one of the most intensively studied anywhere on earth and stretched between Montana, North and South Dakota and Wyoming, overlying the Fox Hills formation where they now trod. Channing had spent his entire career out here, sweating on his knees beneath the ferocious sun rummaging through ancient rocks that had once been brackish clays and sandstones deposited along river channels and deltas at the end of the Cretaceous Period, some sixty five million years before. An interior seaway surrounded by sub–tropical forest had once occupied this area, a stark difference from the arid sun–baked rocks crunching beneath their boots as they descended.

Channing had been approached by Weisler after the reporter had received an anonymous letter from somebody who could only have been an academic working in the same field of science as Channing: paleontology. The precise nature of the script, the naturally flowing choice of words, the carefully placed and equally carefully concealed hints and tips to the location of the subject of the letter suggested a superior intelligence. Channing figured by the postmark that the correspondence had come from out east, maybe one of the prestigious halls of academia in New York City, but he hadn't had the time to investigate and track down his mysterious benefactor due to a single line in the letter:

It's exposed, and will not survive long the harsh elements of Hell Creek...

The crumbling rock faces gave way to slopes, where scattered clumps of hardy grass clung to life amid the scorching rock faces. Channing surveyed the strata around him, colorful stripes across the hills that denoted the passing of history before their very eyes.

'Why are there lines all across the hills?'

Weisler's voice sounded stark in the silence, louder and perhaps a touch more irritating than Channing would have liked. Why the author of the letter, having wanted nothing to do with whatever he had found out here, would then request a media man to assist Channing in his search made no sense whatsoever. The newspapers rarely managed to record anything accurate, their methods diametrically opposed to the careful accumulation of data used by science to ascertain truth *before* revealing it to the world.

'The lines are sedimentary strata,' Channing explained patiently. 'Here in Hell Creek, erosion of softer rock by rivers and wind exposes hillsides formed from other, harder rocks and the strata they contain, laid down over millions of years.'

Weisler considered this for a few moments as they walked. 'So it's a record.'

'Yes, it's a record of geological time, of what happened here over huge periods, like the growth rings in a tree. Different weather, different events, all of them leave a record in the rocks for us to study.'

'And you're the guy that studies the rocks, right?' Weisler said, apparently pleased with himself.

'No,' Channing replied with a quiet joy at the media man's error. 'I'm the guy that studies what we find *buried* in those rocks.'

Channing reached a section of the hillside slope that he recognized and he slowed and crouched alongside a steep cliff face, strips of color clearly visible even to the layman's eyes. Although not a geologist by training, Channing's work involved understanding precisely what he was looking at in order to locate what he was seeking.

'We need to go a little deeper,' he said.

Weisler wiped sweat from his brow and squinted down into the valley. 'Damn me, it's like an oven here. How do you know you need to go deeper?'

Channing pointed at a thin layer in the rocks. 'Because of this.'

The layer was an inch or so thick, light pink or white, and lay beneath another one about a half inch thick and dark gray in color.

'What is it?' Weisler asked as he crouched alongside Channing.

'The K–T Boundary,' Channing replied, 'the division between the Cretaceous and Paleogene period. This boundary bed marks a bolide impactor's arrival on Earth.'

'A *what* now?'

'A massive asteroid impact,' Channing went on. 'See the dark layer above it? That's shocked quartz and iridium, caused by rock being super–heated and compressed. That fell after the layer below it, which was formed by acid rain falling on the earth after the impact as the chemicals churned up from inside the earth hit the atmosphere and poisoned it.'

Weisler stared at the rocks in amazement. 'You can tell all of that from an inch and a half of rocks?'

'It's been studied for decades,' Channing replied. 'See the few inches of banding above the K–T boundary? That's where we find what we call the "fern spike", huge numbers of fossilized ferns. Such plants are usually the ones to grow first in the wake of forest fires, when the rest of the landscape has been decimated.'

Channing could almost hear the media man's mind turning over as he looked at the barren landscape around them.

'And this happened here, turned this land to stone like this?'

'No,' Channing replied. 'It happened on the Mexican peninsular, at a place called Chicxulub, sixty five million years ago. This boundary of rock, the evidence of the impact, is found at the same level in the rocks all around the world.'

Channing stood up and prepared to move out again.

'An Extinction Level Event,' Weisler said, surprising Channing.

'Yeah,' he agreed, 'an ELE. Ninety per cent of all living species went extinct directly after that impact.'

As they moved down the hillside, Weisler hurried to keep up. 'What did you say you studied again?'

'I'm a paleontologist,' Channing replied, his voice echoing away across the lonely canyons. 'I specialize in looking for Tyrannosaurs.'

The descent continued for another few minutes as Channing sought the location specified in the letter. The author's references to *opposing lignite layers* and *tonsteins,* a name for a certain kind of acid leached kaolinitic clay, guided Channing as he searched the rock faces. The sun blazed down upon them and seemed to beat back off the rock faces as Channing hunted for his quarry, but after an hour of crawling across hard rocks on his knees and chipping off samples from the rock face itself he was no closer to locating whatever the letter was referring to.

Channing sat back in his haunches and pulled his hat down further over his eyes to shield them from the infernal sun. Weisler stood over him and looked impatiently at the rocks.

'You found anything yet?'

Channing fought to keep his temper in check as he replied.

'A lot of old rocks and nothing much else. Are you sure you don't know who sent you that letter?'

Weisler shook his head. 'I told you, I have no idea. It showed up, post–marked NYC, no name or identifying marks, with a covering note asking me to contact you and pass it on. I would have binned the damned thing if it hadn't said that what was out here could change the world forever.'

Channing wiped sweat from his brow onto the back of his forearm and shook his head. 'There's nothing here.'

'Nothing?'

'Nothing,' Channing repeated, already suspecting that the letter was a hoax, the party trick of some sad loser with nothing better to do than waste other people's time with their fantasies.

'But then why bring me to you? Why go through this whole charade?'

Channing got slowly to his feet and dusted his jeans off as he replied.

'I have absolutely no idea, but who knows? There are more than enough weirdos and conspiracy theorists in this world. I've lost count of the number of letters I've received from people claiming that the world is in fact flat, or that people walked alongside the dinosaurs, or that the world is only six thousand years old.'

Weisler looked up at the hard, uncaring face of the cliff and sighed, and Channing realized that the media man had been as deceived as he had and was as likely just as disappointed.

'Don't let it get to you,' Channing suggested. 'I'm surprised that you don't get these kinds of pranks all the time too.'

'We do,' Weisler admitted, 'but this one seemed so real, so genuine. He knew stuff, right?'

Channing hesitated. Weisler was right, the author of the letter had known what he was talking about. He wondered whether the prank had been played by one of his colleagues, or perhaps worse one of his competitors.

'Do you have the rest of the letter with you?' Channing asked, wondering if he could identify the prankster by his hand writing on the covering letter that Weisler had mentioned.

Weisler retrieved his covering letter and handed it to Channing, who read it for a moment and then gasped out loud as his hand flew to his mouth.

'What is it?' Weisler asked.

Channing re–read the covering letter and realized that the note contained further concealed information.

Please forward this information to Professor Aubrey Channing, Montana State University, whose knowledge of fossilized remains embedded in Paleogene kaolinitic layering is far and above that of his contemporaries, none of whom would think to seek higher knowledge.

Channing lowered the letter and stared at it in silence for several long seconds.

'Will you tell me what the hell's going on?' Weisler demanded.

'Why not?' Channing whispered vacantly and then stared up at the rock face before him. 'We're in the right place and the wrong place.'

'What the hell is that supposed to mean?'

'This can't be possible,' Channing murmured again.

'Damn it man, what does the letter say?'

'That we're in the right place, but the wrong *time*.'

***

III

Channing broke free from his catatonic shock and hurried up the hillside, scrambling for purchase amid the rocks. Weisler leaped up in pursuit, struggling to keep up as Channing climbed up toward a narrow ledge a few yards further up the hill.

The sun was now beating down with almost unbearable strength as they ascended the hill, Channing's shirt soaked with sweat and his breath coming in short, sharp gasps as he climbed and finally reached the ledge. He clambered up onto it, and immediately he saw what he was looking for as Weisler dragged himself onto the ledge and knelt alongside him, gasping for breath.

'Jesus, where's the fire?'

Channing did not respond as he looked at the rock formation before him.

The face showed obvious signs of disturbance by human hands and tools, and although Channing was no tracker he could see a few scattered boot prints in the dust where somebody had been working the site, maybe for a couple of days or so. But it was what was protruding from the rock face itself that stunned him into a sort of reverential silence.

'That's a bone!' Weisler said, and whipped out a camera from his satchel.

Channing knew that it was a bone, or to be more accurate the fossilized remains of a bone, buried deep in the strata for sixty five million years. His career experience was such that he did not need to study it for more than a few moments to know what he was looking at.

'Tyrannosaur,' he whispered.

The bone that Weisler was now photographing avidly was almost a yard long and lined with razor sharp teeth several inches in length, the whole bone and likely the skull with it still mostly concealed inside the rock from which patient hands had begun to liberate it. The classic lines of a theropod carnivore were obvious, perhaps even to the layman, but as Weisler was clearly beginning to realize, that was not what was odd about the remains.

'Wait one,' he said. 'Scientists have been digging these things up out here for years, so what's the big deal?

Channing didn't know quite where to begin, and suddenly he found himself beginning to understand why whoever had written the letter had no desire to be associated with the spectacular remains they had located out here in the barren Montana wilderness.

'It shouldn't be here,' Channing replied finally.

'Sure it should,' Weisler insisted. 'It's a dinosaur, right? They're buried all over the place out here.'

'But not here,' Channing insisted.

Weisler sighed and lowered his camera. 'I don't get it.'

Channing pointed down the hillside, and across it at the thin line of the Cretaceous–Paleogene boundary running through the rock strata.

'The K–T Event, the asteroid impact that struck the Chicxulub peninsular and caused a devastating extinction level event, occurred down there.'

Weisler looked down at the line, and then turned to the remains in the cliff face.

'The asteroid that killed the dinosaurs,' he said quietly.

'It ended their reign sixty five million years ago,' Channing confirmed. 'Virtually every scientific discipline accepts that the event was the end of the dinosaur line, and no scientist has ever discovered the remains of a dinosaur after that event.' He turned to stare at the jaw bone lodged in the solid Montana rock face. 'Nobody has ever discovered dinosaur remains *above* that line.'

Weisler got it quickly enough and began enthusiastically snapping more shots of the remains, this time ensuring that the nearby line of the K–T boundary was in–shot.

'So, the asteroid didn't kill all of the dinosaurs. I can see why this guy didn't want to go public right away. I guess he'd face a real storm of protest.'

There was a famous saying in science that Channing had first heard at college, from the words of a man named Arthur Schopenhauer: *"All truth passes through three stages: First, it is ridiculed. Second, it is violently opposed. Third, it is accepted as being self–evident."*

Often academic careers were ended by such dramatic discoveries, the truth of those discoveries only coming to light long after the unfortunate scientist's death. Established science would often cut funding to research deemed unscientific, scientific journals would refuse to publish papers on radical hypothesis, and both governments and big business would seek to undermine any research that threatened profits or political stability: researchers into the links between cigarettes and lung cancer had even been issued death threats as a result of their work. To buck the trend, to rock the boat or otherwise oppose the establishment early in one's life was reckoned to be career suicide for any academic, which was why professional opposition to supposedly "consensus" science like climate change was vocalized only by those scientists who had already retired and thus had no career and income to lose.

Suddenly Channing realized why he had been sent the letter, why he had been targeted to travel to this lonely, barren corner of Hell Creek. The scientist who had made this discovery could not afford to promote it, for fear of losing grants and funding for whatever they were researching in their day job. This had been a personal crusade that they could never complete. But Channing was nearing retirement age, had little to lose and himself cared little for the establishment.

'His or her career would be over,' Channing said finally. 'They're handing me the discovery of the century because they know I can afford to take the chance on this.'

Weisler lowered the camera in his hands as he looked at the professor.

'It's not that big a deal, surely?'

Channing stared up at the reporter and shook his head. 'You don't get what this means, do you?'

Weisler shrugged. 'The stone from space didn't kill all of the big monsters. What of it?'

Channing looked down at the rocks before them.

'Tyrannosaurs evolved in the last few million years before the K–T Event,' he explained. 'They represented the largest of their species, the theropods, and those were the first to suffer when the asteroid hit.'

Weisler seemed to forget about his camera as he looked at the huge bones lodged in the rock face.

'How bad was it?'

Channing chuckled bitterly.

'The asteroid, which was about seven miles across, hit the Yucatan Peninsular at about thirty thousand miles per hour. It passed through our entire atmosphere in a few seconds. Meteor Crater in Arizona is a mile across and was created by an impactor with an energy release of about ten megatons. In contrast, the K–T event impactor struck with a force estimated to be one hundred *million* megatons.'

Weisler's voice became quiet. 'Pretty bad, then.'

Channing nodded. 'The impact would have produced a light so bright that it would have penetrated the bodies of living things, making them briefly translucent and blinding them instantly. The crater it left behind, which is now below the Gulf of Mexico, is two hundred kilometres wide. The impact rained down debris across the entire globe, causing worldwide forest fires and a post–event global winter that lasted a decade. The large herbivores that survived the impact event died out first after all the vegetation was destroyed, followed by the large carnivores like Tyrannosaurs which had nothing left to hunt, followed by marine animals poisoned by the chemical fall out from the blast which would have fallen around the globe. Very little life survived the event and its consequences.'

Weisler looked at the rocks around them. 'And all of that's contained in these rocks?'

'Hard evidence,' Channing replied, 'no pun intended. The lowest layers of the K–T boundary are the acid leached rocks, its kaolinitic composition the result of acid rain produced when the asteroid impact blasted anhydrite rock at Chicxulub, which is dehydrated gypsum and forms sulfur dioxide when vaporized. That fell first, followed by the more famous iridium–enriched shocked quartz, the debris from the impact that was hurled into the atmosphere by the blast and then settled on top of the lower layers of the boundary. Finally on top of all that is the lignite, a sort of coal formed in swamps, lagoons and shallow lakes, where peat mires are common, and that lignite contains unusually dense concentrations of fossil fern spores.'

'The growth after the impact,' Weisler remembered. 'The fern spike, after the dinosaurs were all gone.'

Channing nodded, and with one hand he gently brushed the long, hard jaw bone of the Tyrannosaur.

'And yet here it is,' he said softly, '*after* the impact event.'

Weisler frowned. 'Couldn't it have simply survived?'

'Not an entire species,' Channing shook his head. 'Besides, they would have evolved further, changed, adapted over time to the new environment. This specimen simply shouldn't be here unless everything we've assumed we know about the Chicxulub impact is…' Channing hesitated as though he were afraid to say the last word.

'Wrong,' Weisler added. 'But that doesn't mean anything that big, right? Only scientists will be in uproar. Most folks won't give a damn one way or the other.'

Channing shook his head as he ran his hand down the surface of the Tyrannosaur bone again, this time feeling ripples and holes in the bone beneath his touch.

'That's not what worries me,' he said softly. 'What's on my mind is: if the asteroid didn't kill the dinosaurs, then what did?'

Weisler shrugged. 'Climate change? Volcanoes? Rising sea levels?'

Chandler shook his head again and then he stopped moving his hand. He pulled it away abruptly, looked at his palm in shock.

'What, you get bitten by something?' Weisler asked.

Channing stood bolt upright as he sucked in a deep breath and seemed to quiver on the spot as though momentarily no longer in his own body. Weisler took a pace toward him, and Channing thrust his hand out to forestall the reporter.

'Stay back,' he said.

'What?'

'The letter,' Channing said, 'when it was posted to you, when you received it. Was it in a sealed plastic bag?'

Weisler's eyes flew wide in amazement. 'Yeah. Say, how the hell did you know that...?'

'Get out of here, right now,' Channing snapped. 'Get back to town and call CDC.'

Weisler's face drained of color as he stared at Channing. 'The CDC? What the hell for?'

The Center for Disease Control was the country's most elite scientific unit tasked with the containment of infectious diseases. Any mention of it was enough to bring the average person out into a cold sweat.

'Just do it!' Channing bellowed, his voice echoing away across the canyons. 'Tell them what happened here and pray you get there fast enough!'

Whatever Weisler saw in Channing's eyes was enough to get him scrambling away up the rocky slopes as Channing sat down in front of the ancient fossilized bones and waited until the silence enveloped the site once again. The wind moaned across the hillside, laden with boiling heat, and the few scattered clouds drifting across the hard blue sky brought little shade with them.

Channing let his eyes lose focus as he stared at the tyrannosaur bone before him, at the deep pitting that lined the massive jaw. He knew that they were not the scars of some ancient, titanic battle with another tyrannosaur. He knew that they were not the result of an impact of some kind, or bite.

Channing recognized the pitting as the scars of some horrific disease, an affliction deep enough to deform the very bones of a gigantic carnivore that weighed some six tons. He knew that no asteroid impact had killed this huge creature.

The asteroid that hit the earth sixty five million years ago had unleashed something else entirely.

***

Dean Crawford

IV

Logan Circle,

Washington DC

The sound of incessant banging reverberated through the apartment and jerked Ethan Warner out of his slumber. He opened his eyes and saw the faint light of pre–dawn glowing lethargically through the blinds of his bedroom window. One hand reached for the Beretta M9 pistol he kept under his pillow and he whipped the weapon across to point at the bedroom doorway as a figure loomed before him, the bed sheets falling onto the floor.

'Nice piece.'

Nicola Lopez leaned on the door jamb, her arms folded and a mischievous smile on her face as she looked into his eyes, clearly trying not to cast her gaze across his body as he stood up and scowled at her.

'You ever learned how to knock?' he uttered as he grabbed the bed sheets and covered himself.

Lopez dangled a key from one finger. 'You gave me a key, remember? After what happened to…'

Her cheerful mood subsided a little and Ethan nodded. 'Sure. I forgot.'

An awkward silence filled the room for a moment and then Ethan recovered his bravado. 'So, what drove you to cross town and wander into my bedroom at six in the morning?'

'Not your weapon,' Lopez managed a faint smirk as she pocketed the key and jabbed a thumb over her shoulder. 'Jarvis has a fresh lead on Majestic Twelve and we've been summoned.'

Ethan rubbed the sleep from his eyes and yawned mightily as he trudged into the bathroom. 'How come they don't ever get leads at a sociable hour, like three in the afternoon?'

'Beats me.'

Ethan could see her from the corner of his eye as he cranked the faucet and splashed hot water across his face. A diminutive five foot three, with long black hair and olive skin, her petite frame belied a ferocious temper and formidable right hook. Brought up on the tough streets of Guanajuato, and later Washington DC where she served in the blues of the Metropolitan

Police Department, Lopez was an enigma that both fascinated Ethan and worried him. Both of them had risked their lives on numerous occasions in the work that they did as contracted agents to the DIA, and not six months before they had lost an agent on a highly classified mission in Antarctica. That loss had hit Ethan harder than he would ever have believed possible, to the extent that he now found it difficult to form long–term attachments of any kind other than Lopez. He saw his own reflection in the mirror, a man who was starting to look older than his years, the rigors of life etched deeply into his skin.

His hair was thick and light brown in the mirror, his eyes gray and his jaw a little too wide to be considered attractive, and his chest and back bore the scars of numerous confrontations. He pulled on a shirt and jeans, then padded back out to see Lopez scoping the apartment with interest.

'Still haven't bought anything to personalize the place,' she observed.

The walls were bare, as were the cupboards, but then he didn't want to remember much these days about his past and the traumas it contained.

'It's a roof and four walls,' he replied. 'Are we going?'

Lopez shrugged and led the way.

An SUV awaited them by the sidewalk outside, glossy black as always and bearing government plates. Ethan climbed in and shut the door behind him, and two agents in the front seats drove them away toward Anacostia–Bolling Airbase, Washington DC, the home of the Defense Intelligence Agency.

Ethan and Nicola had worked for the agency for several years, both officially and unofficially depending on who was in charge of the agency at the time and who was in the White House. The current Director of the DIA was Lieutenant General J. F. Nellis, a former United States Air Force officer who had been appointed DNI by the current president

Their task was to investigate cases the rest of the intelligence community had rejected as unworkable. The connection to a high level agency like the DIA had come from a former colleague of Ethan's named Douglas Jarvis. The old man had once been captain of a United States Rifle Platoon and Ethan's senior officer from his time with the Corps in Iraq and Afghanistan. Their friendship, cemented during Operation Iraqi Freedom and later, when Ethan had resigned his commission and been embedded with Jarvis's men as a journalist, had continued into their unusual and discreet accord with the DIA where Jarvis continued to serve his country.

Since joining the agency they had completed nine investigations, involving everything from alien remains excavated from ancient cities around the world, free energy devices, technology so advanced it had allowed terrorists to infiltrate the minds of key government and military figures, and alien technology that had crash–landed deep inside the Antarctic. It had been there that Agent Hannah Ford had lost her life, the victim of an extremely well equipped rogue organization that operated entirely outside the US Government.

The SUV reached the DIA building within twenty minutes, blue lights allowing them to bypass the traffic already building up around the Potomac and Capitol Hill. Ethan got out and followed Nicola to a security check point inside the entrance to the Defense Intelligence Agency where a pass was clipped to her shirt by a security guard.

The DIA's south wing entrance, in front of which was a fountain before perfectly manicured lawns, made up only a tiny part of the vast complex. Huge, silvery buildings with mirrored windows contained some of the most sensitive intelligence gathering equipment in the world, including vast 24/7 *Watch Centers* manned by agents monitoring events across the entire globe.

Lopez led the way through a barrage of security measures, enduring full X–Rays and pat down searches. They finally passed through the checks in time for Jarvis to meet them in the main foyer of the building, the polished tile floor emblazoned with a large DIA emblem in the manner of all the intelligence agencies.

'Welcome back,' Jarvis greeted them, his hands in the pockets of his dark blue pants, his white hair stark against his suit and shirt, all a similar shade of blue. 'How are you holding up, Ethan?'

'I'm fine,' Ethan replied without elaborating. 'Where's the fire?'

'Come with me,' Jarvis replied. 'I'll show you.'

Ethan followed him as large numbers of civilian staff strode this way and that through the building. Surprisingly, for a highly secretive intelligence agency, two thirds of the DIA's seventeen thousand employees were civilian, which allowed selected freelance operatives to act in concert with official employees like Jarvis. Represented in some one hundred forty countries and with its own Clandestine Service, to which Ethan and Nicola were now attached, the agency suffered only from a lack of influence in law enforcement, often forcing Ethan and Nicola to work alongside police and federal law agencies around the country who were less than inclined to open up to direct interference from such a clandestine agency.

Jarvis led the way into the Defense Intelligence Agency's *Advanced Research and Intelligence Engineering Section*, otherwise known as ARIES.

Created to support the work of other agencies such as the NSA, CIA and DARPA, ARIES was tasked with emulating the technology of other nations that had been uncovered by overt overseas operations, for the purpose of finding effective defenses against those technologies. In a world where digital and cyber–warfare was more widespread now than ever, where foreign hackers were capable of accessing everything from the computers of major film studios to even the Pentagon and other defense installations, the need for absolute security had never been more paramount.

ARIES was a giant pool of desks arrayed before banks of large plasma screens showing news feeds from around the world. Essentially the hub of the DIA's intelligence gathering force, what came in to the room rarely left except to be investigated by agents like Ethan and Nicola.

As they entered the station they were greeted by a slim, bespectacled and bearded young man with an infectious enthusiasm radiating from his gaze.

'Guys, you've just gotta see this!'

Hellerman had worked for the DIA for less than two years, but already he was one of the chief technicians specializing in novel technologies. Ethan considered him something of a 'Q' character from a James Bond movie, but in truth Hellerman's near–genius level intellect had saved them from certain death on numerous occasions.

Hellerman led them to an area of the Watch Station where a partition wall with a single door had been erected, right outside the cluttered office where Hellerman created his wondrous gadgets.

'What are we looking at?' Lopez asked, as ever amused by Hellerman's excited expression.

'A wall,' Hellerman replied, gesturing with widespread arms as he moved to the center of the space and spun around to face them. 'There's absolutely nothing here but a wall, right?!'

Ethan blinked and folded his arms across his chest.

'Not exactly the bombshell we were hoping for.'

Hellerman smiled, dropped his arms, then turned and reached out. He pushed the door, and it swung open before them. Through the door a huge Bengal tiger leaped at Ethan and Lopez, its shaggy coat shimmering in the light, its jaws agape and lined with brutal yellow fangs, hunter's eyes wide and bright. Ethan flinched and hurled himself to one side as Lopez drew her pistol and flew across the floor, aiming at the savage beast as it soared in full flight toward them.

The beast's roar was deafening as it shot between Ethan and Lopez to vanish like a ghost into thin air. Ethan hit the floor and rolled, coming up on one knee with his pistol aimed at where the huge carnivore had disappeared.

'What the hell?!'

His heart was thumping in his chest, Lopez's eyes wide with alarm as she too aimed into thin air.

'Hard light!' Hellerman yelled in delight. 'Otherwise known as Seven–D technology. You've nothing to fear, there was nothing there in the first place, just a three dimensional projection onto thin air using highly focused pulse lasers. We've built a projection machine that uses a one–kilohertz pulse laser through a three–D scanner, which reflects and focuses the laser onto an exact place in the air above. The laser ionizes the air's molecules in that specific spot, which results in the flashes of light that make up each pixel, if you will, of the image.'

Ethan and Lopez exchanged a glance as they got up, holstering their pistols and stalking toward Hellerman.

'You ever think to warn people about that before you send a tiger flying at their face?' Lopez growled.

Hellerman's delight dissolved into anxiety as he backed up a pace. 'Now, it was just a demonstration and...'

Ethan reached out to grab Hellerman's shirt and almost fell over as his hand passed right through the technician's body.

'Sorry!' a voice called out from within Hellerman's office as the second projection flickered out before Ethan, the partition wall vanishing a moment later. 'Thought you might do that!'

From within the office Hellerman peeked out at them, one hand on his door to slam it shut in case they charged him together.

'Jarvis said to make the demonstration as impactful as possible,' he offered.

'And where did our great and hallowed leader disappear to?' Lopez demanded, looking around them.

'Right here,' Jarvis said as he suddenly materialized as if from nowhere behind them, the nearby offices trembling briefly as though in a heat haze as Jarvis popped into existence.

Ethan could not help but rub his eyes in disbelief. 'You're kidding?'

'I was hiding behind a projection of the office behind me,' Jarvis explained. 'Remarkable technology with huge potential for battlefield evasion.'

'Trust you to figure that out,' Lopez uttered as Jarvis joined them. 'There was me thinking that interactive cinema might be a better use for it.'

Jarvis leaned against the side of Hellerman's office and shrugged.

'All technologies eventually find their way into the markets as profitable enterprises,' he replied. 'That's just the way of the world. This technology could allow an army to advance undetected, aircraft to become virtually invisible. No respectable military is going to ignore that kind of advantage.'

'Why are we here?' Ethan asked.

'We have a name and a location,' Jarvis replied. 'Aubrey Channing, Montana.'

'Who's Channing?' Lopez asked.

Hellerman stepped out of his office with a tablet computer in his hand, which he propped up on a table alongside them.

'Professor Aubrey Channing,' he announced, 'studied at and worked for the University of Montana until 1996, when he disappeared somewhere in the Montana badlands while on an exploratory dig. Until his disappearance, he was the world's leading authority on tyrannosaur remains.'

'What do dinosaurs have to do with Majestic Twelve?' Lopez asked. 'Why would they be interested in paleontology?'

'That's where things get interesting,' Hellerman explained. 'According to a reporter named Rory Weisler who accompanied him, Channing was working out in Montana because of a letter sent to the reporter by an unknown individual who had discovered something out there that he wanted nothing to do with. The reporter had been ordered in the letter to contact Channing and have him locate the remains of whatever it was had been found.'

'So far, so mysterious,' Ethan said. 'And we know all of this how?'

'The reporter wrote the piece up in the Montana paper he worked for,' Hellerman explained, reading from the tablet's screen. 'But the piece didn't get published for almost twenty years, because according to the reporter Channing found the remains but then became extremely agitated and ordered the reporter to leave the scene immediately. That was the last that anybody saw of Channing.'

'Could Weisler have murdered Channing?' Lopez asked. 'Maybe created this whole thing as a ruse to cover his tracks?'

Hellerman scanned down the pages on the tablet. 'According to this, that's what the Montana Police Department thought but they were contacted privately after Channing disappeared by the man who had written the original letter, who confirmed the reporter's story. The only reason the piece got published was because the reporter fell sick in his old age and finally felt able to publish the piece.'

Ethan frowned. 'He waited until his deathbed to write the report?'

Hellerman nodded and looked up at Ethan.

'This would all be conjecture for us, were it not for the communications chatter we've picked up between members of Majestic Twelve since we identified them all. There have been several mentions of Aubrey Channing, Montana, and biological experiments of some kind.'

'What about family members?' Lopez asked. 'Did anybody close to Channing know what happened to him?'

'His wife died a few years after Channing vanished,' Hellerman said as he looked at his screen, 'and their only son, Robert, committed suicide a year after that. The only other person who might know anything is a scientist named Martin Beauchamp who worked as an undergraduate student with Channing, but guess what? He disappeared two days ago, and a missing–persons report was filed by his family in Ohio.'

'You think that MJ–12 took them out too?' Ethan asked.

'Well, Weisler is on the record as saying that he'd been threatened to say nothing of what happened to Channing, that he feared for his life and that of his family if he had written the report any sooner.'

***

V

'Okay, it sounds like MJ–12 are in on this all right,' Lopez said, 'death threats and intimidation are their currency. But it doesn't explain what they wanted with Channing or what he found out there in Montana?'

Hellerman slipped into a seat as he finished reading the document.

'The reporter claims in his article that what Channing was led to was a Tyrannosaur jaw bone,' he said. 'Channing at the time said that it shouldn't have been there because it was located above the K–T boundary, a sedimentary marker that depicts the impact debris from a massive asteroid that hit the earth sixty five million years ago and rendered the dinosaurs extinct.'

'Everybody knows about that, right?' Ethan said.

'Sure,' Hellerman agreed, 'but back then the science was not as solid. This all happened not long after *Jurassic Park* came along and half the globe went dinosaur mad, and science got the kind of funding to finally confirm what many had suspected for years. Even now, the discovery of dinosaur remains above the K–T boundary is a rare but always contentious event.'

'You mean it's still happening?' Jarvis asked.

'The K–T boundary is not uniform,' Hellerman explained. 'Some sections of the formation in Hell Creek mark the boundary as Paleocene in age, not Cretaceous, so the Cretaceous–Tertiary boundary in time does not always coincide exactly with the Hell Creek Formation's position in the rock.'

Lopez blinked. 'Er, and?'

'There have been discoveries of Triceratops fossils supposedly above the K–T boundary,' Hellerman said. 'Most explain this away as the fossils being located in areas where the overlying rock formations have dipped, or erosion in the distant past has caused the sedimentary layer to descend compared to other geographical locations. The process is called bioturbation, and is often used by Creationists as supposed evidence that the historical record is false and so on, when in fact it's not.'

'So what's the big deal?' Jarvis asked. 'Channing finds remains that look like they're above the K–T boundary but aren't? Surely that means they're nothing special?'

Hellerman shrugged. 'Something spooked him, because that's about when he took off. The reporter claims he acted as though he were somehow contaminated.'

'Contaminated?' Lopez repeated. 'I don't like the sound of that.'

'It doesn't sound possible,' Ethan said. 'Fossils are effectively stone, minerals that have replaced the bones of an animal buried in ancient sediment. They can't contain anything that could be considered infectious.'

Hellerman leaned back in the seat and shook his head. 'That's not strictly true.'

'You're kidding?' Lopez asked. 'You can catch a cold from dinosaur bones?'

'Not quite, but researchers working in Montana recently identified soft tissue in the remains of an eighty million year old Hadrosaur fossil. They compared proteins extracted from the tissue to modern birds and confirmed that they were actual dinosaur veins, ruling out contamination from other sources such as bacteria. Myosin was the protein found in the tissue, which is also found in the walls of blood vessels.'

'So they got dino–DNA out of a fossil after all?' Lopez said. 'Michael Crichton would have been proud.'

'Again, not quite,' Hellerman cautioned, 'as red blood cells don't contain DNA. However, collagen–like tissues have also been found in the bones of a Tyrannosaur, and from those hardier substances genetic material could be recovered. Whether it would be intact or even useful after so long is another matter.'

Ethan thought for a moment.

'Is it possible that Channing feared that something in the bones that he found could have been preserved for tens of millions of years? Did they even have that kind of knowledge back then, enough to understand that he could have been in danger?'

'That depends on what Channing saw that spooked him,' Hellerman said. 'The reporter went back to the Montana site shortly before his death, hoping to seek answers to what happened. He said that the bones were gone, that the site had been excavated professionally and that had he not photographed the scene when Channing had been there and known that he was in the right spot, he would never have known that the bones had been in the rock face at all.'

'Somebody cleaned up real good behind them,' Ethan suggested, 'which means they had something to hide.'

'Including Channing,' Lopez pointed out. 'I take it that the author of the original letter is long dead?'

Hellerman shook his head. 'No, quite the opposite, although whether you can get them to talk is another matter. Since the disappearance in 2002 they have never again mentioned what happened, even when the report was finally publicized a couple of years back. They had their name blocked from the report, had lawyers acting for them. We've only got their identity because of the police investigation.'

'You got an address?' Ethan asked.

'Norway,' Hellerman replied, 'which means you're back on a plane again.'

Ethan nodded wearily and turned to Jarvis as Hellerman hurried off.

'What's next for MJ–12?'

'We keep the pressure on,' Jarvis replied with a casual shrug, 'and find out what their connection to Aubrey Channing was. If we can find a body, we might be able to connect it to one of their own.'

'I doubt they would have got their own hands dirty,' Lopez pointed out, 'although if we could locate Mitchell he might know something about what happened.'

'He's on his own,' Jarvis replied, 'and we don't know what he's planning either. I doubt that he'll just retire into the sunset.'

'Me either,' Ethan agreed. 'We've got to track him down and fast before he starts killing off our suspects. It took us long enough to identify the members of Majestic Twelve – I don't want Mitchell knocking them off on a revenge spree and MJ–12 becoming a new set of faces we can't identify.'

Jarvis did not reply, as clear on their dilemma as Ethan was.

Majestic Twelve, a secretive cabal of powerful industrial and political figures, had been formed in the aftermath of World War Two after a series of events involving unknown craft observed in flight around the world. Although unidentified flying objects had been observed throughout history as far back as ancient Egypt, it was only in recent times that any understanding of what the craft actually were and the nature of their purpose had been reached. When one such craft had crashed in New Mexico in 1947, close to a town called Roswell, and aviator Kenneth Arnold had observed "saucer like discs" flying at terrific speed near Mount Rainier that same year, the Eisenhower administration had created Majestic Twelve to coordinate a study of the phenomenon. What the administration had not appreciated was that the founders of Majestic Twelve were men who had been aware of Nazi experiments with supposed extra–terrestrial technology during the Second World War, and involved in spiriting that technology away from the United States Government after the fall of Berlin. Majestic Twelve, as it had turned out, was not just a cabal of industrialists intent on the control of governments – it was actively continuing the work of the Nazis.

'If Mitchell knows anything about Montana, he's going to show up there too,' Lopez said. 'He'll follow the same threads that we do, maybe even have informants of his own showing him the way.'

'Majestic Twelve must have pissed off a lot of people over the years,' Ethan agreed. 'Enough that Mitchell may be able to leverage some of them into helping him.'

That list, Ethan reflected, might even include serving members of the administration. Majestic Twelve was, in effect, a descendent of The Silver Legion of America, also known as the Silver Shirts, an underground American fascist organization founded by William Dudley Pelley in 1933 that had been headquartered in North Carolina. A white supremacist group based on Adolf Hitler's Brownshirts, the Silver Shirts had built a fortified headquarters in the hills of Los Angeles and had been some fifteen thousand strong. The Japanese attack on Pearl Harbor in 1941 killed off public support for the legion, but the remaining members were ready when the Nazis were defeated to bring into America survivors of the *Third Reich* along with all of the wealth stolen from within Germany during the final days of the conflict.

After the war, the founding members of the Silver Legion used their wealth to invest in the industrial–military complex. They prospered, became powerful and when in 1947 the first hints of extra–terrestrial technology coming into the hands of the United States government began to circulate, they were there to pick up the threads of what had begun in Germany many years before with *Die Glocke*, a rumored extra–terrestrial device captured by scientists and designed to bring a crushing defeat to the allied forces. Ethan and Nicola had located just such a device in an abandoned German facility six months before, buried deep beneath the ice floes of Antarctica.

'We need to get onto this first and figure out what it is that brought Channing to the attention of MJ–12,' Jarvis said finally. 'If MJ–12 are making another play for dominance then whatever they've got in mind it won't be healthy, and that mention of biological experiments gives me the creeps. I'll have Victor Wilms transported out of Florence ACX as soon as possible and we'll give him a hint of what life's like in general population to see if he'll fold. Why don't you go down there before Norway and find out if Wilms knows anything about Aubrey Channing?'

'If we make him think he's going into general population, we might lose any trust he has in us,' Lopez pointed out.

'His resolve will fail a lot quicker if he feels really threatened,' Jarvis pointed out. 'We just have to make him think we genuinely don't give a damn about him. What's left of his bravado is due to him believing he's still important, still has leverage.

Hellerman hurried across and handed Ethan a scribbled note.

'The professor behind the original note works in Spitsbergen, at the Doomsday Vault.'

'The what now?' Lopez asked.

'The Doomsday Vault,' Hellerman said in reply. 'It's a facility used to store seeds and DNA in the event of a global extinction event.'

Ethan tucked the address into the pocket of his jeans and looked at Lopez.

'Nothing like doom and gloom, huh?'

***

Dean Crawford

VI

Florence, Colorado

'Damn me it's hot here.'

'Quit whining, this is nothing.'

Ethan Warner drove along Highway 67 beneath the flaring white orb of the sun that scorched the barren deserts surrounding them. The sky was a flawless light blue, the temperature forecast to be in the high nineties.

'It's okay for you, coming from Mexico,' Ethan complained.

Despite the air conditioning in the vehicle, he felt uncomfortably hot as the sunshine blazed through the windscreen. Beside him, Nicola Lopez sat with her boots up on the dash as she played some sort of game on her cell phone. Her dark eyes flicked left and right as she played, long black hair framing a perfect face and sculptured lips.

'That's racist,' she pointed out.

'It's not racist to state a fact,' Ethan defended himself. 'I come from Illinois, remember?'

'I think you're just getting feeble in your old age.'

'So I'm *old* now too?'

'Let's be honest, you're getting on a bit.'

Ethan knew better than to push it. Lopez was several years his junior, a fact that she often reminded him of, and when it came to a chase she usually shot ahead of him like a damned gazelle. It had been many years since he had worn the colors of the Marine Corps, and although he ran three times a week and visited the gym at least once, there was a big difference between civilian and military standards of fitness.

Ahead of them, flaring white against the desiccated deserts, were a series of low angular block–like buildings surrounded by towers and glittering razor wire fences.

'We're almost here,' he told Lopez. 'You ready for this?'

'You betcha,' Lopez replied. 'Just gotta send this last boss–fight down and I'm all yours.'

'Since when did you get into video games?'

'Since I started having to spend hours stuck in a car with you.'

ADX Florence, as the facility ahead of them was known, was America's most secure Super–Max prison, designed to house the country's most feared inmates. The majority of the facility's thirty seven acre complex was above ground, with a subterranean corridor linking the cellblocks to the lobby. Few journalists had ever been permitted entry, and Ethan and Nicola were here only on the authority of the Defense Intelligence Agency's Clandestine Services.

Ethan pulled slowly into the parking lot, stopped at the security gates and showed both their identification and their letter of admittance to the guards before being waved through and parking in front of the southern block.

They stepped out of the air conditioned vehicle and into the hot sunshine that flared off the asphalt, doubling the heat.

'You think that this facility will be able to hold him?' Lopez asked. 'Mitchell managed to get out.'

'Security's been overhauled after Mitchell's escape,' Ethan replied. 'And Wilms is a different man altogether from Mitchell. He's not going anywhere.'

They walked together to the block entrance, where the first of many security gates opened and then closed behind them as they passed through. Prison security teams frisked them thoroughly, checked again their letter of admission before waving them through to a reception area where they were required to leave cell phones, wallets and other personal belongings.

'This way,' a guard assigned to them gestured.

They walked through a corridor that descended beneath the block walls and led to more security gates. Each was governed by operators in remote stations and covered by security cameras: there were no keys, no means for a prisoner to escape even if they did somehow manage to get out of their cell. They passed through the gates, and Ethan saw an X–Ray machine sunk into a revetment in the wall that scanned them as they moved by. No alarm was emitted and they continued under the guard's guidance until they emerged into a cell block.

Unlike most prisons, Florence had no communal areas for prisoners to mingle for they spent their days on permanent lockdown. Exercise time, one hour per day, was strictly organized so that prisoners never crossed paths. Complete and utter solitude was the facility's solution to the brutality of its inmates.

The sergeant led them to an austere room and held the door open for them. They walked in to see a table, steel rings bolted into its surface and poured concrete pillars for seats on either side, more steel rings in the floor either side of the seats designed for ankle restraints. The walls were also built from poured concrete, featureless and bare.

As the guard left, Lopez turned to Ethan. 'Okay, I believe it. Wilms couldn't even think about getting out of here, but there's no reason that Majestic Twelve couldn't get in. We know what they're capable of.'

'We've got Majestic Twelve on the run,' Ethan replied with grim delight. 'They're more concerned with distancing themselves from Wilms than taking him down.'

The door to the room opened, and a thin, pale man shuffled inside, two bulky guards flanking him. Victor Wilms had lost weight since his incarceration for the murder of FBI Director LeMay some months before. The video evidence of the director's demise, surrounded by the members of MJ–12, had become world news, and the other eleven men in the room had been only too quick to point their fingers at Wilms in return for immunity from prosecution. The sacrificial lamb had thus been sent to the slaughter, a once wealthy and powerful man reduced to a trembling wreck in less than half a year.

Ethan noted the handcuffs on his wrists and ankles, joined by chains, and the defeated low–watt glow of life in his eyes as he was shoved into a seat opposite them and the guards left the room. As the door closed, Lopez leaned on the table and flashed Wilms a bright smile and a wink.

'How ya' doin', Vic?'

Wilms did not respond to Lopez's smug smile, as though he occupied another universe and was merely looking in. Ethan eased his way forward and sat down.

'Your friends in high places have forgotten about you, Victor,' he said. 'There's nothing left to fight for.'

Victor sighed, his shoulders slumped and narrow. 'I'm alive.'

Lopez snorted. 'Call this alive, Vic?' she said as she gestured at the walls around them. 'You got a hundred forty years, no parole, no appeals. You're already deader than my great grandparents. How about you open up and give us the low–down on the creeps that left you here?'

Ethan winced. Victor may be defeated, but Lopez's arrogance gave him leverage, the sense that he still had something that the Defense Intelligence Agency did not. He saw the thin little line of Wilm's mouth crease into a weak smile.

'I had a good run,' he replied. 'I've nothing to gain by turning snitch.'

'They turned coat on you Vic',' Lopez insisted. 'I didn't think you were the type to huddle in a corner and weep yourself to sleep?'

Ethan felt a tingle of interest as he realized where Lopez had been going with her charade. She leaned on the table next to him and peered at Wilms.

'Guess you've only got the cajones for this game when you've got money and muscle to hide behind, right Vic'? Cornered and on your own, you're just a limp–dicked nobody afraid of the bad guys in the cells all around you. Tell me, what's it like being somebody else's bitc…?'

Wilms shot up out of his seat, the chains cracking as they were pulled taut.

'I could still have you iced Lopez!' he seethed, spittle flying from his dry, thin lips. 'All I have to do is ask!'

'That's my point,' Lopez smirked, 'you'd have to *ask*. You're a spent force, Wilms, you've got nothing left in the tanks. MJ–12 won't come anywhere near Ethan or me because they're too wrapped up in what happened to LeMay, got their fingers burned and now they're worried about every cop who passes them in the street. And as for you…? You don't get calls, you don't get visitors, you don't got nothin'!'

Wilms' rage withered and he slumped back into his seat.

'She's got a point,' Ethan said. 'MJ–12 have gone into hibernation since LeMay's murder, they can't afford the exposure. You know it Victor, just like I do: you're done and you'll never get out of here alive. You can choose to die on your knees because MJ–12 abandoned you after years of dedicated service, or you can die on your feet and help us ensure that they too end up where you are.' Wilms looked up at Ethan, his eyes rheumy with age now, robbed of the vitality and confidence that had once resided there. 'You can bring them down, Victor, right here, right now. All you have to do is testify.'

Victor chuckled, and shook his head.

'You think that they'll take the word of the man who killed the director of the FBI?' he challenged. 'They took my money, my homes, my boats, left my family destitute.'

'Doesn't mean that they won't use your word to do the same to the remaining members of MJ–12,' Lopez pointed out. 'Or are you okay with the idea of them still living in luxury, sending their kids to private schools, cruising in yachts around the Bahamas?' Lopez leaned in again. 'Think about your replacement, Victor. I guess he's having a real good time right now.'

Victor glared up at her, his jaw set. 'I'm no snitch.'

Lopez shrugged. 'Then I guess you're all set to go here. You just think about that replacement of yours next time you're on your knees in front of one of the other cons in general population.'

Wilms did not respond for a moment, but then his features collapsed as he stared in horror at Ethan.

'Afraid so,' Ethan forestalled his protest. 'You were put in maximum security here because of the nature of your crime, but you're just not considered dangerous enough to warrant your place. You'll be transferred to Colorado State Penitentiary tomorrow.'

Wilms' already pallid skin turned even paler as Lopez smiled at him.

'No more solitary confinement for you, Vic'. You'll be walking among the murderers and rapists and armed thugs. They're real violent men, Victor, but then I guess you know that already, right?'

Lopez whirled away and headed for the door. Ethan took his cue and stood to follow her. He'd reached the door and was almost walking out when Wilms' voice reached them.

'Wait.'

Ethan hesitated at the door. 'What?'

Wilms did not look at Ethan as he spoke, his bony hands clasped together, his knuckles white and his jaw taut as though he were being forced to spit the words out.

'Varginha,' Wilms uttered, and then slowly looked at Ethan, a hatred of everything he was being forced to do and perhaps of himself shining like a cruel star in his expression. 'That's all I'll give you.'

'That's not enough,' Ethan shrugged in reply as he left the room and pulled the door shut before Wilms could protest any further.

'Who's Varginha?' Lopez asked.

'I have no idea but if it's important enough for Wilms to spit it out, it's important enough for us to check it out. C'mon, let's get Wilms checked out of here.'

***

Dean Crawford

VII

Florence, Colorado

The sun was not yet above the horizon, the empty deserts laced with blue shadows and only the peaks of the mountain ranges bathed in a golden glow. The air was brittle with the chill of the night, but he knew that within an hour the searing heat would return. Still, he did not move, utterly motionless on the steep hillside and crystals of frost glistening on the thick blanket that covered his shoulders.

The valley ranged before him for endless miles, the small town of Florence to the north little more than a scattering of twinkling street lights against the wilderness. Between that town and his position on the hillside was a series of geometric buildings set against the nearby highway, glistening razor wire and smoked–glass watch towers.

Aaron James Mitchell watched the facility through the powerful magnifying scope of the rifle before him, cradled in his grasp and set onto a tripod wedged into the rocks. The bolt–action AWM was the world–standard in sniper rifles, chambered with .338 Lapua Magnum cartridges and equipped with a Schmidt & Bender Mk II military scope and suppressor. A British rifle, it had gained a fearsome reputation in the hands of the Royal Marines in Afghanistan and held the record for the longest sniper kill in history with two confirmed lethal hits at over two thousand, seven hundred yards by a British sniper in Musa Qala, Helmand Province. For Aaron's purposes, the weapon was perfect.

Through the scope he had identified the block in which he was interested, and for two days prior he had been encamped out in the desert, watching and waiting for the perfect moment. One had come the previous day, but the tremendous heat rising up from the desert floor had prevented him from taking the shot that he so desperately desired, the thermals sufficient at such range to affect the flight of the bullet and render what otherwise would have been a confirmed kill a miss.

Now, he had received good enough intelligence to make the shot and even better he knew the precise location from which his target would appear because he had once made the same walk himself. All had been planned, all had been carefully organized, and soon would come the time to strike.

*

'Wilms, Victor!'

The bellicose shout of the guard jerked Wilms like an electric shock and his guts plunged within him as he realized that Warner and his team had carried through with their threat.

Outside his cell door, through a narrow slot at eye–height, he could see a guard glaring in at him, two more faces behind his, could hear the jangling of the chains and manacles into which he would be forced. Suddenly, despite the Spartan cell in which he lived and the radical collapse of his world, he felt as though he were leaving home for something even worse. Which, he knew, he was.

He dragged himself up off the thin mattress and shuffled to the cell door, then turned and placed his hands behind his back. A second shutter opened, and strong hands cuffed him before the cell door was opened and the guards barged their way in and began manacling his ankles, and linking them with the heavy chains to his wrists. Within moments, he was weighed down by the steel and turned forcefully to march out of the cell.

'Where am I going?' he asked the nearest guard, hoping against hope that he was not being moved from the security max to a general prison.

'Where we tell you. Move!'

The guards hustled him down the sterile corridor outside; plain walls, no windows, other cells locked and their shutters closed. The doors were sufficiently thick to deaden all sound, and all of the inmates spent twenty three hours per day locked behind them.

Wilms cried out inside for the power that he had once wielded; the ability to end the careers of all three of the guards escorting him with a simple command; the financial power to sway government with a single gesture; the fear and respect that had enabled him to strike terror into the hearts of men far stronger than he. One of the guards shoved him from behind and he realized that his power, his strength had been a mere illusion, Wilms the same thin and fragile man he had always been. He had been abandoned, his assets stolen, his fortune ripped from his hands like candy from a child, no trial, no media coverage, nothing. Victor Wilms had been cast into a pit of despair that he knew he would never escape from, but worst of all was the fact that he had been abandoned by his peers – Majestic Twelve and the Bilderberg Group had watched him fall and laughed as they had done so.

Tears pinched at his eyes and he realized that he was thinking of his parents, of the quiet Ohio town in which he had been raised. *Crying for his momma.* That's what the jocks had sneered at him back in high school, the geeky, bespectacled Wilms no match for their strength and courage. In later years, he had revelled in destroying their careers one by one from afar, and watching them succumb to suicide, prison, drink or drugs. Now he realized he would perhaps encounter them again, in the general population, angry, embittered, aggressive men with nothing left to lose…

His betrayal by Majestic Twelve suddenly burned bright in his mind and he knew that he no longer had a choice. If he was truly to fall, then he would damned well take them with him.

'I want to talk to Douglas Jarvis of the Defense Intelligence Agency,' he announced.

The guards did not respond to him. Wilms, cultivating some of his recently lost superior–air, glared at the man to his left.

'Did you hear what I said?!'

The guard whirled, twisted on his right boot as he brought his left knee up with a brutal jerk into Wilms's guts. The blow ejected the air from Wilms's lungs in a great rush as his legs folded up beneath him and he slumped to the polished floor with a cry of agony. The guards lifted him bodily, twisted his arms painfully up behind his back and dragged him toward the exit gates.

'You're done talking,' the guard sneered into his face as he was hauled out of the cell block. 'By this afternoon you'll be in general population, and by tonight you'll either be in the infirmary with a shiv sticking out of your guts or you'll be in the morgue. Have a nice day.'

The guard shoved Wilms through the gates and he collapsed onto his knees, his aged bones cracking on the unforgiving floor as he finally wept openly. The guards ignored him and dragged him toward the next exit gate, with every step bringing him closer to his doom.

*

Mitchell lay in the silence and ignored the cold that seeped it seemed into his bones, aching there as he waited. Most men his age would have long ago retired from field work, but Mitchell was driven by forces far beyond his control, his desire for not just revenge but the utter annihilation of Majestic Twelve and its Bilderberg representatives of far greater importance than his own wellbeing.

Members of the Bilderberg, together with their sister organizations – the Trilateral Commission and the Council on Foreign Relations, were charged with the post–war take over of the democratic process. The measures implemented by the groups provided general control of the world economy through indirect political means. Originally conceived by Joseph H. Retinger and Prince Bernhard of the Netherlands, they formed a proposal for a covert conference to involve NATO leaders in general discussion on international affairs. The meeting would allow each participant to speak his mind freely because no media representative would be permitted inside. If any leaks occurred, the journalists responsible would be "discouraged" from reporting it. From the outset the American group was influenced by the Rockefeller family, the owners of Standard Oil – competitors of Bernhard's Royal Dutch Petroleum. From then on, the Bilderberg business reflected the concerns of the oil industry in its meetings. Around a hundred and fifteen participants attended the meeting, coming from government and politics, industry, finance, education and communications. Participants were invited to the Bilderberg meeting by the Chairman, following his consultations and recommendations by the Steering Committee membership. The individuals were chosen based on their knowledge, standing and experience – just like the members of Majestic Twelve.

Although MJ–12's origins could be found much further back in time in the wake of World War Two and the flight of the leaders of the Third Reich from Germany to South America, Mitchell knew that their agenda was reflected in the Bilderberg meetings, especially now that the west's obsession with oil was being replaced with a keen desire to develop alternative fuels that would render the relevance of the Middle East's powerful royal families a thing of the past. Mitchell was well aware that a paradigm shift was coming, a drastic alteration of the balance of power around the world, all of it engineered by the heads of state at the annual Bilderberg meetings and influenced directly by the members of Majestic Twelve.

Until now.

The work of the Defense Intelligence Agency had begun to unravel the vast network of informers and employees of Majestic Twelve, and in the course of several investigations they had succeeded in blowing wide open some of MJ–12's most ambitious and secretive programs, agenda so classified that even the President of the United States was completely unaware of their existence.

In the course of those investigations, Mitchell had seen his own position within MJ–12 compromised, and ultimately he had been required to make the choice between killing for employment and killing for a reason. Mitchell, a veteran of the Vietnam War, had long since lost any real sense of sympathy for or empathy with the human race. Dedicated it seemed to destroying itself, mankind was to Mitchell an uncaring, selfish, blind and irresponsible creature for whom the future was somebody else's problem. But the orders to murder a man who had developed a device which provided electrical power virtually for free, simply because his device would remove power from Majestic Twelve and the Bilderberg Group, had been too much for Mitchell. Worse than that, the assassination target had not even intended to make any money from his "fusion cage", as it had been named, despite knowing that he could have made billions of dollars overnight. To Mitchell's astonishment he had intended to give the device away to mankind, for nothing other than the sheer joy of altruism.

The death of Stanley Meyer had affected Mitchell greatly, and when he had then been ordered to murder a former President of the United States he had gone rogue. No longer would he answer to men who were powerful only because of their money and the offices they held. Mitchell would himself do something out of sheer altruism, and destroy for once and for all the incomparable greed that grew outward from MJ–12 like a cancer spreading across the globe.

A door opened from one of the cell blocks, almost a mile and a half away, and Mitchell's train of thought slammed to a halt as he saw four guards exit the block, between them a small, white–haired man in orange prison overalls and weighed down by steel chains that glinted in the sunlight. Mitchell leaned down and pressed his eye to the military–grade optics. The scope did not have any zoom function, designed instead to provide the clearest image of a distant target possible. Mitchell had positioned the scope based on previous prisoners he had seen escorted from the block, and in the meantime he had watched birds of prey wheeling in the sky above to judge the thermals and the light winds between his lonely mountain hideout and the prison before him. Conditions were perfect, light winds, few thermals, clear visibility. Even at such extreme range, Mitchell knew that he could not miss, and with the gentle breeze in his face he knew that not only would his target be dead before anybody heard the shot, they would likely barely hear the shot at all. Mitchell would be long gone before the security guards would be able to pinpoint where the shot had come from.

His gloved finger rested on the trigger as his left thumb turned the rifle's safety switch to *off* as he prepared to fire.

***

Dean Crawford

VIII

Ethan hadn't been sure what he had expected to feel when he saw Victor Wilms being dragged out of the sally port of Florence ADX, but sympathy hadn't been high on his list. Yet despite himself, the sight of an elderly man on his knees was still something that compelled him to reach out, to assist, to help in some way. It was only his knowledge of what a cruel man Victor Wilms had become that forced him to stand firm.

'Doesn't feel so great, does it?'

Lopez's voice was calm but cold on the morning air as they stood alongside four armed guards, who were themselves arrayed before an armored truck. The security around a figure like Victor Wilms was in fact staged by Doug Jarvis back at the DIA: had they really wanted to move Wilms and not have him iced by Majestic Twelve, they would have slipped him out quietly under cover of darkness in a goods truck or similar, the security hidden out of sight. Jarvis had felt that highly visible security would make it easy for MJ–12 to spot and track Wilms to whatever hellish gaol he was destined for, and that Wilms would know it.

'You think he'll fold?' he asked Lopez.

'He'll fold,' she replied, for once in agreement with Doug Jarvis. 'He doesn't have the stones to survive in general population even if MJ–12 weren't gunning for him.'

Wilms shuffled to stand before them, and Ethan looked down at the old man.

'Last chance, Vic',' he said, mimicking Lopez's talent for subtly irritating Wilms. 'You talk now, or you spend what little will be left of your life waiting for a shiv in your kidneys.'

Wilms visibly trembled, and not from the cold. Ethan could see the fear in his eyes, running like poison through his veins. The old man's shoulders sagged, and he spoke softly with the voice of a broken man.

'There was a new player,' he whispered, 'a man who had approached Majestic Twelve a short while before the Antarctic expedition with a proposal.'

'What kind of proposal?' Lopez demanded.

'It was something to do with old bones,' Wilms replied, clearly not sure on the details of a science he probably knew very little about. 'I figured this guy was trying to resurrect extinct species in order to extract living samples of some kind of super–virus from them.'

Ethan shot a glance at Lopez. 'A link with Channing.'

Lopez nodded.

'What's that got to do with Varginha, and who are they?'

'It's not a *them*,' Wilms said, 'it's a where. It's in Brazil.'

Ethan couldn't be one hundred per cent certain that Wilms could be relied upon, but the figure that he cut in the dawn, thin and pale and beaten, suggested that Wilms was a spent force who had finally realized that spilling everything was the only way to ensure that he wasn't murdered in some filthy prison shower by young thugs who would pull off the homicide for nothing more than a packet of cigarettes.

'All right,' he said finally, willing to show Wilms an act of kindness in the hopes that it would encourage him to say more. 'You just bought yourself a reprieve, but we need a name. Who was this new player that approached Majestic Twelve?'

Wilms looked up at Ethan and parted his lips to speak.

There was no sound as Wilm's head snapped suddenly to one side as the side of his skull splattered across the asphalt at their feet and his body dropped in free–fall, the light gone from his eyes.

The sound of the shot boomed across the compound an instant later, even as Ethan and Lopez stood still and watched Wilms's lifeless body collapse into a heap on the ground before them. It took Ethan a full second to whirl and look in the direction of the shot, scanning first the nearest watch tower even as he realized that the delay in hearing the shot must mean that the shooter was much further away.

'Holy crap!' Lopez uttered as she spun on her heel, one hand on her pistol.

The guards around them scattered, weapons drawn as Ethan and Lopez dashed for cover behind the nearest towering walls surrounding the compound. Ethan ran and looked up as he did so, to see a low ridge of hills something over a mile away and silhouetted against the bright dawn sky.

Lopez hit the wall and turned her back to it as she gasped.

'Where the hell did that come from?!'

Alarms began droning across the prison as Ethan checked his pistol's magazine.

'At least a mile to the north east,' he replied and looked up at the sky. 'Sniper rifle, maximum range, perfect conditions, no wind and minimal thermal interference. A professional hit.'

'Mitchell,' Lopez growled.

'It's a fair bet,' Ethan confirmed, 'either that or MJ–12 contracted somebody else to silence Wilms.'

Ethan called across to a sergeant sheltering behind the thick wall of the nearest watch tower. 'You guys got a helicopter here?'

The guard shook his head. 'Marshall's office, or the local airfield, but they won't be up here at short notice!'

Ethan shoved his pistol back into its holster and dashed for the nearest of the prison trucks. Lopez rushed after him, and they climbed into the cab as Ethan started the engine and yelled out of the window.

'Get the damned gate open or the shooter'll be in the wind!'

Ethan crunched the truck into gear and drove it toward the main gates as a guard rushed into the control room and opened the gates. Motors whined as the gates slowly opened, and beyond them a second solid set also rumbled apart to let them through.

Ethan hit the gas and the truck lurched through the open gates and into the parking lot outside, accelerating toward the exit as Lopez leaned forward to peer out to the east at the distant hill.

'Jesus, that's a long way to shoot.'

Ethan nodded as he turned onto the highway, the truck's wheels screeching on the asphalt. The chassis shuddered as the rubber bounced and then caught again, and he slammed the gas pedal down as he replied.

'Bullet drop due to gravity must have been damned near four feet at that range, and there was no way the shooter could have tested the shot without alerting the prison. First time, at a mile: even with the perfect conditions it's the shot of a lifetime.'

'Especially for Wilms,' Lopez uttered dryly. 'He was about to give us another name. That's why I keep telling you, we need these assholes alive. They know enough to give us info on bad guys for years.'

Ethan changed gear and gritted his teeth, but he said nothing. He wasn't sorry to see Wilms fall dead right in front of him, had even felt a brief sense of elation. But he realized too that Lopez had been right all along, as usual: with Wilms dead there was nothing else he could do for them. All of his knowledge of Majestic Twelve and all that it had done had died with him, information that could have brought more of their kind to justice.

The line of hills drew closer, but even as they sped along Ethan knew that their chances of finding anybody up there were almost nil. The deserts beyond were vast and empty. If the shooter was a smart man, and Ethan had to figure that he was, he wouldn't have a getaway vehicle. Instead, he would cross the deserts to another town and slip away into obscurity once more, the deserts themselves far too vast to search effectively. Even basic camouflage and concealment skills would be enough to evade detection, and the heat of the desert would remove any advantage in using infra–red cameras on helicopters until nightfall.

A narrow, dusty track led off the main road toward the hills, the truck bouncing and bumping around and leaving clouds of dust spiralling away across the hot wastelands. Ethan could hear above the engine noise the wailing of sirens as police pursuit vehicles alerted to the crisis raced to catch up with them.

'Call the Sherriff's office,' Ethan said to Lopez. 'Have them send the cars to surrounding towns, and circulate an image of Mitchell in case he shows up somewhere local.'

'Might not be him,' Lopez said, but pulled out her cell without question. 'Besides, he'll have thought of that.'

By the time they had driven to the edge of the hills and Ethan had been forced to abandon the truck, the shooter could have covered a fair distance out into the desert from wherever he had set up his laying–up position. Ethan scanned the hills, and spotted a likely location. He climbed up the hillside, leaving Lopez talking on her cell, powering his way up the steep slopes until he was a hundred feet or so above the plain.

He could see the prison clearly from up here, and down into the entrance compound and some small areas of the exercise yards. The watch towers were close enough to be able to make out the guards patrolling within them, watching over the prison and likely also watching him now climb the hill.

Ethan scouted around the hillside for a few minutes until he found what he was looking for.

Alongside a narrow track on the hill was a shallow depression, and around it had been placed a loose assembly of rocks that was a little too circular to be natural. Ethan climbed down into the depression, and underneath one of the rocks he saw a small slip of paper folded between them.

He knelt down and tugged the piece of paper out, unfolded it, and read the words printed there in a hurried script.

THIS IS THE BEST WAY. DON'T TRY TO STOP ME. A

Ethan folded the piece of paper once more and looked over his shoulder to where the crest of the hill vanished. He stood up and climbed to the top and looked out over the vast empty desert, the sun rising in a blaze of glory before him and the wastes devoid of life and movement.

Lopez climbed up to join him, and he handed her the slip of paper.

'He's on the warpath,' she said softly, and let the piece of paper fall from her fingers. 'That asshole's gonna cost us dear if we don't shut him down.'

Ethan nodded, but he knew that there was no real way they could catch up with Mitchell now.

'C'mon, let's get back to DC with what we've got.'

***

Dean Crawford

IX

Westin Excelsior,

Rome

'In questo modo, signore.'

A concierge attached to the luxury Villa La Cupola Suite guided the eleven men through the silent corridors of the exclusive hotel situated in the Via Veneto district of the city. The suite occupied two entire floors of the hotel, making it the largest in Italy and ensuring absolute security and privacy for its occupants.

The concierge led the men to the room, opened the ornate doors and then stood to one side and allowed the men to file past him. As soon as they were inside he closed the doors behind them and left.

The suite had recently been refreshed with a seven million dollar makeover to ensure that any individual or group hiring the suite would be surrounded by the finest that Italy could offer. Furnished in the grand old style, with hand–frescoed cathedral–like domes and a grand piano in the main conference room, it was also peppered with tastefully incorporated high–tech gadgets controlling heating, lighting, drapes and other extraneous fittings, along with a private fitness room, dining room, sauna, steam bath and Jacuzzi.

Samuel Kruger had never before visited this particular hotel, the location of their meeting chosen by one of his personal assistants, but he approved of her selection as he turned to the ten men who had accompanied him.

'Gentlemen, it is time to discuss our next move.'

Samuel Kruger was a tall, gaunt man who had just enjoyed his sixty fourth birthday surrounded by his family and close friends on an island in the Bahamas that he had hired for the occasion. Throughout his long years Samuel had known only the finest things in life, from his education at Eton College in London to his business life managing the sizeable property empire that his father had built in the wake of World War Two, when so much of Europe had needed re–building. Samuel had inherited the immense fortune and then gone on to swell it further with numerous wise investments and forays into global property development, especially those that allowed him to snap up land cheaply from native populations and then eject them in order to build multiplex hotels and resorts. His last major acquisition, the ravaged shores of Aceh, Thailand that had been shattered in the wake of the tsunami that had taken tens of thousands of lives, had been made possible by considerable bribes to government officials. With the land reclaimed from the families who had owned it, he had built an immensely profitable new development.

Of the families who once lived there, he knew and cared little.

Unlike the smaller, publicity loving buffoons like Trump who paraded their wealth for all to see, Kruger and his companions remained in the shadows, their wealth and power unknown to all but a few politicians. That, in part, was why Kruger was now the *de facto* head of Majestic Twelve.

'Our next move?' uttered one of his companions, a man with a cane who looked old enough to be able to remember Gettysburg. 'You make this sound like a position of choice Samuel, but we are being hunted, our position is precarious. It is likely that our enemy know our identities.'

Samuel nodded sombrely, keen to show that he understood the delicacy of their position. 'The American Defense Intelligence Agency has made great strides in deconstructing our efforts and they have had some victories, but their power will always be limited by the office of their director, General Nellis.'

'Who has the ear of the President,' a man by the name of Felix pointed out, younger, more hawkish and energetic, the heir to an oil fortune whose mind was every bit as sharp as his father's had been. 'That's significant in itself.'

'Presidents come and go,' Samuel replied without concern. 'What one achieves, the next often undoes for nothing more than spite. The current president clearly shares few of our ideals, but he has little power over us. That, my friends, is why the administration is allowed to lead the country: it makes the people think that they can make a difference.'

The other men nodded in silent agreement.

'We almost took too much from them last time,' said another man, the owner of one of the world's largest and yet least known banks. 'The people suspect, Samuel.'

'The people believe conspiracy theories,' Samuel countered. 'That's why we promote them, one after the other: faked moon landings, UFO sightings, economic crashes, shadow governments...' Kruger smiled. 'When they can no longer tell what is true and what is not, the truth remains well hidden within the lies.'

'It was too great a risk,' said another, the owner of a major shipping company. 'Look at the Arab Spring, at Syria, Egypt and others. Push the people too hard and they will rebel, violently if necessary.'

'Indeed they will,' Kruger agreed, 'against their politicians. Not against us. Most of them barely know we exist, and those that suspect that we do don't know who we are.'

Kruger sat down on an ornate chair and folded his hands beneath his chin. He was well aware of the old adage that *power corrupts, and absolute power corrupts absolutely*: that was why Majestic Twelve was formed of twelve men and not one. The cabal's origins in the wake and the rubble of World War Two had been born of more than just the spectacular discoveries made during the time of Einstein and Oppenheimer, for that conflict had resolved in the minds of men made powerful by the sale of weapons that humanity, even democratically governed humanity, simply was not capable of saving itself from tyranny when it appeared. Mankind had lost all sense of the common good, and thus was feeble in the face of violence and greed, traits that Kruger and others before him had encouraged.

A *state of fear* was that which best protected both leaders and the led. That had been the conclusion of the predecessors of Majestic Twelve, military industrial figures who pondered the bizarre way in which the Third Reich had risen to power and so completely brainwashed the population of Germany before setting Europe aflame for five long years. Hitler had used a skillful combination of patriotic rhetoric and fearmongering to galvanize the German people into rising against oppressors that in many ways did not exist; blaming the United Nations for the crippling economic reprisals directed against Germany for the First World War under the Kaiser, despite Germany having been the aggressor in that conflict also; blaming the Jews likewise for the ailing economy, targeting them as an enemy of the state while convincing the people that every other country in Europe would continue to oppress them, preventing Germany from ever holding a place on the world stage. In doing so, he took control of the entire country and won the allegiance of a people who had vowed to fight an enemy that technically did not exist.

In the aftermath of the conflict, Majestic Twelve formed and began planning to emulate the Third Reich's methods, not with conflict but by guile: to sew fear into the hearts and minds of people, to convince them beyond all shadow of doubt that they *needed* governments to protect them, *needed* armies and navies and air forces to protect them, *needed* the skill and knowledge and prestige of well educated men to lead them to safety, *needed* water and electricity pumped to their homes, food in their supermarkets and fuel in their vehicles. Fears arose and were duly cultivated by Majestic Twelve to ensure the allegiance of the masses: the Cold War, The Bay of Pigs, Vietnam, the Gulf War, the War on Terror, global warming: anything and everything that could be created to ensure that the people felt as though the enemy were already at the gates and only the might and expertize of the government could save them…

Kruger knew that he sat among the most powerful men on earth: powerful not because they were wealthy but because they knew precisely how the *vulgar crowd*, as Niccolo Machiavelli had once described them, were always "taken by appearances". The growth of the Internet and the information age, far from hindering this process, had given it even greater reach as the truth was lost amid the inane ramblings of millions of citizens all clamoring for the truth even though they would not have recognized it had it rose up and slapped them across the face. Just as once had hundreds of Jews been subdued beneath the barrels of a handful of German Wehrmacht, simply because of the uniforms that they wore, when they could have risen and overpowered a few soldiers in moments; just as civilians even now suffered beneath dictatorships in so many countries, or cowered in apartments afraid to step out onto streets ruled by gangs, so the citizenry continued to fail to realize that it was their own inability to *unite* that kept them in chains. Hitler could never have reached power without the complicity of ordinary Germans; gangs of street thugs would be crushed in days by the might of the citizens living in houses across every city on earth; dictators would fall easily were the people, including the military, to form a true alliance of peace. Kruger knew that the Defense Intelligence Agency presented little threat to Majestic Twelve. He was more concerned with events like the Arab Spring where truly courageous, ordinary people had risen up and overthrown dictators like Muammar Gaddafi.

'We must choose our twelfth member,' Kruger said to his companions. 'For too long we have been without a full compliment, and Victor Wilms is now either dead or in the hands of the Defense Intelligence Agency. If that is so, he may very well remain beyond our reach.'

'And able to turn on us,' said another of the men. 'And of course, you have not yet even mentioned Aaron Mitchell.'

Kruger shifted uncomfortably in his seat. Mitchell, once their most talented assassin, had performed a remarkable *volte face* and become perhaps their most feared foe. His sudden reversal of allegiance was a prime example of one individual rising up against an oppressor, except that in this case Mitchell knew nothing of Majestic Twelve's true intentions and thus was motivated purely by revenge, in itself a powerful threat.

'Mitchell's whereabouts are unknown, and as far as we are aware he has no knowledge of our identities.'

'As far as we're aware,' a British man named Hampton echoed. He sat bolt upright in his seat, his hands resting on an ornate cane that he used more for show than anything else, the former Etonian as spritely as any man half his age and his clean jaw adorned with a broad, silvery moustache.

'As far as we were aware it was impossible for a man to escape from a security max prison, but Mitchell achieved it. What else are we *aware of* that might also be incorrect, Samuel?'

'A great many things,' Kruger admitted, 'but we are neither omnipresent nor omniscient. Mitchell has chosen his path and sooner or later it will bring him to us. When it does, we will be prepared to eliminate the threat that he represents and continue with our work.'

'And what about the Defense Intelligence Agency?' asked another. 'They have clearly made it their policy to hunt us down and to expose Majestic Twelve. Until now it has been a tolerable threat but we now face greater issues. What are we to do about Nellis's team?'

Kruger examined his hands for a moment as he thought about the consequences of the DIA's mission to expose the cabal. As his colleague had said, the DIA had been directly responsible for obstructing a number of MJ–12 campaigns, but at the same time they had failed also in many others, technology concealed from the American government that could otherwise have changed the face of humanity, at great financial cost to the cabal.

But now things had changed. An expedition to the Antarctic had resulted in the loss of a DIA agent's life, and somehow that had created a personal vendetta of sorts. Kruger was well aware of the identities of the team's members: Ethan Warner, Nicola Lopez, Douglas Jarvis and others, all apparently hell–bent on bringing the cabal down when they didn't really have even the vaguest understanding of what Majestic Twelve represented, what its true mission was and had been for decades: some would say, centuries.

'The DIA are operating with the consent of the current administration, although that in itself is of course a temporary measure for them and could change at the next election. However, I believe we share the view that leaving such measures to chance is never a wise course of action. The DIA's mission to expose us has already cost the life of the Director of the FBI, and that in itself may seed caution in the minds of those who would stand against us.'

'It also handed them Victor Wilms on a plate,' said one of the men. 'There are too many loose ends Samuel, too many problems to be resolved individually. We must strike boldly to prevent us losing control of the situation any further.'

Kruger was about to reply when his cell phone buzzed in his jacket pocket. To be contacted by his assistants during one of the cabal's rare meetings would require a seismic event and he looked at his cell immediately. As he read the simple message there, he felt the first twinge of dread creep like insects beneath his skin.

'What is it?' asked the man named Felix.

Kruger slipped the cell back into his pocket as he replied. 'Victor Wilms is dead. Local media have reported an incident inside the prison walls, but our contact has confided that Wilms was killed by a sniper's rifle from at least one mile away.'

A gust of discontented sighs drifted among them as the old British Etonian replied.

'That's it, Samuel. Enough is enough.'

'I agree,' Kruger replied. 'We cannot afford to take the chance that the next administration will share the same sympathies as the incumbent president. I have placed a team on stand by and they are merely awaiting the command to carry out my order: I have instructed their leader to enact the Extinction Code.'

A deep silence weighed heavily in the room as Kruger judged the reactions of his companions. They were all men of the world, well educated, of proven financial power and success, but those same traits also denied them the experience of the man on the street, the perspective of the ordinary citizen upon whose inadvertent allegiance all men of power relied.

'We have tried this before,' said one of the men. 'Dwight Oppenheimer made a play to pull the plug on civilization and he ended up dead. We're nothing without the masses, if only they knew it.'

'Again, I agree,' Kruger replied, 'that is why, unlike Oppenheimer's broad–brush and clumsy attempt at a worldwide epidemic, this will instead be a precision strike.'

'How?' demanded another. 'Are you suggesting a false–flag nuclear war option of some kind?'

'No,' Kruger replied. 'It has come to light recently that a new perspective on all living species has revealed a means to eliminate life by the flick of a switch, biologically speaking.'

'And this Extinction Code, it is already in place?' asked one of the youngest men in the cabal. 'It has been tested?'

'It is seeing a limited trial in Madagascar,' Kruger replied. 'The man behind it wishes to meet us, to discuss his terms.'

'And the DIA?' asked another. 'If we embark on another campaign now they will be sure to obstruct us, as will Mitchell. We cannot afford to move publicly for fear of an arrest or even an assassination.'

'The Extinction Code I refer to covers two plans of action,' Kruger explained. 'The first is localized and directed at the employees of the Defense Intelligence Agency. If we are all in agreement, I will put it into motion immediately.'

The cabal members all raised a hand in favor, and Kruger nodded.

'So be it. The second plan of action is global and under the control of a man whose opinions and ideas I think that we should listen to. He has been in touch and would like to meet us in Dubai.'

The members of Majestic Twelve looked at each other for a moment, and then they all turned back to Kruger. 'Who is this man?'

***

X

DIA Headquarters

Washington DC

'You're sure it was Mitchell?'

Ethan and Lopez walked into Hellerman's office, Jarvis and the scientist waiting there for them.

'No doubt about it,' Ethan replied. 'He even left us a nice little note.'

'Then it's started,' Jarvis said. 'Mitchell's likely developed a plan to hit them all, one after the other, and they'll start running as soon as they hear about what happened to Wilms.'

'Can't we keep it under wraps for a bit longer?' Lopez asked.

'Unfortunately not,' Jarvis explained. 'There was a media team inside the prison doing a documentary for state television. They've agreed not to broadcast the footage of what happened, but the word's out already that a man died in Florence ACX after a shooting incident. Majestic Twelve won't have missed the event.'

'Okay,' Ethan said, 'then we need to move quickly. The last thing Wilms told us was that a new player had approached Majestic Twelve with a proposal. He died before giving us a name, but what about this place called Varginha? Did you learn anything about it?'

'Varginha, Brazil,' Hellerman said. 'Well, what do *you* know about it?'

'It's probably hot,' Ethan offered, 'but I've never heard of it.'

Lopez also shrugged and shook her head. Jarvis did not seem surprised, and instead picked up a remote and activated a screen on the wall nearby. Ethan turned to see what looked like news reports coming out of the region, some of the footage blurry and indistinct.

'What are we looking at?' Lopez asked.

'A news report, one of several, broadcast in 1996,' Jarvis explained. 'The media went into a frenzy down there after three young girls, sisters Liliane and Valquiria Fatima Silva, and their friend Katia Andrade Xavier, reported the discovery of an injured alien creature hiding in backstreets in the town. They said that they had seen the "devil", a biped about five feet tall with a large head and very thin body, with what they described as V–shaped feet, brown skin and large red eyes. It seemed unsteady and the girls assumed it was injured or sick. Nobody took much notice until a half dozen other people saw the same creature and the police got involved.'

'And what happened then?' Ethan asked.

'That's when things got real interesting.'

'I hate it when he says that,' Lopez murmured.

Jarvis gestured to the screen, which was showing numerous news reports in Spanish, scenes of frightened civilians, police vehicles and cordons, news crews being denied access to areas of woodland and what looked to Ethan like a hospital.

'The police showed up and one or two of the officers involved got a look at whatever it was that had spooked the girls,' Jarvis explained. 'They got all riled up about it too, and the government rolled out some big wheels to take a look and started cordoning off sections of the city. Nothing much happened after that, and the police reported that the girls must have encountered a local homeless man nicknamed "*Mudinho*" who was known to the police and who often squatted in doorways, never washed himself and so on.'

'V–shaped feet and large red eyes?' Lopez replied. 'Could three girls have all made the same mistake?'

'That's what I thought,' Jarvis agreed. 'Then, two days later another creature was reported as being found near or on a road just outside the city, and a convoy of military trucks and personnel were despatched to find it. At the same time the owners of a local farm, named Oralina and Eurico de Freitas, reported a large UFO hovering over their land.'

'Mass hysteria,' Ethan figured, 'maybe even mass hallucination created by the news reports and rumors?

'Again, that's a possibility,' Jarvis agreed, 'but it's what happened *after* these events died down that's got our interest. A third sighting of a suspected alien creature was reported from a local zoo, and in the aftermath of the sighting three of the animals in the zoo in the immediate vicinity of the sighting mysteriously died.'

'Coincidence,' Lopez suggested.

'Gunshots were heard that night from the local area where military vehicles were operating, and at least one police officer was said to have had direct contact with an unknown species of animal out in the woods. One month later that officer, a man named Marco Eli Chereze, died in hospital from an unknown disease.'

Ethan's interest was sparked, and he saw an image of the young officer appear on the screen.

'He was just twenty three years old,' Jarvis went on. 'An expert physician was assigned to treat him, a man named Dr Cesario L. Furtado, who confided later that he had never seen an illness like it. The victim was treated at Bom Pastor Hospital before being transferred to the hospital Regional Do Sul de Minas, where he died on February fifteenth, 1996. The incident itself became brief global news, with a piece written about it in the *Wall Street Journal* and a book by Doctor Roger Leir, *Des Extraterrestres captures a Varginha en Brazil*, said by many to recount what was a "New Roswell" in UFO history.'

'So what's the big deal?' Lopez asked. 'Was he killed by an extra–terrestrial, if there ever was one, or did the military commit some mistake and decide to silence him in order to cover it up?'

'That's what we're interested in,' Jarvis said, 'because the police officer's family fought for information but were denied an independent autopsy. Whatever happened at Varginha, the Brazilian government went to great lengths to cover it up.'

'They denied an autopsy?' Ethan echoed in amazement. 'Even after all the media hype around the incident?'

Jarvis gestured to the screen, which now bore images of heavily redacted military reports that Ethan assumed had been obtained by agents from beneath the noses of the Brazilian military and police.

'The police superintendent who was in charge of the police presence on the night the incident occurred requested to be present at the autopsy, on behalf of the family of Marco Chereze. He was denied, in direct contravention of the laws of the Nation. It was only a year later that the Military Police, bombarded with public outcry over the cover up, were forced to open up some of the files they had created, which is essentially what you're seeing here on the screen.'

Lopez moved closer to the screen, her eyes scanning the documents.

'It says that Chereze died of a generalized infection, but it doesn't give any details.'

'And that's the problem,' Jarvis said. 'This thing, whatever it was, killed him within a month and yet there was no cause of death on the certificate. There is no mention of the symptoms he suffered, no details of those symptoms escalating in any way: it just says he died of an infection and that's it.'

'So they don't have a clue what killed him,' Ethan said. 'What about the family, anything from them?'

'Nothing,' Jarvis replied. 'The victim's sister, a Marta Antonia Tavares, visited the hospital frequently while Chereze was still alive but was always denied access to her brother and was repeatedly denied access to both his medical records and even to the doctors who were treating him.'

'And all of this happened as a result of a close encounter of the third kind that supposedly didn't happen?' Lopez asked.

'That's what I thought,' Jarvis replied. 'You don't cover something up if there's nothing there to cover up. The Military Police claimed that Chereze wasn't on duty that night, among various other claims that were quickly proven false by the local media, not to mention Chereze's own family who waved him off to work that evening. Before long, the whole independent investigation ground to a halt when key witnesses began recounting their statements and refused to talk to reporters.'

'Government sanctioned cover–up,' Lopez said, 'we've seen that before.'

'Death threats were made,' Jarvis confirmed. 'Only people who have since grown too old to care anymore are willing to speak on the record about what happened, and what few records there are remain consistent and independently verifiable. The Policeman Marco Eli Chereze was confronted by a biped of some kind and came into close contact with it, and that contact killed him within weeks.'

'Again, why are we here?' Lopez asked. 'This all happened decades ago, the trail would have long ago run cold.'

Jarvis's normally composed features seemed to Ethan to become somewhat pale, taut with concern. He pressed a button on the remote and the screen changed to an image of some kind of cave system.

'What do you know about the collapse of bat colonies across the United States?'

Ethan blinked. 'Well, nothing?'

'Or the dramatic decline in pollenating insects, such as the common bee?' Jarvis tried again.

'Aren't they being killed off by some kind of fungus?' Lopez asked. 'A bee disease?'

'Partly,' Jarvis agreed, 'although the companies that manufacture chemical pesticides like to play down the correlation between pesticide use and bee decline. What about the dramatic acidification of ocean water, the unprecedented decline in amphibians and the disappearance of more species in the last fifty years than in the preceding five thousand?'

'You're talking about climate change, right?' Lopez hazarded.

'No,' Jarvis replied. 'I'm talking about what's now being described by science as the Holocene Extinction.'

'That doesn't sound so good,' Lopez said.

'It isn't,' Jarvis replied as he stepped away from the screen.

Hellerman took his cue from Jarvis.

'The Holocene extinction, sometimes referred to as the Sixth extinction, describes the decline of global species during the present Holocene epoch that began around ten thousand years ago in the wake of the last Ice Age. The large number of extinctions span countless plants and mammals, birds, amphibians, reptiles and arthropods. According to the species–area theory and based on upper–bound estimating, the present rate of extinction may be up to a hundred forty thousand species per year, which makes it the greatest loss of biodiversity since the Cretaceous–Paleogene extinction event.'

'Since the what?' Lopez asked.

'The K–T event, as it was known,' Hellerman explained, 'the bolid impactor that killed off the dinosaurs.'

Ethan began to pick up the threads of connections between dinosaurs and the Varghina Event of 1996.

'Wait one,' he said. 'Are you suggesting that what happened in Brazil all those years ago might have something to do with this extinction event?'

Hellerman nodded.

'You ever read about the *Conquistadores* and their conquering of South America?'

'Sure,' Lopez said. 'They walked right into the Inca and Aztec Empires and wiped them out.'

'That's right,' Hellerman agreed, 'but they didn't do it using weapons in the classical sense. In fact, what they really did was get lucky by having smallpox and influenza.'

'Wow, that does sound lucky.'

'It was as if you were a tiny force of perhaps a hundred starving men, far from home, facing hundreds of thousands of heavily armed warriors in their native land,' Hellerman explained. 'The native Americans had no immunity to the diseases carried by the *Conquistadores*. When Cortez and the others landed, they inadvertently infected the native populations with diseases that ravaged them as effectively as any weapon of war. The Spaniards did not destroy the ancient American civilizations by courage in battle: they made them sick in huge numbers, sufficient that they were able to win battles with massively inferior numbers.'

'And you think that what's happening now is a similar thing?' Lopez asked. 'That all those species going extinct is being caused by some kind of sickness?'

'Not exactly,' Hellerman cautioned her. 'The Holocene is unique in that it has seen the disappearance of large land animals known as megafauna, starting around ten thousand years ago, which was about when mankind really got going. Megafauna outside of the African continent that didn't evolve alongside humans were massively vulnerable to predation by early humans and many died out shortly after we began spreading across the Earth. It's been suggested that the extinction of the mammoths, whose habits had maintained grasslands, resulted in the growth of major forests and that the resulting forest fires may have resulted in early human–induced climate change.'

'So we're the bad guys again,' Ethan said.

'We were just another species struggling for survival back then,' Hellerman said. 'We did what we had to do, but now there are seven billion of us. Some believe that anthropogenic extinctions may have begun as early as when the first modern humans spread out of Africa up to two hundred thousand years ago, which is supported by rapid mega–faunal extinction following human colonization in Australia, New Zealand and Madagascar. We're a global super predator, Ethan, and our reach as a species that preys on other apex–predators is unprecedented. Extinctions of species have occurred on every land mass and ocean with a human presence, with overfishing, ocean acidification and the amphibian crisis being a few examples of an almost universal decline of biodiversity.'

'What about this virus then?' Lopez asked, somewhat confused. 'How does that play into things?'

Hellerman took the remote from Jarvis and switched the screen to a new image, this time of the caves once more, in which were millions of bats.

'White nose syndrome,' he said. 'It's claimed between six and seven million bats, with the decline in some cave systems exceeding ninety per cent, a truly pandemic and dangerous disease. The disease is caused by a fungus, *Pseudogymnoascus destructans*, to which the bats have no natural immunity. While this in itself is bad for bats, the wider implications are many and varied. The extinction of so many bat species has resulted in the Forest Service estimating that the die off could mean that two and a half million pounds in weight of insects wouldn't be eaten, resulting in wide ranging crop destruction in New England alone, with bats saving farmers in the United States some three billion dollars annually in pest control measures, not to mention bats' crucial pollination and seed dispersal habits that further support ecological balance.'

'You're talking about the butterfly effect, right?' Ethan said. 'That the knock on effects of one event can be blown out of proportion as they spread.'

'Pretty much,' Hellerman agreed. 'The predicted effects of all of this are alarming, and they share similar features with other outbreaks such as Colony Collapse Disorder, the abrupt disappearance of all western honey bee colonies due to an unknown disease, and *chytridiomycosis*, another fungal disease linked to the worldwide decline in amphibious species. These animals are all known as "sentinel species", creatures that underpin the foundation of natural eco–systems around the world. If they go, we all go in an extinction event, and that's what's so frightening about what's happening: it doesn't take a meteorite impact to wipe out all life on earth. If we lose insects and bees, within years everything will die out.'

'Everything?' Lopez uttered.

'Everything,' Hellerman confirmed. 'If you lose the foundation species, the large populations at the bottom of the food chain, then everything up from them dies out in sequence. If you lose the plankton in the oceans due to acidification, then you next lose the small invertebrates that feed on the plankton, then the fish that feed on the invertebrates, then the sharks and dolphins and seals that feed on the fish: it never ends until all species have collapsed in population or become completely extinct, which all depends on how perfectly adapted they are to their environment.'

Ethan watched the images of species flickering across the screen as a new thought crossed his mind.

'The policeman who died in Brazil: did he have any contact with other people or the local environment after his infection?'

'That's what we were afraid of,' Jarvis said, 'so we went and checked out local wildlife populations in the surrounding areas, which are part of what's called the Atlantic Forest. The news wasn't good.'

'The forest once covered over half a million square miles,' Hellerman explained. 'Due to deforestation and logging, that's now down to fifteen hundred square miles: over eighty five per cent of the forest is gone, forever. The extinction rate is staggering, with over seventy per cent of species lost. But that's not all we found.'

The image on the screen changed, and Ethan frowned. 'What's that?'

The image showed a shadowy canopy of dense forest, light filtering down in golden shafts, the camera work unsteady as though the photographer had fought to capture something in motion. In the center of the image, running away from the camera and looking back over its shoulder as it fled through the undergrowth, was a small, gray skinned biped with large, oval eyes.

'The locals have taken to calling them *demonios forestales*,' Hellerman replied, 'forest devils.'

Lopez eased even closer to the screen for a better look.

'You think that's what was captured back in 1996, what they tried to cover up in Brazil?'

'No,' Jarvis replied. 'We think that it's more recent than that and we want you both to go down there and check it out, because there's a damned good chance that whatever that species might be, it's responsible for the extinction rate in the Atlantic Forest.'

Ethan raised an eyebrow as he looked at Jarvis. 'Like the Conquistadores?'

'Just like them,' Jarvis agreed. 'We think that the Brazilian government isn't conducting the logging operations for money. We think that they're using the work to flush out these creatures on purpose to maintain the cover–up, because they're ground–zero for the next great extinction event.'

'The next extinction event?' Lopez echoed. 'You think that it's really happening, here and now?'

Jarvis handed her a sheet of paper, which she read as he went on.

'Intelligence from our sources suggest that Majestic Twelve has a stake in the game,' he explained. 'They're up to something, and I want to know what the hell that might be. Right now, we only have two possible lines of enquiry: the sightings of these supposed forest devils in South America and anybody connected with Channing's work. According to the old police reports we've uncovered the scientist who wrote the letter that led to his disappearance was a man named Eric Schofield.'

Ethan frowned.

'Majestic Twelve won't want to see a mass extinction go ahead, Doug. People of power are only powerful because of the populations they control. Alone, they're nothing.'

'Agreed, but Majestic Twelve were born out of the Nazi Silver Shirts at the end of World War Two, and we all know what Adolf Hitler really wanted: an Aryan Race, a human future of pure blood. MJ–12 have attempted major pandemics before in order to cull the population and remove what they consider to be "undesirables". If they're onto something here we need to find out what it is, get ahead of them, and put a stop to it.'

'Where can we find this Schofield?' Lopez asked.

'That's where it gets interesting,' Jarvis replied. 'He works at the world's premier Doomsday Vault, designed specifically to survive the end of the world.'

***

XI

The deepest, most secretive subterranean section of the Defense Intelligence Agency's ARIES department was its Research and Test facility, concealed not just from the public but from most of the agency's many thousands of employees. Most were informed that it contained the agency's archives, the record of countless covert missions, which was true enough, but Jarvis knew that it did not reveal the whole story.

In a far flung corner of the archives, in an area purposefully allowed to gather dust, was a door emblazoned with an aged warning sign of high voltages within. The door had a single visible lock, to which only a handful of the agency's personnel held a key. The key would not work on its own, however, for most of the locks inside the door were on the far side and controlled from a secure location in the Director's office. One could only access the door with their key if the other locks had been accessed by the director himself, in this case to allow Jarvis and Hellerman access to the secretive bunker.

Jarvis slid his key into the lock, turned it, and waited.

Moments later he heard mechanical and electrical locks open and the door hissed open before him. He walked with Hellerman into a narrow tunnel filled with old fuse boxes, cables and pipes, and strode down it until he reached another door. Above this one, a dusty looking camera flashed a red light, and as the door behind them closed again so the one in front of them opened.

The laboratory within was large, manned by a dozen or so people Jarvis had picked from the agency's thousands of staff. One of them was Hellerman, who hurried away through the laboratory toward a single experiment shrouded inside a large, transparent cubicle.

'What progress have we made, Hellerman?' he asked.

Hellerman controlled himself and pointed down the laboratory. 'It's complicated.'

Jarvis followed him to the cubicle, inside which was an array of robotic arms surrounding a Perspex box that contained a perfect chrome sphere of material that looked to him like a ball of mercury, the liquid flowing around itself as though it represented the weather patterns on a tiny planet. Beneath it was a golden disc, broken now into two pieces.

'That's not what I asked,' Jarvis pointed out as Hellerman sat down at a workstation that allowed him to control the robotic arms.

'The technology we're looking at here is hundreds of years in advance of our own,' Hellerman said.

'Hundreds?' Jarvis echoed. 'I figured that you'd say thousands, or even millions.'

'No, believe it or not we're not too far behind this kind of memory storage device,' Hellerman explained. 'We know at the moment that it is a highly advanced computer drive, a liquid metal, variable state memory system.'

Jarvis knew that the device was something that Majestic Twelve had spent decades trying to acquire. The problem for them had been that the device had been aboard a structure that had been orbiting planet Earth for some thirteen thousand years, and only when it had come crashing down into the Antarctic ice had there been any opportunity to obtain it. Ethan Warner had led a team into the icy wastelands of the continent and managed to retrieve the device, but at a great cost in lives.

'The thing is, we have something similar already,' Hellerman went on as he reached down and picked up a small, transparent disc that looked to Jarvis to be made of plastic. 'This is a 5D photonic or light–based memory chip, developed by researchers at Oxford University and Germany's Karlsruhe Institute of Technology. It uses waveguide technology to move light from lasers to and from a germanium, tellurium and antimony alloy nano–coating, creating a memory chip a hundred times faster than anything we have today.'

'Is it as fast as that thing?' Jarvis asked, pointing at the silvery sphere.

'No, but it's already been surpassed by another non–layered glass chip developed by scientists at the University of Southampton in the United Kingdom. The University's Optoelectronics Research Centre also used femtosecond laser writing, but their disc has a three hundred sixty terabyte disc data capacity, thermal stability up to a thousand degrees Celcius and virtually unlimited lifetime at room temperature – that is, it could last as long as the age of our universe, some fourteen billion years. They've already saved the Universal Declaration of Human Rights, Newton's Opticks, the Magna Carta and the Kings James Bible on a single chip and barely made a dent in its capacity. They're calling the devices "Superman memory crystals", because they're like the memory crystals seen in the *Superman* movies.'

Jarvis leaned closer to the sphere. 'So we're catching up with whoever made this.'

'In a sense,' Hellerman agreed. 'It's been in orbit around our earth for thirteen thousand years, and we have no idea how long it took to get here, so it could have been constructed millions of years ago, but the level of technical ability is almost within our grasp.'

'Can you access it yet?'

Hellerman shook his head.

'I've deconstructed the way that 5D crystal memory works, and we're applying it now to computer models of this sphere to see what happens. The use of fluid dynamics *and* crystalline memory storage means that this device is infinitely more powerful than our new 5D chips. It's a bit like asking our current weather technology to accurately predict global weather for the next ten years or so, when we struggle to get an accurate local forecast for the next twenty four hours. It's going to take time, boss, a *lot* of time.'

'We need a computer to decipher the computer,' Jarvis mused as he watched the silvery sphere's surface coil and swirl like weather patterns across the surface of the earth. A thought occurred to him as he watched those swirls. 'Does it spin?'

'What?'

'Does it spin, the sphere? Have you measured any rotation?'

'We hadn't got that far yet,' Hellerman admitted. 'We've mostly been preoccupied with getting it into a stable state in the cubicle. Why?'

Jarvis gestured to the swirling patterns on the sphere.

'Those patterns look a little like the Coriolis Effect,' he observed, the force that caused circular weather systems on earth driven by the planet's rotation.

Hellerman stared at the patterns for a moment. 'You're a genius.'

'I've often said it myself.'

'I'll get the tech team on it right away,' Hellerman said, agitated and excited all at once. 'If we could map the Coriolis to known fluid dynamic forces in closed–state spheres and…'

'I'll take your word for it,' Jarvis said as he stood to leave. 'Call me if you figure anything out.'

Jarvis left Hellerman where he was and walked out of the Research Department and back through the eerily quiet surroundings of the basement complex. To travel back to the ARIES Watch Room and then up to the fourth floor took him several minutes, but before long he was knocking on the door of the Director DIA's office. He heard a muffled *enter* from within and he strode inside and shut the door behind him.

'Take a seat, Doug.'

Jarvis sat in a comfortable leather chair. Opposite him sat Lieutenant General J. F. Nellis, the Director of the DIA. Nellis was a former United States Air Force officer who had been appointed DNI by the current president.

'Where are we with MJ–12 and Mitchell?' Nellis asked. 'I heard about Wilms.'

'Mitchell's made the hit,' Jarvis confirmed. 'Ethan and Nicola couldn't locate him but he left his calling card.'

'What's your best assessment of his plan?'

'Mitchell served MJ–12 as an assassin having come in at the ground level after the Vietnam War,' Jarvis said. 'He doesn't consider himself one of them, especially now after all that's happened. He considers them weak men in positions of great power. My best guess is that he'll hit them one after the other, drive the remainder underground and then finish them off. Do we know where MJ–12's members are right now?'

Nellis nodded, glancing at an intelligence report on his desk.

'Most of them,' he acknowledged. 'But it's not easy keeping tabs. Many of them use doubles, and travel incognito as much as they can. Now that Mitchell's targeting them they'll go to ground and that's only going to make our job harder.'

Jarvis shrugged. 'Maybe that's not a bad thing?'

'What do you mean?'

'Let's just let Mitchell do our work for us,' Jarvis replied, 'see how many of them he can take down.'

Nellis raised an eyebrow. 'You're talking about agency sanctioned homicide.'

'I'm talking about justice,' Jarvis said. 'General, you and I both know damned well that even if we arrested every member of that cabal tomorrow, laid out everything we have on them in front of the Attorney General and assembled a prosecution team allied to our administration, not one of those self–serving bastards would see the inside of a jail cell.'

Nellis exhaled noisily and leaned back in his seat as Jarvis went on.

'Look at all the bankers, the politicians, the corporate CEOs who have screwed the people of our country over and over again only to retire on pensions that make our salaries look like a joke while we all have to abide by the same laws that they ignore, laws that often they created!'

'It's not our job to cherry pick policy, Doug.'

'It's not my job as a human being to waste years chasing convictions that will never stand in court. Majestic Twelve's members are too powerful, too well connected. We can't go after them ourselves, so why not let him do it for us?'

'Because then we're no better than they are. Mitchell hit Wilms, but he doesn't know the identities of the other members, right?'

Jarvis shook his head, looked away from Nellis. 'As far as we know, but he'll follow the same leads that we do, figure things out as we have done. He's been quiet for six months – for all we know he's onto them already.'

'It makes sense,' Nellis agreed. 'He wants revenge on MJ–12, wants to take them down himself while he's still capable enough to do it. If he succeeds, he'll be satisfied, but others will rise to replace the dead members as they always have done and we'll be back to square one. I want this mission to completely destroy Majestic Twelve, Doug, nothing else will do. We have to stop them, and we have to apprehend and imprison them before Mitchell can put a bullet in their heads.'

'You realize that, effectively, you're asking me to protect MJ–12, right?'

'I'm asking you to protect our right to see them rot in security max prisons for the rest of their lives, Doug. A painless bullet between the eyes isn't good enough for these people, we both know that, after all that they've done and all that they no doubt plan to do. Your job is to bring them to face justice Doug, our country's justice, not Mitchell's. You need to make a choice right here and now about which side of the law you're standing on: theirs, or ours.'

Jarvis stood up, and without another word he strode from the General's office and closed the door behind him. He turned down the corridor and kept walking, then pulled out his cell phone as he dialled a number from memory.

**

Dean Crawford

XII

Svalbard Global Seed Vault,

Spitsbergen, Arctic Circle

'Damn me it's cold!'

Lopez looked at Ethan as they stepped out of the warm cab of an Arctic track vehicle, puffs of warm vapor spilling out into the frigid air.

'Do you ever stop complaining?' she asked. 'Too hot one day, too cold the next.'

'C'mon,' Ethan protested, 'just take a look around at this place!'

The estuary of a nearby river spilled into the bitter black water of the Greenland Sea, which was littered with a silent armada of icebergs visible through the dense mist cloaking the island and its soaring mountains. The frigid air and midnight–sun location was hardly somewhere that Lopez felt at home despite the thick Arctic jacket she wore, her face barely visible within her fur–lined hood.

'Agreed,' she capitulated, and turned with Ethan toward a large rectangular building built directly into the side of a nearby mountain.

Spitsbergen was the only permanently populated island of the Svalbard archipelago in northern Norway and bordered the Arctic Ocean, the Norwegian Sea and the Greenland Sea. After landing on an ice strip and checking in with the local authorities at Longyearbyen, Ethan had travelled with Lopez to this, one of the most remote scientific establishments in the world. Only the Russian mining community of Barentsburg, the research community of Ny–Alesund and the mining outpost settlement of Sveagruva accompanied the vault on the archipelago.

'What the hell do you think that somebody like Schofield would be doing out here?' Lopez asked as they crunched through thick snow coating the path to the seed bank.

'He's a scientist,' Ethan pointed out, 'they do this sort of thing all the time.'

'He's a long way from home,' she said in reply. 'I'd want my job to be well worth it to be stuck out here for any longer than one day.'

As they neared the building's entrance a small, stocky looking man wrapped up in dense layers of protective clothing and flanked by two armed soldiers approached them.

'Eric Schofield?' Ethan asked and introduced Lopez.

Schofield looked far older than he had in the picture that they had been given from his days in Montana.

'Welcome to Spitsbergen,' Schofield greeted them. 'Let's get inside, shall we?'

Schofield led the way at an impressive pace to the building's entrance, where they were required to undergo a number of security checks by a pair of armed guards, who confiscated Ethan's and Nicola's weapons before they entered the building proper. A blessed wave of warmth washed over them as they walked into a bizarre tunnel carved into the living rock, which extended into another tunnel lined with blue lights that encircled the tunnel walls.

'What is this place, exactly?' Lopez asked.

'This is the world's premier Doomsday Vault,' Schofield explained. 'It was built in 2006 into this sandstone mountain and is designed to withstand a direct nuclear attack and even a meteorite impact on our planet, an Extinction Level Event. Spitsbergen was considered the perfect location for this vault because it has no tectonic activity, has permafrost which aids preservation of materials and is over four hundred feet above sea level, meaning it will remain dry even if all the world's ice caps melted.'

'The Norwegians built this place in case of a mass extinction?' Ethan asked.

'No,' Schofield replied. 'They built it *because* of a mass extinction, which has already begun. This facility is designed to protect the diversity of life on earth after mankind has gone.'

'You sound like you think that's a certainty,' Lopez pointed out.

'That's because it is,' Schofield replied. 'That's why it's here. There are no permanent staff based here, and even if all the power was lost the contents of the vaults would remain safe for many weeks afterward, time for us to rectify the problem. It's been estimated that many of the seeds and grains held here could survive for thousands of years without human intervention.'

Schofield slowed as he reached a set of vaults arrayed before them, all behind air–locked doors.

'We can go no further,' he told them. 'In the vaults are contained around one and a half million agricultural seeds and other flora considered either endangered or crucial to human survival in an apocalyptic event.'

Ethan folded his arms for a moment as he looked at the vault.

'But if there's nobody left to eat them, what's the point?'

Schofield smiled, as though pitying Ethan.

'Not exactly the pioneering spirit of optimism are you, Mister Warner?'

'You're the one working in a Doomsday Vault,' Lopez said.

'Truth be told,' Schofield replied, 'even a major apocalyptic event such as a meteorite impact with our planet would be unlikely to eradicate every last human being from existence. Our species, despite becoming rapidly unable to survive in the wild as our ancestors once did, possesses the means to make a rapid technological comeback in the aftermath of such a crisis. Petrochemicals, solar plants, bacterial energy generation, the growing use of insects for food in many countries, nuclear bunkers and so on all lend weight to the theory that even something as cataclysmic as a ten mile wide bolide impactor such as the one that forced the dinosaurs into extinction would not necessarily render humanity likewise extinct. The survivors would be aware of these vaults and use would no doubt be made of their contents.'

'What made you come all the way out here from Montana?' Lopez asked.

'I've worked here and for other conservation projects for almost twenty years. How did you know that I worked in Montana?'

Ethan took a pace closer.

'You worked for the Montana state University, and we're chasing a lead on a man named Aubrey Channing.'

Ethan noted that Schofield's eyes widened slightly and his skin paled at the mention of the name.

'I don't recall that name,' he said, and made to move past them. 'I have work to do.'

'You wrote a letter to a reporter named Weisler describing a find you made in Montana's Badlands,' Ethan said, and moved to his right to cut Schofield off. The smaller man came up short before Ethan and squinted up at him. 'Aubrey Channing was never seen again, Eric.'

Schofield raised his chin.

'I was cleared of any involvement in whatever happened to Channing,' he snapped back. 'That's all far in my past now, if you'll excuse me?'

Ethan didn't move. 'Channing found something, didn't he, out there in the wilderness? He was directed by your letter. We would very much like to know what you found.'

'I don't know,' Eric insisted. 'Even Channing did not know or couldn't figure it out.'

'He disappeared before he had the chance,' Lopez said, 'and you wouldn't have gone to those lengths if you hadn't known what it was buried in those rocks.'

'A young scientist,' Ethan said, 'somebody who could not risk their career by unveiling a truly world–changing discovery, wrote that letter. You were young at the time.'

'Yes,' Schofield agreed. 'That much is true.'

'And then he disappeared,' Ethan went on. 'When did you last see him?'

'I told this all to the police at the time,' Schofield protested. 'I worked the site and found remains that contradicted the theory that the dinosaurs were wiped out by an asteroid impact. I couldn't write a paper on it, or even attempt to describe what I'd found, because the university would never have dared to employ me again, such would have been the fallout from such an announcement. So, instead I wrote an anonymous letter to a reporter and directed him to Channing. That was the last I ever heard of him.'

'And what you and he found, in the rocks?' Lopez asked. 'What happened to that?'

'It was gone,' Schofield replied, 'just like I said at the time. When I went back, there was a cavity in the rocks where the remains had been.'

'Remains,' Ethan echoed. 'Remains of what?'

Schofield faltered and then tried again to push past Ethan. 'I don't recall.'

Ethan's hand stopped Eric in his tracks. 'Try harder.'

'You don't understand,' he hissed angrily.

'Then help us out,' Lopez suggested.

Schofield gritted his teeth and almost spat his response. 'They'll kill me.'

'Who will kill you?'

'Them,' Schofield insisted. 'They came to see me the day after Channing disappeared, after I'd spoken to the police.'

'Who?' Ethan demanded.

'I don't know! Guys in suits, serious men, angry men. They questioned me for over two hours like I was under arrest in my own home, wanted to know everything that Channing had told me. When they were done they said that if I breathed a word of what I'd witnessed to anybody they'd make sure I paid for it with my life. I believed them!'

Ethan and Lopez exchanged a silent glance and then Ethan reached into a pocket and retrieved his cell phone. He quickly thumbed through a series of images and showed one of them to Schofield.

'Guys like this?'

Schofield's eyes almost popped out of his head as he nodded frantically. 'Yes, that's one of them! How did you…?'

'Long story,' Ethan replied as he closed the image of Aaron Mitchell on his phone and looked at Lopez. 'Mitchell's likely to be following the same threads that we are.'

'Which means that he might come here,' she agreed.

Schofield's eyes widened further and filled with fear. 'Here?'

'You didn't tell us why you're here,' Lopez said to him.

'You're a scientist,' Ethan pressed also, not willing to let Schofield go just yet. 'You wouldn't have just walked away from a discovery like that to come out here and babysit barley.'

Schofield seemed sobered by the image of Aaron Mitchell, and spoke freely.

'I looked into Channing's disappearance again after I heard that his son Robert had committed suicide, started to make links to people, powerful people,' he said. 'That's when the heavy mob showed up. They made it real clear I should back off or else, so I did. But I didn't stop looking into what I'd already found.'

'Which was what?' Lopez asked.

'Channing wasn't just a specialist in Tyrannosaurs. He also worked extensively on alternative theories for why the dinosaurs died out. His work on Tyrannosaurs coincided with the asteroid impact period, because creatures like T–Rex were some of the last of the dinosaurs to walk the earth before they went extinct, so the two subjects kind of went hand–in–hand. When I did a little digging into other people working in the same field, I started to see a pattern. They were coming to the conclusion that the dinosaurs were already dying out *before* the asteroid impact that sent them extinct.'

'Before it?'

'Yes, quite some time before it,' Schofield confirmed. 'There were lots of things going on geologically at the time that could have contributed to their demise, but Channing and a few others seemed to have realized that there was more to it than our own Earth.'

Ethan frowned, uncertain of where Schofield was going.

'What, you think they were really onto some other reason for why the dinosaurs died out?'

'Oh they absolutely were,' Schofield nodded. 'They were working on something so unbelievable that I couldn't really begin to accept it myself at the time, but when I finally did and I realized what it meant for us as a species, I decided to work instead in conservation.'

Ethan felt a chill down his spine as Lopez questioned Schofield further.

'What did you learn?'

Schofield sighed and shrugged.

'That we're doomed,' he said finally. 'Few terrestrial species last more than a couple of million years before they go extinct, which is about how long modern man, *Homo sapiens*, has existed. Humanity will not survive for more than a few decades at the most. Our extinction event is already here.'

***

XIII

'We know,' Ethan said. 'We were briefed before we left on the Sixth Extinction.'

'We really need to know what you found in Montana,' Lopez insisted. 'What convinced you to leave and go into conservation?'

Schofield seemed to hesitate for a moment longer, and then he sighed and looked around him at the rocky walls and the vaults beyond.

'I guess if I'm not safe speaking a hundred forty meters inside a secure mountain facility, I'm safe nowhere,' he said finally. 'Aubrey Channing had discovered a...'

Ethan did not hear Schofield's last as a clatter of machine gun fire echoed down the corridor from outside. He whirled, one hand instinctively reaching for the pistol at his side and finding it not there. Ethan cursed as he hurried across to one side of the tunnel, Lopez following and dragging Schofield with her.

'What's happening?' Schofield gasped in terror. 'Could they have heard me speaking even down here?'

Ethan shook his head as he heard the guards returning fire. From somewhere ahead in the facility he could see the distant flashes of muzzle fire as rifles were aimed out into the bitter wastelands outside.

'I'm afraid we're not the only ones interested in what happened to Aubrey Channing,' he shouted above the noise as he looked at Lopez. 'Our weapons are inside the office.'

'Sounds like multiple targets outside,' she replied. 'We're gonna be sitting ducks.'

'Any other way out of here?' Ethan asked Schofield.

The scientist shook his head. 'Kind of the point of the place.'

Ethan cursed under his breath as he heard another rattle of gunfire and saw in the distance one of the facility guards stagger backwards and collapse onto his back, his weapon falling uselessly alongside him.

'There's too many!' cried the remaining guard, his features stricken with fear as he looked over his shoulder at them for assistance.

'Get him out of sight,' Ethan snapped at Lopez as he dashed forward toward the entrance.

The remaining guard fired another few rounds into the snow outside, falling back as a hail of gunfire raked the wall alongside him and sent clouds of debris spraying across the hall. Ethan slid down alongside the fallen guard and grabbed his rifle, checked the chamber before he tucked in alongside the wall opposite the remaining guard's position.

'How many are there?' he asked.

'Ten, maybe twelve,' the guard replied, adrenaline coursing through his veins and causing him to breathe heavily. 'We got three of them but I'm almost out of ammunition.'

'Any way to call for back–up?'

The guard shook his head. 'There's supposed to be a secure underground communications link to the town but it's out of action. They must have either cut it or jammed it somehow, and we're too far away from the town for anybody to hear the gunfire!'

Ethan ducked down as more gunfire raked the wall nearby, scattering clouds of stone chips across his jacket as he retreated down the corridor.

'Where the hell did they come from?!' Lopez shouted.

'They must be following us!' Ethan yelled back above the clatter of gunfire now being amplified by the confines of the tunnel. 'Maybe Majestic Twelve have taken the gloves off and decided it's time to get rid of us for once and for all!'

'Good place to do it!' Lopez shot back. 'We're unarmed and there's no way out of there but through that entrance!'

Ethan looked back at the entrance, where the guard was still trying to hold off the attackers outside. 'There's no way out of here!'

Lopez looked back at him but she said nothing, clearly knowing just like Ethan that the only way out of the facility was right through the hail of fire coming from the entrance.

'You got any smart ideas, now would be a good time to use one of them!' she finally yelled back.

Ethan looked at the beleaguered guard and the entrance, and made his decision.

*

'Forward!'

Jake Viggen waved his arms forward and urged his men on, half a dozen of them breaking cover from behind their vehicles and rushing the entrance of the massive vault. Viggen saw the security guard loose off a few more rounds, and then his courage failed him before the charge and he disappeared inside the facility.

'Go, now!'

Viggen leaped out from behind the jeep in which he had arrived and sprinted up the icy track to the entrance. His men plunged into the facility ahead of him as a salvo of gunshots burst out and thumped into the walls around them. Viggen hurled himself against a wall as he saw one of the rounds smack into the forehead of one of his men and exit the back of his skull with a puff of scarlet blood that splattered the pristine ice around his boots. The gunman, a former Army trooper named Granger, dropped almost vertically, the life gone from his eyes as his rifle toppled from his grasp and landed beside his corpse.

More gunshots rattled out and Viggen crouched out of sight as he watched his men advance by sections into the building. Of the twelve he started with, three were already dead, but he knew that he outnumbered those inside by better than two to one, and that only the guard was armed. He risked a peek down the corridor that led to a gigantic tunnel and saw the guard retreating, firing as he went. Closer, his men jumped over the dead body of the second guard sprawling face down in the entrance.

'Let's finish this!' he bellowed as he stood up and opened fire down the corridor, spraying the walls with gunfire and forcing the security guard to cower out of sight behind a metal stanchion that supported the rocky ceiling of the tunnel entrance. 'Advance!'

The men plunged into the facility, rushing through the shattered glass of the airlocks as Viggen sprinted along behind them and jumped over the dead guard's body, firing as he went. Bullets hammered the walls of the tunnel and one of the arcing blue lights shattered and spilled glass down onto the rocks beneath their boots as they rushed into cover against the walls of the tunnel.

The gunfire ceased, and Viggen peered ahead. He could see in an office at the far end of the tunnel a man and a woman crouched behind a desk for cover, and to his left near them he could see puffs of breath from the security guard glowing in the blue lights.

'There's nowhere to go!' Viggen yelled. 'Come out now with your hands up and we'll talk!'

The guard's voice shouted back at them, heavily accented with Norwegian. 'If you'd wanted to talk, you wouldn't have opened fire on us!'

Viggen shrugged. 'We're not here for you! We're here only for the Americans! Stand down, and you'll live!'

The guard's reply echoed down the tunnel. 'Go to hell!'

Viggen grinned and shouted back. 'You first! Take them all down!'

His men burst from their hiding places, and Viggen heard a crescendo of shots blaze down the tunnel. He was about to follow his men when he realized that they had not yet opened fire. Bullets smashed past Viggen and he saw them hammer into the backs of his soldiers, cutting them down like an invisible scythe as he whirled, brought his rifle around and caught sight of the "dead" security guard standing in the entrance, his rifle blazing.

Viggen tried to take aim, but the first round hit him in the chest before he could pull the trigger, and then the second slammed into his shoulder and he spun as he collapsed onto the ice, his rifle tumbling from his grasp.

*

Ethan, standing in the dead guard's ill–fitting uniform, fired his final rounds just as one of the black–clad soldiers realized what had happened and turned to try to return fire. Two rounds cut him down and he tumbled aside as the last of the soldiers was cut down with a bullet landing square between his shoulder blades. A cloud of bright blood burst from his chest and his cry of agony was cut short as he collapsed onto the rocks.

'Clear!' Ethan yelled as the gunfire ceased and echoed away through the tunnel and out toward the entrance.

Lopez and Schofield broke cover along with the remaining security guard and hurried to Ethan's side as he crouched down to where one of the soldiers was lying on his back on the icy rocks, blood spilling from a wound in his chest that had caused massive trauma to his back as the bullet had exited his body. More blood spilled from a second wound in his shoulder as Ethan grabbed his rifle and used the ammunition to reload his own weapon.

'Nice move,' said the guard as he joined Ethan, who began shrugging off the dead guard's uniform. 'Who are these people?'

'That's a long story,' Lopez said as she joined them and looked down at the fallen soldier.

He was alive but he wasn't moving. Ethan figured that the bullet had probably severed his spinal cord on the way out of his back, but he was likely still able to talk. Ethan crouched down again alongside the man and spoke in a quiet but firm voice.

'You have about three minutes to live,' he informed the injured man. 'Tell me who sent you, and I'll patch that wound and you'll survive this. Refuse, and we'll walk out of here and leave you to it.'

The soldier offered Ethan a grim smile. 'Drop dead.'

'You already have,' Ethan replied.

He stood up and marched away. 'Come on, let's get out of here.'

Lopez, Schofield and the guard moved to follow, but they were stopped by a shriek from the fallen man.

'Wait!'

Ethan turned and moved to stand over the fallen soldier, his rifle resting on his shoulder. 'Make it fast.'

'They sent me an e–mail, from Italy,' the fallen man gasped, tears welling in his eyes as blood snaked across the rocks around him and his skin began to turn pale. 'Named you as a target, you and the Chiquita.'

'Who sent the mail?' Ethan demanded.

'No names,' the soldier whispered, struggling to stay conscious. 'But the e–mail was sent from a top hotel in the city, some super luxury pad, I can't remember the name…' The soldier's eyes flickered as a tear spilled down his cheek. 'Please, fix the wound.'

Ethan looked at the lake of blood already drenching the ice around the fallen soldier, and knew that there was nothing that he could do to save him, but of course the dying man didn't know that.

'Go fix it yourself,' Ethan uttered, and marched away.

He led the way out of the tunnel, walking fast as the pitiful cries for mercy faded away behind them. Lopez, Schofield and the guard followed.

'What the hell was that?' Lopez asked as they strode outside.

'He was already dead,' Ethan replied without looking at her. 'There was nothing that we could do.'

'Yeah, but..?'

Ethan glared at her and she fell silent. 'They started this war,' he pointed out. 'They wanted it, and they'll damned well get it.'

Lopez lifted her chin as she confronted him, the snow whipping around them. 'I just don't want to see you turn into another Aaron Mitchell, is all.'

Ethan pulled his cell phone from his jacket and dialled a number as he walked across to their vehicles and tossed the rifle into the trunk. Jarvis answered on the third ring.

'What's up?'

'MJ–12 have taken the gloves off,' Ethan growled in response. 'We just got out of a shoot–out with some of their boys. I need you to do a search on e–mail traffic coming out of Italy's most expensive hotel: they must have been there recently, and it's our only new lead.'

'I'm on it,' Jarvis replied. *'What are you going to do?'*

Ethan slammed the trunk and made for the driver's door.

'Repay them in kind,' he said simply. 'Let me know when you've tracked them down.'

Ethan shut off the line and looked at Schofield. 'Tell me everything, before we all end up dead.'

Dean Crawford

XIV

Burj Al Arab Hotel,

Dubai

The huge hotel looked spectacular in the dawn light, glowing golden against Dubai's vivid beaches, the city skyline glittering like a jewel encrusted into the ancient deserts as the helicopter descended toward a landing pad jutting out from the side of the immense building's rooftop.

Professor Rhys Garrett gazed down upon the building's incredible opulence, built as were the churches and cathedrals of old by the hands of the poor, and in this case on land reclaimed from the ocean to create an artificial island almost a thousand feet from Jumeirah beach that had taken longer to create than the gigantic teardrop shaped hotel itself, connected to the mainland by a private curving bridge. The entire city was the poster–child for wealth over practicality, substance over style, Dubai a city built into deserts woefully unable to support it without the arterial lifeline of supplies and land expensively altered to allow the cultivation of green spaces.

Despite his own personal wealth, Garrett had never before visited Dubai and this was in fact his first visit to the Middle East. He had never set foot on their ancient sands and, if he was able, he never would. Garrett looked beyond the glittering, crystalline waters of the bay and out beyond Dubai's bustling streets and glittering tower blocks and saw there the stain of poverty and disease that was the hallmark of the developing world. He knew, like so many others, that the only wealth in this land was in the hands of the Royal families, and that without their export of oil this city would be as dead and desiccated as the endless deserts that surrounded it. In truth, it wouldn't even exist. It stood near the site of the old Chicago Beach Hotel, which had its origins in the Chicago Bridge & Iron Company which at one time welded giant floating oil storage tanks, known locally as *Kazzans,* to fuel the export trade that had made so few wealthy and so many desperately poor.

The helicopter settled onto the landing pad, which was just under seven hundred feet above the waves below, and the engines wound down into silence as Garrett unstrapped his harness just in time for a white–suited concierge to hurry to the helicopter's door and open it. Garrett saw the man smile and bow graciously, and managed to hide his face as he stepped out of the helicopter and into the dawn air.

Even at this early hour he could feel the heat building from the equatorial sun as it rose swiftly in the east, the bright orange sky tiger striped with thin banners of cloud already being burned off by the rising temperature.

The concierge closed the helicopter's door and beckoned for Garrett to follow him toward a doorway that led into the hotel's interior. Garrett followed in silence, a single chrome briefcase in his hand that shone like gold in the sunlight. Many people would have preferred to enter the hotel through its main entrance, to boldly state their presence and revel in the opulence of the towering lobby or dine in the exclusive *Al Muntaha* restaurant, which was reached via a panoramic elevator and had views across the Persian Gulf, or perhaps the *Al Mahara* restaurant, accessed via a simulated submarine voyage and replete with a two hundred sixty thousand gallon fish tank. Garrett, however, was appalled by such extravagance, not to mention the publicity it risked by being seen in such a place. Now, more than ever, it was important for him to maintain a low profile.

For this reason, his reservation for the Royal Suite that night had been booked under one of his assumed names by one of his secretaries, and had cost some nineteen thousand dollars.

The concierge guided him to the suite and opened the door for him. Garrett strode inside, aware of the continued opulence around him as the aide began speaking.

'Welcome to the Royal Suite sir, our finest and most luxurious accommodation.'

'I'd like to be alone,' Garrett said softly.

'As you wish sir,' the concierge continued smoothly. 'If you require anything at all, please simply press the call button on the wall by the door'

Garrett smiled his thanks, and handed the man a thin wedge of notes that made the young man's eyes bulge in amazement.

'Sir, I couldn't possibly…'

'Make sure nobody interrupts me, understood?' Garrett said as he pushed the money into the man's hands.

The aide turned on his heel with another deep bow and hurried away. Garrett waited until the door to the suite was closed before he set the briefcase down on the immense leather couch that dominated the suite and looked around. He walked to the balcony doors and threw them open to take in the extraordinary view. Fresh air billowed in from across the Persian Gulf, devoid of the stench of the human stain.

Soon, that stain would no longer be a problem.

Inside the chrome briefcase was a simple laptop computer, one that before the end of the day would have its hard drive removed and crushed to a pulp, while the rest of the device would be thrown from Garrett's helicopter on the flight over the bay to the airport and his private jet. Now, all he needed to do was tend to his guest and await the arrival of a very powerful group of men.

Garrett walked to the bathroom door, which had been locked on his instructions after his package had arrived about an hour before he had. Delivered just as he had been by helicopter, it had been placed here for safe keeping. Garrett unlocked the door and walked into the spacious bathroom, saw the marble tiles, the gold–plated taps, the polished floors. He ignored all of it and walked across to the shower, then yanked the curtain back.

Curled up inside the shower was a man, dressed only in soiled shorts, his body covered in bruises and his face swollen and puffy. The beating he had endured had been designed more to terrify than to cause permanent injury, and that was important to Garrett. He needed this man to be in good shape when his guests arrived – not *perfect* shape, obviously – for he also needed them to see that he would perform any act in order to achieve his goal. Then, once the information the man held in his mind was delivered in person before his guests, he could again demonstrate his resolve in a final and undeniable act of loyalty.

Garrett reached down to his wrist watch and pressed a button. Moments later, the door to the suite opened and two burly men strode efficiently inside and joined Garrett in the bathroom.

'Get him ready,' Garrett ordered as he turned and walked from the room. 'They'll be here within the hour.'

*

ARIES, DIA Headquarters,

Washington DC

'We've got something.'

Hellerman hurried across the Watch Room to Jarvis's side, carrying with him a tablet computer that he handed to Jarvis as he explained what was on the computer.

'Surveillance at the NSA picked up some shielded chatter coming out of Dubai International Airport. There are not one but *three* private jets landing there right now that are known to be on the books of members of Majestic Twelve. Given that they've been laying low for some time I thought that you ought to know.'

Jarvis nodded, immediately sensing the urgency of the situation. 'What assets do we have in play in Dubai?'

'The FBI has a field office there, as do we, and two safe houses inside the city,' Hellerman replied. 'We could probably put a tail on any one of them right now, maybe even ask local law enforcement to...'

'Not a chance,' Jarvis cut him off, 'police there are far too vulnerable to bribes. We'll have to keep watch using trusted assets. Put any available agents that we have on watch, find out what they're doing out there and where they're going, understood?'

'Got it,' Hellerman agreed. 'What about Ethan and Nicola?'

'They're in Norway,' Jarvis replied, 'but I'll fill them in on this and get back to you.'

Hellerman rushed off as Jarvis walked into his office and closed the door behind him. He pulled a cell phone from his jacket and dialled a number, waited for the line to connect. A voice answered on the third ring.

'Yes?'

'We've got contact, confirmed sightings of at least three of the cabal in Dubai. Where are you?'

'I'll be there by tomorrow and will pick up the trail.'

'There won't be much time. They must know about Wilms by now.'

'You let me worry about that.'

The line cut off abruptly and Jarvis pocketed the phone, conscious of his surroundings and hoping that the shielding on the burner cell was sufficient to protect the call. Although he was inside one of the most secure buildings on earth, there remained in all government facilities an institution known as "trust". People like Edward Snowden existed because without trust there was no security. The DIA monitored signals from all over the world in conjunction with the National Security Agency, but unless a specific search was made they would have very little control over who was calling out from within the building. Jarvis knew that as long as he kept his calls short and infrequent, there was little chance of his duplicity being noticed.

Jarvis had worked for far too long in the intelligence game to be certain that the apprehension and trial of figures as powerful as those within Majestic Twelve was at best a futile gesture and at worse a waste of time, resources and even lives. He had himself seen massively wealthy and powerful drug lords negotiate "deals" to avoid lengthy prison sentences, politicians found guilty of massive fraud given jail sentences less prolonged than those daily dispensed with joy against less powerful citizens for shoplifting. In a society where the powerful lived under a different set of laws to the general populace, there would never come a day when Jarvis would see Majestic Twelve's cabal rotting behind bars for mass murder. He knew that even if caught, tried and prosecuted, not one of them would ever likely serve a day in a real prison, their lawyers too numerous and too powerful, their wealth too great, their friends in the Capitol and even the administration able to pull strings and quote laws that he would never be able to oppose.

Jarvis looked in the mirror, saw his rheumy eyes looking back at him. His white hair was thinning now, his features tired and drawn. He had spent far too long in this game already and he knew that it was only a matter of time before his role went to another, younger and more energetic soul than he. But he was damned if he would go down without first seeing one of the most dangerous cabals ever conceived brought to its knees, crushed from existence. Jarvis knew that the greatest punishment he could mete to the members of Majestic Twelve was to take away their *power*, for it was that upon which they feasted, that and the fear of the powerless citizenry who suffered as they profited.

Jarvis's hand clenched the burner cell in his pocket tightly, threatened to crush it. He forced himself to relax a little, to breathe. Anger at the hopelessness of the ordinary man when confronted with people like MJ–12 was as clear to him as the next man on the street, perhaps even clearer because he, uniquely, was in a place to do something about it.

Jarvis took a breath and opened his office door, headed out to a desk in the Watch Room and quickly accessed a terminal. Within moments he was able to identify his own out–going cell signal from the DIA building, and then identify the nearest cell tower from which the answering cell had pinged.

He smiled ruefully as he noted the location of the cell.

'Saudi Arabia,' he whispered to himself as he deleted the call trace and data from the server.

Aaron Mitchell was already in a position to strike.

***

Dean Crawford

XV

Burj Al Arab Hotel,

Dubai

Professor Rhys Garrett stood on the balcony of the Royal Suite and watched the distant waves of the Persian Gulf hundreds of feet below roll serenely toward the beach behind him, which was covered with tourists from countless countries blissfully unaware of the cataclysm rushing toward them.

His men had dressed their victim and planted him firmly on a chair in the lounge, to which he was heavily bound and his mouth gagged. That anybody would venture up here by chance was unthinkable, especially now that there were literally dozens of discreetly placed security agents scattered throughout the hotel and watching the movements of every single person who entered or exited the building.

Majestic Twelve had sufficient power to topple governments, provoke stock markets and engineer economic crashes, create or destroy lucrative drug trades and even influence the President of the United States depending on who held office at a particular time. Thus, creating a security perimeter around an already highly exclusive hotel was not a stretch for them.

A soft buzzing intruded on his reverie and he turned with some reluctance from the stunning vista outside and closed the balcony doors behind him. He pulled the blinds closed to prevent any observation from outside, and then moved across the lounge to the entrance and opened the door.

Outside stood a tall, gaunt looking man whom he recognized instantly although most people could have walked past him in the street and had no idea who they were looking at.

'Good morning, Rhys,' the man greeted him with a hand shake and a sombre voice. 'May we come in?'

'Of course,' Rhys said as he backed away from the door and gestured for the men outside to enter.

One by one they walked into the room, each wearing a tailored suit that would have cost most people a month's salary, wrist watches worth more than many luxury cars and colognes from brands too exclusive to even be available to the general public.

For the most part Garrett did not recognize the men as they filed into the room, accompanied by two armed escorts. The apartment door was closed behind them and they variously sat or stood as he turned to face them. Of those that he did recognize, he knew them to be reclusive trillionaires who had forged their fortunes in stock markets, real estate, agriculture and military technology. Not one of the men was less than fifty years of age, and there were just eleven of them, not twelve. Their number had been reduced a few years previously when a Texan oil billionaire named Dwight Opennheimer had met his maker, and his replacement had recently disappeared from the streets of New York City, never to be seen again. That disappearance weighed heavily on Garrett's mind as the eleven men looked at him and then at the man strapped into the chair nearby.

'What brings us here, Mister Garrett?' asked Samuel Kruger, the gaunt man who had greeted him at the door.

Garrett took a breath and began.

'As you know, gentlemen, I have spent most of my career involved in the study of genetics, and have achieved my status both profesionally and personally as a result of the patenting of novel coding techniques that allowed mankind to map his own genome, among other things. In more recent years I have been involved in a new study, and during the course of that work a groundbreaking discovery was made which I would like to share with you all.'

'We didn't come here for a lecture,' one of the men said in a dismissive tone that suggested he felt his time was being wasted. 'You've got two minutes.'

Garrett reeled momentarily, but he forced himself to smile at the man through his teeth. 'Unless you have a degree in biogenetics, you won't know what hit you.'

'One minute fifty,' the man replied without interest.

'Let him speak,' Kruger chided his companion gently. 'Rhys, if you will?'

Garrett turned to the man trussed up in the chair beside him.

'This is Professor Martin Beauchamp, a leading expert in the field of palaeontology,' he introduced his victim. 'Believe it or not, this man holds the key to the survival of the human species.'

Garrett was met with silence this time, but an expectant silence that urged him on. He reached down and pulled the gag from Beauchamp's mouth as he went on.

'Professor Beauchamp here would like to share with you a discovery that was made by Doctor Aubrey Channing on a hillside in Montana some decades ago, when Martin was his undergraduate student.' Beauchamp looked up at the men surrounding him, his eyes bleary and his shoulders slumped. 'Just tell them what you told me.'

Beauchamp worked his mouth as though getting up the strength to speak, and then he turned his head slightly and spat a globule of phlegm onto Garrett's polished shoes. Garrett looked down at the mess as he heard a ripple of muffled laughter from the powerful men before him.

Mastering his dignity, he turned to his guards. Without a word they stalked toward Beauchamp and grabbed his arms, then lifted him almost off the ground and carried him toward the helipad outside. Garrett ignored them as he turned to the men of Majestic Twelve.

'Professor Beauchamp is the former undergraduate of a scientist who worked in Montana,' he said. 'That scientist received a letter in 2002. I believe that you know about that letter and intervened in the excavation performed by Aubrey Channing.'

The eyes of several of the men raised up to his at that point, their interest piqued.

'Go on,' said their gaunt leader.

'Channing discovered the remains of a species of dinosaur in the rocks of Montana's badlands, something that has rarely been seen before: a dinosaur that was alive after the asteroid impact that supposedly sent them extinct.' Garrett said. 'Channing has never been seen again since and nor have the remains that he found. I contend that you intervened, and had them taken from him. Would that be correct?'

Kruger raised his chin as he peered at Garrett.

'I cannot confirm nor deny that.'

Garrett smiled. 'I understand that you do not wish to implicate yourselves without good reason. That's why I brought Beauchamp along with me, to redress the balance.'

Outside the helicopter lifted off the helipad and turned away from the suite, climbing high into the hard blue sky as Garrett strolled across to the balcony doors and watched it fly away as he spoke. 'It's a remarkable thing, a temperature inversion. It's what creates mirages in the desert and on roads, bending the light so that the impossible seems to occur and objects float in the distance above the horizon, or ghostly lakes shimmer in the desert. It's all about bending light, and what few people know is that it can also occur somewhat in reverse: that is, something that should be visible is not under certain conditions, which are most often experienced when air is being rapidly heated.'

Garrett watched as the helicopter performed a wide circular flight, swinging back in toward the platform once more, and through the faint haze they all saw something tumble from inside the helicopter and fall rapidly toward the ocean a thousand feet below. Garrett saw a tiny white splash in the ocean a mile away as the object plummeted at lethal speed into the water. The pilot skillfully brought the helicopter in to land outside and Garrett's guards climbed out. The seats behind them were empty, Beauchamp no longer aboard. Garrett turned to his guests.

'Beauchamp had seen your faces and connected them to me, so naturally he could not be allowed to live. Now, we are even.'

Kruger continued to peer at Garrett, a hint of suspicion in his eyes. 'What is is that you want, Garrett?'

Garrett walked back to face them more closely, in control of the situation once again.

'I have an island,' he said simply, 'upon which I have built a test facility that is currently involved in developing the genetic capability to influence the evolution of any species on our planet, whether extant or extinct. I have used it to explore species that have not walked this earth for millions of years.'

One of the oldest men before him, who stood with one hand resting on a glossy black cane, squinted as though confused.

'You're trying to tell us that you've built *Jurassic Park*?'

'No,' Garrett smiled, 'although to do so would technically not now be beyond our capabilities. What I have built is a means to study the fundamental building blocks of DNA and one of the discoveries that I have made is that all life on earth, literally every single species in existence and that has ever lived, all shares one common gene, a piece of DNA that has no business being there and has defied explanation ever since it was discovered.'

'And?' another of the men challenged. 'Stop pulling the chain and get to the action.'

Garrett grinned.

'Why rush the finale?' he asked. 'I take it that you have heard of the experiment that led to the term "behavioral sink"?'

Met with silent stares, Garrett elaborated. 'The experiments were conducted in Rockville, Maryland from 1947 until 1995 using mice and rats. They were placed in controlled environments with readily available access to food and water, and protection from predators: essentially, rat heaven. Their numbers were controlled and their behavior measured and recorded. The interesting things started to happen when the number of creatures in any one closed–environment was increased. To cut a long story short, they devolved in nature and swiftly became extinct, having created the "behavioral sink". Many believe that this process is ongoing in society today.'

'That's not telling us anything that we don't already know,' said another man.

'True,' Garrett countered, 'but did you know that as with all other things in nature there is a natural counter–balance, an automatic response triggered by environmental factors that is designed specifically to cull or even destroy a population of any one species from within without any external influence whatsoever?'

None of the men moved now, all silently awaiting Garrett.

'That's the gene that we discovered,' he said finally. 'Within our bodies, within every living thing on earth, there is a gene specifically designed to trigger an auto–destruct mechanism within us.'

Garrett moved to where Beauchamp had once sat, and patted the chair.

'That mechanism has been triggered several times in the past, usually once every thirty or so million years, and has been responsible for the greatest extinction events in history, those that have eradicated ninety per cent of all life on earth in one fell swoop.'

Kruger frowned. 'That's not possible. Viruses are typically species specific, and cannot make the leap easily from one to another.'

'Correct,' Garrett agreed, 'but that ignores some of our most recent discoveries, including the revelation that DNA can communicate in a telepathic sense.'

'Say that again,' one of Majestic Twelve uttered, his face stony with disbelief.

'Intact, double–stranded DNA can recognize similarities in other strands of DNA *from a distance*,' Garrett repeated. 'The recognition of similar sequences in DNA's chemical sub–units occurs in a way unrecognized by science until now. There's no known reason why the DNA is able to combine this way, and from a current theoretical standpoint this feat should be chemically impossible, and yet it happens. The research was recently published in the ACS Journal of Physical Chemistry. It's not telepathy of course, that's just the word the scientists involved in the research gave to the phenomena, but I've recreated the event in my laboratories.'

'To what end?' asked another of the cabal, a man named Felix.

'Eight percent of our genome is made up of retrovirus DNA,' Garrett explained. 'These are viruses that have been passed down for so long that most have mutated and are held powerless in your system. But some retroviruses can take on new life, such as in people with HIV and several viruses that trigger cancer. When we isolated the DNA of both HIV patients and healthy people, we found a virus they called K111, sometimes intact and sometimes not. It is also found in the genome of chimpanzees, so the virus would have infected our ancestors before humans split off over

6 million years ago. When people are infected with HIV the ancient K111 virus becomes activated.'

'So?' Kruger asked. 'Are you saying you're able to cure people of HIV?'

'No,' Garrett replied, 'I'm able to cure people of something much more ancient and far more deadly. Our DNA contains genes that we share with every other living thing on earth, so ancient that they cannot have evolved here.'

'Alien DNA,' Felix said. 'You're going to tell us that we were seeded here by little green men.'

'No,' Garrett replied, 'although that technically is not impossible. Life exists between the stars as chemicals in giant molecular clouds that collapse with gravity and form new stellar systems pre–loaded with the ingredients for life. That foundation of chemical life means that we all share some level of genetic material, no matter how small, with all other life in the universe. When populations become too dense, that combines with DNA's ability to recombine at a distance to produce a virus so incredibly dangerous that it can literally wipe life from the face of our planet.'

Garrett sat in a chair and folded his hands calmly in his lap.

'The last time it happened, it was wiping the dinosaurs from the face of the earth both before and *after* the asteroid that hit the planet sixty five million years ago. I have successfully extracted that virus from the living bones of a dinosaur, and contained it at my facility. Nature has evolved a kill–switch, gentlemen,' he said, 'an extinction code, and I know how to control it.'

'The *living* bones of a dinosaur?' Hampton gasped, to a nod from Garrett.

Kruger peered at Garrett suspiciously. 'Prove it.'

Garrett grinned. 'I already have,' he replied. 'It's been released into the wild.'

***

XVI

Parc National Andasibe Mantadia,

Madagascar

'Don't go in there.'

The air was thick with moisture, so dense that Michael Arando could see it hanging in before him like mist and curling around thick vines and trunks in diaphanous swirls. The tropical forest was like a wet oven, Michael's skin slick with sweat that simply would not evaporate and the heat gripping his body and making even the slightest movement seem a gargantuan task.

His aide, a local Madagascan, remained beside him but was clearly spooked by what lay ahead.

'Relax, Lucien,' Michael soothed. 'This won't take long.'

In truth, it already had taken two days and drained them both of their energy. The Parc National Andasibe Mantadia was some twelve miles north of Andasibe and had been created primarily to protect the indri, also known as the babakoto. A primate, the black and white ruffed lemurs were unique to the island and had been a subject of Michael's studies since he had moved here four years previously. What he had found, along with his discoveries around the rest of the world, had profoundly changed him as a man and as a human being.

'Come on,' he urged Lucien as he moved off through the forest. 'We've come this far.'

Michael led the way, Lucien trudging wearily along behind him as the vast tropical forest swallowed them whole. The cooler breezes that had chased them daily from the east coast disappeared entirely, and the deep silence of the rain forest consumed the world around them.

Michael had spent enough time in such forests to know that the wildlife inhabiting them would often fall silent as humans passed through. Long and likely weary experience had taught them that mankind was a dangerous foe, willing and able to hunt any of the creatures of the forest with near impunity. However, despite that knowledge the silence that confronted him now was unearthly, deep, bottomless it seemed. The only sound was the chorus of water droplets falling from the immense heights of the canopy far above, where weak sunlight filtered down in glowing shafts, too broken to ever hope to reach the forest floor.

Michael followed a path that was far from the tourist tracks of Circuit Rianasoa and Tsakoka, the trail littered with leeches and entombed in thick vines, creepers and dense foliage that clogged the untrodden forest. They passed a waterfall that thundered down from overhanging cliffs into a limpid pool of green water, and crossed a narrow trail on a hillside that offered a tremendous view to the east, dense forest cloaking the hills and swathed in veils of mist. To get this far out into the rain forest had required permits from the MNP office in Reserve Speciale d'Analamazaotra, and Lucien's skills had been hired by Michael there too, for he alone had seen what was up here and reported it just three days before.

Michael pulled a machete from his rucksack and slashed his way off the animal trail they had been following, hoping to make his way onto higher ground, when he caught the first scent of it.

The heady aroma of the rain forest was often deadened by the sheer weight of moisture in the air, but some scents it seemed could penetrate anything. Especially the scent of death.

Michael halted, and beside him Lucien sniffed the air and nodded to himself, a sombre expression on his features. His dark Malagese eyes looked into Michael's but he said nothing, for there was no more for him to say. Michael felt a little chill ripple up his spine despite the cloying heat, but he forged ahead anyway and followed the scent through the forest.

It rapidly became thicker as they moved, seemed to cling to the trees and to the foliage, and Michael swatted at a cloud of tiny insects buzzing in the hot air as he pushed his way between giant ferns and a thick waft of putrid air stained his throat and caused him to gag reflexively.

Michael coughed and his eyes filled with water as he struggled to control his stomach as it turned over inside him. The unbearable stench was heavier and more oppressive even than the tropical heat, thick with loathing and the choking odor of rotting flesh and decaying skin and fur.

The carcass was perhaps ten feet from him, sprawled across the forest floor and seemingly alive with a seething mass of maggots that swarmed through the interior of the corpse in sufficient numbers that areas of unbroken skin rippled and limbs rolled lethargically this way and that.

'How long?' he uttered to Lucien, his voice thick with nausea.

Lucien, still anxious but impervious it seemed to the stench, shrugged. 'A day, perhaps two. They do not remain long here for they are consumed swiftly.'

Lucien's voice was heavily accented but his English was exemplary, years of guiding tourists through the forests rewarding him with perfect fluency.

But that was all over now. There hadn't been a tour brought up into the mountains since he had warned the government about what was happening here.

Michael had been informed the very next day.

'Stay back,' Michael said.

He pulled a handkerchief from his pocket and tied it around his mouth and nose to protect him as he edged forward toward the remains. For the most part, they had been eviscerated, entirely cleaned out not by the ferocious jaws of some hellish predator but by the living jungle itself. The sheer weight of diversity in the rain forest meant that the remains of creatures that had died here survived only days before they were completely absorbed once again by their surroundings. Michael had written an entire thesis on this single fact: that the very living jungle around him was entirely comprised of the remains of living things, created to be finally absorbed once again to become a part of some new species of animal or plant. Nature's perfect recycling machine was a marvel to him, an icon to natural selection and the harmony of living species, but this was different.

He saw the second corpse a moment later, further ahead in the forest.

'There are more,' Lucien offered, staying back, 'many, many more.'

Michael edged past the remains on the forest floor, the fur a ruffled black and white where the lemur had fallen and died. Its skull looked up at him, mouth agape and swarming with insects, its eyes sunken black orbs staring accusingly into his.

Michael pushed on into the forest, and as he saw one corpse so he saw another, and another, and another still. His pace slowed, the air thick and black with insects feasting on the gruesome banquet that nature had provided, and his brain slowly fell almost silent as he witnessed the scale of the catastrophe.

Michael knew that such events occurred occasionally in nature but that this was something new. Within five hundred years of human arriving on Madagascar some two thousand or so years previously, nearly all of the island's native and distinct megafauna had become extinct, with smaller species following swiftly due to hunting pressure and an expanding human population. Smaller fauna experienced a brief spike in population due to decreased competition but then they too died out under the human onslaught, victims of habitat loss and aridification of forests.

But this...? This was unprecedented, almost impossible.

The forest floor was littered with the carcasses of lemurs, all in various states of decay. Some were bare bones, still retaining the form of the animal due to the tough tendons remaining intact, the skin and flesh hanging in tatters from the bones like limp rigging on an abandoned ship. But a few were fresher, their corpses intact but bloated from expanding gases trapped inside their guts, and Michael stepped toward them, swatting dense clouds of mosquitoes and flies from his face as he looked down at the nearest victim.

He could tell at a glance that predation was not the cause, for the lemur had been neither bitten nor eaten in any way. Although the eye sockets had already been consumed, all animal's softer parts the first to decay or be eaten after death, its flesh and fur remained almost untouched, and that was when Michael saw what he had feared the most.

The lemur's snout was enveloped in a thick mass of white, gloopy fluid that looked almost like fungus. Michael crouched down alongside the remains, and with one hand he pulled a sample kit from his jacket and carefully scooped a globule of the mess inside and then sealed the kit, careful to wipe the exterior with an alcohol solution before slipping it back into his pocket.

He was about to leave when something else caught his eye, a bright patch of color amid the dense foliage. He got up and moved across to it, and looked down to see the colorful plumage of a Malagasy warbler, a small bird native to the eastern forests that survived on insects. Michael took another pace closer and then he froze.

The warbler's beak was smeared with white fluid.

Despite the intense heat cloaking the forest, Michael's blood ran cold in his veins as he looked around and saw more birds lying dead amid the foliage, their beaks and bills choked with the fungal fluid. He took another horrified step back, then turned and hurried away from the grim killing field, holding his breath all the way but already knowing that it was too late. He stumbled to Lucien's side and thrust the specimen he had collected into the guide's hand.

'Take this to Reserve Speciale d'Analamazaotra, as fast as you can, and never come back here again.'

Lucien took the sample, his dark eyes fixed on Michael's. 'What did you find?'

Michael could barely speak of it, but the sight of the lemurs and the birds lying dead together on the forest floor was something that he would not forget as long as he lived, which may not be all that long at all. Two distinct and unrelated species, struck down by the same affliction, dead within hours.

'I found the end,' he gasped. 'Go, hurry!'

Lucien whirled and ran down the hillside, vanished within moments into the forests further down as Michael ran his hands through his hair and looked back over his shoulder into the depths of the gloomy forest as though death were watching him even now from within.

***

Dean Crawford

XVII

Narryer Gneiss Terrane,

Canadian Sheild Formation,

North–West Territories

Ethan clambered out of the jeep that had carried them far out into the wilderness of one of the most rugged landscapes on earth. Although the sun was shining high in a perfect blue sky the air was so cold he felt as though he could reach up and crack it with his hands. Spruce forest dominated the undulating hills, which were peppered with streams that flowed into a large lake to their east, endless beaches of rock lining the frigid water.

'They like their wilderness, these guys,' Lopez noted as she pulled the collar of her jacket closer about her neck and checked a map she held in one gloved hand. 'He should be around here somewhere.'

Ethan slammed the jeep door shut and looked around briefly for any sign of bear spoor before he set off toward the river. They were right in the heart of big bear country and although Ethan was armed, he didn't fancy his 9mm pistol's chances against an eight hundred pound bear with a bad attitude.

Schofield had sent them in pursuit of Doctor Gregory Lysander, a scientist who would understand what Channing had been involved in. That Beauchamp was already missing in itself troubling, but Lysander was allegedly in the field somewhere out on the Canadian Shield and so far nobody had reported him as missing.

'Jarvis said that Lysander was looking for something far older than what Channing was working on,' Ethan said as they walked, their hiking boots crunching on the heavy rocks beneath them. 'I'm not sure but didn't they find some of the oldest rocks on earth out here?'

'Beats me,' Lopez said with a shrug. 'I'd Google it for you, but we're about a zillion miles from the nearest cell tower so I guess we're on our own.'

They made their way down to the shoreline for a better look both up and downstream in the hopes of spotting Lysander's camp. As soon as they got there it was obvious that the scientist was camped nowhere near their location.

'Nothing,' Lopez said, her voice seeming louder in the deep silence of the terrain surrounding them. 'Damn it Ethan, this guy could be anywhere out here and it might take days to find him.'

'You never know,' Ethan shrugged, 'he might just walk up to us.'

'Yeah, sure we'd get that lucky.'

The reply was called out from behind them. 'Good morning!'

Ethan turned and saw a man standing beside the jeep they'd arrived in, waving cheerfully as he descended the beach toward them. Ethan smirked at Lopez, who in reply stuck a sharp little tongue out in his direction.

'You'll freeze like that in this cold,' he warned her.

The man, bespectacled and bearded and wearing thick thermal jacket, pants and boots, stuck a hand out in Ethan's direction.

'You're from the Institute,' he said in delight. 'I heard your jeep from across the valley. Did they approve my funding for the next semester?'

'I'm afraid we're not from the Institute, Doctor Lysander,' Ethan replied as he shook Lysander's hand. 'We're from the Defense Intelligence Agency.'

Lopez managed to show Lysander her ID badge using her gloved hand, unwilling to expose even the smallest patch of her skin to the cold. Lysander's expression faltered.

'What brings you out here?' Lysander asked. 'And how did you know my name and where to find me?'

'The Institute gave us a rough idea and we just followed our nose after that.'

Lysander frowned. 'What would the Defense Intelligence Agency want with me?'

'Nothing,' Lopez said, 'it's what you know about other people that interests us. Do you know a man named Aubrey Channing?'

Lysander seemed surprised. 'I did, he worked out of Montana, made quite the name for himself before he disappeared some years ago. I think that most people thought that he'd injured himself while working alone in the field and perhaps succumbed to the elements or wild animal attack, it does happen from time to time. I've encountered quite a few bears out here since I arrived.'

'We think that Channing was murdered,' Ethan said. 'We're not sure but we have some leads we're following, most of them surrounding a Professor Martin Beauchamp.'

'Beauchamp?' Lysander said. 'He's working similar fields to me, we met at Harvard only last year. How is he?'

'He's missing,' Lopez replied, 'hence our interest. There's something linking the two men, Channing and Beauchamp, and we wondered whether you could help enlighten us on what they might have been up to? Beauchamp worked as Channing's undergraduate during the early part of his career, and helped Channing to find something buried in Montana. Channing found it but then disappeared.'

Lysander stared at them for a moment. 'What you're describing sounds like some kind of conspiracy theory or something.'

'Trust us, we've seen far worse,' Ethan assured him. 'You say that Beauchamp works in a similar field to you? What is it that you do here?'

Lysander gestured to the wilds around them.

'You're standing on the Canadian Shield, what's known as a physiographic division, essentially a large divide between different kinds of rock. The whole thing together is a maze of Archean Plates, terranes and sedimentary basins formed in what we call the Proterozoic Eon, one of the formative periods of earth's formation.'

Ethan and Lopez stared blankly at Lysander in silence for a moment and the scientist chuckled as he went on.

'I'm studying the very earliest stages of the formation of life on our planet, and have made some incredible discoveries only in the last few years. Come, I'll show you.'

Lysander set off at a spritely pace, leaving Ethan and Lopez with no choice but to follow him across the rugged terrain. They walked until Lysander crouched down and pulled a claw hammer from a satchel slung across his shoulder. Moments later, he hacked a piece of rock from a sloping formation near the water's edge and turned to show it to them.

'There, what do you think of this?'

Lopez stared vacantly at it. 'It's lovely. What is it?'

'It's a rock,' Ethan smiled helpfully at her.

'This is part of an Archaean igneous core of an ancient mountain chain, exposed by glacial forces that formed this valley millions of years ago. A form of this rock discovered in 2008 at the Nuvvuagittuq greenstone belt contained zircons inside it that were successfully dated to over four billion years old.'

Ethan blinked. 'So, from around when the earth itself formed then?'

'Precisely,' Lysander confirmed. 'We're talking about rocks that have escaped the normal process of tectonic absorption and recycling that is a feature of our planet's active geology. The zircon crystals within those rocks can survive such activity anyway though so even if the encasing rock was younger, the age of the crystals remains measurable.'

'Okay,' Lopez said cautiously, 'so what does this have to do with dinosaurs?'

'Nothing, and everything,' Lysander explained. 'The dinosaurs would not emerge as a species until billions of years after this rock was formed, and in fact no recognizably complex forms of life would have existed at this time.'

'*Sooo*,' Lopez ushered Lysander on.

'This is the really exciting bit,' Lysander enthused as he pointed at the rock in his hand.

'I'm on the edge of my seat,' Lopez whispered.

If Lysander noticed the jibe, he didn't react to it as he went on.

'Similar zircons recovered from the Jack Hills in Western Australia and aged at nearly four and a half billion years possessed an isotopic composition that suggested there was already water on the earth when they were formed.'

If Lopez was blown away by this information, Ethan could see no evidence of it.

'But the earth was just a molten ball of fire back then, right?' she said.

'Apparently not,' Lysander continued. 'In a paper published in the journal Earth and Planetary Science Letters, it was suggested by a team that continents and liquid water have existed on this planet for some four point three billion years, and were subject to weathering from the elements and an acrid climate.'

'So there was water early on in earth's history,' Ethan said. 'I don't get the connection yet.'

'That was what Beauchamp was working on,' Lysander explained. 'He was attempting to connect the discoveries of water on the early earth with the parallel discoveries being made in cosmology and physics. Essentially, what they had found was further evidence of panspermia, of the existence of life not from this earth but from elsewhere.'

'We know about that,' Ethan said, 'the idea that life can exist inside comets and other celestial bodies and travel between the stars, seeding life on new planets.'

'Precisely,' Lysander agreed, 'but these new discoveries suggest that something more than just the chemicals of life arrived on our planet with comets and other bolide impactors. There is a growing collaboration between physicists, biologists and chemists that seeks to identify something known as "directed panspermia".'

'What's that?' Lopez asked.

Lysander appeared uncomfortable as he sought words to express his explanation.

'Essentially, the idea that life did not begin naturally on our planet or anywhere in the universe, but was *deliberately* directed here: seeded, if you will.'

Lopez frowned. 'By whom?'

Lysander shrugged. 'Well, that's the big question isn't it?'

'And do you think that Beauchamp, or Channing, might have found the evidence that proves it's possible?'

Lysander sighed again.

'I don't think it's possible,' he replied. 'I know it is, because the evidence has already been discovered.'

***

Dean Crawford

XVIII

'You're kidding me?' Lopez uttered. 'They've actually found alien DNA?'

Lysander's smile faded and he let the rock fall from his hands to clatter against the countless millions of others beneath their feet.

'For some decades now, it has been proposed that the most likely place for us to find the signature of a higher intelligence is in our very own DNA,' he explained. 'The reason for this is that unlike physical structures that could be erected by higher civilizations as a marker and evidence of their presence, a signature in genetic material could survive intact for millions, perhaps even billions of years, whereas physical structures would decay and erode far more quickly. Therefore, a concerted effort in some academic fields has been ongoing for many years to identify any evidence of such tampering or intervening in the natural code.'

'That gives me the creeps,' Lopez said.

'It's supposed to,' Lysander agreed. 'The idea that life was purposefully seeded on earth in the form of RNA or DNA, which led to the development of cells and ultimately life, means that all life on earth is ultimately ancestral to some other species that did not originate on this planet.'

Ethan turned to Lopez. 'The Black Knight.'

Lopez nodded. 'Could be something to do with it.'

'What's the Black Knight?' Lysander asked.

'Never mind,' Ethan said. 'How did they find out about this supposed alien DNA, and why the hell isn't it being talked about on every news channel on earth?'

Lysander chuckled bitterly. 'Human foibles and failures. There is considerable concern among governments around the world about just how some people would react to this kind of news. Some argue that it would be an irrecoverable blow to religious faith that would see some form of societal collapse in the wake of such devastating news. Others, that the faithful of the world would simply assume it as further evidence of divine intervention in human evolution. I personally would like to see this news around the globe too, but for now it's considered far too sensitive and is thus passed over by most of the media.'

'I don't believe they'd block something like that,' Lopez said.

'No?' Lysander challenged. 'In a recent study of Israeli and Palestinian Muslim Arabs, more than seventy per cent of the Jewish men and over eighty per cent of the Arab men whose DNA was studied had inherited their Y chromosomes from the same paternal ancestors, who lived in the region within the last few thousand years. In short, Israel's people are not a distinctive race after all and have no right to claim to be. Israel promptly blocked the report wherever they found it, and it was distinctly under–reported around the world for fear of upsetting Jewish beliefs, their faith and their perceived right to a country with an undivided Jerusalem as its capital. Faith trumps fact once again, with media compliance.'

'But this alien DNA is sensational, right?' Lopez argued. 'I'd have thought that they'd be all over this no matter who it upsets?'

'Do not underestimate the power of politics over science and the media,' Lysander cautioned her. 'This isn't the first time scientists have been censored over what they can release publicly. The International Committee on Climate Change has repeatedly used its governmental connections to suppress any evidence suggesting that climate change is anything other than man–made. Manufacturers of everything from toothpaste to major drugs repeatedly do the same to conceal the long–term effects of the products they produce, and tobacco firms long fought to suppress evidence of their efforts to create cigarettes capable of crossing the blood–brain barrier, increasing addictiveness. In the case of alien DNA, however, the suppression appears genuinely motivated by a desire to prevent a paradigm shift in human nature and understanding: mankind has never been able to answer questions of this magnitude until now, and the reaction of the general public is notoriously difficult to predict. Ask any presidential candidate.'

'How did they find this alien DNA?' Ethan asked. 'Are you sure this isn't just some Internet Meme or something?'

'It was part of the Human Genome Project,' Lysander explained. 'Scientists worked for thirteen years to unravel the code, and in doing so they discovered that some of the non–coding sections of our genetic sequences, once referred to as "junk DNA", were in fact extra–terrestrial in origin. The research published in the open access journal *Genome Biology* focused on the use of horizontal gene transfer, or HGT, the transfer of genes between organisms living in the same environment. Scientists from the University of Cambridge in the United Kingdom proved that HGT has contributed to the evolution of many, perhaps all, animals and that the process is ongoing.' He smiled as though in wonder at it all. 'We're full of extra–terrestrial material, and nobody knows where it came from.'

'Could it be a mistake?' Lopez asked.

'Regretfully, no,' Lysander replied. 'Maxim Makukov of the Fesenkov Astrophysical Institute supported the Cambridge researchers' conclusions, which were essentially that our DNA consists of two versions: a large structured code and a simple, shorter one. The larger part of the code is non–terrestrial, inherited from some other place or species, while the shorter section of the code is the result of biological and chemical evolution over the history of our planet. The research, along with other material on directed panspermia, has featured in the prestigious journal *Icarus*, among others.'

'Can this code be read?' Lopez asked.

Lysander seemed uncertain.

'The human genome contains many millions of lines of code but in principle yes, any message contained therein should be decipherable in the same way that binary code can be converted into words, images and mathematics. Precisely such a code was found in the human genome in 2013, in the form of mathematical and semiotic patterns within that code.'

'Mathematical patterns?' Ethan echoed. 'Like a *message*?'

'Precisely,' Lysander agreed. 'However I haven't heard anything about the work since, which leads me to believe that it was rapidly covered up by the governments in question and the scientists involved in the work prevented from elaborating any further on what they had achieved.'

Ethan thought for a moment and then he thanked the doctor for his time and marched back up the shore with Lopez.

'The Black Knight contained information,' Lopez said as they walked, 'that device inside it and the quantum computer that Hellerman's been working on. This whole thing is connected to Majestic Twelve. Maybe this is what they've been working on the whole time?'

Ethan nodded in agreement. Ever since they had begun the seemingly endless task of attempting to bring Majestic Twelve down, they had seen connections with what appeared to be a vast conspiracy to cover–up a major discovery that had occurred some decades before, perhaps centuries even. Ethan had always felt that beyond their investigations, buried deep somewhere in archives so classified that even the President of the United States knew nothing about them, was a clue that could unravel the entire mystery and reveal just what it was that the members of Majestic Twelve knew and why they were so opposed to it becoming public knowledge.

'What if everything they've been doing over the years is to keep this single big secret?' he suggested. 'Majestic Twelve were formed right after the supposed alien crash at Roswell, New Mexico in 1947, and they've had a presence at virtually every major paranormal or supernatural event that we've investigated.'

'And they keep silencing people who are working on this stuff,' Lopez agreed, 'Lucy Morgan in both Israel and Peru and the site in Antarctica where we found the Black Knight.'

'Most of what got them started seems connected to the ancient alien hypothesis,' Ethan said, 'those monoliths around the world, the Nazca Lines, everything pretty much ties them into some kind of knowledge about bigger things than we've been looking at over the past few years.'

Ethan reached the jeep and looked back down the rocky shore to where Lysander was busily collecting samples and examining them with a magnifying glass, already oblivious to Ethan and Lopez. The fact that so many scientists were involved in programs of one kind or another that Majestic Twelve had shown an interest in made him wonder whether any of their twelve members were themselves academics. He'd heard of various scientists who had become fabulously wealthy as a result of patenting their various inventions either within universities or as private ventures outside of them.

'Has Jarvis released the names of all of MJ–12's members yet?' he asked Lopez.

'Not so far,' she replied. 'They're keeping it under wraps right now, presumably to prevent them from becoming aware that we know who they are.'

Lopez, while working with a former FBI agent in New York City, had been able in a previous operation to use a small robotic drone to hover in front of a towering hotel and snap a single image of the entire group assembled in one place. There had been twelve men present, plus one more, the Director of the FBI, a shocking revelation that had ended the director's career and ultimately his life.

'Twelve men, and one of them was Victor Wilms, right?'

'Sure,' Lopez agreed, and then caught onto Ethan's train of thought. 'Wilms is dead, so they're one short.'

'I wonder if their new member, Wilms's replacement, is a geneticist of some kind?'

Lopez yanked open the door to the jeep and was about to climb in when Lysander hurried up the shore to them, a satellite phone in his hand and an amazed expression on his face.

'It's for you!'

Ethan blinked in surprise as he took the satellite phone from Lysander.

'Ethan, it's Jarvis. You need to get to the nearest airport immediately, I'll have a plane meet you there.'

'Where are we going?'

The reply chilled Ethan to the core.

'Madagascar,' Jarvis replied. *'The extinction has begun.'*

***

XIX

Rome

Waiting was always the hardest part.

The car was parked on a side street just a quarter mile south of the iconic Colosseum, which he could see now and which provided a handy datum for orientation in the city. He kept an eye on the shadows falling on the buildings on the opposite side of the street too, gauging both the time and direction.

Aaron Mitchell had little time for modern technology, preferring instead to rely on his wits and years of training. Electrical gizmos had a nasty habit of failing when the batteries ran out, or glitching at crucial moments. The beautiful golden glow of the sunlight hitting the ornate buildings on the opposite side of the street reminded him of an operation deep inside a frigid town in southern Bosnia, where the snow and ice was encrusted around the shelled fragments of what had once been a town house. Mitchell had crept through the shattered interior of the building in search of two men who had been gunning down civilians passing through the area and robbing them before erecting the corpses on stakes in streets nearby.

A low sun made visibility difficult, bright beams of misty golden light passing through bare windows and gusty corridors littered with debris and chunks of fallen masonry. Mitchell had advanced with all due caution, but sometimes all the skill in the world was no match for sheer bad luck and the unpredictable.

He had eased around the corner of a corridor to see a remote machine gun emplacement staring straight at him, likely installed by mercenaries paid to take down whatever Serbians or Croats their employers had decided no longer had the right to life. Sunlight glowed in beaming shafts through mortar holes in the corridor wall and fell onto the ugly black barrel, damp with moisture that glistened in the light. He had seen the operators a moment later, huddled excitedly over some little black box that controlled their new toy and tucked safely out of easy shooting range around the far end of the corridor. Mitchell had heard the motors of the machine gun whine and the barrel shift slightly to the right, and then he had heard the laughter as the two operators pressed the fire button. The empty click that had echoed down the corridor revealed the flaw in trusting one's life to circuits and electrodes: the bitter cold had caused ice to form on the machine gun's attached auto–trigger circuitry, breaking up the flow of electrons and denying the signal when the sunlight had hit the weapon and melted the ice.

Mitchell had lunged forward, yanked the machine gun round to aim back down the corridor and pulled the trigger himself. A deafening few seconds later and the opposite side of the corridor was peppered with rounds that punched easily through the crumbling walls, long since exposed to the elements. Mitchell had passed by what was left of the two operators sprawled across the corridor with a deep mistrust of such gadgets and a conviction never to fall prey to their lure of an easy kill.

A distant bell chimed and woke Mitchell from his reverie. He cursed himself silently, aware more now than ever that his advancing years were blunting his skills and his senses, that he would not much longer be an effective asset in the field. That, of course, meant that sooner or later a younger, fitter, more able man would be the one pulling the trigger on Mitchell. He recalled his being bested by Ethan Warner not much more than a year ago, in Nevada. He had barely escaped from that encounter with his life, and once again only good fortune had been on his side – without it, he had no doubt that Warner would have finished him for good.

Movement on the opposite side of the street, and again Mitchell cursed his drifting mind as he saw four men exit an exclusive restaurant. Suits, shades, broad shoulders, glances cast carefully up and down the street. It amused Mitchell sometimes that the security teams wealthy men assembled to protect them were also the very thing that drew attention to them: a man walking alone, ironically, was much harder to spot from a distance than somebody who walked with five bodyguards to protect them.

Mitchell watched as one of the guards opened the door to a glossy black Mercedes, and then a man walked from the restaurant. Perhaps fifty years of age, smartly dressed, empowered by money but not by honor. Mitchell glanced at a high resolution photograph in his hand and confirmed that this was indeed the mark he had followed from Dubai.

Time to go to work.

The Mercedes pulled smoothly away from the restaurant, a second vehicle moving into view to follow it a few car lengths behind. Mitchell knew that this would be the vehicle carrying two of the security team, with the other two driving the Mercedes. There would likely be a third vehicle that would now have pulled out somewhere ahead, which would have two further agents inside who would recon' the route ahead, looking for obvious trouble spots like traffic bottlenecks or perhaps unplanned roadworks which would signify a possible assassination attempt.

Majestic Twelve were worried, Mitchell realized, and smiled.

The two vehicles moved off, and Mitchell pulled out into the traffic flow and followed them a discreet distance behind. The security team, if they were sharp, would have noted his vehicle among all of the others and would monitor their presence, looking for some sign of a tail. Mitchell's vehicle plate began with the letters *Delta Echo Zero Four,* easy to memorize for a keen–eyed agent and pick up again if he was seen too often following the Mercedes.

Mitchell had a map of the city open beside him, and he began noting where the Mercedes was headed through the city. The airport was in the opposite direction so his target was not intending to leave the city today. Having just eaten would mean that a social engagement was unlikely at least until the evening. That meant a likely route was to one of the exclusive hotels, of which Mitchell knew they would pick only the absolute finest. Sometimes, men of power revealed their hands far too easily, their love of luxury an Achilles Heel. Mitchell had already circled the three most expensive hotels in the city, and now he identified one of them in particular as being the most likely destination. He could be wrong of course, but the closer they got, the more likely his judgement was correct.

Mitchell followed and waited, all the while glancing at the map and plotting an alternative route to the hotel, one that would allow him to park up and observe from afar. When they got within a mile of the hotel, he turned into a side street and left the Mercedes and its escort, driving his car through a maze of narrow back roads until he found the spot he was looking for and eased into the sidewalk.

Aaron Mitchell, an African American standing six foot three and two hundred forty pounds, was not at his anonymous best in an urban environment in daylight. He remained in his car on the Via Della Minerva, where he had deliberately parked behind a goods vehicle to help conceal his location and his vehicle's license plate.

Before him across a large, square open plaza was the Grand Hotel de la Minerva, one of the city's most exclusive. Milling crowds of tourists further helped conceal his presence as he saw three vehicles move into view. The first was a non–descript white sedan, which Mitchell realized was the recon' car and noted its number immediately. The Mercedes followed a moment later, and finally the rear guard vehicle. As Mitchell watched, his target exited the Mercedes with two men swiftly flanking him and walking with him through the hotel's large double doors.

Mitchell turned and looked at the buildings surrounding the Palazzo Severoli. Most looked inaccessible, but one stood out to his right: The Pontifical Ecclesiastical Academy's doors were open, and as Mitchell looked up he could see that its rooftop terrace stood just a little higher than that of the Minerva Hotel.

Mitchell got out of his car, a briefcase in his hand as he walked across to the academy. The interior visible from outside was as luxurious and decadent as he would have imagined, neoclassical Italian architecture and art transformed into hallowed halls of the Roman Colleges of the Catholic Church. Mitchell neither knew nor cared much for the faiths of the world, and had merely used his burner phone to discover that the academy was dedicated to the priesthood's diplomatic Corps and the secretariat of State of the Holy See.

Mitchell walked with a purpose, one of the key skills provided to field agents when they began their training. If you look like you know where you're going, nobody thinks that you don't and therefore you do not stand out. None the less, Mitchell kept his face away from the hotel across the plaza as he walked not into the Pontifical Academy but into a small trinket shop right alongside it.

There was little chance of Mitchell getting through such a building as the academy without raising the alarm, much less escaping again. But the rows of little shops nearby provided a second route, built as they were into the same massive edifice shared by the academy.

Mitchell ducked inside the shop and closed the door behind him, a small bell tinkling to alert the shopkeeper to the presence of a new customer. Mitchell turned the door's "*chioso*" sign to show out to the street outside as he saw an elderly man hobble out to greet him with a smile.

'Buongiorno signore,' Mitchell intoned as he set the briefcase down beside him. 'Avete accesso al tetto?'

The shopkeeper's smile faded into confusion as he wondered why this new customer would want access to his roof.

'Sissignore,' he replied and then switched to English as he detected Mitchell's American accent. 'But you can't go up there because it's owned by...'

Mitchell's hand was faster almost than the old man's eye. He scythed the blade of it across the shopkeeper's throat, just below the thorax, in a loose blow designed not to kill but to incapacitate. The old man staggered backwards, both hands flying to his throat as it collapsed in the wake of the blow and he wheezed as he tried to suck in air. Moments later, his legs gave way beneath him and he collapsed to his knees.

Mitchell locked the shop door and gently pulled down a blind, then turned and walked across to the old man, who was gasping for air. The shopkeeper raised a hand defensively to protect himself from Mitchell, terror in his old eyes. Mitchell grabbed the old man's hand, and then gently lifted him up onto his feet and spoke softly.

'You are in no danger,' he said. 'You will not be harmed, and I need only a few moments of your time.'

Mitchell turned the old man around and used a length of fabric from a nearby rack of scarves to bind the old man's wrists before he walked him out into the back of the shop and sat him in a chair. Moments later, the old man was bound in place. Mitchell rested one giant hand on his old shoulder and squeezed gently.

'I will be a few minutes,' he said. 'Don't try to escape, understand?'

The old man looked into Mitchell's eyes, and what he saw there made him nod slowly, conveying that he did indeed understand that the consequences of disobedience would be severe.

Mitchell retrieved his briefcase from the shop out front, and then walked past the shopkeeper and out toward a storeroom out back. It took him only a few moments to find an old door behind stacks of tinned goods that had been likely sealed decades before. Access to other sections of the same original building would also be in place, but Mitchell knew that he had only one direction in which to travel.

Up.

He slipped a small leather case from his jacket, and within a minute had picked the lock of the old door, hardly a major task given its antiquity. Mitchell tried the lock, and to his delight it opened, the owners not having sealed the door from the other side using more robust locks. It was possible that they did not even know of its existence, furthering Mitchell's advantage.

The door opened onto a stone staircase, one that had probably once climbed between rooms in the now separate buildings. He could smell damp and dust, stale air cool on his skin as he closed the door carefully behind him and climbed up the stone stairs to a small landing where two more doors awaited, one to each side, both locked.

Mitchell knew that the academy likely awaited on both sides, occupying all of the upper floors, so he tackled the door to his right in the hopes of avoiding the main building. Mitchell waited for a few minutes, listening intently, and having satisfied himself that whatever awaited on the far side of the wall was devoid of human presence, he picked the lock as quietly as he could and then opened the door.

A wide staircase faced him, climbing ever up toward the roof.

Mitchell shut the door behind him and eased silently upward.

***

XX

Grand Hotel de la Minerva,

Rome

Felix Byzan strode into the penthouse suite of the hotel as though he owned the place, which of course he could at any moment he chose, if he actually had liked the city. Rome, to him, was a city built on the foundations of a former glory that it had never recaptured: an icon, a relic to something that had once been great and was now forgotten in all but school text books and historian's libraries.

The doorman opened the room's windows for him to allow a breeze to drift across the sumptuous furnishings, and then waited beside the open door for Felix to tip him. Felix looked him up and down for a moment, and then smiled.

'Giornata piena, Signore?'

The man smiled to be spoken to in fluent Italian, and replied in perfect English.

'Very busy sir, the tourist season is beginning.'

Felix handed the doorman a fifty Euro note. 'Buona fortuna.'

'Grazie, Signore.'

The door closed, and Felix slipped out of his jacket and tossed the three hundred dollar garment across the leather couch as though it were trash, then unbuttoned his collar and pulled off his tie. The fresh air was welcome and he could see from his balcony the view across the plaza below, and the small obelisk that dominated the square. He had seen similar obelisks across the country, even in front of the Vatican itself, and marvelled again that so many people could worship here when the country's history of Egyptian and other civilization's presence even now told the true story of Italy's heritage. Rome had long since been stripped of all reference to its mighty imperial past, the museums filled instead with the religious iconography that the church believed the people wanted to see. Felix himself had been deeply disappointed to find that even the famed Colosseum was devoid of any true history, stacked instead with cheap religious trinkets.

He turned from the window and poured himself a drink, his mind filling with other more pressing concerns. The meeting had not gone well, at least he did not feel that it had. Garrett's claims had unnerved him, and did not sit well with the cabal's preferred method of probationary membership before a newcomer was welcomed into the fold. Then again, he had not enjoyed watching Gordon LeMay die earlier in the year either, but it was not his place to dictate Majestic Twelve's choice of actions, only to *advise*.

Felix sipped the single malt he'd poured and then felt his cell phone buzz in his pocket. He answered it, set it onto speaker phone on a coffee table nearby.

'Felix,' Kruger's voice greeted him, 'your thoughts on our potential new member?'

'I don't like him,' Felix replied. 'He's too confident in what he's doing when we all know that he's dabbling in something we cannot control. We've been fighting the threat of a new extinction age for decades and if there's one thing we've learned it's that no volume of technical wizardry is going to stop seven billion people from ultimately self–destructing. There are just too many of us.'

A long silence filled the suite until Samuel Kruger finally answered.

'You know that we're losing influence, Felix. We need a man like Garrett to bolster our position, perhaps in the face of an extinction level event. The FBI no longer represents a valuable asset to us, despite our links to the agency remaining strong despite the loss of LeMay.'

Felix let a bitter little smile flicker across his features.

'Loss,' he echoed. 'Waste, is a word I would have used. As for Wilms, I take it that you believe that Mitchell was behind the attack?'

'It would appear so,' came the reply. 'It was only a matter of time before this happened Felix, you and I both know that. Wilms would have talked eventually, and it's only convenient that Mitchell struck before somebody in our own employ was able to make Wilms a historical irritation.'

'Wilms was a servant of our organisation for many long decades and you hung him out to dry,' Felix snapped back. 'One of the pillars of loyalty is that said loyalty is shown to those who work for us. The walls start falling when people come to believe that loyalty is a one way street; that it only applies to those at the top. I predicted this would happen if either LeMay or another of our assets was compromised.'

'I don't appreciate the lecture.'

'Which is why we're in the state we're in,' Felix shot back. 'Garrett is dangerous, more so than I think any of us realize. He's not here to join us; he's here to take control. He says he has the cure for a disease so powerful that nobody on earth can stop it, and yet he won't allow us access to that cure? Since when do we allow ourselves to be blackmailed?'

'Since we started becoming the hunted,' Kruger growled back. 'Mitchell rightly has every reason to believe that we will kill him the first chance we get, therefore he is now making the first move. It is only a matter of time before he reaches one of us, before he finds out who we are and is able to target us directly.'

Felix shook his head.

'The Defense Intelligence Agency already knows who we are,' he corrected, 'but they cannot use the imagery they obtained in New York against us. It would be inadmissible in court without letting the world know that the President of the United States is merely a cipher for power in our country. No self–respecting Congressman or Senator is going to say that they're a powerless pawn in our geo–political games.'

'We can't be sure of that.'

'No?' Felix challenged. 'So, what's the news saying about Wilms? Are they suddenly now reporting that he's been shot by an assassin?'

Another long silence before the reply came. 'No, there was a brief report an hour ago that a prisoner in Florence ADX facility had died of a self–inflicted chest wound.'

Felix nodded and smiled. 'And the coroner's report will reflect that and no mention will ever be made of Mitchell's kill, the weakened security of Florence ADX or the fact that Mitchell escaped from the damned place! The government still fear us, are still unable to admit to the people of the world just who really pulls the strings for the greater good. If they find out that people like us control nations and remain unaccountable there would be riots on the streets of every capital city on earth!'

'And arrests,' Kruger pointed out.

'Perhaps,' Felix agreed, 'but I trust in politicians' shared desire for the illusion of power, their propensity to lie and their spineless nature to ensure that none of them would ever upset the status quo. No matter how strong the DIA's agents become, or how deeply ingrained Mitchell's hatred of us grows, they won't be able to bring us down.'

'Unless somebody at the DIA is feeding Mitchell information.'

Felix stopped pacing again. 'That's unlikely, they want him brought down as much as we do.'

'Our people have so far failed to derail General Nellis's effort to expose and arrest us,' Kruger reminded him. 'The longer they have, the greater the chance that they will succeed, and there is always the chance that one of our weaker members might decide to turncoat if things get too tough.'

Felix nodded again to himself, a concern of his own that some of the cabal's other members might not entirely share Majestic Twelve's vision of the New World Order.

'We must talk more on this, in person,' he agreed.

'Garrett's invited us to his island,' the director said. 'Most of us have accepted.'

'That's dangerous.'

'It's necessary,' the director insisted. 'We need a way forward and a means to maintain a hold on the United States Government. Without that, we're as vulnerable as we've ever been. And if Garrett's threat of a global pandemic is real, we need to be with him when that unfortunate event occurs. We're no longer *safe*, Felix, we have little choice.'

Felix sighed. 'When?'

'Forty eight hours from now,' the director said. 'I'll send you the details. Delete them as soon as you've memorized them and then destroy the cell entirely.'

'Understood.'

The line went dead, and seconds later the cell phone beeped as Felix received a message.

ILHABELA, BRAZIL. BE CAREFUL

Felix smiled. 'I don't think Mitchell will come after me first, old man,' he said as he moved his thumb across the screen to delete the message.

'Don't be so sure.'

Felix froze, his eyes staring into space as the hairs on the back of his neck went up. He turned slowly and saw the huge man standing in the suite, a pistol aimed between Felix's eyes.

Felix knew of Mitchell only by reputation and a brief description once given him by a former member of Majestic Twelve who had since passed away. Still he was not prepared for the man's immense presence in the room, something more than just his considerable physical size. The light seemed to have dimmed, as though Mitchell projected an aura of darkness around him. Felix managed not to swallow or show any fear.

'You're after the wrong man,' he said simply.

'How so?'

'We're not all hell–bent on world domination, Mitchell. Some of us have other plans.'

'So I heard,' Mitchell replied as he glanced at Felix's cell phone. 'Toss it on the couch.'

Felix obeyed, let the cell phone fall onto the soft leather as Mitchell moved around him and picked it up.

'How did you get in here?' Felix asked.

'The balcony was open,' Mitchell replied without looking at him, 'via the roof next door. Why are you going to Brazil, and who is Garrett?'

'You know I can't tell you that,' Felix said, 'won't tell you that.'

Mitchell turned to face Felix, seemed to appraise him for a moment, and then he put the pistol away in its shoulder holster. Felix sighed in relief.

'You're doing the right thing,' he began. 'I know who you should be...'

'In two minutes you will be dead,' Mitchell said in a soft but threatening growl. 'I would choose your words with care as they'll be your last.'

Felix swallowed now, glanced at the suite door.

'You won't make it,' Mitchell promised.

'I'll just scream at the top of my lungs,' Felix replied.

'You won't finish that scream,' Mitchell said. 'You have a choice: die on your knees or on your feet like a man. But whatever you choose, it's all over for you.'

Felix felt desperation swell like poison inside him and his legs felt weak. He considered sprinting for the balcony and hurling himself out of the apartment but somehow he figured that Mitchell would overpower him.

'That's right,' Mitchell said as though reading his mind, 'there's no escape.'

'Why me?' Felix asked finally.

'You were the closest.'

'How did you know?'

'It doesn't matter.'

'It bloody well matters to me!'

Mitchell looked at him without interest, as though he had no soul, and then he reached into his pocket and produced a small polythene bag filled with a clear fluid, attached to which was something that looked like a fishing hook.

'Your kind will never know true justice,' Mitchell replied finally, 'at the mercy of your peers, devoid of political help, so there are those at the DIA who have decided that there is only one kind of justice that we can subject you to.'

'Nellis?' Felix asked, and was rewarded with a shake of the head.

'Nobody that you would know,' Mitchell replied.

'I want to know the name of the man who ordered my death,' Felix insisted.

'So would many thousands of people who have died because of what Majestic Twelve has done, what I have done for them. Families who will never know what happened to their loved ones so that people like you could get rich.'

'I've never killed anybody, nor ordered any such thing!'

'You know well what you're into,' Mitchell said as he loomed before Felix. 'This can either be easy or it can be hard. Decide.'

Felix felt his courage finally abandon him and his voice cracked as he spoke.

'There must be some other way...'

'The hard way, then,' Mitchell said.

Mitchell's fist flashed across Felix's face and struck him with a blow that seemed to echo around the room. Felix opened his mouth to scream for help, then realized just too late that the blow was merely a distraction. Mitchell's knee slammed into Felix's solar plexus like a wrecking ball and the air blasted from his lungs in a rush as he folded over the blow and sank to his knees.

Mitchell bowed over him and in his silent, rasping pain Felix felt a tiny prick of pain in the side of his neck, felt the polythene bag against his skin as Mitchell's iron hands pinned him in place and squeezed the bag. Something cold leeched into Felix's body, Mitchell's weight and the terrible pain surging through his guts rendering Felix unable to move.

Then, suddenly, the cold was gone and Mitchell stood up and backed away from him. Felix looked up through blurred eyes and saw Mitchell quietly lock the apartment door and then move silently back across the suite to pick up Felix's cell.

Felix opened his mouth to ask what Mitchell had done to him, and then he realized that his voice no longer worked and that a pain was building in his neck and across his chest. As soon as he noticed it, the pain intensified and then soared. For a brief moment while he was still capable of coherent thought, Felix believed that Mitchell had set his body aflame as white pain seared his every pore, deep inside his body and even across the surface of his eyes. He opened his mouth to scream in agony but even his lungs burned as his vision faded to black and he heard Mitchell's voice reach him as though from afar.

'It's the venom from a snake known as the western taipan, an Australian species,' he said matter-of-factly. 'It's a specialist mammal hunter and the most venomous snake on earth, much worse even than sea snakes, its toxicity specifically designed to efficiently kill warm blooded species. One bite contains enough venom to kill at least a hundred grown men, and you've received the equivalent of around thirty bites.'

126

Felix's mind disintegrated into a swirling maelstrom of unimaginable agony as he collapsed onto his side, his lungs seared with naked flames and his eyes wide and unseeing as his body went into complete and total organ failure.

'I keep a couple of them on stand–by back in America,' Mitchell said as he stood over Felix and looked down at him, 'for special occasions. They're a surprisingly docile snake that likes to avoid confrontation, but are utterly lethal if provoked or handled incorrectly. I like to think that's a trait I share with them, Felix. I'll let myself out.'

Felix saw a halo of light, something shadowy receding into the distance before him as his brain was overwhelmed by the volume of toxins flooding through his veins and poisoning his every fibre. His last thought was that he was glad to die, such was the unimaginable pain blazing through every cell in his body.

***

Dean Crawford

XXI

DIA Headquarters,

Anacostia–Bolling Airbase,

Washington DC

'Lucy.'

Doug Jarvis stood up as a young woman entered the room in which he was waiting with Hellerman. His granddaughter was tall, with blonde hair and intelligent green eyes who none the less flung her arms over his shoulders as though she were still the child he remembered her as.

'Please, take a seat,' Jarvis said to her as he closed the door behind her and they sat down.

'I'm not sure what I can do for you,' she said as she looked at them.

'We figured you owed us a favor or two, over the years,' Jarvis replied with an easy smile. 'Do you know much about Aubrey Channing?'

'Aubrey died so many years ago now, and I only know of him by name. He's something of a legend in the field.'

'You say that he died,' Hellerman pointed out, 'but isn't he still just missing?'

'Officially, yes,' Lucy agreed, 'but in most minds he died many years ago. Aubrey was just the sort to just wander off for weeks in the wilderness, you see. To be gone for so long, he must have died somehow.'

'What do you know about what he was working on when he vanished?' Jarvis asked.

'Just rumors mostly,' Lucy said, 'but he spent most of his time in Montana so I would have to assume that he was studying Tyrannosaur remains. They were his passion, one that was vastly inflamed by the movie *Jurassic Park*, which he said was the first time in history that mankind got to see what a real Tyrannosaur would have looked like in the flesh.' She smiled. 'I heard that he often showed the T–Rex scenes from the movie to his students, and I think he did the same at a lecture I once saw him give in Chicago.'

'And you now also work in science?' Hellerman asked.

'Anthropology,' Lucy confirmed. 'My latest research is in the field of novel medicine and ancient diseases, specifically seeking drugs to combat what is known as the antibiotic apocalypse.'

'The what?' Jarvis asked.

Hellerman replied for Lucy.

'The antibiotic apocalypse is the rising inability of medicine to effectively combat even basic illnesses, due to the growing resistance of bacteria to all known medicines. It has been suggested that by 2050 we could be seeing a mass extinction of humanity as it falls prey to diseases that were eradicated generations ago.'

Lucy inclined her head at Hellerman in respect of his knowledge.

'Precisely,' she said. 'It is considered to be one of the greatest threats to human existence that we have ever faced, and there has been a concerted effort to play down the impending crisis in the media for fear of the panic that it will cause.'

'You're saying that people can die of colds now?' Jarvis asked.

Lucy nodded.

'Potentially, yes,' she said. 'Antibiotics have been used as a wonder–drug for half a century, prescribed by physicians for the mildest of ailments. Most are broad–spectrum, which means that they simply attack all and every bacteria in the body. This destroys the sickness but also harms other bacteria within us that protect us, which can make us vulnerable to other illnesses. The problem that has developed has its cause in two issues; one, the over–reliance of medicine on antibiotics to fight infections that could otherwise have been defeated by the human body's own immune system, and two; the fact that despite doctors always telling patients to complete the entire dose of antibiotics, they often do not.'

'What difference does that make?' Jarvis asked.

'It leaves some of the infection present,' Hellerman explained, 'if the dose is not completed. People take the anti–Bs, start to feel better, and then stop taking the medicine. This gives the infection within them, and more specifically the bacteria that caused the infection, the chance to evolve. Some of them will develop a resistance to the antibiotics, and are then spread to other people, whereas if the dose had been completed by the patient the infectious bacteria would have been totally destroyed and would not have been given the chance to develop resistance or pass on to other hosts.'

'Again,' Lucy said, 'very precise. 'Bacteria able to resist the drug of last resort, colistin, have been identified in patients and livestock in China. That resistance will spread around the world and is already raising the spectre of untreatable infections. If the antibiotic apocalypse should occur, medicine could be plunged back into the dark ages within years. Common infections will kill again, while surgery and cancer therapies reliant on antibiotics will be under threat. The resistance we're seeing has already spread between a range of bacterial strains and species, including E. coli, *Klebsiella pneumoniae* and *Pseudomonas aeruginosa*, with strains seen in Laos and Malaysia. When the gene responsible, MRC–1, goes global, and I promise you that it will, then there will no longer be an effective medicine against the majority of human ailments.'

'How often is this happening?' Jarvis asked.

'Five years ago, discovering antibiotic resistance to most illnesses was a non–event', she replied. 'Now we're seeing a dozen cases a month in every major medical facility in the United States. MRC–1 connects with other genes extremely easily, creating pan–resistance across many forms of infection and exacerbating the problem. It will only be a matter of time before bacterial resistance extends to all illnesses, even the common cold. It may surprise you to know that for any species never before exposed to it, the common cold is as much as a killer as influenza, because untreated and without natural immunity it will eventually lead to pneumonia and death.'

'And there's nothing that we can do at all?' Jarvis asked.

'There's *always* something that we can do,' Lucy replied, 'which is why I now work in the field that I do. We're attempting to develop narrow–spectrum antibiotics which target bacteria with laser–guided efficiency, so that a patient's immune system is not compromised during treatment, and we're searching for new antibiotics in nature, scouring jungles and forests worldwide in an effort to locate new treatments.'

Jarvis saw the link between what they knew about Aubrey Channing and the fossilized specimen that he had discovered out in the brutal Badlands of Montana.

'We think that Channing discovered evidence that the dinosaurs may have been succumbing to some kind of virus or illness that was wiping them out long before the asteroid that hit the Yucatan Peninsula,' Hellerman said.

'Really?' Lucy replied, evidently shocked. 'But the asteroid impact theory is as solid as they come.'

'That doesn't mean that something else was occurring at the same time or prior to the impact,' Jarvis pointed out. 'We have evidence that when he made the discovery, Aubrey became agitated and refused to let the reporter who accompanied him come anywhere near the find.'

Lucy shook her head, confused.

'That makes no real sense,' she replied. 'Any infection that killed an animal sixty five million or more years ago would not have survived the fossilization process. DNA is not robust enough to maintain integrity over even a fraction of that time.'

'We'll, that's not quite true,' Hellerman interjected. 'We now have DNA successfully extracted from fossilized remains in excess of sixty five millions years, tendons, blood cells, bone tissue and other organic material from Tyrannosaurs and even genetic material extracted from insects trapped in amber for hundreds of millions of years.'

'Not to mention bacteria revived after hundreds of millions of years encased in sodium crystals in New Mexico caves,' Jarvis added with a knowing glance.

'Yes,' Lucy conceded, 'but recovering material and recovering viable material that can be used in modern processes are two different things. Having material doesn't count for much if you cannot use it.'

'But it may be important if whatever Channing found was able somehow to have survived inside the rocks for millions of years,' Hellerman argued, 'which is what we're really talking about here. Aubrey acted as though he was in danger of being infected by something, and he refused to let anybody come near him. That was the last anybody saw of him. When the Center for Disease Control arrived with the reporter, Weisler, Channing was gone and so was his discovery.'

'If Channing had contracted some kind of exotic infection the Federal Food and Drug Agency would have had him locked down within hours because that's where I would have taken him, so that the infection could be studied and hopefully a cure found while not risking a pandemic.'

'Which begs the question why Channing didn't do that and wait for the CDC,' Jarvis said. 'He could have quarantined the site and got the help he needed. His vanishing act doesn't make sense unless somebody abducted him.'

Lucy nodded, stared at her lap for a moment before she replied.

'His disappearance remains a mystery that crops up in conspiracy theories all the time, even on television.'

Jarvis looked at Hellerman and nodded once.

'We made a discovery, recently,' Hellerman said, picking his words with care. 'There has been an outbreak of some kind, of an unknown and highly exotic disease.'

Lucy frowned. 'I didn't hear of anything. Where is it located?'

'Madagascar,' Hellerman said. 'I take it that you are already aware of the growing scientific hypothesis that earth is currently entering a new extinction age that some are calling the Sixth Extinction?'

'I am,' Lucy admitted, cautious now. 'The markers are there for all to see among sentinel species around the world, as well as the population collapse among bats, bees and other pollinating species.'

Hellerman nodded. 'This is not one of those situations. Information is sketchy and the Malagasy government appear to be trying to keep a lid on things. We only found out about this after an American scientist working in the jungles out there managed to get word out to the United Nations via satellite phone.'

Lucy leaned forward in her seat. 'Do we have any information on the nature of the outbreak?'

Jarvis replied.

'The only definitive communication we have from the man on the ground there is that the disease is pan–species and one hundred per cent lethal.'

Lucy's features paled and she stared blankly into the middle distance. Jarvis had seen fear in the eyes of people many times in his career, especially in war zones when traumatized civilians had crawled from the smoking ruins of buildings, and he saw that same fear now in his granddaughter's eyes: primal, deep, terror.

'Pandemic,' she whispered finally. 'Madagascar is just the sort of place that we might expect to discover novel diseases with no known cure.'

'How so?' Jarvis asked.

'Because it's geographically isolated,' Hellerman replied, 'and much of it is virgin rain forest upon which people have never set foot. There could be viruses, bacteria and other such nasties that the world has literally never seen just waiting to find their way into the wider food chain and propagate themselves across the globe.'

Lucy nodded.

'For a long time now, biologists have feared the emergence of a super–strain of some kind, a disease so virulent and yet so easy to distribute that it would infect humanity in weeks, wipe out millions, perhaps billions. It's happened in the past often enough. But I have never heard of a species of bacteria or virus that was pan–species in its ability to infect. You're saying that it's killing flora *and* fauna?'

'Everything it touches, that's what we've been told,' Jarvis replied.

Lucy's shoulders slumped and she dragged a hand down her face.

'This is it then,' she said finally. 'This is where the end begins.' Then she looked up sharply at Jarvis. 'You haven't sent anybody anywhere near it, have you?'

***

Dean Crawford

XXII

Ambila Lamaitso,

Madagascar

'Right this way.'

Ethan and Nicola stepped off the deck of the boat and onto the jetty as a young man with short black hair and a hassled expression ushered them away from the small dock toward the shore. The sun felt unusually subdued due to the hazy overcast, the island's dense humidity cloying and uncomfortable.

'You're agents Warner and Lopez, correct?'

'DIA,' Ethan confirmed wearily as he showed the man his badge, tied around his neck beneath his loose white shirt. The flight from Canada had been long and uncomfortable in the hold of the C–17 Globemaster transport aircraft.

'Agent Christiano Rabinur, South African field office.'

'What's the story?' Lopez asked.

'Quarantine on the island, up in one of the national parks,' Rabinur explained. 'We got called in because the local Malagasy teams couldn't figure out what they were looking at.'

'How bad is it?' Ethan asked as Rabinur led them along a jetty toward what looked like another small dock, this one enclosed within a man–made harbor.

'Reports are sketchy but we've had one team make it through to the site and they've reported that at least fifteen local people are dead already, and that half the damned forest animals are literally falling out of the trees.'

Lopez shot a concerned glance at Ethan. 'You're kidding? On what timescale?'

Rabinur stopped at the edge of the jetty and turned to face them.

'Hours,' he replied, his features taut with what appeared to be an almost superstitious fear. 'I've never seen or heard of anything like it. The local wildlife experts and conservation teams have tried to preserve evidence at the site, but we lost two more of them last night. Whatever's up there it's too lethal to even think about handling directly. We pulled the remaining teams out and have sealed off the forest.'

'How far is it to the site and what's the access like?'

'That's part of the problem,' Rabinur replied. 'The forest is one of the deepest on the island, no roads in or encampments large enough to take a helicopter. The only way in was by foot and it's taken teams two days to reach the site in the past. Things are moving too slowly to contain whatever it is that's up there.'

'We don't have two days,' Lopez pointed out. 'We need to figure this out and fast.'

'I agree,' Rabinur replied, and gestured to the dock before them.

There were rows of old fishing boats, some of them little more than dug—out canoes, nets stacked in their sterns where local fishermen had plied their morning's trade out in the dark waters before their catch dove once again into the deep. Among the boats was a white craft that Ethan realized was not a boat at all but a remarkably small aircraft, its wings folded behind it to decrease storage space.

'You're kidding?' Lopez asked as they walked along the jetty toward the aircraft.

'Jarvis informed me that you have a microlight license,' Rubinar said to Ethan.

'Sure,' Ethan agreed, 'I was trained to use them in the Marines, part of an initiative to improve reconnaissance techniques. But that looks like a real aeroplane and I don't have the qualifications to…'

'It'll be fine,' Rabinur promised. 'The laws here aren't quite as strict as back home, and right now getting the two of you into that site is of far greater importance. Besides, it's just like driving a car.'

Ethan blinked at Rabinur's confidence as they moved to stand alongside the tiny craft.

'This is the Icon A5, an amphibious light aircraft designed to be simple enough for anybody to fly,' he announced.

'Even *him*?' Lopez asked as she jabbed a thumb at Ethan.

'Even him,' Rabinur agreed as he opened the cockpit.

Ethan looked inside and was startled to see that it looked almost exactly like the interior of a normal car, with the exception of the control column in place of a steering wheel and a small box of emergency flares tucked in the foot well. The aircraft had two seats, and the engine was a large propeller mounted atop the fuselage and just behind the cockpit. Small outriggers kept the aircraft balanced on the surface of the water, and a large T—tail completed the configuration, the aircraft painted a glossy white that shone as it reflected the surface of the harbor.

'It's fully fuelled,' Rabinur assured him, 'and produces about as much power as a twin–engine microlight with a similar handling style, so you should feel at home.'

Ethan peered doubtfully at Rabinur as he manually folded down the wings and locked them into place. 'And the small matter of landing the thing when we get there? You said that the site is deep in the mountains?'

'There is a river to the east of the site, within a mile or so,' Rabinur assured him. 'It empties into an estuary just south of here, so you can follow it all the way in. Navigation data has already been programmed into the aircraft's GPS screen, so you'll be able to pick the best spot to land. Be careful though as the river does have some rapids at the higher elevations. You'll need to pick your spot and tie the aircraft down firmly once you've landed.'

'Sounds easy if you say it fast enough,' Ethan murmured in reply as Rabinur handed him a set of keys.

'Starts just like a car and it has an internal parachute safety system in case things go horribly wrong,' he said cheerfully, 'so even you won't be able to crash it.' But then his humor faltered as he remembered the task at hand. 'Biohazard suits will await you, and you'll be met by a member of our team who is camped outside the quarantine zone. Be careful, both of you.'

Rabinur turned and hurried away as Ethan looked at Lopez.

'Oh well,' he shrugged, 'ladies first.'

They climbed into the aircraft and Ethan unmoored it and pushed away from the jetty, the Icon rocking gently on the waves as they strapped into their seats and Ethan pulled the canopy down and latched it into place. He shoved the keys into place, checked the fuel taps were open and that the fuel pump was *on*, set the throttle to a quarter–inch open and then turned the key.

Lopez jumped visibly as the engine roared into life, and they donned headsets as the hundred–horsepower Rotax powerplant settled down to a steady hum. Ethan kicked the rudder to turn away from the jetty and eased the power open and the little Icon turned willingly on the waves as it rotated on the water to face into the wind blowing across the harbor.

'Are you sure about this?' Lopez asked.

Ethan shrugged as he pressed a button to lower the aircraft's flaps a single notch to increase take off lift.

'Only one way to find out,' he said, and opened the throttle fully.

The engine roared gamely and the Icon leaped into motion, Ethan kicking in opposite rudder to counter the torque from the propeller as the little aircraft accelerated across the smooth water, the jetty on the far side of the harbor rushing toward them.

'Christiano didn't say how fast this thing takes off!' Lopez pointed out.

Ethan kept his hand on the throttle, holding it wide open as he kept the Icon straight on the water and replied.

'Safest speed is too fast,' he shouted as the Icon climbed through forty knots and he pulled back on the control column, the whole aircraft trembling and rattling.

The waves thumped against the fuselage below them and he felt the wings wobble as the Icon gained a little more airspeed and then suddenly they were off the water and the rush and rumble of the harbor fell away from them.

The jetty drifted by beneath them, local townsfolk looking up into the sky and pointing at them as Ethan retracted the flaps and turned the Icon gently to starboard, gaining height as they climbed up into the sky. The sun broke through some of the haze and the ocean glittered far below, boats scattered at anchor in the bay as Ethan searched for the estuary to the river.

As he looked across the cockpit, he saw Lopez smiling as she gazed down upon the bay below them.

'See, not so bad?' Ethan said.

A jolt of turbulence shook the little Icon and it bounced and gyrated on the wind currents as Ethan fought for control. He levelled the wings, checked his airspeed, and looked again at Lopez's suddenly furious face.

'It's a riot,' she growled. 'How about we get where we're going, real fast?'

Ethan didn't argue as he spotted the estuary glittering green against the blue ocean, the water filled with sediment drawn from the banks of the river further upstream. Soaring mountains dominated the skyline to their right as Ethan flew over the river and turned east to follow it into the forests.

He spotted a magenta line on the GPS display that roughly followed the path of the river, and a red marker to the west buried deep in the mountains.

'Looks like our spot,' he said as he pointed at the screen. 'Fifty miles inland, we should be there in about twenty minutes if this thing can climb fast enough to avoid us hitting anything high and hard.'

'That's reassuring,' Lopez replied. 'That river looks plenty big enough to put down on.'

'It is at the coast,' Ethan warned her. 'I'm not so sure how wide it'll be when we're fifty miles inland.'

The Malagasy shore gave way to a few dusty looking roads and then the jungle, thick carpets of tropical forest swathed in veils of mist. The sunlight faded slightly as the overcast moved in again, and Ethan eased the Icon into a gentle climb that he hoped would match the terrain around them.

The river wound its serpentine way through the canopy far below, its effect on the landscape sufficient that Ethan could follow it even when it disappeared beneath the thick canopy itself. The warm, moist air did nothing for the aircraft's wings, hot air less dense than cold and he realized that the little aircraft was already struggling to maintain altitude.

'You sure we can make it?' Lopez asked again, noting the altimeter reading and the forest canopy that seemed to be getting closer by the minute.

'We can make it,' Ethan promised, judging his height above the forest and the distance to run. 'What bothers me is getting airborne again.'

Ahead the mountains soared into the haze above them, an impassable barrier into the Madagascan hinterland.

***

Dean Crawford

XXIII

'Ten miles now.'

Lopez watched the altitude dial with a furtive expression as the Icon A5 climbed through veils of mist and light cloud gathering around the mountain peaks and spilling like white rivers down into the valleys below. Ethan leaned forward and switched on the pitot heat to avoid icing inside the aircraft's sensitive instruments as he sought to maintain a track on the river far below.

'There's not a road in sight out here,' Lopez said. 'If we can't take off again, we'll be stuck out here for days.'

'We need to be quick,' Ethan agreed. 'Once it heats up in the jungle the air won't have enough density to get airborne again. I hope they're ready for us down there.'

A dense swathe of cloud drifted by below them, and then Ethan glimpsed the river winding like a silvery serpent beneath the jungle canopy toward a deep chasm between two terrific mountain ranges cloaked in thick tropical forest.

'Down there,' he said and pointed ahead.

As they closed in on what looked like a fairly open stretch of water they glimpsed a sudden burst of what looked like blood spilling into the air. Ethan recognized the red stain for what it was, a smoke grenade marking the landing zone for him, something he'd seen many times in his service years in Iraq and Afghanistan.

Ethan glanced at the terrain around them. He knew that the rising temperatures would send the air over the jungle up while the cold air from the mountain tops would plunge down, creating lethal vortexes of turbulent air close to the base of the mountains. But he knew that he also had to turn into the wind to land, which would be blowing in from the distant shore. He angled the Icon to pass to the south of the smoke marker, and his eye traced an imaginary line through the sky he would follow to descend and land on the river.

'You're overshooting,' Lopez said as she leaned over to look at the smoke marker a thousand feet below them.

'I know what I'm doing.'

'I feel *so* reassured.'

Ethan banked the Icon over and felt the wings tremble and the fuselage gyrate as it hit the violent downdrafts sweeping across the mountain slopes toward the valley below. The engine strained as he allowed the aircraft to descend, turning slowly as the jungle loomed toward them until he lined up with the river and the turbulence died down.

'Remind me not to do this again,' Lopez said as she gripped her seat, her jaw clenched as they descended.

Ethan did not reply as he focused on the green surface of the river, which kinked left and right maybe a half mile ahead. The red smoke was drifting toward him in a listless cloud, revealing not much in the way of lift-generating headwind as the water began to race past them just a few feet away, tree limbs reaching out for the little aircraft as it skimmed the surface of the river at almost fifty knots.

Ethan pulled back on the throttle and eased the nose a little higher, and then the Icon's hull thumped gently down onto the water and the aircraft slowed dramatically under the extra drag until it settled on the surface, drifting slowly downstream with the current. He heard Lopez's sigh of relief as he kicked in the rudder and guided the Icon around in a gentle turn, adding power to cruise upstream to the landing zone.

On the bank stood two figures, both of them encased in Level Four Hazmat suits, their faces visible behind the transparent face plates, even their hands shoved into thick white gloves. Each carried another identical suit in their arms as Ethan guided the Icon into the bank and let her nose bump up onto a narrow shore. He killed the engine as one of the Hazmats grabbed the aircraft's nose with his free hand to prevent the Icon from slipping back into the river.

Ethan opened the canopy and Lopez tossed the two suits a line. They understood immediately and by the time Ethan and Lopez had disembarked the aircraft was secured to a nearby tree by the line.

'Put these on, right now,' one of the Hazmats ordered. 'We don't know how far this thing has spread.'

'It's airborne?' Lopez asked as she hauled on the Hazmat suit.

'We're not sure, but we know how infectious it is. One touch folks, and you're history.'

Ethan felt his blood run cold as he hurriedly pulled on the Hazmat suit. 'One touch?'

'I'm doctor Michael Arando,' came the reply, 'and yes, one touch. I'm damned lucky to be alive myself. It's this way.'

Ethan said nothing more as he pulled on his headgear and mutually checked Lopez's suit for any gaps or tears before they moved to follow Arando into the forest.

If the climate had been hot before they had reached the shore, it was as nothing compared to the intense humidity of the jungle as they clambered through its interior in the heavy, uncomfortable suits. Ethan felt as though he was walking inside an oven, his lungs feeling hot as he stumbled and struggled through the dense undergrowth, conscious of any sharp objects that might tear his protective suit.

'How long have you been up here?' Lopez asked Arando, coping somewhat better with the conditions.

'Five years, studying lemurs,' Arando replied. 'I was working out here when I discovered the site. I didn't know for sure what I was looking at, other than it was highly dangerous. That's when I called for the quarantine zone to be put into place, in an attempt to prevent the contamination from spreading.'

'How long do you think the disease, or whatever it is, has been at work?'

'No more than a few days,' Arando replied, 'which is what's so terrifying. I checked on the lemur population here a week ago and there were no problems at all. I came back for the following weeks' check–up and they were all dead.'

'All dead?' Lopez echoed. 'How many is all?'

'About a hundred fifty,' Arando replied, and Ethan noted the suppressed grief in the naturalist's tone. 'Just gone, overnight. And that's not all.'

'What do you mean?' Ethan asked.

'You'll have to see that to believe it,' Arando replied.

Ethan followed the scientist along what looked like an animal trail that ran through the densely packed trees. Listless rays of sunlight that had managed to break through the overcast penetrated weakly through the canopy far above, but the forest floor itself was a gloomy and uninviting place. Heavy creepers clung to the thick trunks, foliage blocking every path between them except for the narrow trail Arando was now following.

He slowed, and Ethan waited as the scientist raised his hand to halt them and then pointed at something lying in the bushes. Ethan saw what looked like a delicate bird, it's once colorful plumage smeared with a mess of ugly white foam.

'It's fungal,' Arando said, 'and it's spreading fast. This path was clear of infection yesterday.'

'The birds,' Lopez guessed. 'If they're susceptible to this disease they'll spread it faster than anything else.'

'Agreed,' Arando replied, 'which is why we're so lucky the outbreak is occurring here on Madagascar and not on the African mainland. But it's only a matter of time before a migratory species picks up the infection and reaches other shores, if it hasn't happened already.'

Ethan frowned again at the tiny corpse.

'But this is the same infection as the one hitting bats in the USA, isn't it? White nose syndrome?'

'Oh no,' Arando said in reply as he pushed on through the foliage, 'this is far worse than that.'

'Why?' Lopez asked.

Arando didn't answer, pushing on through the dense undergrowth until he reached what looked like a clearing ahead, the forest appearing brighter as the sunlight was able to reach the earth. Ethan would be glad to get out of the dense forest and...

He slowed as Arando moved to stand next to the edge of the clearing. For a moment, Ethan's mind could not quite understand what he was seeing, for the forest seemed to be cloaked in snow. He heard Lopez gasp, and as they moved to stand next to Arando so they got their first glimpse of the terror that had struck the forest.

Everything before them was coated in a thick, white fungal growth so dense it concealed the details of everything hidden within, as though the jungle were indeed beneath a few inches of snow. Ethan could see trees, ferns, creepers and vines all likewise coated in the bizarre foam and the forest floor was littered with the smooth, white, indistinct forms of dead animals, their corpses entombed in the thick fluid that stretched for hundreds of yards in a near perfect circle amid the dense greenery of the surrounding jungles.

The only markings visible on the white blanket were patches of forest growth that had fallen since to litter the forest floor, dead leaves and vines, all decaying and slowly being consumed by the white mess oozing from within them.

'What the hell?' Ethan uttered.

Arando spoke slowly, as though also still in shock at what he was witnessing.

'All I've managed to ascertain so far is that this fungus affects something that is in all of us, and by all of us I mean *all living things* on this planet. The disease can penetrate skin, thus devouring the victim from within. It attacks at the cellular level, and is the first and only time I've ever encountered a disease which affects all flora and fauna alike. Even insects are not immune. This, thing, kills anything and everything it touches and it's spreading fast.'

Ethan crouched down, and with one gloved hand he touched the edge of the white film coating the forest floor. It came away in gloopy strings, sticking to his gloves easily.

And then he saw it was moving.

Ethan stood bolt upright and took a pace back from the edge of the white film, a sudden and deeply primal horror filling him as he took a sharp intake of breath.

'That's exactly what I did when I first realized it,' Arando said as he noted Ethan's reaction. 'It's *alive.*'

***

.

XXIV

Lopez backed away from the white goo, a look of disgust on her face. 'That's like something from a fifties horror movie.'

'That's exactly what it's like,' Arando agreed. 'This is like nothing I've ever seen before, and my only conclusion is that it cannot have come from this island. It exists at ambient temperature, and although it could have lain dormant for millions of years I don't know of any major event that could have brought this thing out of hibernation and to have manifested itself so fast.'

Ethan looked at Lopez, who appeared transfixed by the horrific scene. 'This is what must have been going on when Channing disappeared from Montana. Maybe he thought that he'd found evidence of an outbreak like this before, maybe as far back in time as the dinosaurs?'

Lopez nodded, her gaze vacant as the stared at the horrific sight before them.

'Channing sends the reporter away, isolating himself. Then what? He excavates the bones himself and flees with them?'

'I doubt it,' Ethan said. 'Too much work for one man to complete in one day. Somebody else might have got there first, taken Channing with them. They might then have figured out what scared him so much and...'

'Started work on it,' Lopez finished his sentence. 'What if they figured out what happened and started developing a weapon from it? It could have escaped.'

Arando looked from one of them to the other in confusion. 'What the hell are you two talking about?'

Ethan turned to the scientist. 'A few years back a specialist in Tyrannosaurus remains named Aubrey Channing disappeared after finding a fossil in Montana, to which he was directed by another younger scientist who wanted nothing to do with what he'd found. That younger scientist now works in a remote facility charged with preserving bio–specimens in case of an extinction level event.'

Arando looked at the thick gloop covering the forest. 'You think that he figured the dinosaurs succumbed to this same infectious disease? It's not possible. We would have found evidence of this in their fossils long ago, the cellular destruction would leave markers in the bone that would be obvious, just like any other infection.'

Ethan's train of thought slammed to a halt. 'You're sure?'

'Damned sure,' Arando replied. 'You don't get an outbreak like this, big enough to remove eighty per cent of all living things from our planet, and not have any evidence of it ever having been here. Besides, the dinosaurs are now agreed to have been forced into extinction by an asteroid strike in the Yucatan Peninsula – all of the available evidence points to it.'

'Then what the hell was Channing so afraid of?' Lopez asked Ethan.

Ethan stared at the glutinous mess before them that was consuming the jungle alive, creeping ever outward with the remorseless, unstoppable patience of a glacier swallowing entire continents, and then he thought about what had happened to the dinosaurs so many millions of years ago.

'Schofield said that the dinosaurs were already in decline before the asteroid hit,' he said, 'or so Channing had told him.'

'Yeah, sure,' Lopez agreed. 'But they weren't taken out by this infection, right?'

'No,' Ethan replied, having to assume that a specialist like Arando knew far more about the science of extinction than he did. 'But what if they were suffering from it, and the asteroid was what brought it to an *end*?'

Lopez seemed to consider this for a moment. 'An impact with the strength of a billion Hiroshima bombs would lay waste to most things, maybe even this,' she agreed.

Ethan turned to Arando. 'Does fire kill this stuff?'

'Sure,' Arando agreed, 'fire kills all living cells if directly exposed to it, but it would take a hell of a blaze as this stuff smothers everything. Flames need a constant supply of oxygen to burn.'

Ethan thought for a moment.

'The global damage after the impact that wiped out the dinosaurs spread around the globe, right? There were forest fires, lava flows and then a nuclear winter that lasted for a decade and wiped out pretty much all of the flora and fauna on the planet.'

'It was a devastating blow to life,' Arando agreed, 'and the lava from the Deccan Traps covered most of what we now call Asia. Very little life survived on the surface or in the oceans, which were poisoned by the chemicals falling out of the sky.'

Ethan turned to Lopez.

'If this fungus feeds on living cells, it would have a tough time surviving the wake of an impact like that,' he said. 'That asteroid might also have been responsible for bringing to an end an extinction level event, rather than just creating one.'

Arando shook his head, uncertain. 'Many species did survive,' he pointed out, 'and even thrived in the wake of the impact. They would have been surrounded by debris and carcasses, highly exposed to any surviving examples of the infection. No, it couldn't have happened like that, but...'

'But what?' Lopez pressed.

'But it could have brought the disease down with it,' he replied.

Ethan thought again, about what he knew about panspermia and tardigrades and the knowledge that some forms of life could remain locked up inside comets and asteroids for millions, perhaps billions of years, just waiting for that perfect moment to burst into life on a new world and replicate.

'If it did, then it could have infected some species that survived the impact,' Ethan speculated, 'which then died out before the infection took hold due to the devastation around them in the wake of the impact.'

Arando nodded.

'It couldn't spread far and eventually vanished again, until your man Channing discovered those bones in Montana. If he recognized the fossil to have been infected by something, perhaps something that might have survived the fossilization process, it might have been enough to scare him into quarantining himself.'

'And that act might have cost him his life,' Ethan went on.

'Somebody extracts the infection from the fossilized bones,' Lopez figured, 're–animates it or whatever, and then starts testing it out.'

Ethan looked at the mess before them and suddenly he knew that what he was looking at was not a natural act, the evolution of some new and lethal weapon of disease. This was something ancient, primal, captured by men and released on the island to wreak its havoc on species that had no natural defense against it.

'Somebody put this here,' he said finally.

'You're saying that somebody killed this forest on purpose?' Arando said in horror. 'Why?'

'To test it,' Ethan guessed. 'And now they won't want it to spread too far and get out of control.'

'It's too late for that!' Arando wailed in horror. 'It's out, they can't stop this now!'

Ethan was about to reply when he heard a distant sound, like a horn echoing in from the mountain peaks. The echoing, indistinct sound grew stronger with each passing moment, and with a near–clairvoyant certainty Ethan knew that this part of the forest was about to become an inferno.

'Move, now!' he yelled. 'Get back to the river!'

Ethan bolted from the scene and crashed through the undergrowth, Lopez following right behind him and Arando bringing up the rear and calling out to Ethan.

'What the hell is going on?!'

'Your site is about to disappear for good!' Ethan yelled as they ran, stumbling in the heavy suits across fallen trees and dense foliage. 'Keep moving!'

Ethan heard the noise more clearly now above the sound of his own laboured breathing inside the oven–like mask, a distinctive whine of a jet engine that rocketed through the valleys nearby. He couldn't see anything in the sky above them through the mask and the dense canopy, but he knew the jet was coming around toward them by the sound of its engine.

'They must have followed us!' Lopez gasped as she ran behind Ethan toward the river. 'They'll see the smoke from the landing zone!'

Ethan did not reply as he ran, focusing on moving as fast as he could though the dense undergrowth. The sound of the jet engine became much louder, howling toward the site from what sounded like directly ahead as Ethan burst from the treeline onto a shore of wet, dark sand and looked up to see a small jet fighter soar overhead, a faint trail of smoke from its engines as it vanished over their heads. Ethan tore off his mask and ripped off the suit as he cried out.

'Get down!'

Ethan shouted the warning as he hurled himself into the water, Lopez crashing in alongside him as Arando turned and looked back into the forest.

The blast thundered as though a storm had broken directly overhead, a shockwave of pressured air radiating outward at supersonic speed, crashing through the forest and flattening trees in its path. The blast hit Arando with the force of a freight train, the Hazmat suit disintegrating as the explosion tore his body apart to hurl what remained far out across the river in a hail of debris that crashed into the water around Ethan.

He broke the surface and shielded his head as burning debris plummeted out of the sky all around them and plunged into the water. Lopez burst from the river alongside him, her long black hair snaking down her shoulders and streaming with water as she shielded her face from the onslaught and shouted to Ethan.

'We've gotta get out of here!'

'The Icon's down there!' Ethan pointed.

The aircraft remained where it was, shielded from the blast by the steep banks alongside the river. Lopez kicked out and began swimming for the aircraft as Ethan heard the jet coming around for another pass, this time in the opposite direction. Already he could see towering flames roaring through the rainforest, thick black smoke coiling up into the gray sky above as the napalm bombs being dropped by the aircraft incinerated the forest below.

Ethan swam to the Icon's port side and dragged himself up onto the shore as Lopez yanked the mooring line away from the tree. They hauled open the canopy together and climbed into the cockpit as Ethan glanced up into the sky and saw the jet wheeling around for another pass.

'They're coming back,' Lopez said.

Ethan leaped into his seat as Lopez kicked off the shore with one boot and the Icon slid backwards into the green water. She jumped in alongside him and pulled the canopy down as Ethan fired up the engine and turned the little aircraft around with a healthy stab of rudder and throttle.

'He's lining us up!' Lopez shouted as she saw the jet fighter rocketing in toward them.

Ethan slammed the throttle wide open and the Icon surged away from the shore as he saw a tiny speck drop from the jet fighter's wings and it pulled up sharply, vapor trails spiralling from its wingtips.

'Incoming!'

The Icon accelerated across the water and away from the shore, and Ethan glimpsed the slender projectile rocket across the sky behind them and plunge into the forest barely a hundred yards from their position.

'He's still hitting the forest!' Lopez said. 'We need to get out of here while we can!'

The dense jungle nearby was ripped apart by a blossoming fireball that burst from the banks of the river and soared above the water, and the Icon was hurled sideways as the shockwave hit them.

***

XXV

Ethan pushed the control column all the way to the right in an attempt to stop the aircraft's wings from flipping over under the blow and the Icon skittered this way and that on the water rushing beneath its wings. Burning debris rained down across the water around them and clattered against the canopy as the Icon reached full power, billowing streams of flame flickering across the sky as the tiny aircraft blasted clear of the explosion.

'We're at full power!' Ethan shouted above the engine noise. 'She won't lift off!'

Lopez craned her neck around and searched the sky for any sign of the fighter jet as the clouds of smoke and tongues of flame receded behind them.

'I can't see him!' she shouted.

'He'll be there,' Ethan replied grimly as he looked ahead and saw the river arcing around in a bend to the right.

He knew that there was no way that they could take the bend at full power, and so he eased back on the throttle and the Icon settled down more heavily into the water.

'You're slowing down!'

Ethan eased the aircraft around the bend in the river, affording Lopez a better view aft.

'Jesus,' she uttered, 'they virtually nuked the place.'

Ethan glimpsed walls of flame and smoke as the forest burned fiercely in the wake of the attack. There was no way that whoever cultivated this particularly horrible form of life would want it to get out of control, and the only way to achieve that was to utterly destroy it once the experiment had been completed. *Fire will destroy it*, Arando had confirmed before he too had been obliterated in the attack.

The river twisted back around to the left and as Ethan turned he saw in the far distance a line of white foam, the river churning its way over a series of rapids.

'Er, we've got a problem,' he said.

'Yeah,' Lopez replied, 'and it's right behind us.'

Ethan looked over his shoulder and saw the jet fighter sweeping around in a turn low over the forest, banking steeply as it turned toward them, vapor trails twisting from its sharply raked wings again like white streamers rippling against dark gray clouds in the distance.

Ethan knew that the Icon's white fuselage and wings would be an easy spot for a fighter pilot against all this green water and forest. He looked at the distant rapids.

'We'll never make it into the air before we get there,' Lopez said. 'There's nothing we can do.'

'We're too heavy,' Ethan agreed, then looked at her. 'Would you mind jumping out?'

Lopez shot him an appalled look, then scowled as the saw the humor in Ethan's eyes.

'How can you joke at a time like this?!'

'Who said I was joking?'

'*You* get out before I throw you out!'

Ethan smiled as a new idea crossed his mind and he looked down at the controls. He saw what he needed and flipped a switch.

'Here goes nothing,' he said, and opened the throttles wide once more.

The Icon accelerated gamely across the smooth water, racing toward the rapids ahead, churning white water tumbling into an abyss beyond and likely laced with black rock that would shatter the Icon's fragile hull in an instant.

'I hope to hell you know what you're doing!' Lopez said as she gripped the edges of her seat and began to try to push herself backwards into it, as though she could somehow escape their fate.

Ethan focused in on the airspeed indicator as he selected half flaps, the throttle pushed to the firewall and the Rotax engine screaming close behind him. The other gauge he watched closely was the fuel gauge, and suddenly Lopez realized what he had done.

'You're dumping gas?!'

'It's no good to us if we're dead,' Ethan shot back, 'and it's a short flight home.'

Lopez craned her neck back once again and almost screamed. 'He's right on us!'

Ethan risked a glance back behind them and he saw the fighter sweep in low over the trees, following their path down the river as it screamed toward them, and he saw the fighter's nose suddenly vanish behind flickering lights.

'He's firing!'

Ethan saw the water to one side of the Icon suddenly churned by a blaze of twenty millimetre rounds that smashed into the river and swept in toward him as the fighter pilot dragged his line of fire onto the Icon.

'Hold on!' Ethan yelled.

The rapids loomed before them and Ethan saw a gap between ragged chunks of damp, black rock. He nudged the rudder to the right and aimed for the gap as the cannon fire ripped into the water just feet from the Icon's fuselage, and then the aircraft's nose hit the rapids and Ethan hauled back on the stick and shut off the fuel dump valve.

The Icon soared off the surface of the water and the airspeed plunged as she clawed her way briefly into the air. The cannon fire shot ahead of them, the fighter pilot taken unawares by the Icon's sudden loss of airspeed, and the jet roared overhead and shot away over the jungle as Ethan pushed hard on the control column and the Icon's nose fell away.

The aircraft plunged toward the turbulent rapids below, her engine still at full throttle as Ethan retracted the flaps and let the airspeed build in the shallow dive. The swirling green and white water loomed up toward them, but freed from the surface friction of the river the Icon's airspeed rocketed and at the last moment Ethan gently eased back on the control column and the aircraft levelled out barely three feet above the churning river and began to climb slowly into the misty air.

'Jesus,' Lopez uttered, her heart hammering in her chest.

The Icon climbed away from the river, the engine labouring to lift the aircraft in the dense and humid air, but as they climbed so the temperature began to drop. Ethan knew that the lower temperature meant denser air, and as if by magic the Icon's rate of climb increased.

'Where is he?' Ethan asked as they climbed out above the jungle.

Lopez looked around them but she could see nothing. 'I lost him in the mist.'

Ethan nodded and headed for the nearest cloud bank he could find.

'We'll do the same, 'cause we won't stand a chance against his guns.'

Lopez shook her head. 'He'll wait for us, we can't make it all the way back to the coast.' Ethan guided the Icon toward the clouds. 'I wouldn't be so sure. He'll run out of fuel before we will, so he can't stay out here forever. Besides I recognized the aircraft type, a MiG–17 Fresco that must belong to the Madagascan Air Force.'

'They're in on this?!' Lopez uttered in shock.

'The government likely isn't,' Ethan cautioned, 'but in an out–of–the–way country like this I don't suppose it's hard to bribe a few personnel.'

Lopez kept searching the skies but she couldn't see the enemy jet anywhere.

'Maybe he's gone.'

Ethan was about to take the chance that she might be right when something appeared from the clouds dead ahead and a stream of tracer fire rocketed past the Icon's wings.

'Incoming!'

Ethan banked hard right and the Icon veered away from the onrushing gunfire as the MiG shot past at high speed. G–Force pushed them down into their seats as the Icon turned tightly, and then Ethan levelled out and looked back over his shoulder.

The fighter was climbing steeply toward the gray sky, her swept wings arcing over gracefully as the pilot turned back toward them.

'Slashing attacks,' Ethan said through gritted teeth as he gripped the controls more tightly. 'We're just damned lucky that he doesn't appear to have missiles.'

Lopez swivelled in her seat and saw the fighter descend back down toward them at terrific speed.

'Here he comes!'

Ethan made to move the control column, but then he had a better idea and he relaxed in the seat. He looked ahead and he knew that they would never make the safety of the cloud banks before the jet fighter's bullets tore into the Icon, and therefore into both of their bodies. They would be shredded in an instant and the aircraft would tumble from the sky in pieces to fall into the dense jungle, and who knew how long it would take for anybody to find their remains, if they ever did. Nobody involved in this attack was going to report the incident.

'Turn, damn it!' Lopez snapped at him.

Target fixation. The words drifted unbidden through his mind as he recalled the Gulf War. There had been occasions when fighter pilots had fixated on a target so much that they had literally flown their aircraft into the target itself. Snipers had focused so much on long range shots that they hadn't noticed the ranks of enemy soldiers advancing on their position.

Ethan weaved the Icon lethargically about the sky as he descended toward the forest, trying to give the impression that he was attempting to evade the attack but instead looking for somewhere down below to land on the river.

'Ethan!' Lopez snapped as she grabbed his collar. 'We, are going, *to die.*'

Ethan looked over his shoulder at the onrushing MiG, one hand on the controls as he waited for the inevitable sight of the bullets rocketing toward them. With his free hand he reached down and twisted the rudder trim to one side.

The little Icon pivoted in the air, her nose shifting to the right slightly.

'What are you doing?' Lopez asked.

'Spoiling his aim,' Ethan replied. 'Get ready, we're leaving.'

'We're *what*?!'

The Icon was still five hundred feet above the river as the MiG descended in behind them. Ethan twisted his shoulders and craned his neck as he saw the jet line up and then a burst of cannon fire ripped toward them.

Ethan did not touch the controls, and in a heartbeat of terror he saw the bright tracer rounds rocket it seemed directly toward his eyes. Then the bullets flashed past the Icon with scant feet to spare, and Ethan hit the fuel dump gauge once again and pushed forward on the control column.

The Icon descended sharply, trailing a cloud of fuel vapor behind it as the MiG rocketed overhead and climbed sharply away. As soon as it was past them, Ethan reached across and pulled a bright–red lever as he pulled back on the throttles.

The emergency safety parachutes deployed with a loud double–bang and the Icon slowed to a halt in mid–air, Ethan and Lopez thrown forward in their harnesses as the jungle canopy loomed ahead of them. In an instant the Icon crashed down onto the tree tops, her wings collapsing as the aircraft settled at an awkward angle amid the dense branches, leaves and vines.

'Go, now!'

Lopez pushed the canopy open and clambered from the cockpit, the sound of the jet aircraft's engine echoing around the forest as she climbed clear of the Icon and hurriedly began climbing down the tree.

Ethan clambered out of the cockpit and grabbed one of the emergency flares as he scrambled onto the tree. He pulled the flare and tossed it into the cockpit, smoke and flame spitting from the device as he clambered down in pursuit of Lopez, who was almost on the forest floor.

'Run!'

Ethan jumped down behind her and dashed away as he heard the jet engine rocket closer, and then a deep *brrrr* sound. Bullets smashed through the canopy above them and hammered the forest floor as Ethan hurled himself down alongside a large tree trunk and Lopez rolled into deep undergrowth.

The MiG's bullets hit the Icon's fuselage and the searing heat from the tracers hit the fuel vapor spilling from the dump valve. The Icon exploded in a massive fireball in the tree tops as the MiG rocketed by overhead. Ethan covered his head with his arms as burning debris rained down from the canopy and the roaring of the jet fighter faded into the mountainous distance.

He rolled out from his hiding place and looked up to see the remains of the Icon burning furiously, clouds of thick black smoke spiralling up into the humid sky.

'Lopez?' he called out. 'Are you okay?'

There was no response from the jungle nearby, and Ethan scrambled to his feet and bolted toward the place he had last seen Lopez disappear into the undergrowth. He saw her legs poking from the thick foliage and rushed to her side, reached out for her.

'Lopez?'

She groaned and he gently helped her up into a sitting position. His hands searched for any sign of injury, but he could find nothing. He looked at her and she scowled back at him wearily.

'We'd like to thank you for flying Warner Air. Please be sure not to leave anything behind, like body parts.'

Ethan fought to conceal his relief as he helped her to her feet.

'Hopefully, they'll think that we're dead,' he said.

'Are you sure we're not?'

'You're complaining, so everything's normal,' Ethan replied and orientated himself toward the coast. 'Come on, we've got a long walk ahead of us.'

'We could use the satellite phone, call for help,' she said.

Ethan pointed up to the burning remains of the Icon A5. 'The phone's up there,' he replied, 'but I don't want anybody knowing we're still alive. MJ–12 is going all out to finish us off, let's make them think that the job's done.'

***

XXVI

Ambila Lamaitso,

Madagascar

'Sweet Lord above, what happened?!'

Christiano Rabinur stood in the doorway of his office in a ramshackle safe house near the coast, the night air filled with a heady mixture of wild Indian Ocean and dense jungle foliage.

'We ran into a little trouble,' Ethan replied.

He stood in the doorway with Lopez, both of them bedraggled and weary, smeared with grime and foliage from their impromptu trek through the jungle.

'Is my aeroplane all right?' Rabinur enquired anxiously.

'Well, it's technically still airborne.'

Rabinur peered at Ethan suspiciously and then ushered them inside the safe house and slammed the door behind them. 'You didn't break it did you?'

'We're fine, thanks for asking,' Lopez uttered, her black hair entwined with soil that hung in thick clumps around her shoulders. 'We just spent an hour hiding in a mud hole waiting for sundown so we could get here unobserved. How about you quit with the questions and tell me where the shower is before I take what's left of your airplane and shove it up your as...'

'Straight up the stairs, turn right,' Rabinur said quickly. 'You can't miss it.'

Lopez stalked up the stairs without another word as Ethan walked with Rabinur into the kitchen, where the agent poured him a glass of filtered water.

'We came under attack from a Malagasy fighter aircraft,' Ethan said after he had guzzled two full glasses. 'I'm afraid the Icon didn't make it out in one piece.'

'Mother alive, how will I explain this to General Nellis?' Rabinur wailed softly, his hands pressed to his head. 'We only received it last week.'

'Don't worry,' Ethan promised, 'Nellis is used to me breaking the agency's toys, I'll take full responsibility. I need to know how many MiG–17 Frescos the Malagasy Air Force operates?'

Rabinur laughed. 'One, maybe two,' he replied. 'They're older than the hills and barely get airborne these days.' His tone became sombre. 'You think that they were hired out to hunt you down?'

Ethan nodded, draining another glass of water. 'We need to talk to the pilot of that aircraft. I didn't get a good enough look to pick out a registration or anything, but if the Air Force only operates a couple of jets then there can't be many pilots on the island qualified to fly them.'

'I'll get on it in the morning,' Rabinur promised. 'What are you going to do next?'

'We can't question the pilot,' Ethan replied. 'He most likely believes us to be dead and I want it kept that way. I'll need to speak to Jarvis though and I'll need you to conduct the interrogation of the pilot, make it look like a homicide case: if he thinks he's up for killing two Americans, and the government suspects the same, he might be willing to talk. Likewise he would have been paid to attack us, as would the crew who fitted the aircraft with live missiles, maintenance and so on. Track them down, and we'll find out who was behind the attack.'

'Got it,' Rabinur replied. 'We've got a secure link here to Washington if you need to use it.'

Ethan checked his watch: ten in the evening in Madagascar made it roughly five in the evening in DC. 'Do it,' he replied, 'and no visual images, just audio.'

'Okay, it's this way.'

Ethan followed Rabinur to a small room that looked like a little library, with bookshelves and a wicker rocking chair. Rabinur pulled one of the books from the shelves, and the entire wall revolved to reveal a communications station replete with radio set and a telephone.

'Very James Bond,' Ethan said as he picked bits of mud and foliage out of his hair.

'It's a Cold War safe house,' Rubinar replied as he sat down and switched on the communication panel. 'The radio is state of the art though, untraceable as it runs direct through DIA satellites: no way to intercept the signal, and even if somebody could they would still have to break the encryption.'

'Good,' Ethan replied. 'I want you to shut all of that off and make this a normal–sounding call, routed out of the city and not this safe house. Can you do that?'

Rubinar seemed surprised. 'Well, yes, but why would you want to…?' Then he got it, and smiled.

Ethan watched as Rubinar contacted the DIA Headquarters and was passed on to Jarvis in the ARIES Watch Room.

'Jarvis?'

Ethan let Rubinar vacate the seat as he sat down and spoke clearly to Jarvis, hoping that his own voice carried clearly enough to be recognizable to his boss.

'This is Agent Foxx, Madagascar Station, I'm afraid I'm here to report the loss of two agents in the field this afternoon, local time.'

There was a moment's pause and Ethan felt he could almost hear Jarvis thinking thousands of miles away.

'That's truly regretful,' Jarvis replied. 'Do you have the names of the agents in question?'

'Warner, Ethan,' Ethan replied, 'and Lopez, Nicola. We believe that they were killed during a routine investigation in the interior. We only have limited witness reports suggesting an attack by a Madagascan Air Force jet, but reliable intelligence is thin on the ground at this time.'

A brief silence this time.

'I will arrange to have their next of kin informed as soon as possible,' Jarvis said. 'What is the investigative plan to find out who was behind this attack? You do realize that if this was indeed an attack by a Madagascan Air Force jet then this will become a national incident involving both governments and may be considered an act of war?'

Ethan smiled. Jarvis was well on the ball already and knew that any Madagascan government listening post would be hearing the radio chatter and panicking like never before.

'We will endeavour to ask the government here to detain all personnel capable of flying the aircraft in question within the hour,' Ethan replied. 'Any injury that they might receive before we question them will likely be seen as government complicity in the crime, so either way we're going to get to the bottom of this. Wherever it takes us, we'll follow.'

'Understood, Agent Foxx,' Jarvis replied. 'I'll inform the Secretary of Defense of what's happened, and we'll brief the President in the morning. Let's hope the Malagasy government do the smart thing and hand over the pilot behind this as soon as possible. I'd hate to think what would happen if the American people heard of the death of two US agents in the country and demanded military reprisals? Madagascar would cease to exist overnight.'

'Precisely,' Ethan agreed. 'I'll have Agent Rubinar contact the consulate first thing in the morning and find out what's happening, and report back as soon as we know what the Malagasy position on this regrettable incident is. Foxx out.'

Ethan switched off the communication suite and looked around at Rubinar. 'It's all yours, Christiano. Find out what you can when they hand the pilot over and pass it directly to Jarvis on behalf of "Agent Foxx". Whatever trail you uncover, we'll pursue.'

Rubinar was about to reply when the sound of rattling pipes was followed by a screeched *'For Christ's sake"* that echoed through the safe house as Lopez's voice cried out.

'Have you people never heard of hot water, damn it?!'

Rubinar sighed and headed off to the antiquated boiler somewhere else in the house.

*

ARIES Watch Room,

DIAC Building, Washington DC

Jarvis had only moments ago set the phone down after his mysterious call from Ethan Warner when Hellerman knocked at his office door and peeked in.

'Boss, we've got something.'

Jarvis pushed himself up and out of his chair as he followed Hellerman through the Watch Room to his office, where Hellerman closed the door and pointed at the chromium sphere in the vacuum chamber. The scientist had brought the object up from the ARIES R&D department earlier that day.

'I've figured out something about how this thing operates, and more importantly why.'

'Go on,' Jarvis encouraged.

Hellerman recounted something of the history of the device first.

'You'll recall that the first mention of *Die Glocke*, or "The Bell" in German, appears somewhere around 1937, when an object matching its description was described as having crashed into a Bavarian lake. Another sighting was made in 1945. Then there was another sighting in Kecksburg, Pennsylvania, in 1965, this time of an airborne object that was witnessed by hundreds of citizens in the town and later covered up by the military. Both objects appear identical in their descriptions to the object that was first detected in orbit around our planet by Nikola Tesla in 1899.'

'I know the history, Hellerman,' Jarvis said. 'Cut to the chase.'

Hellerman, enthused as ever, pointed to a monitor displaying historic events.

'Well, each of the purported sightings and captures of these devices, referred to later as Black Knights, corresponds to major events in human history. The production of continental scale electrical signals by Tesla, the atomic bomb attacks on Japan that ended the Second World War, the Vietnam War and the first true operational satellite launches: each of these years seems to have triggered the appearance of one of these Black Knight, bell–shaped objects to have appeared on Earth.'

Jarvis frowned. 'So, they're responding to something?'

Hellerman nodded eagerly.

'More than that, I think that they're *programmed* to respond to significant events,' he replied. 'They're orbital platforms and they're designed to come down to Earth when certain events occur. It's already been noted by many observers that the frequency of UFO reports increased dramatically during and after the Second World War.'

'And it's been noted by many that paranoia and fear also provokes rashes of UFO sightings,' Jarvis countered.

'Maybe, but here we have evidence that *Die Glocke* or whatever you might want to call it is a real object,' Hellerman insisted, 'and it came down recently due to further human activity on our planet. Maybe climate change or something.'

'And how would it know to do that?' Jarvis asked.

'Because of its shape,' Hellerman explained. '*Die Glocke* is a bell, a shape specifically designed to emit sound but one that is also particularly good at detecting those same sound waves. Our planet emits radiation, sound and so on across all frequencies on a daily basis and *Die Glocke* appears particularly well designed to detect those frequencies.'

'I'll need more than that to take this to General Nellis.'

'I know,' Hellerman agreed, 'which is why you'll need to understand what this sphere does. We've managed to crack some of the fluid dynamics after you suggested that the patterns in the sphere might correspond to a small–scale Coriolis Effect. It's fearsomely complex, but combined with the shape of *Die Glocke* that we have on record from Ethan and Nicola's expedition to the Antarctic, I'm pretty sure that what we have here is a form of monitoring device.'

'Monitoring?' Jarvis echoed. 'Like a spy satellite?'

'In a sense,' Hellerman agreed, 'although I can't say that it's designed specifically to spy on anybody. Apart from the signals that betrayed its presence to humanity in 1899, 1926 and more recently during our expedition, *Die Glocke* appears to be a mostly passive device: it reacts accordingly to a set of parameters that we're still trying to identify. So far, we've managed to figure out the following: that *Die Glocke's* signals corresponded directly to the experiments conducted by Nikola Tesla in Colorado Springs in 1899, to the dropping of the atom bombs on Hiroshima and Nagasaki in 1945, and to recent changes in the composition of Earth's atmosphere that many believe are the product of human activity on the planet.'

Jarvis thought for a moment.

'You think that it's designed to respond to the emergence of technology,' he said finally, 'to the presence of intelligent life.'

'Precisely,' Hellerman confirmed. 'More than that, I think that it also would have sent other signals out into the cosmos as that intelligent life emerged, as technology appeared and began to transmit signals into outer space, which we've been doing as a species for over a hundred years now. Because radio waves propagate at the speed of light, it is highly probable that any intelligent extra–terrestrial species on any planet within one hundred light years of Earth knows that we're here.'

The room suddenly seemed oppressively silent as Jarvis considered the implications of what Hellerman was saying.

'You think that such a civilization exists?'

'It must,' Hellerman said as he gestured at the sphere, 'because we're looking at something that is highly technical and could not have been built by human hands. Not only that, but at what I can only assume was a predetermined time these things started dropping out of Earth orbit so that we could collect and examine them. They're out there, Doug, and they're listening in on us. These devices didn't fall from orbit by accident. They're here to tell us something.'

Jarvis stared at the sphere for a moment longer. 'So, if the Black Knight is the bell, the sensor, then what's this thing for?'

Hellerman grinned. 'It's the data chip,' he replied. 'It records everything in three–dimensional quantum foam.'

'Quantum foam?'

'Yes, the tiny particles zipping in and out of existence in their billions all around us, patterns so complex that only fluid dynamics is capable of the variation in appearance required to record such vast quantities of data in a manageable form. Just like the 5D memory discs I was talking about, but immensely more powerful.'

'Can we use it?'

Now Hellerman's grin was as wide as a mountain range. 'By altering the magnetic field around the sphere, we can input data and retrieve information relevant to that data. It's just a numbers game, so if you input sufficient data regarding say, bank accounts, you retrieve the codes to those accounts in *seconds* because this device will run through every possible numerical calculation in the universe in a matter of moments. It is, in effect, a miniaturized universe of possibilities.'

Jarvis peered at the device. 'So you could use it to hack the accounts of Majestic Twelve, freeze everything?'

'Just give me the accounts and I'll give you the access codes.'

'I'll send them,' Jarvis said, 'you send me the codes by return. Let's keep this to ourselves okay? I don't want to run to Nellis with something this big until we know for damned sure it will work.'

'You got it,' Hellerman agreed.

Jarvis's cell phone buzzed. He retrieved it and answered, heard General Nellis's voice on the end of the line.

Jarvis, we've had a report from Rome. Felix Byzan, one of Majestic Twelve's members, has been found dead in his apartment. It's a homicide.'

Jarvis gripped his cell tighter. 'Mitchell.'

'How the hell did he identify Byzan?'

'I don't know,' Jarvis replied, maintaining an even tone, 'but we're going to have to find him and fast, or he'll take the entire cabal down.'

***

XXVII

Ethan awoke to the dull light of another gloomy Madagascan dawn, thick fog banks rolling in off the cool ocean and the forested mountains draped in veils of ethereal mist. He dragged himself out of bed and padded to the open windows, then out onto a veranda that was damp and yet warm to the touch.

The entire village was silent, the hills and jungles steaming in the humid air and creating a scene that it seemed could have just as easily been seen a hundred million years before by dinosaurs and not by a DIA agent in the twenty first century. Ethan turned back inside and poured himself a coffee, boiling the water in an antiquated kettle.

Lopez emerged from her own hotel room a half hour later, apparently equally lethargic in the oppressive heat and humidity. Only the gentle breeze gusting in off the nearby ocean offered any relief.

'You heard anything from Jarvis yet?' she asked as she strolled in wearing shorts, sneakers and a loose T-shirt and flopped down onto a wicker chair in the corner of the lounge.

'Ball's in our court,' Ethan replied. 'Rabinur should be working the pilot of the MiG over by now, if our ruse worked. As soon as we have what we need we can get the hell out of here and back on the trail.'

Moments later, Rabinur knocked on the door to the hotel room and Ethan let him in. The agent hurried inside and shut the door behind him, excitement emanating from his every pore.

'It worked,' he gasped in delight. 'The Air Force investigated the sortie the moment I contacted them and they sent the pilot over late last night.'

'What happened?' Lopez asked.

Rabinur took a seat on the couch, gesticulating wildly as he marvelled at the conspiracy going on right beneath the noses of the air force.

'The mission sortie was a navigation exercise,' he explained, 'totally standard training for our pilots. However the aircraft was supposed to be unarmed, fitted only with fuel tanks. Somewhere along the line those tanks were replaced with munitions, giving the pilot the ability to attack the site in the forest.'

'And us,' Ethan reminded him. 'What did the pilot say?'

'The Air Force was unaware of the incident until the reports of blasts and fires in the jungle,' Rabinur said, 'which it was already investigating when somebody high up must have been informed of the radio chatter between our station here and Jarvis in DC. They already knew that they had a jet in the area at the time, and they folded the moment we showed up. As for the pilot…'

Rabinur opened a folder as he read from the contents.

'The pilot was paid an undisclosed sum to carry out the attack. He claims that he was approached by two men who offered him the money a week ago, but he turned the offer down and refused to carry out the attack. He was intending to report the incident to his superior officer, but when he got home he found an envelope in his doorway that contained photographs of his wife and children. The two men returned the following day and made it clear that they wouldn't offer the money again and that if he declined, his family would pay the price.'

Lopez frowned. 'He could just be saying that in order to offload responsibility for the attack.'

'That's what I thought,' Rabinur said, 'so I got the names of the maintenance team who fitted the live weapons to the MiG. Their stories matched identically: some happily took the bribe, but others refused and were subject to similar threats as the pilot.'

Ethan sipped his coffee thoughtfully. 'And you're sure that the air force was unaware of these events, that nobody higher up the chain was approached by these men?'

'I'm not seeing anything that says there's been a cover up,' Rabinur replied. 'As soon as the air force feared reprisals of any kind from the USA, they folded totally. We're investigating the accounts and movements of a number of senior figures who perhaps could have orchestrated this, but we're coming up blank right now. It looks like an outside job.'

Ethan nodded.

'Which means whoever is behind it doesn't have much sway with the government here,' he said. 'They targeted lower–level servicemen rather than trying to buy politicians. Did you manage to follow a money trail?'

'Tried,' Rabinur said, slightly deflated, 'but it went cold at a shell corporation in the Cayman Islands. Maybe the team back at the DIA could figure it out but I'm stuck here.'

Lopez gritted her teeth as she looked at Ethan. 'Back to square one again. We're chasing our tails here.'

Ethan looked out across the jungles once more. The disease that had been placed out there had to have got there somehow. The only way into the interior was via the dangerous tracks through the jungle, unless an aircraft like the Icon A5 was used, or perhaps a similar design from which samples of the disease could have been dropped into the jungle.

'There must have been a very specific time frame for all of this to have occurred,' he said, thinking out loud. 'If they planted the disease as a test, then they must have had a time limit before it had to be destroyed, before it got out of control.'

'Agreed,' Lopez said, 'but if MJ–12 is behind this then why didn't they just send one of their own aircraft to deposit and later destroy the disease? They could have avoided any contact with the Malagasy people all together.'

Ethan knew that Lopez was right, that Majestic Twelve had more than enough assets to organize a covert operation even out here in the Madagascan jungle. However, that ability could also be their Achilles Heel, requiring a presence of some kind that could likewise be tracked to an individual or perhaps a charter company. A bribed pilot, whose family had been threatened directly, was much less likely to talk than an honest charter.

'If they came here, we could track them,' Ethan summarised his thoughts. 'So they play the blackmail card against local people instead and hope that it's enough to cover their tracks.'

'Which it is, right?' Lopez said. 'Even though the pilot talked, we're no closer to the perpetrators now than we were yesterday.'

'Except that we are,' Ethan said. 'Christiano, you said that the air force knew what aircraft were in that area at the time of the blasts, so they must keep records of all flights made by military aircraft, right?'

'Sure,' Rabinur replied, 'the Malagasy air force isn't very big, it's easy for them to keep tabs.'

Ethan looked again out across the distant jungles and mountains. 'Although it would be easy for a helicopter or similar to fly out over there and drop the fungus that caused the outbreak, somebody would have noticed, right? They couldn't sneak it in and out, and the scientists in the area would have noticed.'

Rabinur shrugged. 'I suppose so, but nobody mentioned anything about aircraft operating in the area.'

Ethan looked at Lopez, who got it straight away.

'Drone,' she said.

'Small, silent at altitude and easy to crash into the jungle to disperse whatever biological terror it is they've cooked up, but practically impossible to find afterward,' Ethan agreed. 'Plus it would have been incinerated in the napalm attack we witnessed.'

'But that won't lead you to whoever was behind this,' Rabinur said. 'It's untraceable, surely?'

'A drone also has a very short range,' Ethan pointed out, 'and it would be hard to smuggle one through X–ray machines at customs, if not impossible. Therefore the only likely way to have done it would be to have launched it from a ship that never made landfall here.'

Rabinur's eyes widened.

'They could have sailed straight on by,' he said, 'nobody would have known a thing.'

'Especially if the drone had climbed high enough by the time it reached the shore,' Lopez agreed. 'They could even have placed a GPS beacon on it, so they could locate the drone once the disease had spread and target the right area with the napalm.'

Rabinur's eyes widened further and he suddenly shuffled through the paperwork in his folder.

'The pilot,' he said quickly, 'he said something about how he used a GPS device to locate the target area, and then he aimed his weapons visually once he saw the white patch in the forest!'

Ethan nodded, clenched his fist at their minor victory. 'If we pick up the record of every vessel that's sailed these waters in the past few weeks, I'm willing to bet that one of them will lead back to Majestic Twelve.'

'I'll get right on it,' Rabinur said. 'It won't take more than a few hours to collate the data.'

'As fast as you can,' Ethan urged him. 'If we're lucky, any ship we can link to this might lead us directly to the person responsible.'

*

Ilha Ferando de Noronha,

Atlantic Ocean

The deck of the yacht flared white in the brilliant sunshine as Professor Garrett leaned back in a chair and let the warm sunshine wash across his body. Anchored in a harbor off the bay of an island most people on Earth had never even heard of, the massive vessel dwarfed most of those around it.

One of an archipelago of twenty one islands in the Atlantic Ocean and over two hundred miles from the Brazilian coast, Fernando de Noronha was one of Garrett's favorite bolt–holes. Although the island promoted tourism, it was a difficult place to reach and some three quarters of the entire island was designated as a national maritime park. Thus, the population was less than three thousand and the interferences minimal, especially when Garrett remained on the deck of his vast vessel and had local cuisine shipped aboard at his pleasure.

He was soaking up the sunshine when a crew member approached him with a satellite phone and coughed discreetly.

Garrett reached out for the phone without otherwise moving or acknowledging the crewman's presence, and the young man handed him the phone and walked out of earshot across the deck as Garrett put the phone to his ear.

'Yes?'

The voice that replied was gruff but recognizable as one of many freelancing mercenaries employed by Garrett through shell companies in the Cayman Islands, a man named Forbeck.

'It is done,' the voice said. *'Initial reports suggest the entire area is now toast.'*

'Good,' Garrett replied. 'Make your way back to Brazil and await further orders.'

'There was a problem.'

Garrett felt irritation rise up inside him and he clenched his jaw as he replied. 'What problem?'

'Two agents from the Defense Intelligence Agency were apparently at the site when the attack occurred, and both were killed. We picked up radio chatter last night confirming their deaths and suggesting the USA would enact reprisals if the matter was not dealt with immediately. The pilot we coerced into making the strike sang like a canary when he was picked up.'

Garrett cursed under his breath. He generally disliked hiring unknown third–parties to carry out such delicate work. A scientist would not have used such blunt instruments to perform such sensitive task. Now, there would be US agents crawling all over the site and questioning locals, and although there could be little physical evidence of what had occurred remaining at the site, it was not impossible that the presence of the yacht off Madagascar could be identified and linked to the outbreak.

'We will leave immediately,' he replied, unable to keep the anger from his voice. 'Meet me in Brazil, and make damned sure you aren't tailed or I swear when you get here I'll feed you to the local wildlife myself!'

Garrett slammed the satellite phone down onto the deck and it shattered into several pieces that skittered along the polished wood. The deckhand hurried across and began picking up the pieces as Garrett lay back on his chair and forced himself to calm down.

'Inform the captain to get underway and head for our facility off Brazil, no radio contact, understood?'

'Yes sir.'

The crewman hurried away as Garrett closed his eyes and thought. The DIA would not take long to figure things out, if they weren't already on his case. He would have to act faster than he had hoped, but that would be fine: he would soon have fresh test subjects now that the sample was almost ready to distribute.

Whoever reached his island first would get a great deal more than they bargained for.

***

XXVIII

'We've got something!'

Ethan heard Rubinar's voice before he even reached the hotel door, and then he realized that the agent's voice was coming not from the corridor but from the ground floor outside the veranda.

Ethan hurried across to the veranda and looked down to see the agent waving wildly in his direction.

'Get down here, now! It's time to leave!'

Lopez was already on her feet as Ethan ducked back inside, as keen to leave the stifling heat and humidity as he was, a day bag slung over her shoulder. Ethan grabbed his own meagre belongings, already tucked into a similar bag as he followed her out of the hotel room and shut the door behind them.

Rubinar was waiting for them outside in the parking lot as they stepped out, sitting in a small jeep with the engine running as they hurried across to him and Ethan climbed into the passenger seat.

'Start talking,' Ethan said.

'A man named Ryan Forbeck,' Rubinar said as he drove out of the lot and onto the coast road toward the airport. 'American national, landed here three months ago on a tourist visa. He's been staying at one of the local hotels barely a mile from here.'

'Why is he a person of interest?' Lopez asked.

'Financials,' Rubinar explained. 'He's having a thousand bucks a week wire–transferred to his accounts, which he's drawing a bit at a time. That wouldn't raise alarm bells on its own, but we got in touch with the DIA in DC, who pulled in the National Security Agency to back trace the accounts from which the funds were originating, and we got a hit on a company called Pacific Leasing Corp.'

'Shell corp?' Ethan guessed.

'Yep,' Rubinar agreed, 'except that this time that corporation is also linked to maintenance payments on a luxury yacht named *San Ferdinand*, registered in San Diego, California, and guess where that yacht was sailing six weeks ago?'

'Damn me,' Ethan said, 'good work, Christiano! Who owns the yacht?'

Rubinar handed Ethan a folder, and he opened it up to reveal an image of a middle aged man with thin–rimmed spectacles and a refined, almost superior expression.

'Professor Rhys Garrett,' Rubinar said, 'American national and biochemist, made his name selling advanced genetic profiling kits. He has countless patents to his name, many of which have earned him tens of millions of dollars. He no longer works in general science and has instead opened his own labs which are rumored to be working alongside departments of the United States military, which might well make this whole investigation a great deal more difficult than we thought it might be.'

Lopez looked at the image and frowned.

'If this guy's tied in with DARPA or something then we're going to run into big trouble once we show up on their radar,' she said.

'Does Jarvis know about this?' Ethan asked Rubinar.

'I sent him the same file,' Rubinar acknowledged. 'He's in the loop as though he's the only person who is aware of what I'm working on. This hard copy was one I made at home, so nobody knows that you're either alive or in on this.'

'Good,' Ethan said, and then looked at the agent. 'You know that this means you're a part of the loop as far as Majestic Twelve are concerned. If this Garrett is involved with them, this chink in their armor could lead right back to you.'

'I agree,' Rubinar said as he drove, 'which is why we're headed to the airport. Ryan Forbeck's on the move and in a hurry. Following him and locking him down is the only way I can be sure that word won't get back to MJ–12 on who broke through their security. If Forbeck shows up wherever he's headed, with two agents on his tail whom I reported dead in Madagascar, I don't want to think about what kind of knock on the door I'll get.'

Ethan nodded.

'Fine, we'll take Forbeck down.'

'What about DARPA?' Rubinar asked.

'They're not the bad guys,' Lopez replied for Ethan. 'Sure, they're government and they can be as shady as the CIA but they're not in the revenge game. Doing your job won't bring them down on you, but if Forbeck walks out of here you're right, MJ–12 will back track him and clear up any loose ends. How much of a head–start does he have?'

'Not far,' Rubinar said, 'and the next charter flight out of the country doesn't depart for another hour. He bought tickets last night, so he's planning to leave.'

Ethan rubbed his face to keep himself alert and urged Rubinar on.

'Step on it,' he advised. 'If Forbeck suspects the authorities might be on to him he'll try to conceal his trail. The tickets might be a ruse to do that. Do you have a tail on him?'

'No,' Rubinar admitted. 'He left his hotel real fast, but he took a cab and we have the company name and the registration number of the vehicle.'

'Find it,' Ethan advised, 'as soon as you do, we'll take over.'

Rubinar nodded as he pressed on the accelerator pedal and the jeep surged forward along the highway, the wind rumbling past outside.

*

'How much further?'

Forbeck checked his watch as the irritable cab driver replied in heavily accented English.

'Twenty minutes sir, please.'

The heat inside the cab was oppressive and the stench of what might have been weed stuck to the back of Forbeck's throat as he tried to ignore the garish decorations inside the cab's interior and focus instead on the rear view mirror, which was angled sufficiently for him to maintain a watch behind the vehicle on the road.

Forbeck had worked in surveillance and as a mercenary for over a decade, and the military for twenty years prior, and he knew well what dangerous and powerful men were capable of. Professor Garrett did not frighten him physically in the slightest: at two hundred thirty pounds and six foot three, not many people frightened Forbeck at all. But Garrett's threat was one to be taken seriously by anybody who wanted to survive in this cut–throat world of espionage. Forbeck had learned early in his military career that a weak man at the top of the chain was vastly more powerful than a strong man at the bottom, and that care and caution was essential in dealing with men who considered themselves to be a law unto themselves. What frightened him about Garrett was the fact that he was a man dabbling with powers that were far beyond Forbeck's comprehension. Hired five years previously to maintain security on a facility on an island that Garrett apparently *owned*, as if that itself wasn't enough evidence of the man's tremendous financial power, Forbeck had already seen enough to know that the further he was from Garrett the safer he was. The professor's experiments were both fascinating and terrifying by turns, and Forbeck wanted nothing to do with them. He had decided a year previously that he wanted out of the contract, but the lure of tens of thousands of dollars per month had kept him in place until now.

Two DIA agents were dead and it was without a doubt that within hours the island would be crawling with more agents driven by typical patriotic desire to root out those responsible and ship them back to the states for a public trial. With their forensic power they would soon uncover whatever the hell it was Garrett had unleashed in the Madagascan jungle, along with whatever was left of the drone Forbeck had purchased to deliver the samples into the wilderness.

Forbeck had no intention of flying out of Madagascar, and certainly no intention of showing up in Brazil so that his jumped–up squirt of an employer could have him fed to sharks or something as an example of what happened to people who "failed" in their duties. There were plenty of other ways off the island, provided one had cash, and Forbeck had ensured that he had sufficient funds to bribe his passage on a private vessel bound for just about anywhere but Brazil.

'Head for the docks,' he instructed the driver.

'But you said that you…'

'I changed my mind,' Forbeck growled. 'The docks, as fast as you can.'

The driver obeyed, sensing the threat of violence in Forbeck's voice. He kept one eye in the rear view mirror as they headed toward the docks, and after a couple of minutes he spotted a distant vehicle following them on the road. Forbeck was not the world's most paranoid former soldier – he had learned long ago that while paranoia was a useful defense mechanism, it also could prove one's undoing just as quickly. But now he found himself staring at the jeep whenever it appeared in the mirror far behind them. Something about it sent alarm bells ringing in his mind, but he couldn't tell what it was that had sparked his instincts.

The cab driver continued blissfully unaware of the drama unfolding in the rear seat as Forbeck's hand reached down beneath his thin jacket and rested on the butt of his pistol, nestled in a shoulder holster. Reassured, he watched the vehicle behind them and noted that it was closing in, moving faster than they were.

He realized the source of his concern. The vehicle was moving with a great purpose, its lines on the road sweeping, moving fast, dust spiralling from its tires as it turned corners. But it was when he saw it move out and pass another vehicle on the road behind them that he suddenly and clairvoyantly knew that it was a threat.

'Go faster,' he ordered the driver.

'This road is for vehicles driving at no more than…'

The pistol was out of Forbeck's holster and pressed against the driver's head before he could finish his sentence.

'I go faster, I go faster!' the driver squealed, his features flushed with panic as he pressed the accelerator to the floor.

***

Dean Crawford

XXIX

'He could be anywhere!'

Lopez leaned between the jeep's front seats as the vehicle descended a coastal road toward a small town nestled against the endless rollers of the Indian Ocean, a busy dock filled with countless boats and yachts.

Ethan raised his hands and used his fingers to make a box before his eyes, an old trick he'd learned in the Marine Corps, focusing on one small area at a time just as he searched the road ahead and the docks themselves, seeking anything unusual or out of place. A few moments later he spotted a vehicle that was weaving in and out of traffic barely a mile ahead of them.

'There!' he shouted, pointing ahead. 'He's in that cab!'

'Are you sure?' Rabinur asked.

'Only one way to find out,' Lopez said.

Rabinur slammed the accelerator down and the jeep flew down the hillside, Rabinur showing considerable driving skill as he weaved in and out of the traffic on the main road, horns hooting him and angry shouts whipped away on the hot wind as they rocketed toward the docks.

'Told you he wouldn't make for the airport,' Ethan said. 'Too easy for him to be traced. He'll have paid for a ride out of here on a private vessel.'

Rabinur replied as he drove, gripping the wheel tightly.

'There are a lot of tourist vessels that run out to the islands or across to the African mainland! He could pay for a ride on any of them, and the captains will easily turn a blind eye to him getting ashore in Africa without paperwork.'

'If he makes it there, he'll be in the wind,' Lopez warned.

'He's not getting away from us,' Ethan said, checking his pistol before he tucked it away again beneath his shirt. 'Christiano, are there any agency vessels down there?'

'Nothing worth having,' Rabinur replied as he swerved around a fast right–hander, the jeep rushing down into the small town and the docks ahead of them, glittering green water enclosed in a man–made bay and filled with boats.

'I can't see the cab anymore!' Lopez said, even her keen eyes unable to track the vehicle as it disappeared into the myriad streets.

'Ignore the cab,' Ethan said, 'just get to the docks. We can cut him off from there!'

Rabinur was about to agree when he spotted the vehicle. 'There it is!'

He swerved across the oncoming traffic as the jeep's tires squealed on the asphalt and he changed direction.

'Get to the docks!' Ethan insisted. 'It's the only way!'

'I can catch him before he gets there,' Rabinur insisted. 'Trust me!'

Ethan remained silent as he saw the cab ahead, a battered old vehicle that looked perhaps Russian or maybe French as it clattered down a street, puffs of brown smoke coughing from its exhaust as the driver pushed the geriatric engine far harder than it was designed for.

Ethan gripped the door beside him as Rabinur yanked the wheel this way and that, the jeep's engine screeching as it zoomed in behind the fleeing cab.

'Holy crap, take it easy!' Lopez yelled as the cab loomed before them.

Rabinur, his features twisted with grim determination, failed to hear her as he stomped on the accelerator and swerved out, pushing the front of the jeep alongside the rear of the battered old cab, and then he pulled back in hard.

A crash of metal clattered out above the combined roar from the two engines and Ethan held on for dear life as the cab's rear wheels spun out and the vehicle shot to the right, out of control as clouds of blue smoke billowed from its tires and the cab spun a hundred eighty degrees and slammed into the wall of a small house barely a hundred yards from the dock entrance.

Rabinur let out a whoop of delight as he stamped on the brakes and the jeep screeched to a halt in the centre of the street. Ethan managed to prevent his head from smacking into the windshield as he pulled his pistol from its holster and shoved his door open. Lopez vaulted from the rear of the jeep, her own pistol drawn as together they dashed across to where the cab sat awkwardly against the wall of the house, steam hissing from beneath the hood and the acrid stench of burned rubber tainting the air.

Lopez rushed the passenger door and shoved her pistol in at the driver, who Ethan glimpsed with his hands in the air beside his head and his face stricken with terror.

'Don't shoot, don't shoot! He made me, he made me!'

Rabinur hurried up alongside Lopez and pointed at the horrified driver. 'You're under arrest and so is your passenger!'

Rabinur looked across at Lopez and winked casually. 'Not so bad, huh?'

An old woman hobbled from inside the small house and began yelling in Malagasy at them, brandishing what looked like a length of broomstick as though it were a broadsword. Ethan steered clear of her and yanked open the rear door of the cab to look inside, then slammed the door shut.

'He's gone.'

Rabinur's jubilation withered as he peered inside the cab. 'But he...'

'He jumped out when we lost sight of him,' Ethan scowled, 'and paid the driver to flee, which given his traumatized state he did willingly.'

Rabinur's bravado collapsed into despair and he whirled to Lopez. 'But I thought we could cut him off and...'

'He can't have gone far,' Lopez said soothingly as she holstered her pistol and backed away from the old woman and her baton. 'You deal with her, we'll find Forbeck.'

Rabinur stared at the angry woman as she bore down upon him, and Ethan shoved his pistol back into its holster and started running toward the dock. Lopez caught up with him easily and they sprinted down to the water's edge in time to hear another engine cough into life.

Ethan dashed onto the quay and saw a sleek blue and white speedboat turn sharply on the water and a burst of white foam explode from its stern as it accelerated away toward the harbor exit. In the water behind it a middle aged man bobbed about on the waves and screamed obscenities at the fleeing vessel.

'There!'

Lopez pointed to another similar vessel, upon which stood a man who had watched the entire exchange and now stared at Lopez as though she were about to shoot him. Ethan stormed across to the boat and jumped down into it as he held up his badge.

'Defense Intelligence Agency,' he announced. 'We'll need your boat.'

'No way!' the man snapped in perfect American. 'This vessel is my personal property and we're not in United States territory. You have no right to...'

Lopez landed cat–like into the boat and pulled the mooring line while one small, flat hand thumped into the man's chest with enough force to propel him backwards over the side of the speedboat to crash into the water.

Ethan turned the key in the dashboard and the boat's powerful engines roared into life. He grabbed the polished throttles and pushed them forward, cautious of applying too much power and flipping the boat, but the vessel still surged forward with surprising speed and almost toppled Lopez off the stern as it rocketed away from the quay.

Ethan guided the speedboat into a steep turn, white water spraying in glistening clouds as they plunged through the harbor exit and out toward the open ocean. The harbor walls flashed past on either side as they raced in pursuit of Forbeck, the white trail of his vessel's wake clear on the ocean before them.

'He's got nowhere to go!' Lopez shouted above the wind. 'All we gotta do is cut him off!'

Ethan pushed the throttles wide open as they soared in pursuit. The speedboat was maybe a hundred yards in front of them and Ethan could see Forbeck looking over his shoulder at them, one hand to the side of his head.

'He's calling for help!' Lopez said.

The speedboats were both following the coastline south and Ethan knew that there was nowhere for Forbeck to hide unless he made it ashore and was able to disappear into a major town. He was surprised that Forbeck had even stolen the speedboat in the first place, as if he'd simply hidden out for a while they might never have found him and…

'This is part of his plan,' Ethan said out loud, 'he's already got a rescue coming!'

'Where the hell from?!' Lopez asked.

'Gotta be a helicopter or something!' Ethan shouted in reply. 'He's got MJ–12 financing him, he can afford anything! We need to control him before his support can arrive!'

Lopez did not reply. Instead, she clambered up onto the bow of the speedboat and lay herself flat as she drew her pistol and aimed it dead ahead. Ethan knew instantly what she planned to do and he steered the speedboat gently to port, clearing the turbulent wake of Forbeck's boat and seeking the smoother ocean to either side.

The speedboat levelled out a little on the waves and accelerated as it carved a smoother path. Lopez aimed carefully and then opened fire. The shots cracked out but were snatched away by the hot wind as Ethan watched for impacts on Forbeck's boat. Lopez's second shot appeared to hit the hull, the third moving close enough to Forbeck to force him to duck in surprise.

Forbeck whirled and two shots zipped back toward them. Ethan crouched down a little to avoid making such a big and obvious target as Lopez fired two more rounds. This time, Ethan thought he saw a spurt of gray smoke from one of Forbeck's two engines.

'I got him!' Lopez yelled in delight.

Ethan saw a thin stream of smoke spilling from the casing of Forbeck's starboard engine, saw the gunman look behind him. Then, without warning, the speedboat suddenly turned sharply to the right amid a huge burst of white water as Forbeck hauled the vessel around and charged back toward them.

'Get off the bow!' Ethan yelled.

Lopez hurled herself back into the speedboat as Forbeck charged, his pistol aimed ahead of him as he opened fire at Ethan. Ethan spun the wheel and the speedboat's hull shuddered as it turned hard, and then the bow waves of the onrushing speedboat slammed into their hull as Forbeck raced past in the opposite direction.

Ethan was hurled sideways away from the wheel and tumbled across the deck as the speedboat beside them accelerated away, still trailing a thin plume of smoke. A salvo of gun fire rattled off the decks, showering Ethan in sparks as he ducked his head down low.

Lopez rolled alongside him and let her arms fall onto his body to use him as a rest as she fired four more rounds from her pistol at the fleeing speedboat. This time a thicker cloud of smoke burst from Forbeck's engine as Ethan scrambled across to the wheel and slammed the throttles wide open again.

'He's losing the engine,' Lopez called, 'he can't outrun us now!'

'Take the wheel and get us as close to him as you can!' Ethan yelled at her.

Lopez responded instantly and dashed to the wheel as Ethan drew his own pistol and leaped onto the speedboat's bow, gripping the mooring posts as the vessel crashed through the waves. There was no way that he could hit a target under these conditions but he didn't want Forbeck dead anyway: he only needed to keep his head down. As they closed on the fleeing boat he fired two or three wild shots in Forbeck's general direction, and through the spray Ethan saw the gunman flinch and duck his head down.

Ethan crept forward onto the bow and shoved his pistol into its holster as he prepared to make the leap. Lopez eased the speedboat in toward Forbeck, who immediately turned away from them toward the open ocean.

Lopez anticipated the turn with admirable accuracy and the speedboat surged through a tighter turn, cutting across Forbeck's wake while also cutting the corner off the turn. Ethan saw his chance as the two vessels surged together on the turbulent ocean, and he tucked his legs beneath him and then thrust forward with all of his might.

Ethan leaped from the bow of the boat and seemed to hang in mid-air for what felt like an age between the two speeding vessels.

***

Dean Crawford

XXX

Forbeck looked over his shoulder even as Ethan plunged down toward the stern of his boat and he pulled the vessel away, turning hard to starboard in an attempt to send Ethan crashing into the ocean.

The speedboat turned broadside amid a wall of white water, its propeller whining and spraying clouds of water vapor onto the hot air as Ethan crashed down and slammed into the rear of the speedboat, the stench of overheated engines and smoke filling the air around him as Forbeck spun the wheel with one hand as he desperately tried to aim his pistol at Ethan with the other.

Ethan reached for his pistol but found the holster empty, saw that the weapon had been dislodged by the impact of his landing and had skittered away across the deck. Forbeck fired and a round smashed through the fibreglass hull beside Ethan's leg as he scrambled to his feet and hurled himself at the gunman before he could take another shot.

Ethan plowed into Forbeck and they slammed down onto the deck, the speedboat crashing out of control across the waves. The gunman thrust the pistol toward Ethan's face, attempting a point–blank–range kill shot. Ethan swept one arm across Forbeck's and diverted the weapon just as it fired, the gunshot deafeningly loud in his ear as Ethan pushed his arm forward and jammed it against Forbeck's armpit, locking the arm away and denying him another shot as Ethan got one knee up and forced himself upright. He swung a left–handed punch that smacked across Forbeck's temple with a crack loud enough to hear above the engines, wind and waves, but the blow seemed to barely effect the gunman as he swung one knee up into Ethan's chest.

The blow punched the air from Ethan's lungs and his vision starred as he gaped for air and forced himself to focus on keeping Forbeck's gun from pointing at him. Forbeck lurched upright, using his body weight to counter Ethan's block and turn his grip into a disadvantage. Ethan felt himself twisted over to the right, his arm being locked into Forbeck's grip as the gunman attempted to change pistol hands, grabbing for the weapon with his free hand.

Ethan swung his left fist around, two fingers pointed at Forbeck's face as he plunged them into the gunman's eyes as hard as he could. Forbeck screamed as Ethan's fingers bit deep into the soft wet tissue of his eyeballs and he scrambled to get away, temporarily blinded by the unexpected move as Ethan fought for position and tried to turn the pistol toward Forbeck.

Blinded and desperate, Forbeck jerked his arm to one side and his pistol flew into the air and crashed into the ocean speeding past the hull. A chunky fist flashed toward Ethan's face and he ducked his head down as Forbeck's knuckles crunched across the top of his head. Ethan reeled backwards and crashed into the seats at the stern of the boat, made to scramble to his feet again as he looked up.

A heavy boot thumped across his chest as Forbeck staggered upright and lashed out. Ethan's lungs convulsed and he slammed onto his back in the boat's stern, Forbeck rushing toward him and raising his boot again to stomp it down on Ethan's face and end the confrontation.

Ethan threw his hands up to attempt to block the blow when the terrible sound of splintering fibreglass and metal crashed out and the speedboat lurched across the waves. Forbeck stumbled sideways and crashed into the wheel as Ethan saw Lopez briefly as her boat smashed into Forbeck's vessel's hull and threw him off balance.

Ethan scrambled to his feet even as Forbeck recovered himself and the gunman's hand fell upon a crowbar lodged behind the wheel. Forbeck grinned maliciously as he yanked the crowbar from its braces and staggered toward Ethan, blood spilling from where his head had hit the wheel during Lopez's collision.

Forbeck raised the thick crowbar and brought it crashing down toward Ethan, who leaped to one side and let the weapon smash down onto the deck as he dashed past Forbeck and rolled along the deck.

Forbeck turned and raised the crowbar once again as Ethan's hand rested on his lost pistol and he whirled, aimed at Forbeck's left knee and fired.

The gunshot smashed through bone and muscle and Forbeck screamed as his leg gave way beneath him amid a fine spray of crimson blood that splattered the boat's pristine deck. The gunman slammed down onto the deck as Ethan, his chest heaving, crawled to one side and reached out to close the speedboat's throttles. The vessel slowed on the ocean until it became stationary on the swells, and Ethan could hear Lopez's craft turning nearby and closing in on them.

'Are you okay?' she yelled as she guided the speedboat in alongside Forbeck's and saw the gunman writhing in agony on the deck, both hands clasped around his knee.

'Never better,' Ethan gasped and wiped blood from a cut on his lip that stung sharply. 'You wanna call an ambulance for this asshole?'

*

Ambokala Hospital,

Manakara

Madagascar did not possess the kind of medical facilities that most western people considered a human right, and that was something that Ethan was determined to capitalize on as he stepped out of Rubinar's jeep and looked at the building before him. A hospital designed to treat mental patients that had recently been refurbished, it had only a rudimentary emergency service, which he and Lopez witnessed as they walked into a small ward of bare walls and minimal furnishings to see Forbeck lying on his back on a metal bedstead with a mattress that might possibly have been older than the town itself.

A saline drip had been inserted into Forbeck's right arm and his leg had been set and dressed, but Ethan had quietly ensured that there was little in the way of pain relief for the wound Ethan had inflicted. The dressings were clean but thick blood stained the mattress beneath the wound and Ethan knew that Forbeck could hardly expect to escape without an infection at best and the loss of his leg at worst.

Ethan eased alongside the bed and looked down into Forbeck's strained eyes.

'Greetings,' Ethan said. 'Remember me? We took a little boat trip a couple hours ago?'

'Go to hell,' Forbeck seethed through gritted teeth.

'How's the leg?' Lopez asked, then looked at it and sucked her teeth as she shook her head. 'I wouldn't put much on you walking out of here on that thing. Mind you, I wouldn't put much on your ever walking again if you stay here too long.'

Forbeck glared at her.

'I'm an American citizen,' he snapped over his pain. 'I demand that you contact the consulate and have me repatriated so that I can receive proper treatment after I was attacked and shot by this assho....'

'Ahh that's the problem you see,' Ethan cut across him. 'You're an American citizen all right, but there's no record of you entering the country. That makes you an illegal immigrant and therefore not eligible for medical treatment here other than at your own expense.'

'Furthermore,' Lopez went on smoothly, 'not only do we have witnesses who saw you steal that speedboat from the docks, but also witnesses who saw you open fire on us. You do know that we're Defense Intelligence Agency, right?'

Ethan saw trepidation on Forbeck's face, and then shock as both he and Lopez flashed their badges at him.

'Opening fire on an intelligence agent carrying out the course of their duties is a federal offence anywhere on earth,' Ethan said, 'and the attempted homicide of not one but two agents will get you... what do you think, Nicola?'

'Ooooh, I'd say about thirty years, no parole,' Lopez replied. 'You look to be about forty Forbeck, so you'll get out just long enough to use what's left of your leg for a year or two before you drop dead of old age.'

Forbeck scowled and spat weakly in her direction. 'Get me a doctor or I'll sue the pair of you and your department for a breach of my human rights!'

Ethan smiled as he leaned against the wall and folded his arms.

'Well, you see that's the other problem. You travelled here without visas or passport, so there's no record of you actually being here at all. So, we figured, y'know what? If Forbeck doesn't play ball, that's just fine. He's not going anywhere on that leg and since we just froze his bank accounts and recovered his cash assets, we'll just pretend this whole thing never happened.'

Forbeck frowned in confusion and Lopez smiled brightly.

'That's right,' she said. 'We'll just let you go.'

Ethan pushed off the wall and took a moment to look around the hospital ward at the stained walls, the emaciated bodies of two dying men laying in nearby beds, the sickly aroma of lousy disinfectant and urine heavy in the air.

'This is as bad a prison sentence as you'll ever get back home,' Ethan said. 'We already know who you're working for so I guess there's not so much you can do for us anyway. I doubt you'll make it out of here alive. Best of luck with that.'

Ethan walked away from Forbeck's bed, Lopez turning on her heel and following him toward the ward exit. He got to within two paces of the door when Forbeck's strained voice cried out.

'Wait!'

Ethan turned at the door and looked at Forbeck expectantly. His face was flushed red both from pain and the incessant heat. Ethan knew that he wouldn't last long in here, that he would probably not survive the wound in his leg if he wasn't shipped to America real fast.

'Talk,' Ethan said, 'and make it damned fast and equally good or I'll walk out of here right now, something that you'll never be able to do.'

Forbeck grit his teeth, but he knew that he had no place left to go.

'I work for a man named Garrett.'

'Tell us something we don't already know,' Lopez insisted.

'He has an island,' Forbeck gasped as a fresh wave of pain washed over him and he squirmed in agony, 'off the coast of Brazil.'

Ethan walked back to the bedside. 'An island?'

Forbeck nodded.

'I don't know exactly what he does there but he leases the island from the Brazilian government for experiments of some kind, and whatever it is that he's up to is not good. I don't go there if I can avoid it.'

'Why?' Lopez asked, interested now. 'What is it that you don't like about the place?'

Forbeck clasped his wound with both hands. 'I need pain killers,' he whimpered.

'You'll get them,' Ethan promised. 'Talk.'

Forbeck managed to get himself under control and spoke in a weary, ragged voice, the tone of a man in total defeat.

'I saw some of the things they have there,' he whispered, 'creatures.'

'Creatures?' Lopez echoed, almost nervously.

'People,' Forbeck said, 'but they're not people, not really. They're... they're not human.'

Ethan felt the hairs on the back of his neck stand on end as he considered what Forbeck was saying. If the man was trying to stall for time he was doing a damned good job of it: nobody in their right mind would make up such an outlandish story if they were trying to convince government agents that they were telling the truth. The pain alone wasn't enough to make Forbeck delirious.

'This island,' Ethan asked. 'What's it called?'

***

XXXI

'It's called Ilhabela, and is two hundred miles south west down the coast from Rio de Janeiro.'

The interior of the Lockheed C–5 Galaxy was blessedly cool compared to the dense humidity of Madagascar. Ethan sat at a communications terminal inside the aircraft's cavernous fuselage, just behind the cockpit, the immense Galaxy having been diverted south from a flight out of Iraq to collect them under the pretence of collecting the dead bodies of two US agents killed in the line of duty in Madagascar. At the same time, Forbeck had gotten himself a ride back to the USA and the medical attention he so desperately needed.

A monitor before Ethan showed an image of Doug Jarvis in his office in Washington DC, while a small window to Ethan's right revealed the twinkling lights of Madagascar's coastal towns vanishing beneath swathes of cloud as the Galaxy climbed out toward the African coast and the vast South Atlantic Ocean beyond.

'Tell me about it,' Ethan said as he leaned back in the seat. 'Forbeck is convinced that whatever Garrett's up to, it's happening on that island.'

Hellerman's face appeared on the screen as he briefed Ethan.

'Ilhabela is Portuguese for "beautiful island",' Hellerman said, 'it's a few miles off the coast, far enough to be clear of most tourists.'

'How could this guy Garrett hide some kind of experimental facility from so many people?'

'Because it's not exactly hidden,' Hellerman explained. 'Garrett leases the western side of the island from the Brazilian government, and that side of the island is rarely visited by tourists. The island's interior is densely forested and virtually impassable, which means that access to the island on the far side of the channel is possible only by boat. Most folks don't venture inland from there, staying on the secluded beaches.'

Ethan watched as Hellerman's features disappeared to reveal a satellite image of the island.

'The facility itself appears to be mostly underground, with thick forest canopy concealing what little is visible from the air. Access is strictly controlled, and as far as we're aware nobody but employees of Garrett have set foot inside that facility since it was constructed some ten years ago.'

'Ten years, huh?' Lopez echoed, 'plenty of time for somebody to have been busy creating who–the–hell–knows–what. Forbeck claimed that there were creatures on that island, something not quite human. Who the hell is this guy Garrett, anyway?'

'Professor Rhys Garrett,' Hellerman explained, 'a former Professor of genetics at Harvard. Made himself a billion or two during the early rush to decode the human genome among other things, by licensing a series of coding protocols for DNA that allowed computers to crunch biological data more efficiently.'

Ethan saw an image of the professor appear on the screen, a hawkish looking man with thin–rimmed spectacles balanced precariously on the end of his beak–like nose, eyes with an ominous hint of radicalism glittering in them like a distant, volatile star.

'When was he last seen?' Ethan asked.

'Garrett slipped the net at Dulles International two weeks ago,' Jarvis explained. 'Went as far as to use a body double, which fooled the tail we had on him. The flight he took was private and was headed to South Africa, but from there the trail goes cold until Madagascar and his yacht, which you both connected to the events on the island.'

The image of the island vanished and Jarvis spoke to them again.

'As far as Garrett's aware, you two are dead,' he reminded them. 'There's no way that we can gain rapid access to this facility through normal diplomatic channels. The Brazilians are allies, sure, but they are likely generating huge revenue from whatever Garrett's doing down there and we've got to assume that he's already well in with the government and other heads of state.'

'They wouldn't stand against America,' Ethan pointed out. 'We have direct evidence linking assets of Garrett to the attack in Madagascar. Can't we just point the finger and force the Brazilians to open the place up to an inspection?'

'They already tried,' Jarvis replied. 'Three years ago the US tried to convince Brazil to open the island up for investigators, but Brazil closed ranks around Garrett. It turns out that they're not particularly trusting of America's history of concealing UFO events, and they seem to think that this island has something to do with the Varginha event.'

'You think that the creatures that Forbeck mentioned are the same things that were seen at Varginha?'

'Maybe,' Jarvis replied, 'but without boots on the ground it's all conjecture. Many witnesses claim to have encountered strange creatures on the island, but few have come forward in recent years.'

'How come?' Lopez asked.

'Recanted their statements,' Jarvis replied, 'either as a result of intimidation or bribes. Garrett can do both. The only person I could find who might talk is a former military police officer name Martinez who was a witness to the original sightings in Varginha. He'll meet you when you arrive in Brazil.'

'And Garrett?' Lopez asked.

'I don't know what the hell this guy's up to out there but right now our best bet is to ignore official protocol and get you both onto that island,' Jarvis replied. 'You're off record anyhow, so anything you can gather intelligence–wise will have to pass through an anonymous source in order to be admissible as evidence before Congress.'

'You think that this can get to the Capitol?' Ethan asked, somewhat amazed.

'I think that it's time to open this up beyond the Defense Intelligence Agency's walls,' Jarvis replied. 'The public needs to know what's happening here. We've been pursuing Majestic Twelve for years and we're not really any closer to bringing them down, and the attacks you've endured on this mission prove that they're out to finish us off any way they can. Our best bet now is to publicly expose them for what they are and embarrass them in the media as much as possible to force them to back off.'

'They'll find another way,' Lopez pointed out. 'They won't stop hunting us.'

'They might,' Jarvis said, 'if we can get Garrett to admit his involvement with the cabal.'

Ethan raised an eyebrow. 'Garrett wasn't one of the eleven men we imaged in New York City.'

'Indeed,' Jarvis said, 'and that's why we think that he's involved in an attempt to join Majestic Twelve. He has the financial power and the expertize, but there must be something else up his sleeve that he's using as leverage to win himself a place. It's your job to find out what that something is. I'll have the Navy send a ship before you head to Brazil so you can intercept Garrett's yacht. Report back in when you have him in custody or you reach his island.'

'Done,' Ethan replied. 'We'll get some sleep while we cross the Atlantic.'

'Be careful. If Forbeck is right, whatever Garrett has on that island won't be friendly.'

*

Washington DC

'Did you get the codes?'

Jarvis turned to Hellerman as soon as the link with Ethan and Nicola had been switched off. Hellerman eagerly handed him a thick wad of papers.

'Most of it's the account details,' the scientist explained. 'The bread's on the first couple of pages, all of the codes. They're held in off shores around the world and the codes change regularly, so we'll have to be quick to catch them all and freeze up the money.'

'How much is there?' Jarvis asked.

Hellerman actually swallowed, as though nervous to say it out loud.

'Almost four trillion dollars in assets,' he said. 'More than some countries.'

Jarvis nodded, and then clapped Hellerman on the shoulder. 'We've got MJ–12 by the balls now, don't we?'

Hellerman grinned. 'You gonna take it to Nellis now?'

'Right this instant,' Jarvis confirmed. 'Get on the horn to the NSA and set up a meeting will you? You deserve the credit for breaking this.'

Jarvis walked from the ARIES watch room as Hellerman hurried to his office to make the call. He strode up to the ground level of the DIA's Headquarters building and walked toward the lobby, his pass card checked by security as he logged out of the building and walked through the south exit.

Broad lawns basked in the afternoon sunlight and a fountain glistened as Jarvis strolled casually toward the parking lot and slipped a cell phone from his pocket. He dialled, and after three rings Mitchell answered.

'Yes?'

'Ilhabela, off the coast of Brazil, just south of Sau Paulo,' Jarvis said simply. 'Target is Rhys Garrett, private facility, defenses unknown. All of Majestic Twelve are likely to be there.'

'Understood.'

'I'm sending you some codes, an unexpected bonus,' he added. 'This is what I need you to do.'

As soon as Jarvis had finished speaking the line clicked off and Jarvis switched off the burner and yanked off the rear of the device. He pulled out the SIM card and dropped it down a drain as he walked, then broke the cell phone in two. He would deposit the remains of the phone in two dumpsters at least a mile apart on his way home, having taken a suitable detour that would avoid any blocks monitored by CCTV.

*

'Flash traffic, south lawn.'

Hellerman sat at a monitor and watched as the automated "crawler" program he had initiated locked on to the cell phone signal burst that had been emitted from a local tower just moments before.

'Where's it from and where is it going?'

General Nellis stood behind Hellerman with his arms folded and watched as the kid worked his magic on the computers, which were linked from his office to the vast data servers of the National Security Agency, the Federal Bureau of Investigation and the Central Intelligence Agency. Within moments the combined resources of all of the agencies and the local telephone company's willingness to comply provided Hellerman with the information that Nellis needed.

'The call originated from our own south lawns and was received by an unregistered cell phone in Tijuana, Mexico.'

'Can you trace the location of the receiving signal?' Nellis asked.

Hellerman shook his head. 'No, it's already gone. My guess is that they're using multiple burner cells and destroying each one after a single use. There's no trail to follow.'

Nellis nodded. 'Okay, just bring up the CCTV on the south lawn and wind it back.'

Hellerman obeyed, picking up the relevant camera feed and winding it back to the time of the call. Moments later a still image of Douglas Jarvis appeared, a cell phone pressed to his ear.

Nellis sighed heavily as he looked at the image. Hellerman stifled his own gasp and looked up at the general.

'You've been tracking Jarvis? Why?'

'That's why,' Nellis said as he gestured at the screen. 'Ever since Felix Byzan was killed in Rome I've suspected that the hit required inside knowledge. The only people who know the identities of Majestic Twelve work in this building, and Jarvis has made no secret of his desire to see the cabal liquidated.'

Hellerman stared at the still image of his boss. 'You're sure there can be no mistake?'

Nellis shook his head.

'No other calls went out south of the border from this location in that timeframe, and we're a long way from Mexico. Get the tech team to place a GPS tracker on Jarvis's car. I want to know where he is at all times, okay?'

'Who do you think he's been calling?'

Nellis rested a reassuring hand on Hellerman's shoulder before he turned and walked from the office.

'I have a few ideas, but I'll deal with this. Share it with nobody, understood?'

'Are you going to arrest him?' Hellerman asked. 'He's served his country his entire life and his record is impeccable.'

'That doesn't give him the right to act as judge and juror,' Nellis snapped. 'The moment we start acting like that, we're no better than MJ–12.'

The General turned and stalked out of Hellerman's office, closed the door behind him and headed swiftly for the elevators. It was only once the doors were closed that he let out a long sigh of relief, grateful for the brief moment of privacy as he pondered on his next course of action.

Jarvis's work had led directly to the death of a member of Majestic Twelve, and Nellis had not the first idea of what to do about it.

***

XXXII

USS Independence,

Gulf of Mexico

'Do we have a location?!'

Ethan had to shout over the noise from the blades of a US Navy Black Hawk helicopter that was winding its engines up as they walked out onto the stern deck of the littoral ship.

'We're working on it now! Stand by!'

USS Independence was one of the Navy's newest combat ships, a small–crew corvette capable of multiple roles. She was a futuristic looking trimaran design, with a wide beam supporting a very large flight deck and capable of sustaining speeds of more than forty knots.

Ethan climbed aboard the Black Hawk alongside Lopez, and around them were packed a small but elite team of US Navy SEALS, heavily armed and their features concealed behind bandanas and camouflage paint that made them somehow look less human and more machine.

Ethan strapped into his seat with Lopez alongside him as the helicopter lifted off the corvette's deck and turned, her nose dipping as her tail rose and the Black Hawk accelerated away from the ship and skimmed over the waves of the Gulf of Mexico, the broad and flat greenery of the Yucatan Peninsula crouched against the horizon before them.

The loadmaster's voice in Ethan's earphones was barely audible as he sat in his seat and watched the glittering seas race by.

'The yacht is still in international waters, but she's making a run for Cancun by the look of things!'

'We've got to get to her first,' Ethan insisted. 'Can we cut her off?'

'Coast Guard already ordered her to heave to, but there was no response,' the loadmaster replied. 'She's making for the dock no matter what, and once inside she's beyond the reach of our government.'

Ethan checked the 9mm pistol in his shoulder holster one last time as he replied.

'We don't have time for political wrangling. Either we stop them now, or this is already over.'

The loadmaster smiled grimly. 'Don't worry, these guys can be aboard her in sixty seconds, and have her engines shut down right afterward. We're ten miles out, it's gonna be close, but they'll make it.'

Ethan nodded, and looked at the lieutenant of the SEAL team.

'Make for the bridge,' he said. 'Turn the ship away from the coast as a priority.'

'Yes sir,' the officer replied. No questions. No concerns.

The Black Hawk turned as it swept along just above the surface of the ocean, and Ethan could see in the distance the exotic beaches of Cancun and San Miguel, strips of dark green and white sand against the blue expanses of ocean and sky. The interior of the helicopter was hot and smelled of grease and aviation fuel, the whole fuselage rattling as the pilots drove the helicopter at its maximum velocity over the ocean in an attempt to catch the private yacht before she reached the safety of the harbor a few miles away.

'We've got a visual,' came the voice of the pilot through the earphones, and Ethan leaned forward in his seat to look into the cockpit between the two pilots.

Beyond the myriad controls and screens, the broad windshield revealed the vast panorama of the Gulf of Mexico beneath scattered cumulus clouds trailing shadows that drifted across the clear blue waters. Dead ahead, a tiny white speck was dwarfed by the immense ocean.

'That's her,' Ethan said as he spotted the shape of the yacht fleeing them.

'We're sixty seconds out,' the pilot informed him. 'They're about two minutes from Mexican waters.'

'Don't try to cut them off or block their course,' Ethan said. 'That yacht's big enough and they'll be ordered to ram you regardless of any risk. Just get overhead her and try to stay stable enough to get the SEALs aboard. We'll do the rest.'

The pilot nodded, his focus on the ship before them as Ethan turned back to the SEAL team.

'They'll try to evade us, prevent you from getting aboard. This could get a little rough.'

The SEALS regarded him in silence for a moment, and then as one they cocked their M–16 rifles in response. Ethan nodded and glanced at Lopez.

'You ready?'

'I'll cope,' she replied. 'I feel better knowing that you're not flying us in this time.'

Ethan rolled his eyes as he prepared for the exit. The SEALs were briefed to go first, followed by Ethan and Lopez if the pilots deemed it safe to do so. Ethan knew that there was little chance of that, so he had decided that he'd drop onto the line the first chance he got. Both he and Lopez had performed this action many times before, but never against the clock.

'Thirty seconds, hatches open!'

The loadmaster hauled open the two side doors flanking the fuselage as the SEALs got out of their seats and hung on grimly, the rappel lines coiled on the deck at their boots. Ethan held onto his seat with one hand, the other gripping his buckle, ready to release it as soon as he could.

'They're evading!'

The Black Hawk tilted over sharply as the fleeing yacht turned beneath them, hoping to throw off the pursuing helicopter for long enough to reach safety. Ethan leaned around and glimpsed the giant vessel's shining white decks and crashing foam around her stern as she twisted on the ocean, the Black Hawk's pilot following her carefully and descending toward the large helipad on her stern.

Ethan knew that the pilot couldn't attempt to drop them anywhere else, even though the ship was so large. Her erratic manoeuvring was enough to make landing anywhere else on the deck hazardous in the extreme, but at least Ethan knew that the captain of the ship would be forced to keep heading toward the coast and therefore couldn't deviate too far from…

'Incoming!'

Ethan heard the pilot's panicked yell as the Black Hawk jerked upward and her engines and rotor blades thundered as Ethan heard a strange tinkling sound, like metal cooling. The SEALs ducked back from the open hatches as a couple of stray rounds clattered against the Black Hawk's fuselage in a spray of sparks.

'Get us down!' the SEAL officer yelled. 'Ten seconds!'

The pilot responded, and in a remarkable display of flying skill he turned the Black Hawk side on to the fleeing yacht, maintaining his flying speed and bringing the rifles of the SEAL team to bear on the gunmen flooding the landing pad on the yacht's stern. Ethan watched as the SEALs opened fire, the Black Hawk descending and rocking on the wind as the soldiers directed a deafening crescendo of withering fire onto the yacht.

Ethan saw two or three gunmen go down as the others fled out of sight, and then the SEAL officer jumped into oblivion, one hand on the rope, the other holding his rifle. The other SEALs plunged out of the helicopter in pursuit, eight men gone in a matter of seconds. Ethan twisted his seat buckle free and launched himself after them, heard the gunfire and the clattering of the rotors above as he clipped his belt harness to the rappel line and leaped out into mid–air even as the loadmaster yelled at him to stay where he was.

The rappel line gyrated wildly in the wind as Ethan plummeted toward the deck, the SEALs fanning out, their rifles firing in a broad semi–circle facing toward the ship's bow. Bullets clanged off the yacht's bodywork as more bullets flew back at them, zipping past Ethan as he slid down the line and then opened the clasp on his belt. He dropped away from the line and landed hard on the deck, rolling forward and bringing his pistol up as he aimed at the nearest gunman hiding on a walkway that lined the bridge and fired.

His shot missed, but the gunman ducked his head and scurried away. The SEALs advanced by sections, sweeping forward as Ethan moved to follow them. Behind him, the Black Hawk's rotors hammered the air and it rose up and away from the yacht, trailing the rappel lines. Ethan checked for Lopez but could see nobody. The loadmaster had probably grabbed her and prevented her from following Ethan out.

The clatter of rifle fire led Ethan forward through the ship. He entered the main cabin, its doors open to the stern, saw two dead gunmen sprawled across the ornate sofas as he made his way forward down a long, carpeted corridor toward the bow. He heard more gunfire, shouts of alarm from somewhere ahead of him, and moved more quickly. There was no time to search the ship, only to stop it and keep it in international waters.

Ethan reached a doorway that led outside to a series of steps with polished chrome grab–rails that climbed up to the bridge deck. He hurried up them, and found another door that led into the bridge itself. He stepped in and came face to face with three rifles.

'Warner, Ethan,' he said.

The rifles dropped as the SEALs now occupying the bridge recognized him and turned away. The officer in command was at the controls but he didn't look happy.

'The crew's neutralized,' he said, 'but the controls are jammed wide open!'

Ethan was about to say something when he felt something hard jam into his back. He turned and experienced an almost supernatural tingle of alarm as he looked into the eyes of a man he had seen lying dead in the stern of the ship only minutes before. Behind him were a half dozen more men, likewise smeared in blood but pointing weapons at him.

Ethan cursed beneath his breath as he backed into the bridge and the gunmen pushed their way in, the SEALs responding instantly but not firing as the yacht's crew moved inside and one of them, a stocky, foreign looking man smiled grimly.

'No sense in shooting us,' he said as he glanced at a GPS screen. 'We'll be in Mexican waters within a minute and you'll all be free to leave.'

Ethan noted the bullet proof vests on the crewmen, and although two members of the yacht's team must have taken hits to the head when the SEALs double–tapped them, the rest were back on their feet, the blood likely fake.

'Shut the engines down,' the SEAL leader ordered, glaring at the crewman down the barrel of his rifle. 'My men could drop you all before you got a single shot off.'

'If that were true, you would have fired by now,' the crewman replied. 'You have no jurisdiction here, and the yacht's controls will not return to us until we're safely inside Mexican waters. Leave, now, or I'll take my chances and put a bullet in this asshole's guts just for the hell of it!'

Ethan felt the pistol jammed harder under his ribs and saw the SEAL team's expression alter, become cold and calculating. Ethan knew that he was weighing up the odds, and he likewise knew that no Special Forces soldier would risk failing the mission for collateral damage.

'Take the shot,' Ethan snapped, and flinched as he started to turn to try to disarm the crewman before he could send a bullet plowing through Ethan's body.

But before anybody could move the yacht suddenly began to slow. Ethan froze as he heard the distant hum of the engines fade away into silence, the crash and whisper of waves flushing past the gleaming hull break up. He glanced at the yacht's controls and saw the engine dials wind down to zero, the border of Mexican waters still a few hundred yards away.

The SEAL commander raised an eyebrow at their captor.

'You were saying?'

Ethan heard the Black Hawk helicopter thunder back in toward them, its rotors hammering the air.

'Reinforcements,' Ethan lied as he looked over his shoulder. 'You guys fancy a crack at two Navy SEAL teams?'

The leader of the crewmen scowled as he saw his men throw down their weapons and put their hands in the air. A SEAL pushed past Ethan and grabbed the pistol from his captor's hands before driving his forehead into the man's nose with a dull crack that sent him plunging onto the deck.

The SEALs quickly locked down the ship's crew, as Ethan looked at the lieutenant. 'What happened?'

The lieutenant shrugged, but another voice answered. 'A woman happened.'

They both turned to see Lopez appear and lean in the bridge doorway, her hands shoved casually into her pockets as she smiled at them. 'While you cowboys were blowing brains out up here, I *used* mine and went down below to shut off the fuel valves.' She tapped her temple with one finger.

Ethan heard the helicopter settle on the stern as his earpiece crackled.

'Ethan, it's Jarvis. What's going on down there?'

'The yacht's ours, but Garrett must already be ashore as there was no helicopter on the landing pad when we caught up with it. I don't think Garrett's aboard.'

'Have the ship searched,' Jarvis advised. *'Maybe it'll turn something up. You both get down to Varginha and speak to Martinez, find out what you can about that island. Hellerman will be in touch soon.'*

'What about you?' Ethan asked, and suddenly frowned as he realized that Jarvis was outside, the sound of passing traffic clear on the line. 'Where are you?'

'Goodbye, Ethan.'

Before Ethan could say anything more, the line went dead.

*

Washington DC

Jarvis climbed into a hire car three minutes after calling Ethan, having tossed the cell phone into a trash can on Sumner Road. His own car had been GPS tagged, a basic precaution that he felt sure General Nellis would have undertaken the moment Felix Byzan had died. Jarvis had quickly taken care of that before walking into a convenience store and purchasing a change of clothes.

He drove out of the car hire lot having paid cash and then used a fresh burner cell to call Lucy Morgan. When she answered, he gave her no time to ask questions.

'Tortola,' he said. 'Get there and wait for me. It's very important, Lucy. Just trust me and do it, I'll explain everything when I get there.'

Jarvis rang off and then dialled another number, this time only getting an answer on the fifth ring, his heart being faster with every passing second.

'Yes?'

'It's done,' he said. 'Can you finish what we've started?'

'*I can,*' came the reply. '*Are they on their way?*'

'We've tracked Majestic Twelve as far as Sao Paulo,' Jarvis confirmed, 'but I'm out of the loop now and headed south. We have agents following them, try to ensure they don't get caught up in all of this. It's all down to you now.'

'*Oh, don't worry,*' came the reply. '*I've waited a long time for this.*'

***

XXXIII

Varginha, Brazil

'Now *this* is more like it!'

Lopez climbed out of the ramshackle taxi and opened her arms to absorb the sweltering sunshine blazing down from a flawless blue sky as Ethan paid the driver, whom they had hired in a nearby village to avoid being tracked in their hire car from Sau Paulo into the town. He watched the cab trundle away with a cough and splutter of oily brown smoke from its exhaust, then turned and found himself looking at a towering silver cylinder that was topped with a gigantic silver disc that looked alarmingly like the classic UFO "saucer".

'You're kidding me?' he uttered as he moved to stand beside Lopez.

'They're proud of their UFO heritage,' Lopez said as she slipped a pair of sunglasses over her eyes and pushed her hair back into a ponytail. 'It's not every day that a small Brazilian coffee town finds itself becoming international news. I think that this monument is actually a water tower.'

Ethan looked around for any sign of Jarvis's contact in Brazil, a man named Rodrigo Martinez, but none seemed to emerge from the listless pedestrians shuffling along the baking sidewalks.

'You think he's running late?' Ethan asked.

Lopez turned a pitying smile on him. 'Honey, in South America *everybody's* running late and nobody cares. C'mon, let's go take a look around, y'know, catch some rays?'

Ethan felt irritation rise up inside him, but then he saw Lopez's infectious smile as she slipped her arm through his and urged him to walk with her.

'You could do with the rest,' she advised as they strolled toward a small market. 'All this stress, being shot at and all, it's no good for your heart and soul.'

'Are you my doctor now?'

'I think so,' Lopez opined. 'Your treatment should begin with a leisurely examination of this market, followed by a soothing lunch that you can buy me.'

Despite himself, Ethan laughed. 'How kind of you.'

'It's all for your benefit,' she assured him as she patted his chest with one hand. 'You'll be thanking me later.'

'I'm sure I will,' Ethan replied.

They were walking through the market place when a man in casual clothes, his features partially concealed by a hat, approached them and moved to walk alongside Ethan.

'I am glad you could make it here,' he said in a heavy South American accent.

'Rodrigo Martinez?' Lopez asked as she peered around Ethan to look at the man and saw the white collar of the priesthood about his neck.

He looked older than in the photographs that Ethan had seen from the original incident, his black moustache now white, his hair gray at the temples, but his eyes were unmistakably the same.

'I must remain incognito if possible,' Martinez said as they walked, purposefully keeping his head down. 'There is a coffee shop, a hundred yards ahead on the right that has a secluded garden at the rear where we can talk. I will go there, please join me in a few minutes.'

Martinez moved off, while Ethan and Nicola perused the wares of a trinket stall in the market place.

'It's been decades since the incident,' Lopez said as they waited. 'Surely he doesn't fear for his life after all this time?'

'We've seen this before,' Ethan pointed out. 'People are scared out of their wits when a close encounter occurs, and sometimes it's not by the extraterrestrials they claim to have seen but by the government soldiers who visit them afterward. This kind of intimidation goes on in every country on earth.'

'But for this long?' Lopez repeated. 'You know what I think that means?'

'Yeah,' Ethan nodded, 'that whatever started back then is still going on. Come on, let's see what he has to say about it.'

They walked together down through the market until they reached a tiny coffee shop, one where they had to descend two steps and duck into the entrance, the building probably as old as the hills that surrounded it. The interior was dark but cool and filled with the aroma of fresh coffee as Ethan followed Lopez between the empty tables that filled the shop and beyond, through a set of open double doors that led into a small, shaded courtyard with more tables.

Martinez awaited them, a small cup of coffee before him on the table and two more waiting, the table shielded from the sunshine and prying eyes by an open umbrella that was larger than the table itself. Ethan sat down opposite Martinez with Lopez alongside him.

'So, what can you tell us?' Ethan asked.

'First, I want you to tell me something,' Martinez said. 'You have come a long way to seek me out and to ask me questions about something that happened here twenty years ago and which people are afraid to talk about even now. I need to know why: why are you here, now? What's happened?'

Ethan sensed that behind Martinez's paranoia and fear there was a shrewd mind, and decided to simply tell him everything that he wanted to know in the hopes that he would reciprocate.

'There have been some reports of small, unusual bipedal creatures in the forests around this area and further south along the Atlantic Coast,' he said. 'We've been sent here to check them out, especially around the island of Ilhabela.'

'From America,' Martinez said, making it sound like an accusation. 'Forgive me, but I fail to understand what interest your great country would have in a little town like Varginha.'

'I think we all know what interests us about this town,' Lopez replied. 'You have a big water tower advertising what happened here.'

Martinez scowled.

'An abomination,' he said, 'the commercialization of something so important that it has turned it into a circus, something to be laughed at over coffee, as though it never even really happened. Do you know that the media says the entire thing was invented by the mayor at the time, to bring tourists into the town? They say he copied what happened at Roswell, as if the two were even remotely similar.'

'And what did happen here, Martinez?' Ethan asked.

'You haven't answered my question,' Martinez replied.

A silence grew in the courtyard, and Ethan knew that Martinez was not about to divulge anything without first knowing to whom and why.

'The truth is we're not entirely sure yet why we're here,' Ethan said finally. 'We have a handful of threads of information that don't seem to tie up, but are all related to what happened here in 1996. We were hoping that talking to you might give us some insight into what's going on.'

'What other threads are you talking about?' Martinez asked, now genuinely interested.

'A missing paleontologist from Montana who found dinosaur remains that apparently scared the life out of him,' Lopez said.

'And media reports of a new mass extinction taking place all around us even now,' Ethan added. 'Something links all of these things and we think that you might know what it is, even if you're not aware of it yourself. We just need you to tell us what happened here.'

Martinez seemed momentarily distracted, as though he were suddenly considering something that he had never thought of before. His eyes seemed haunted as he looked at Ethan.

'I saw it,' he said finally, his voice almost a whisper. 'I saw it while it was still alive.'

'You saw the creature that the three girls saw that night?' Lopez asked.

Martinez nodded, one hand on his coffee cup as though for an anchor to reality as he spoke.

'I was working with the military police,' he said, 'ranked a corporal at the time. We were called to an incident just on the edge of town that was said to be an aircraft crash of some kind. We'd expected to see the fire services or other emergency vehicles on the way too, but there was nothing, nothing at all. It was just us and a handful of military police trucks.'

'The aircraft crash was a cover, then,' Ethan said.

Martinez nodded. 'We never saw anything like that, which is why that damned water tower is such a ridiculous construction: there were no craft, other than a local farmer who reported lights over his land the same night, which I did not see.'

'But you did see the creature,' Lopez pressed.

'We drove into the scene,' Martinez went on, 'and as my men began interviewing the witnesses I followed their directions in the hope of capturing whoever had scared the girls. They were wound up pretty tightly, crying mostly as though they'd seen a ghost or something. I wasn't too worried, but I thought that maybe some drunk had dressed up in a suit and was scaring locals, or similar. Then I smelled it.'

'Smelled what?' Ethan asked.

'Ammonia,' Martinez replied, 'so much of it that my eyes watered and I could hardly breathe. It was as though a hundred drunks had urinated all over the sidewalk right there, but I could see no evidence of anybody else having been there. I drew my pistol at that point and managed to keep moving. The smell got even worse, and then it appeared and ran away from me. I only saw it for a few seconds, but in God's name I swear to you I'll never forget a moment of it in my life.'

'What did it look like?' Ethan asked, trying to remain calm even though his own curiosity was heightened now.

'Like the devil,' Martinez said, 'just like the girls had claimed. 'It's eyes were wide and blood red and it ran in a low crouch, as though it were ducking under a bridge that wasn't there. Its arms were long, three fingered, and it had only a tiny mouth like a slit. Its skin was gray, dirty, and it had no hair or ears that I could see.'

Lopez leaned forward on the table.

'Any chance that it was a child in a suit or something?'

'No,' Martinez shook his head vigorously, staring at the tabletop as he replied but his mind clearly back in that alley decades before. 'The physiology was all wrong, the limbs too long, the head too large, the feet the wrong shape. It wasn't proportioned like a child, and the smell, oh God the smell. You couldn't have got close to it without breathing apparatus, it was that awful. I practically was physically ill when it appeared.'

Ethan glanced at Lopez. 'Maybe some kind of defense mechanism?'

'Like an octopus squirting ink, or a skunk,' Lopez agreed, then turned to Martinez. 'What happened next?'

Martinez sighed, looked over his shoulder as though he was being watched.

'That was when the dying began.'

***

Dean Crawford

XXXIV

'The dying?' Lopez echoed.

Martinez nodded, clearly still disturbed by what had happened all those years ago.

'You have to understand that much of what I'm about to tell you was suppressed by the military and doesn't appear on any official documents in the media or the government. Most of it remains only in the memories of those of us who were there that day.'

'Tell us,' Ethan urged him. 'It might help us uncover what's been going on out here, and if everything else we've heard is true it might help prevent some kind of major extinction event.'

Martinez nodded, aware now that his knowledge affected more than just his own life but those of countless billions of people around the world who had likely never even heard of what had happened in this tiny coffee town deep inside Brazil.

'The key investigator who operated outside the military and was here within days of the events was a lawyer named Ubirajara Rodrigues. I spoke to him on numerous occasions after the event until I was ordered to remain silent by my superiors.'

'They actively muzzled you over this?' Lopez asked.

'Yes, they silenced us all and made it very clear what would happen if we attempted to speak to anybody about the events, which is why I'm so concerned now about speaking openly about this and why I asked you to come here, where observation would be difficult.' Martinez took a breath and went on. 'The basic story that you have already likely heard is true enough: three young girls taking a short cut through a vacant lot on the afternoon of January 20th, 1996, came across a bipedal, humanoid creature that scared them so much they ran almost a mile away without stopping. What you don't hear is that military police had already captured one of these creatures that morning in woods just three blocks away from where the girls had their encounter.'

'There were more of them,' Ethan said.

'Yes, that's why the military police were so quick to deploy for the rest of the sightings.'

'How many were there?' Lopez asked.

'I'm not sure,' Martinez admitted, 'but the sighting in the woods was followed by gunshots, as witnessed by a man who was jogging in the area. He reported seeing soldiers march out of those same woods later with two body bags, one of which was moving about while the other was still. A third creature was reportedly captured that evening in the same area, but I don't have a reliable source to verify that information. What's interesting is that the following April, a similar creature was spotted near the local zoo, and in May a motorist spotted another creature on a highway to the east of town, while a possible seventh sighting was reported in Passos, a city to the north of here.'

'Okay,' Lopez said, 'so we have multiple sightings but that doesn't mean there were seven of these things running around the town, and you've heard of mass hysteria, right?'

'Of course,' Martinez snorted, 'but the details of this case are what make it so different, because most of the initial reports came in independently of each other. Most of the incidents occurred in woods between the Jardim Andere and Santana districts, just east of downtown Varginha. Only a single street bisects those woods, east to west.'

'So what marks this out as special?' Ethan asked.

'Because prior to everything that I've just told you, NORAD had tracked a UFO in the skies over Minas Gerais on January 13th and had notified the Brazilian authorities, who in turn notified the army base at Tres Coracoes, east of town. That morning, an ultralight pilot named Carlos Souza was driving north toward Belo Horizonte, about ten miles south of town, when he heard a strange noise. He figured there was something up with his truck and stopped, got out, and saw a cigar–shaped craft hovering to the left of the highway. He reported windows in the craft, a hole at the front and what appeared to be damage, a sort of crack, down the side from which vapor was coming out.'

'Holy crap,' Lopez uttered, and then blushed before the priest. 'That's a technical term we sometimes use.'

Martinez went on.

'Souza followed the craft in his truck, until it went into a steep dive and disappeared into the woods. He continued to search for it and eventually found the wreckage, which was already being watched over by forty or so soldiers, with trucks, a helicopter, ambulance and several other vehicles.'

'So NORAD actually works with foreign military to capture these things when they land?' Ethan said.

'That's right,' Martinez said, 'and that in itself is one of the most perplexing facts about this case. When it comes to UFOs being sighted, politics apparently goes out of the window. It doesn't matter whether the country you're contacting is friend or foe: they get notified, immediately.'

'What happened to Souza, and how can you know his testimony was true?' Lopez asked.

'Souza was spotted by the troops and hounded out of the site. He fled the area and stopped at a local restaurant to gather his thoughts. Before long, two men in civilian clothes but with military bearing and haircuts confronted him, told him a great deal of personal information about him, and warned him not to talk about what he'd seen.'

'And he just decided not to talk to anybody?' Lopez asked.

'You have to understand that Brazil had spent twenty years under a military dictatorship that had only ended a few years before this event occurred. Most people were genuinely frightened when warned by military figures to stay quiet, and Souza himself had seen family members "disappeared" during the dictatorship. He stayed quiet for many months until he saw an article in a magazine about the Varginha event and realized that the cat was out of the bag and he could speak about what happened.'

'And the couple on the farm who witnessed a UFO, you think that was the same object?'

'Yes,' Martinez agreed, 'most likely, as their description matches precisely that given by Souza. Investigations at the time by local reporters unveiled a lot of military activity in the Tres Coracoes–Varginha area at the time, centred on the woods where the creatures were supposedly found and captured.'

'What about other witnesses?' Lopez asked. 'Are there any reports of people seeing what happened who may also not have been able to come forward?'

'Many,' Martinez confirmed. 'The original spotting of a strange creature came not from the three girls but reports that a wild animal had been spotted near the Jardim Andere district. Here in Brazil, all firemen are members of the military police and one of their responsibilities is the recovery of wild animals. Four of them were despatched to the scene of the sighting and found a man, woman and three young boys standing by a steep bank leading into the woods. They described the creature in great detail, and that the boys had been throwing stones at it to try to get it to move until the woman stopped them.'

'And the firemen reported this, word for word?' Ethan asked.

'All of it,' Martinez confirmed, 'and it was all out in the open before the military could really begin to cover it up. The firemen followed the creature, and it took them two hours to finally corner and capture it, a task made extremely difficult due to the hilly terrain, dense foliage and the creature's attempts to escape. Not to mention the stench of it.'

'Ammonia?' Lopez guessed.

'It was terrible,' Martinez confirmed.

'You saw it again, with the firemen?'

'Yes,' Martinez confirmed. 'Once we had captured the creature I radioed my commander and asked him to join us because, frankly, we were terrified of what we had found and didn't know what to do with it.'

'And what *did* you do with it?' Lopez asked.

'My commander arrived, and with him were a sergeant and two officers in an army truck. The creature was handed over, they left and we were told in the strictest terms never to speak of what had happened again.' Martinez sighed. 'The remaining sightings all followed ours, with several creatures being captured or killed during the course of the day and the following night.'

Ethan leaned forward on the table, his coffee forgotten.

'You said something about people dying?'

Martinez nodded, haunted again now.

'At around 6 p.m, after our encounters with the creature, the town was hit by a violent hailstorm, bad enough that it broke windows and windscreens and caused considerable damage to local buildings. During the storm, a military policemen spotted yet another creature in the Santana–Jardim Andere area near the woods. I was there when one of them was attacked by the creature as it attempted to flee. He died a month later.'

'Marco Eli Chereze,' Ethan said, and Martinez nodded. 'He was infected with something.'

'The autopsy reports were never revealed,' Martinez explained, 'and the military altered official documents to make it appear that Marco had never been on duty that night, even though I myself knew that he had been. But his story was not the only one where the government attempted to cover up what really happened here. One night in the May of that year, four men dressed in dark suits knocked on the door of the Silva home, that of the original three girls who had reported the strange creature in the vacant lot. The men made their way into the house and insisted on talking to the two sisters. The men never identified themselves but spent over an hour trying to persuade the girls to change their story and even implied they would be paid if they made their denials publicly on television. Afraid to object, the girl's mother said they would think it over. The men left but told them not to follow them to try to see what kind of car they were driving.'

Ethan thought for a moment. 'The girls never recanted their story.'

'No,' Martinez said with some pride, 'they remained firm to their story and have done so ever since. Because of the publicity around their sighting, which was the only one that actually made the press, it would have been tough for the government to threaten them or carry out that threat as it would have leant further credence to the girls' story.'

Lopez glanced at Martinez' collar.

'And you?' she asked. 'You left the military and joined the church?'

Martinez nodded.

'I thought that an experience like that might have taken you away from religion,' Ethan said.

'I believe that we are all God's creatures,' Martinez said, 'regardless of which planet we came from. Ultimately, it is up to each of us to make our choices over what we should or should not believe, but the one thing I lost all faith in was my government, the military. They lied, Mister Warner, repeatedly, and threatened those who did not comply. I have no idea whether they ever carried out those threats, but it would not surprise me to find out that they had.'

Ethan sat for a moment in deep thought.

'We're here in part to investigate recent sightings of more of those creatures. Do you think that they're back?'

Martinez shook his head.

'No, Mister Warner, I do not think that they have returned. I think that our government used the creatures that they captured to do experiments, and that Marco Eli Chereze was merely the first victim of those experiments.'

'You said he was attacked,' Lopez pointed out, 'not experimented on.'

'He was,' Martinez confirmed. 'And he died within a month from little more than a scratch. Something in that creature was toxic to us, to humans, perhaps to all life, and something as potent as that would be a powerful weapon in the wrong hands.' Martinez leaned forward on the table, his voice lowering to almost a whisper. 'There is an island, off the coast, where nobody goes. It is said that only death resides there. Fishermen avoid it, and have reported seas filled with the corpses of millions of sea creatures and birds that fall out of the sky, stone dead.'

'Ilhabela,' Lopez said. 'Birds falling dead out of the sky, bee colonies decimated, amphibian decline, it all matches up.'

'You said that there are creatures being seen again, that they're being experimented on,' Ethan said. 'How come they're being seen here?'

Martinez continued to whisper as though his life depended on it.

'They're escaping from that island,' he replied. 'Some of them make it to the shore here and disappear into the forests. The problem is that the forests are constantly being cleared, and the number of places for the creatures to hide are getting smaller. It's only a matter of time before whatever disease it is that they're carrying takes a hold in the population here, and from there…'

Ethan nodded as he realized what Martinez truly feared.

'Extinction level event,' he said.

Martinez touched his finger to his forehead and then both of his shoulders. 'If God wills it.'

Ethan sat back in his chair and glanced to the east, where he knew the endless shores of the Atlantic Ocean stretched into infinity to the north and south.

'This island,' he said, 'is there a way we can get to it?'

***

XXXV

'Oh, not again.'

The coast of Brazil was every bit as beautiful as Lopez had expected, and Ethan could see in her eyes that she was delighted to be working in South America. What she didn't like was the battered looking aircraft sitting on the water before them, its white fuselage shining brightly in the sunlight in a way that helped to hide all the dents and scratches.

'You'd better have a damned good reason for draggin' me all the way down here, Warner! There were babes all along the beachfront in Antigua!'

Arnie Hackett's grizzled head popped out of an observation bubble, one of two that flanked the PBY Catalina's hull. The amphibious aircraft was like a gigantic version of the Icon A5 that Ethan had unfortunately destroyed back in Madagascar, a World War Two vintage airframe powered by two huge engines mounted atop her broad, straight wings.

'You'll get paid!' Ethan called back. 'We both know that your only real mistress is cash!'

Arnie scowled back at him and vanished from sight into the aircraft, which was moored alongside a large jetty and was attracting glances from passers–by both on foot and aboard vessels in the harbor. A Catalina of this vintage was a rare sight anywhere in the world, although Ethan suspected that many of the dents and marks in her hull had been garnered back in the Second World War and hadn't changed since.

'Ethan,' Lopez said politely as she turned to him, 'you recall what happened last time we got into an airplane?'

'Yeah,' Ethan shrugged, 'we got out fine.'

'You landed in a tree.'

'Any landing you can walk away from is a good one. Besides, I won't be flying the plane this time.'

Arnie Hackett stepped out of the Catalina's side hatch and onto the jetty. His vibrantly colored shirt and khaki shorts made him look something of a cross between a dazed, sunburned tourist and a badly disguised foreign agent. Two days' worth of stubble and a crazed light in his eye completed the image of the fearlessly insane pilot for hire.

'Ethan,' he said as he shook Ethan's hand, 'thought we'd seen the last of you in Antarctica.'

'Like a bad penny I guess.'

Arnie turned to Lopez and folded her into his arms, lifting her off her feet as he hugged her. 'Still hanging around with this jerk?'

'Just about,' Lopez replied with a smile as she returned the embrace.

Arnie set her down and folded his arms. 'So, what is it this time? No, wait – let me guess: DIA, no questions asked, money's in my account, nobody can know.'

'Perfect,' Ethan replied, 'shall we go then?'

Arnie raised a hand to stop Ethan. 'Go where, my good man? Details first or you can damned well swim wherever the hell it is you're trying to get to.'

Ethan nodded over Arnie's shoulder at an island barely a few miles away off the coast. 'Ilhabela.'

Arnie turned and looked at the island, then back at Ethan. 'You're pulling my chain. I could swim that far.'

'The island is well protected by security personnel,' Lopez explained. 'They monitor the beaches and keep an eye on all access routes into the interior of the island to prevent anybody from getting too close.'

Arnie frowned. 'And you think that me landing this great thing alongside the beach is going to sneak you in without being noticed? Wow guys, you intelligence operatives are really on your game these days.'

'It's the distraction we want,' Ethan said. 'The Catalina gets attention, and while everybody's looking at you, including those monitoring any cameras set up on the island, we'll be making our way up the cliffs out of sight.'

Arnie stared at Ethan. 'You made me fly a couple of thousand nautical miles to give you a lift to an island a dozen miles away, as a *diversion?*'

'Nobody knows how to showboat like you, Arnie,' Ethan said by way of an explanation. 'Oh, and by the way, we don't have passports or visas as technically we both died yesterday in an aviation accident in Madagascar.'

Arnie peered at Lopez, who nodded and shrugged. 'What happened to the plane?' he asked.

'It's seen better days,' Lopez replied.

'Come on,' Ethan said as he walked past Arnie and clambered through the hatch into the Catalina's interior. 'The sooner we get this over with, the sooner you can get back to Antigua and watch the sunbathers roast.'

Arnie muttered something under his breath as he followed Ethan into the aircraft and lumbered his way toward the cockpit. Lopez boarded after him, and Ethan untied the aft mooring lines before he hauled the boarding hatch closed. The interior smelled of metal, old leather and grease, the accumulated scents of seventy years of continuous operation. Arnie clambered up onto the Catalina's nose and untied the bow mooring line, hauling it in before he climbed back into the cockpit in time for Ethan to appear.

'I've got a bad feeling about this,' Arnie muttered as he began strapping in.

'You have a bad feeling about everything,' Ethan replied.

'Where's the location on the island you're trying to get to?'

Ethan handed Arnie a satellite photo of the island, a small white cross demarking the spot where the facility was believed to be located.

'Right about there,' he said, 'which means the best place for you to drop us off would be somewhere around here.'

Ethan pointed at the map to a series of cliffs to the south west of the marker.

'And the small matter of how you'll be getting out?' Arnie asked.

Ethan pointed to a low ridge of hills that curved around the southernmost tip of the island, ending in cliffs that soared above the ocean waves.

'That spot there is a weak point in their defensive line,' Ethan said. 'It's unlikely that they'll have troubled themselves to install cameras on the cliff face as it would be impossible to mount the cliffs from a boat on the surface, the rollers there are much too rough and dangerous.'

'But leaping onto a cliff from an airplane sounds fine to you?'

'We'll parachute out the hatch and make for the cliff face,' Ethan explained. 'The cliffs will shield our jump if you fly low enough, and you'll pop back into view of the beaches and cameras as though nothing has happened.'

Arnie rubbed his temples with one hand. 'You're insane, you know that?'

'You got any better ideas?'

'Stay here and get drunk?'

Ethan patted Arnie on the shoulder and made his way back through the airplane as Lopez strapped herself into a seat.

'We could be dashed against the rocks,' she complained as Ethan joined her, 'or washed out to sea.'

'The wind blows from sea to land during the day,' Ethan explained, 'and the greatest turbulence along a cliff will be at the top as that wind is forced up the cliff face and then rolls over in a vortex when it breaks free at the top. We'll be fine as long as we get a decent foothold on the cliff face. You got the climbing gear?'

Lopez showed him a bag full of lines and metal hooks and braces as Ethan strapped in and the Catalina's engines burst into life one after the other, the fuselage suddenly alive with noise and vibrations.

'Then we're good to go,' Ethan shouted over the cacophony of roaring cylinders and spinning propellers.

The Catalina turned to face out of the bay and into the wind, the engines roaring as Arnie accelerated the big old airplane and the waves thundered beneath the hull before she lifted off, white vapor billowing from her hull and outriggers as they folded up into place.

Ethan peered out of the large bulbous viewing ports as the bay dropped away from them, Arnie keeping the Catalina low over the waves as they flew out of the bay and toward the hazy looking island crouched low on the ocean horizon. Although the island could be visited by tourists, they were in the off season and there would be few people who would have ventured out so far from the mainland.

The number of yachts and boats dwindled as they flew until there was nothing but the vast expanses of the ocean all around them, a handful of wispy white cumulus clouds reflected on the glassy surface below.

'We're coming up on the island,' Arnie yelled from the cockpit. 'If you want, I can fly straight at the cliffs when you jump – you'll stick better that way!'

Ethan grinned tightly and stuck two fingers up at the pilot as he and Lopez unstrapped and made their way across to the Catalina's side door. Ethan steadied himself and then hauled the door open, a brisk wind buffeting into the aircraft as it descended low over the ocean and the island suddenly swept into view.

The shores were dense jungle, sweeping beaches and a couple of small, crumbled jetties poking out into the crystalline water that rushed by below as Arnie banked the Catalina to the left and followed the shoreline. From the beaches rose cliffs, and as Ethan watched he saw a series of saw–tooth rocks poking out from the sea near the shore, the perfect marker.

Ethan clipped his cord to a rail line on the fuselage wall, tucked his hands across his chest and prepared himself, Lopez mirroring his actions alongside him.

'Go, now!' Arnie yelled.

Ethan took a deep breath and leaped from the Catalina. He tumbled out and the cord yanked his parachute open as he hit the slipstream, the aircraft's hundred forty knot airspeed opening the chute violently. Ethan was swung high as the chute billowed open with a thunderous crack and he grasped for the control handles as he saw Lopez's chute blossom open nearby.

The Catalina's thundering engines faded into the distance to be replaced by the crash of waves on the shoreline below as Ethan turned his parachute toward the cliffs and sought a place to grab hold. The buffeting wind carried him swiftly in, barely fifty feet below the cliff tops, and he swung in toward a broad ledge.

The rock face loomed up and Ethan hauled down on his handles, bringing the parachute almost to a halt before the cliffs. The updrafts hauled him upward for several seconds until the parachute caught on the cliffs and the lift spilled from it as Ethan's boots touched down on the slim ledge, barely twelve inches deep but running for tens of yards across the cliff face.

Ethan released the handles and grabbed for a climbing pick on his belt, swung it over and slammed it into the rock face as with his other hand he released his parachute. The chute rumbled as the wind carried it away and it spiralled down toward the ocean below.

He saw Lopez clambering onto the same ledge fifty yards away and a little higher, and her own chute spilled away toward the waves crashing into the rocks far below.

Satisfied that she was safe, Ethan grabbed hold of the nearest secure rock, tested it, and then pulled his pick from the rock and swung it higher as he began scaling the cliff while forcing himself not to look down.

***

XXXVI

The dense jungle was a far harsher environment than Ethan could possibly have imagined, even the undergrowth so deeply entwined that progress was almost impossible. Swamps to the left and ahead prevented any passage to the south or west, forcing him to hack his way through the jungle on a north–easterly course in the hopes of intercepting one of the game trails that led toward the facility.

'Hot enough for you now?'

Lopez was just behind him, her olive skin sheened with sweat, her shirt damp and her thick black hair laced with fallen leaves and pollen. She looked for all the world like a sunburned Lara Croft.

'I take it back,' Ethan admitted as he searched for a clearer path through the jungle.

They had scaled the cliffs only minutes before, and immediately found themselves in this harsh and unforgiving jungle. His best estimate at their position suggested they were within about a half mile of Garrett's facility, but that distance could take hours to cross if they were unable to break free from the deep jungle. Ethan could appreciate now why Garrett had chosen this Godforsaken island to host his facility, one with an interior so totally inhospitable to humankind that only the insane or the desperate would make any attempt to infiltrate it.

'Only thing we can be sure of,' Lopez went on, 'is that nobody knows we're here yet. They couldn't have placed any surveillance in here.'

Ethan nodded. 'Even if they had it wouldn't be able to see very far. We'll have to be careful though – if we blunder directly onto a game trail we might be spotted.'

Lopez was about to reply when she hesitated. Ethan caught the tension in her frame and saw the expression on her features, that of a person listening intently. He said nothing as she remained frozen in place for a moment, and then she looked at him.

'A ship of some kind,' she said finally, 'maybe that yacht of Garrett's.'

Ethan could hear nothing above the hissing of the jungle heat and the incessant whispering of insects crawling in their billions through the undergrowth. Mosquitoes buzzed in dense clouds, the entire chorus deadening all sound to him. Lopez, a few years younger, seemed to possess keener senses that he.

'Maybe we're not the only visitors that Garrett's getting today,' Ethan suggested as he tried to listen.

Lopez turned her head this way and that. 'It's passing us by, heading east around the island. Maybe Majestic Twelve are coming here after all.'

'If Mitchell's given them the frights, then maybe this is the safest place for them to be,' Ethan replied. 'They'll think that nobody can get to them here.'

Lopez's features split into a grin that was almost cruel. 'Let's ruin their day then.'

Ethan pushed on through the jungle for another hour before he reached an area of the terrain where the arm–thick creepers and vines began to thin out and he realized that he could see a faint passage through the forest running west to east. He raised a clenched fist to halt Lopez as he surveyed the trail before he reached into his satchel and retrieved a small electronic device that he switched on and aimed at the trail.

The device was designed to detect electromagnetic radiation, a signature of modern electronics. He slowly scanned the forest ahead, ignoring the buzzing insects and the intense heat as he searched for any sign of surveillance equipment within the device's range.

'It's clear,' he whispered as he slipped the device back into his satchel and they moved forward together onto the trail.

The island was host to many species, but none of them were much larger than a dog. The trail was faint but discernible beneath the dense foliage, and it carved an unerring path to the east through the ancient jungle.

'Why is it that you think a trail like this will lead us directly to the facility?' Lopez asked as they walked slowly along the trail, relieved to be free of the denser jungle surrounding them.

Ethan replied quietly, his voice a whisper as they moved.

'Trash. Wherever you find people you'll find their rubbish, and scavenging animals will always make a beeline for what we leave behind. Garrett's facility is legal and doesn't need to be concealed, so he won't have to worry about burning waste here. My guess is that it's compacted and shipped out on a regular basis. Follow a game trail headed east, and we should end up finding the facility.'

'And all the other trash,' Lopez replied. 'Not bad, for an old timer.'

'Cut it out, I still give you a run for your money on a daily basis.'

'More of a jog, really.'

'There's something up ahead.'

Ethan crouched down in the jungle and noted from hanging leaves that they were downwind of the facility, which could by now only be a few hundred yards away at the most. Something had moved against the deep greenery of the forest, something that to his eye didn't quite belong there.

Lopez moved alongside him, instinctively detecting his own caution as they crouched together and waited in silence. Ethan had done this many times before during his training with the Marines, waiting out for another person, perhaps a potential target, to get bored first and move, thus exposing their position. Given enough time, any human being would throw caution to the wind unless specifically trained to do otherwise, even if their lives depended upon it. Ethan had shot and killed at least three Taliban insurgents during his time with the Marine Corps as a result of their lack of patience and training to...

Something moved ever so slightly ahead of them in the jungle. Ethan squinted, unable to pick out its lines against the backdrop of the jungle. It was well camouflaged, perfectly almost, the dappled light reaching the jungle floor merging with black and gold fur, and suddenly Ethan's brain resolved the scene before him and he gasped softly.

The leopard paced silently away from them through the jungle, the fortuitous direction of the wind preventing the predator from detecting their scent and the easier passage on the game trail having silenced their approach.

'Did I just see that?' Lopez whispered.

Ethan nodded slowly. 'What's Garrett doing out here on this island?'

'More to the point,' Lopez replied as she looked over her shoulder into the jungle behind them, 'what the hell else does he have wandering around out here?'

Ethan moved cautiously forward as he replied.

'It's no wonder people won't come to the island. Anybody who did might not have made it back. Whatever he's hiding out here, it's not good.'

Ethan slowed as he saw more objects before him in the jungle, and this time he caught a glimpse of what could have been geometric stone, stark in contrast to the elegant sculpturing of nature's freehand. He slowed again, crouched down as Lopez joined him and they finally got their first look at Garrett's facility.

The entrance had the appearance of a bunker not dissimilar to the one they had visited in Norway, a large angular concrete entrance protected by large blast doors and a couple of smaller access doors to either side. Surrounding the entire entrance were ranks of razor wire fence, and Ethan could see cameras mounted on posts inside the fences, too far away to be tampered with, as well as ranks of powerful lights that he presumed would illuminate anything detected moving close to the entrance.

A single dirt road led to the security fences, where the double rows were fitted with sliding sections to allow vehicles in and out.

'No easy way in or out of there,' Lopez observed. 'My guess is that's the only door. Odd that there are no guards, though.'

'There won't be a rear section,' Ethan agreed as he looked at the structure of the entrance building. 'It looks like it descends downward, so most of what he's got in there is probably underground.'

'So, how do we do it?'

Ethan smiled at her casual assumption that, one way or another, they'd find a way in. However he did not have the slightest idea how they could possibly sneak past the cameras, fences, light sensors and whatever else Garrett might have set up to deter intruders. He was only certain of one thing.

'If those creatures that were seen in Varginha were something to do with this facility then they must have escaped somehow. If they were able to get out...'

'Then we can get in,' Lopez nodded slowly. 'If it's an underground facility it must have ventilation, and I don't see any vents on that entrance.'

Ethan scanned the surrounding forest thoughtfully. 'Maybe they built the vents somewhere out in the forest away from the main entrance. Metal grills would stop animals getting inside, but they wouldn't necessarily stop some kind of intelligent humanoid from getting out.'

Lopez led the way, pushing off into the forest, but before she took a single pace Ethan grabbed her arm.

'Wait,' he whispered.

A whispering sound reached their ears, and Ethan watched as from further down the dirt road he saw a flash of sunlight on metal. As they crouched, he saw three jeeps driving toward the facility, each leaving a plume of golden dust from the track behind them as they drove.

Ethan watched as the jeeps rolled by toward the facility, the fences opening automatically, and he saw immediately the men sitting in the jeeps. Most wore suits, expensive ones, and all were middle–aged or older.

'That's Majestic Twelve!' Lopez gasped under her breath as she saw the passengers in the vehicles rumble past and go through the entrance gates.

Ethan had never before directly laid eyes upon the cabal that they had hunted for so long. Now, he was surprised to find himself somewhat underwhelmed. In his mind they had taken on a sort of demi–god status, untouchable men, surrounded by ranks of powerful politicians and governments, unreachable by ordinary men. Now that he saw them, he finally saw them for what they truly were: just men, and mostly old men at that. Without their protective shield of money and influence, they were as weak as Victor Wilms had been.

A final jeep entered the compound, this one filled with six security guards that Ethan took to be the personal escorts of Majestic Twelve. As the vehicles came to a halt, Ethan counted the suits and allowed himself a grim smile.

'Only ten of them,' he said to Lopez. 'Mitchell's been hard at work.'

'Yeah,' Lopez said, 'and he won't want to miss an opportunity like this. If he knows that the entire cabal is right here on this island he'll move heaven and earth to get here and take them all down at once.'

Ethan felt himself galvanized as he nodded.

'And we're not going to let that happen,' he replied. 'I want those bastards rotting in a cell for the rest of their lives, not being switched off in the blink of an eye by a bullet to the brain. C'mon, let's get in there and finish this.'

Lopez held his forearm to stop him.

'General Nellis,' she said. 'He'll need to know that MJ–12 is all here at once.'

'And do what?' Ethan asked. 'Garrett hasn't committed any crime because we haven't proved his involvement in anything illegal. Nellis can't send a team in here unless he's got a damned good reason to infiltrate the borders of an allied nation and arrest ten of the most powerful men on earth.'

Lopez bit her lip. 'We could call him now and then hope that we can pin something on Garrett by the time they get here.'

Ethan smiled. 'That's Mitchell talkin' right there, or maybe even Jarvis. No, we can't afford to let these men walk out of here. We get the evidence we need and then we call in the entire Air Force, Navy, Army and Marines if we have to, but we don't do it until we're ready.'

'And what if they leave before we manage that?' Lopez protested.

Now, Ethan's smile grew wider.

'Who said anything about letting them leave?'

***

Dean Crawford

XXXVII

The heat was unbearable.

One of the hardest things to do in extreme environments is to maintain focus when all the human mind wants to do is try to deal with the discomfort and find a way to endure it as best as possible.

Aaron Mitchell lay on his front amid a dense thicket of ferns, looking down toward the compound. The gentle rise of the slope behind Garrett's facility provided a natural vantage point, and Mitchell had known that his only real chance of success lay in his ability to enter the facility without being seen. It also was dependent on his ability to endure the insects, snakes, mosquitoes and other horrors that inhabited this island, and survive them long enough to gain an opportunity to infiltrate the compound.

Although surrounded by razor wire, cameras and lights, Mitchell had already identified weaknesses in the compound's defensive structure. The movement–sensitive lighting had sensors that faced only out toward the jungle. This was often done to allow defensive troops to move freely without tripping the lights, ruining their night vision and exposing their position to enemies that might lay in wait in the jungle. However, it also meant that if anybody *were* able to get inside the compound, they too could move without detection. Mitchell had been positioned in his laying–up point for almost forty eight hours, and though his muscles and weary bones ached for release from their torture he remained silent and still, poised like a coiled cobra for the perfect moment to strike. Mitchell could imagine a fairly sizeable armoury inside the facility, with plenty of ammunition should any defenders require it, although strangely he had seen no guards. He had quickly discarded any thoughts of a full–frontal attack, and instead opted for stealth and patience.

The jungle played tricks on his mind, the dense canopy above and the heat sending him back decades. Mitchell was reminded of his time in the Vietnam conflict, and during his silent vigil had often looked over his shoulder for the reassuring presence of a platoon commander who was no longer there, momentarily forgetting his place in time and space. The long hours forced the brain to make its own entertainment, shockingly vivid hallucinations drifting before Mitchell's very eyes as he lay in silence in the jungle; his mother, washing dishes near a massive tree; his father, driving past on the dirt road to the east and waving from the window of his old Chevy. Sometimes he thought he saw Viet Cong soldiers crouching in the shadows, watching him with predator's eyes, and once he'd seen a leopard stroll by not fifteen yards from where he lay, had even heard its growl. He was busy thinking about the animal when a flash of metal caught his eye and he looked up to see three jeeps approaching the facility.

The fences and gates opened automatically, the jeeps entered the compound, and Mitchell's eyes widened as he watched the entire cabal of Majestic Twelve exit the jeeps. Ten men, all of them matching the faces in the image that he had carried with him for so long. Felix had been right: the meeting here was not just important, but enough so for MJ–12 to all be in the same place at once. The last time it had happened, more than six months before, the Director of the FBI had died as these men had watched and laughed, Victor Wilms among them.

Mitchell calmed himself by force of will. Now, the game was truly afoot. He knew that he could not afford to miss this opportunity, that indeed he would be willing to risk everything for one decent shot at these men with any weapon on automatic fire. His long–cherished dreams of hunting them one by one and prolonging their deaths as he had done Felix's vanished as he saw the chance to cleanse them as one by fire.

The jeeps remained parked near the facility entrance, their roofs just visible on the far side of the facility entrance to Mitchell from where he lay. As he watched, two of the guards disappeared from view as they accompanied the cabal inside, leaving four outside to guard the jeeps.

Mitchell wasted no time.

He pulled from a Bergen lying beside him in the foliage a weapon that resembled a crossbow. Installed upon it was an arrow made of titanium with a steel core, its tip barbed, extremely strong and with enough mass to create considerable momentum. Attached to the rear of the arrow was a five hundred pound rated para–cord, the other end of which was secured to a tree limb ten yards behind Mitchell in the forest.

He raised the crossbow, took careful aim, and fired.

The titanium arrow rocketed across the open space between Mitchell's hideaway and the rear of the facility entrance. The arrow hit the concrete surface and buried itself six inches into the wall, its barbed head lodging itself firmly. Mitchell turned around and grabbed a greased leather strap from his Bergen, looped it over the line and locked it in place. Then he stood, reached around and pulled another line that ran through a simple pulley driven deep into a tree trunk to his right.

The line stiffened as he increased the tension and then locked it in place, the leather strap now inches above his head. Mitchell slung his weapons across his shoulders, turned and grabbed the overhead line, then pulled on it as he picked up his legs and sailed down the line, his feet brushing the foliage until he swept out of the forest, the gentle incline dropping away from him.

The line was silent, the grease helping both the strap to slide and reducing both friction and noise as Mitchell glided down the line toward the roof of the entrance. The motion sensors nearby were aimed at the forest floor, not in mid–air where passing bird life would set them off too often to be of any use. He glided over the fences and hoisted his boots up to slow his approach onto the roof.

Mitchell had originally planned to drop directly down into the compound at night and stealthily kill any guards one by one, but now there was no time to waste. He could not know how long MJ–12 would remain in the facility, and the only way to ensure that he could kill them all was to ensure that they could not leave.

Mitchell's boots landed against the wall of the entrance and he clambered quietly up onto the roof. He turned, unclipped the wire from the arrow's tail with a slice of his knife and watched the high–tensile line recoil away from him with a soft whiplash noise, carried far over the fences once again. Then, he reached down and twisted the rearmost half of the arrow's shaft. Deep inside the concrete, the barbed arrowhead was unscrewed and Mitchell pulled the shaft out, leaving only a small hole in the concrete to betray that he had ever been there.

He rolled over once more, out of sight on the surface of the roof, and pulled an AR–15 Armalite rifle from over his shoulder, the weapon fitted with a SWR Octane suppressor. Although the suppressor was not the kind of device capable of silencing a weapon as people saw in the movies, Mitchell knew that the concrete walls of the entrance would likely be able to prevent anybody deep inside from hearing the shots.

He quietly positioned himself near the front of the entrance, and waited.

The four guards reappeared in less than fifteen seconds. Mitchell rested the rifle's tripod on the surface of the roof and slowed his breathing as he watched the four guards fan out before him, two to the left heading for the gates, two to the right heading for the guardhouse.

Two breaths, slow, measured.

Mitchell selected the two guards heading for the guardhouse, settled the AR–15's iron sights on one of the soldier's backs, and fired once. The bullet impacted with an audible thud into the man's back and his body arched backward as his hands flew into the air in shock and he began to fall. Mitchell fired the second round even before the first man's knees had hit the ground, striking his companion in the upper chest as he whirled to bring his weapon to bear as he heard the gunshot that had killed his colleague. Mitchell saw the round exit the second guard's chest at a different angle to that which it had entered, the bullet striking the dusty soil ten yards to the soldier's right.

Mitchell switched aim as the other two guards whirled, saw them swinging their rifles to bear but initially unable to spot him concealed on the building's sloping roof, only his head and the barrel of the rifle visible, both well camouflaged against the backdrop of forest on the rising slope behind him.

Mitchell fired a third round and saw the guard hit in the shoulder, his rifle firing high and left as he staggered backwards. Mitchell could see that he was hit but not down as he flicked the AR–15 to the right as he saw the muzzle flash from the final guard's weapon as he spotted Mitchell's position and fired.

Mitchell squeezed the trigger even as a clatter of bullets smashed into the concrete roof and sent clouds of stone chips spraying across his face amid a cloud of cement dust. Mitchell squinted behind the clear eye protectors he wore, fired again and saw the gunman collapse as a round passed through his chest and pierced his heart, killing him instantly.

Another salvo of shots hammered the roof as the remaining standing guard fired at Mitchell as he tried to run back toward the entrance. Mitchell dropped the AR–15's barrel to the guard's running boots and released his grip on the weapon as he switched to automatic fire and squeezed the trigger. The AR–15 shook as it fired three rounds in quick succession, the first missing the guard's running boots, the second striking him low in the belly, just above the groin, and the third plowing through his left shoulder and down through his chest as he stumbled.

The guard tumbled onto the ground and sprawled there, his eyes staring lifelessly up into the hard blue sky as Mitchell aimed back at the other guards, two of whom were groaning and one of whom was crawling toward the guard house, dragging himself with his one good arm.

Three more rounds cracked the jungle's silence and the men stopped moving permanently. Mitchell scrambled to his feet and threw the AR–15 over his shoulder as he grabbed the edge of the roof and swung himself over and down before dropping ten feet to the ground. He landed hard and rolled to take some of the impact, but the toll on his ageing body was more noticeable now than ever and he winced as pain bolted through his ankles and knees.

Mitchell crouched for a second, regaining his breath and checking for any sign of life before he hurried across to the dead guards and dragged their bodies out of sight alongside the entrance building's walls. He pulled a pair of 9mm pistols from the belts of two of them, checked the magazines and then stuffed them beneath his shirt before he turned his attention to the entrance building's doors.

Both were heavily armored, far too tough to blow through and he wouldn't have wanted to alert anybody inside the building with explosives anyway. Plus, he needed to be fast: it was only a matter of time before somebody inside the building noticed the absence of the guards at their posts and raised the alarm.

Mitchell searched the guards' bodies and found what looked like some kind of pass–key, a piece of plastic the same shape and size as a credit card. He pulled it from the soldier's neck and then jogged across to the guard house. Inside, a series of simple controls governed the gate motors and two other doors, which Mitchell figured were the two smaller access doors into the facility.

Mitchell swiped the card over the sensors, and a screen offered him several touch–options, one of which was to unlock an access door for thirty seconds. Mitchell selected the option, then jogged back across the compound and reached for the door handle.

The door opened, and Mitchell slipped inside into the darkness.

***

XXXVIII

The vent was small, barely large enough to fit a small mammal through let alone a human being. Ethan stood alongside Lopez and stared at the vent, which was surrounded by vines and creepers but showing signs of being recently altered, reduced in size.

'Well, it was a thought,' Lopez said.

Ethan sighed and turned back for the facility, creeping through the jungle to try to ensure he didn't alert the guards to their presence. He was half way there when he heard three distinct "popping" sounds from ahead and flinched instinctively, dropped onto his haunches as he stared ahead.

'That was gunfire,' Lopez whispered urgently.

Ethan moved cautiously but quickly ahead, until he reached the edge of the treeline and saw the compound before him. Everything was silent, and nothing appeared to have changed, but then he saw the bodies of the four guards lying alongside the entrance building's walls.

Lopez crouched alongside him and peered at the compound. 'Who the hell…?'

As Ethan watched, a large, dark figure emerged from the guardhouse and jogged across the compound toward one of the smaller access doors. He reached out and opened the door, and then slipped inside.

'Mitchell,' he realized. 'Come on, quickly!'

Ethan burst from the undergrowth and dashed across to the fence, Lopez right behind him as he scrambled in his satchel for a pair of bolt croppers and quickly cut into the chain link fence.

'They'll see us!' Lopez snapped.

Ethan didn't reply as he cut a ragged hole in the fence and then shouldered his way into it. The fence folded down as he drove his boot onto it and he broke through and sprinted for the access door into which Mitchell had vanished. He reached out and grabbed the handle and twisted it, and was relieved to feel it click as he eased it open a fraction.

Lopez hurried up to his side, her pistol in her hand as she shot him an enquiring look.

'Time delay lock,' Ethan whispered, 'had to move fast.'

Lopez nodded and aimed at the opening as Ethan pulled the door fully open and she marched inside. Ethan followed and pulled the door shut behind him, closing it carefully and letting his eyes adjust to the darkness within.

A corridor adjoined the main entrance, which was large enough for vehicles to drive through and led onto a small parking lot with four spaces. The fact that the jeeps in which MJ–12 had travelled had remained outside suggested to Ethan that they were not intending to remain inside the facility for long, which was what Ethan was relying on. With only one way in and one way out, he could seal the facility from the outside and keep MJ–12 in place until General Nellis could gain the political leverage to arrest them all.

Only Mitchell's mission of vengeance now stood in their way.

There was no sign of Mitchell, who had moved on past the main entrance and disappeared further into the facility, no doubt moving fast in the hopes of trapping MJ–12 inside the facility. Ethan had half–expected to find the assassin planting explosives all around the exit, intending to bury them in the rubble, but then he realized that nothing less than seeing them die with his own eyes would be enough for Mitchell.

'If he gets to them first he'll take them all out, no matter what odds he encounters,' Lopez whispered as she advanced with her pistol pointed out in front of her.

'So we let him,' Ethan said, following her closely behind.

'I thought you'd agreed that we'd arrest them if possible?'

'I did,' Ethan replied, 'but if Mitchell's going to get to them first then we let him. He'll provide the distraction we need.'

'I admire your confidence.'

'He won't kill them outright,' Ethan said. 'He'll want them looking into his eyes, to know the face of their killer before he pulls the trigger. He's come too far to just blow them to hell.'

The tunnel that emerged before them descended into the depths of the island, a row of lights leading the way into the darkness beyond. The tunnel itself was only about eight feet wide, but otherwise bore a remarkable similarity to the one they had encountered in Norway, that had led to vaults where the world's seeds were stored for after doomsday.

'How many of these places are there?' Lopez wondered out loud, her whisper still echoing back and forth around them.

'Hellerman said there were many vaults, all of them protecting species from extinction,' Ethan said. 'Maybe this was one of them that Garrett bought and uses for his own projects?'

Lopez shivered visibly as she walked, the air much cooler inside the tunnel. Ethan recalled that subterranean structures such as this one maintained much more regular temperatures regardless of the environment outside, one of the reasons why they were so popular as doomsday vaults and nuclear bunkers.

As they walked, a series of revetments in the walls of the tunnel appeared, and Ethan looked into them and slowed, horror creeping up his spine with a cold chill. Lopez moved alongside him, both of them equally silent as they looked inside the coffin–shaped revetments and their gruesome contents.

The figures were humanoid, perhaps four feet tall, with large oval heads and thin limbs. Tiny mouths, no nostrils and large, oval eyes filled with an empty blackness stared back at them, the figures evidently long dead.

'These are what the girls in Varginha saw,' Lopez whispered, morbidly fascinated by the remains. There were almost a dozen, each in its own case like some kind of macabre showroom. 'You think that he's been cloning them?'

'I wouldn't put anything past this guy,' Ethan replied.

He retrieved the satellite phone from his satchel and checked the signal. As expected, down here there was no way to contact the outside world, no means to call in support or inform the DIA of whatever they might find.

'Let me guess,' Lopez whispered as she glanced at the phone, 'we're on our own?'

Ethan nodded and dropped the phone back into his satchel.

'Afraid so.'

*

ARIES Watch Room,

DIA Headquarters,

'Where the hell is Jarvis?' General Nellis thundered as he stormed into the Watch Room.

Hellerman flinched as he emerged from his office. 'I've been trying to reach him for hours but he's not answering. He dropped the GPS tail right after he left the city. We found it attached to a Greyhound bus headed for Canada.'

Nellis followed Hellerman into his office and shut the door behind them. 'Did you tip him off?'

'I haven't said anything,' Hellerman insisted. 'If he's taken off, it's not because of anything we've done down here.'

Nellis sighed, controlled himself. Jarvis was a professional, a man more than used to the machinations of the intelligence community and the procedures used to track felons. He would have likely searched his car for GPS tags, or perhaps switched to another vehicle the moment he got clear of the DIA. Nellis was angry instead at himself, for not taking greater precautions in tracking the rogue agent, and he wondered at himself and whether somehow, secretly, he'd wanted Jarvis to get the hell out and finish what he'd started on his own terms.

Nellis reigned his anger in and focused on the task at hand.

'What about Warner and Lopez? Have you located them?'

'I've got their last known location based on the satellite phone ping,' Hellerman replied as he swivelled around in his chair to give the general a better look at one of his three computer monitors. 'It puts them a quarter mile south of Ilhabela Island, off the coast of Brazil.'

Nellis peered at the island for a moment.

'Connection to their case? Jarvis didn't inform me about any island?'

'It's owned by the Brazilian government, but has been leased for the last eight years to a shell corporation in the Cayman Islands. Garrett is the owner of the leasehold.'

'Some kind of hideaway, maybe?' the director ventured.

'Garrett owns a couple of islands in the Bahamas,' Hellerman said, 'both of which are tropical paradises filled with luxury villas and private docks. Ilhabela, in contrast, is a nature reserve and filled mostly by impenetrable jungle and mosquito swarms. I can't imagine what the hell he would be leasing it for.'

Nellis thought for a moment.

'It's not likely to be anything good,' he said. 'Why not do a check of local shipping companies based in Brazil, or even here in the United States, that might have done supply runs of any kind down there. If Garrett's got something on that island, it would have required building materials, manpower, everything. That stuff doesn't get spirited into existence out of thin air.'

Hellerman complied immediately, his fingers rattling across the keys as he sought answers to questions that were forming rapidly in his own mind. Moments later, a series of shipping manifests appeared on the screen.

'Daeyong Industrial,' he said, 'a Korean shipping firm, delivered multiple consignments of building materials to a dock on the Brazilian coast eight years ago, all of which were subject to import taxes and are on the record. Those consignments were then privately shipped off-coast, but the work was done without any official paperwork other than that signing the goods over to the owner. The company doesn't appear on any US records, so it's probably another shell.'

Nellis drew a hand down his jaw.

'Okay, pull up satellite images from before the dates of the materials being signed away, and then images from two years' later.'

Hellerman accessed the National Reconnaissance Office archives and pulled up the respective images before placing them side–by–side on his screen. The general leaned in close for a moment, and then pointed at a small patch on the island.

'There,' he said, 'that area's been cleared in the intervening period.'

Hellerman nodded and zoomed in on the area. 'Looks like a small track was cleared also, leading in from the west coast, but there are no docks or jetties.'

Nellis stared at the screen for a long moment.

'We're sure that Garrett is behind all of this?' he asked. 'He's controlling the creation of this plague?'

Hellerman nodded. 'Garrett is the only person on earth right now who has the technical skill, the independent financial power and a suitably psychopathic determination to follow his plan through. If that facility on his island really is a bunker of some kind, then you can bet your life that it's the only safe place on earth right now, and he's hiding there with the entire cabal of Majestic Twelve. What are the chances they're just visiting for tea and cakes?'

Nellis drew in a deep breath that inflated his broad chest as he stood up and considered the only likely reason for the cabal retreating to what was in effect a nuclear bunker.

'They're hiding from the coming extinction,' he said finally, 'and Garrett's about to launch his pandemic.'

'We need to cut him off, now,' Hellerman said, 'blast him to hell if we have to. There is no defense on earth for the disease that was spreading in Madagascar, and it was only the limited area of the infection that allowed it to be napalmed out of existence. If it gets out completely, everything dies.'

Nellis knew that he had absolutely no choice in the matter now, and that he had sufficient evidence to connect Garrett to the outbreak on Madagascar. If he didn't take what he had to the administration now, while MJ–12 were within reach, it could take decades to arrest and imprison each of them.

Likewise, he could not stand by and hope that somehow Ethan and Nicola would get inside the facility, defeat the armed guards there, overpower and apprehend Majestic Twelve while also preventing the spread of a sickness that would likely kill them within hours on infection anyway.

Nellis would have sent in the Army, Navy and Marines all at once but he knew that there was no time left for a major invasion of the island that would only alert Majestic Twelve and perhaps force them to release the contagion immediately. If it were capable of airborne transmission, then the mission would fail and humanity might not survive the consequences.

Nellis rested a firm hand on Hellerman's shoulder and squeezed it briefly before he turned away for the door. He got only a couple of paces before Hellerman got out of his chair.

'Sir? Lopez? And Ethan?'

Nellis hesitated at the door, but he did not look back at the scientist as he replied.

'We did everything that we could,' he said. 'Keep trying to reach them, but we have to ensure that Garrett cannot release that disease and I can't sideline the White House on this. It's the President's call now. Fire destroyed it on Madagascar – it'll do the same on Ilhabela.'

***

XXXIX

Samuel Kruger followed the two armed escorts down the long steel tunnel, which was lit with overhead strips that cast a harsh white light around them as they walked, their polished shoes clicking on the metallic plating that lined the floor.

Kruger had installed his own apocalypse bunker back in the states many years before, concerned about the rise of the Kremlin and its power–hungry former KGB leader. Although nuclear conflict was still considered an unlikely outcome in any new confrontation between east and west, Kruger had learned through long experience that it was best to be prudent when you had no control over the larger forces of the world. It was why people built hurricane proof houses in Florida, homes on stilts on flood plains; you prepared for the worst, and hoped for the best.

That life policy had served him well for decades, but now he felt exposed and uncomfortable. The rush to get here to this facility, buried on a remote and to all intents and purposes useless island off the Brazilian coast had distinctly lacked the care and professionalism normally attributed to any of the cabal's gatherings. Garrett's warnings of the coming apocalypse, however, combined with the loss of yet another member of the cabal to Aaron Mitchell's enraged revenge attacks had convinced some of the cabal that they should step cautiously and accept Garrett's offer of shelter. The trouble was, in being cautious about their own safety they had then travelled here, together, with only the scantest protection and with no back–up plan or means of escape should things go wrong. In short, Garrett held all the cards over Majestic Twelve, and that was something that no individual had ever achieved since the cabal was first formed in 1947. *Nobody* on earth had held power over Majestic Twelve, until now.

The guards led them through a series of steel doors that had been propped open, each of them ringed with inflatable seals. Kruger could see air ducts with filters in place, designed to clean air of pollutants and whatever horrific contagion Garrett had cooked up in this awful place. Kruger's nuclear bunker, and those possessed by his companions, contained many rooms all with plush furnishings, stately grandeur designed to make their confinement as comfortable as possible for many years, decades even. In contrast, Garrett's bunker was stark metal and bare rock, power cables hanging in long loops from the walls between the lights, and the air was cool, cold even.

The guards reached a set of double doors, and opened them to reveal an interior of control panels and seats, much like the command center of a warship or similar, but there were no staff, no bustle of people. Kruger walked in and was strangely relieved to see Garrett standing there waiting for them: relieved, because if he was here then it was far more likely that he intended to go through with precisely the plan he had outlined to the cabal in Dubai.

The nine men behind Kruger followed him in, and the guards behind them pushed the doors closed and sealed them in with a deep boom and a hiss of pressurized air.

'Gentlemen,' Garrett greeted them with an open–armed gesture and a bright smile. 'I'm so glad that you could make it.'

'We've travelled a long way, Garrett,' Kruger replied as he looked around the command center. 'Why are we here? What is this place for?'

Garrett gestured around them to the screens and the terminals.

'This, my friends, is a place where for the last five years great work has been done,' he announced grandly. 'It is here that computers, technology, the Big Brother of all mankind has rooted out the most awful, brutal and dangerous infection the world has ever known and decoded its veils of security and protection. It is here that the cure has been found, the most sacred details of the scourge of mankind finally exposed for all to see.'

Kruger frowned as he looked at the screens and saw images of different areas of the world. He recognized famous landmarks; Machu Picchu in Peru; the CERN nuclear fusion generator in Caradache, France; the US Consulate General building in Hong Kong; and then a final image that sent a lance of concern bolting through his spine.

A buried facility deep in the Antarctic ice, built by Nazi Germany during the Second World War, that only a handful of people in the world even knew about.

'What is this, Garrett?' Kruger demanded.

Garrett stepped down off the central podium on the command center and walked to face Majestic Twelve, his smile never slipping.

'This, Samuel? This is about what it's always been about. This is about the Extinction Code. This is about eradicating the scourge of humanity from the face of the earth. This is about saving the best of people while eliminating the worst of mankind's many, many scum.' Garrett's features turned angry, his eyes cold and hard. 'This is about eradicating those that would bring humanity to its demise.'

A loud crack echoed through the facility and Kruger turned to see mechanical bolts on the double doors twist and hiss as they turned automatically, sealing them inside the room.

'What is this, Garrett?!' demanded one of the men behind Kruger. 'What are you doing?!'

'Saving humanity!' Garrett replied joyously as he stepped away again and strode up onto the platform.

With a swish of a remote control Garrett changed the screens above them, and Kruger saw images of men replace those of the sites around the world. Among them he saw his own likeness, a long range shot taken in Frankfurt years before when he had attended one of the Bilderberg Meetings just outside the city.

Garrett turned to face them and now the smile was completely gone. His features reminded Kruger briefly of a bird of prey, staring with black eyes at its victim, knowing that in moments the predator would have killed it, an emotionless expression of utter ruthlessness that chilled the blood in his veins.

'You lured us here,' Kruger spat.

'At last!' Garrett chirped in delight, the scowl returning again with frightening speed. 'The most powerful men on earth, duped by a mere chemist. Not feeling quite so majestic now I take it?'

Kruger stepped forward. 'What do you want?'

Garrett smiled without warmth, his eyes strangely black in the harsh light.

'It's not what I want, because there is nothing that I could want from an animal like you, Kruger. It's what I *know*, and I know that like rats in a barrel none of you will ever leave this room alive.'

*

Ethan eased his way down the tunnel with Lopez close behind. The harsh lighting created deep shadows as black as night, and the chilly atmosphere suggested that whatever this place had been designed for, it wasn't for a cabal like Majestic Twelve to be luxuriating as the rest of the world died in a horrific plague.

'What the hell is this place?' Lopez whispered, her breath condensing in the darkness and glowing in the faint light. 'It's damned cold!'

Ethan had no answer for her, and so instead he pushed on into the facility toward a pair of sealed double doors that marked the end of the corridor. As they approached he could see closed–circuit cameras mounted on the walls, monitoring the approach and the adjoining corridors that presumably travelled further into the facility.

There was no way that they could avoid being seen by anybody monitoring the feeds, so Ethan abruptly dropped the covert act and began walking quickly toward the double doors. Lopez followed without question, seeing the cameras at the same time as he had done.

A sudden, low growl stopped them in their tracks and Ethan felt a primal fear ripple like a cold lance up his spine.

'I didn't hear that,' Lopez whispered. A rumbling, rattling growl followed, immensely deep and terrifying. 'I didn't hear that either.'

In the dim light Ethan sensed rather than saw something move in the shadows, and that something was frighteningly large and quite some distance away despite the volume of the growl. A hefty thump, muscle glinting in the pale glow from the distant lights, the fall of a foot with hundreds, perhaps thousands of pounds of weight behind it. Ethan involuntarily backed up a pace, Lopez mirroring his movement, and then before them a huge shape lumbered into view.

Ethan was no expert on extinct species, but he knew a carnivorous dinosaur when he saw one. It stood perhaps three meters at the hip, cold yellow eyes like those of a tiger staring it seemed directly at him, ranks of fangs overhanging the lower jaw from a head as long as half Ethan's body. The leathery skin was covered in tiny, fine feathers that were colored with elaborate stripes, its small forearms flexing as it inhaled a rush of air, sniffing at them.

'We don't move, right?' Lopez whispered. 'It can't see us that way?'

Ethan shook his head. 'Won't make a difference even if it were true. It can smell us.'

Ethan recalled the species from a documentary: Allosaurus. Up to five tonnes in weight, voracious hunter and scavenger and a younger cousin of the infamous Tyrannosaurs Rex. It padded toward them, heavy footfalls thumping down onto the cold, bare rocky floor of the tunnel. Ethan could hear its heavy breathing, huge lungs sucking in air and expelling it, and he began backing up the tunnel.

'Now what?' Lopez uttered as she aimed at the huge creature.

Ethan saw her breath condense on the cold air, and then he looked at the Allosaurus looming toward them. Something tripped in his mind and he stopped moving, kept his pistol aimed at the dinosaur's enormous skull but held his ground.

Lopez backed past him but shot him an anxious glance. 'Ethan, *move!*'

Ethan felt his legs go rubbery beneath him as the sheer size of the carnivore became apparent, filling the corridor as it moved closer to him, rippling muscle and swinging jowls, those yellowing fangs cruel and stained with old, dried blood.

'Ethan!'

Ethan stared at the huge mouth and flaring nostrils for a moment longer, and then he lowered his pistol, realizing that the weapon was useless against such a huge creature. The Allosaurus accelerated, lifted its huge head and opened those massive jaws, and with a brief hellish roar it slammed its jaws down on Ethan and clamped them around him.

And then vanished.

Ethan could have sworn that he had felt the breeze from the animal passing him as he peered through one half–open eye and saw the empty corridor before them. Lopez, her pistol still gripped tightly in her hands, moved alongside him.

'7–D technology?' she whispered. 'Like Hellerman showed us?'

Ethan, still somewhat shaken, nodded uneasily.

'That's why there are so many rumors about this island,' he replied. 'Garrett's got carnivores wandering all over it, but none of them were real.'

'How did you know?' she asked.

'Its breathing,' he replied. 'It's cold enough down here to see human breath, but the dinosaur wasn't producing any. My guess is that the leopard we saw was also a projection.'

'So Garrett doesn't have any live dinosaurs,' Lopez said with relief as she walked up to the main doors. 'Good to know.'

The double doors were solid steel, locked in place and with elaborate seals that Ethan assumed contained whatever was within and kept it there. He recalled seeing similar seals at the site in Spitsbergen, designed to prevent external contaminants from getting inside the delicately controlled seed vaults.

'They must be inside,' Ethan said. 'These doors will prevent any of Garrett's plague from reaching them.'

Lopez frowned as she examined the seals. 'This doesn't look right.'

'What do you mean?'

Lopez ran her hand up the seals, stepped back and looked at the doors and their overall design.

'They don't look like they're set up to keep something out,' she said finally. 'They look like they're designed to keep something in.'

Ethan scanned the exterior of the doors and with a shock he realized that Lopez was right. The seals that he had seen in Norway had been on the opposite side of the doors at the seed vault.

'Why would he want to keep something *inside?*' Ethan asked out loud. 'That would completely defeat the object of poisoning the rest of the world and...'

He was about to walk across to a pair of small observation windows alongside the doors when his train of thought slammed to a halt and he stared vacantly at the gigantic doors before them as he considered a new and startling conclusion. He couldn't believe that it was possible, that even somebody as bold as Garret would even be able to conceive of such a brazen and yet brilliant idea.

'What is it?' Lopez asked.

Ethan's mind could barely begin to form words with which to reply, so staggering was the revelation that had just been fired across the bows of his awareness. The reply came not from his own lips but from behind them.

'He's just figured it all out.'

Ethan and Lopez whirled to see Aaron Mitchell standing behind them, his rifle pulled into his shoulder and its wicked barrel trained upon them.

'Figured what out?' Lopez asked, her voice more than a little strained.

'That this is where it all ends,' Mitchell replied. '*This* is the Extinction Code.'

***

XL

Samuel Kruger took a pace toward Garrett, his fists clenched and his jaw aching with fury as he pointed at the scientist.

'What are you talking about?! None of us will ever leave this room alive?! We came here in good faith!'

Garrett's smile returned, rather like the one that great white sharks wore, a permanent toothy grimace that preceded their next meal, their eyes black with soulless fury.

'Good faith,' he echoed softly, his voice carrying remarkably well inside the control room. 'How can a man of your nature speak of *good faith*? Was it not you that ordered the murder of Stanley Meyer, a man who had invented a device that would have made fossil fuels redundant overnight and intended to give it away to humanity for free? Then you buried his fusion cage so that it would never see the light of day?'

Kruger's eyes flew wide and he stared at Garrett for a moment before he replied.

'The device would have been released eventually,' he uttered. 'To hand it over to people for nothing would have been suicide for the world economy.'

'It didn't do the Internet any harm,' Garrett replied, 'when the British scientist Sir Tim Berners–Lee gave us the World Wide Web for free. He could have been a billionaire overnight had he sold the rights, but instead he gave us the information age.'

'The man is a fool,' spat another of Majestic Twelve's members.

'The man is a hero,' Garrett countered calmly, 'and one of the reasons I got into chemistry in the first place. I wanted to do for medicine what he did for computers and for mankind at large.'

'Don't lecture us,' Kruger snarled. 'We saw what you did in Dubai! You're as much a killer as all of us, except that you can't pin a damned thing upon any of us.'

Garrett smiled again, chillingly calm. 'What man in Dubai?'

'The man you had thrown from a helicopter!' Kruger raged. 'Do you think us all imbeciles?!'

Garrett pointed behind them. 'You mean that man there?'

Kruger whirled and felt the bottom drop out of his world as he saw Professor Martin Beauchamp emerge from a small adjoining office, the same man whom he had last seen tumbling a thousand feet to his death in the Persian Gulf.

Kruger whirled back to Garrett, his eyes wide as the chemist spoke softly.

'Only true imbeciles would have believed so easily that I would brazenly hurl a man from a helicopter a thousand feet above the water, wouldn't they?' he asked rhetorically. 'Surely you would not fall into such a category, men of status and power like yourselves?'

'What do you want with us, Garrett?!' Kruger demanded, trying to use bravado to dominate the situation and veil the cold fear crawling like insects beneath his skin.

'I want you to understand,' Garrett replied. 'I want you to feel, for the first time perhaps, how powerless you all are. Everything you have become, Majestic Twelve, is built upon the suffering of millions, billions of other people who are no less human than you. But you don't see them that way, do you? Like politicians, you know that there are too many people with too many problems for you to effectively care for them all at once, so instead you care only for yourselves.'

One of MJ–12's oldest members, a former Senator, stepped forward.

'We can give you anything you want,' he promised. 'This confrontation is senseless. There is nothing we cannot do if we work *together!*'

'Noble sentiments,' Garrett said. 'If only you had applied them to the world at large then perhaps it would not have come to this. If the people, bless them all in their streets and towns and cities, were only to come together as one they would hold more power than any politician, than any government. They could bring down corrupt corporations overnight, transform drug–ridden, gang–controlled ghettoes into paradises within days, find answers to the greatest questions in the cosmos as geniuses lost in the masses are found and brought to their proper glory in universities and colleges instead of living in trailer parks or slums.'

Kruger winced.

'Dreams of Utopia are futile,' he spat back. 'We all know that people cannot pull together like that. Mankind's peace is only ever a prelude and a preparation for war.'

'For some,' Garrett conceded, 'but not for most. Evolution, my dear Samuel, is what drives life of all kinds. Those decent people, the majority of our kind, would shut out the evil and the cruel or would embrace those who suffered mental illness and learn to treat them effectively. To be outnumbered is to be outgunned, and with seven billion or so decent people of all races around the world, the minority of those who would do the rest harm would be as nothing compared to the might of a unified human race.'

'This is a waste of time,' Kruger spat. 'Let us out of here or I'll have you shot.'

'Feel free,' Garrett said as he extended his arms. 'I have already achieved what I set out to do, so long ago.'

Kruger frowned. 'What do you mean?'

Garrett shook his head slowly, tutted. 'Such ignorance and yet you're so used to being feted as the elite, the leaders of great corporations and even countries, yet you can't see what stares you in the face right now. Of all the murders you and your kind have committed, there is one that matters most to me: Montana, 2002.'

Kruger raised an eyebrow. 'Aubrey Channing?'

'Aubrey Channing,' Garrett affirmed. 'He was killed by MJ–12 over the discovery of some bones in a Badlands valley.'

'Channing was a danger,' said another of the cabal.

'Channing was doing his *job*!' Garrett screamed, his voice unnaturally loud in the confined command center. 'Channing was learning about history, passing that knowledge onto others, and you had him killed for it! You took my family away from me!'

Kruger stared at Garrett and the realization hit him square in the face, his voice almost a whisper.

'You're his son?'

Garrett nodded. 'Robert Channing,' he said, softly now. 'It didn't take much effort to fake a suicide and change my name after my parents had both died, given the unnatural way in which my father disappeared. The police did not pursue my case very far, which allowed me to slip away. I somehow knew that he had been murdered and it became my life's work to find out by whom, and why. Why, Samuel, did you kill a man over nothing more than bones in the desert?'

Kruger raised his chin.

'We didn't,' he replied simply. 'He was murdered by a man named Dwight Oppenheimer, a Texan oil billionaire who was searching for the secret to immortality and one of our former members. He believed that he could find the secret to immortality inside the bones of extinct species, bacteria of some kind. None of us condoned the killing, but Oppenheimer had lost his way and died himself a few years later pursuing his immortality in New Mexico.'

'Indeed,' Garrett said, 'as you will here and now.'

'Killing us will achieve nothing,' spat the ex–Senator. 'The world will keep turning just as it always does. Your little fantasy mission will be forgotten, Garrett, and Majestic Twelve will continue on with new men at the helm.'

'Yes, it will,' Garrett replied.

Kruger's eyes narrowed, uncertain of the chemist's response. 'You won't kill us, Garrett, it's not in you. Besides, if you're stuck in here with us then you'll die too.'

Garrett nodded. 'If only that were true. You have perhaps a few minutes left before this facility will be annihilated. I would enjoy them, if I were you.'

Kruger whirled to his escort. 'Kill him!'

The escorts aimed and fired instantly. The gunshots were deafeningly loud and Kruger flinched and his hands flew to his ears as four shots blasted Garrett. As the infernal noise died down, Kruger looked up and saw Garrett still standing before them, smiling calmly.

Kruger rushed up onto the platform and reached out for Garrett. His hand vanished into the projection and reappeared on the other side of Garrett's neck. The chemist smiled at Kruger, even this close his projection seeming impossibly solid and lifelike.

'Did I forget to mention?' he intoned, looking Kruger square in the eye. 'I'm not here at all. Seven–D technology, remarkable stuff, almost indistinguishable from the real thing, y'know?'

'Where are you?!' Kruger roared.

'Somewhere safe.'

'Let us out of here!'

Garrett shook his head. 'Like you let my father live? Like you let Stanley Meyer live? The world could have changed dramatically for the better countless times by now if it were not for people like you, Kruger, and your heinous little band of arrogant, selfish little scumbags hiding behind their money.'

'You're no better than us!' another of the cabal shouted. 'You sold chemicals to corporations for billions, denied the medicine to those that needed it!'

'A means to an end,' Garrett replied. 'I assure you that very soon a series of remarkable independent discoveries by scientists in the field will unleash a wave of new medicines onto the market, all of which will be free.'

'You can't do that!' yelled another. 'You'll collapse the pharmaceutical industry!'

'Oh *no*,' Garrett intoned theatrically, 'wouldn't *that* be a shame? Then we'd need individual scientists to independently develop cures and have them distributed for a fair price to all... What a horror.'

'The plague,' Kruger snapped. 'You created the plague to destroy mankind!'

'I discovered the plague that my father feared,' Garrett corrected him, 'and promptly went about finding the cure. That's what we've been doing out here, far from anybody, so that there was no danger of the infection spreading. As soon as we found the cure we distributed it across the globe, some years ago in fact. There will be no pandemic, gentlemen, for humanity is already immune.'

'That's impossible,' Kruger snapped, 'the plague is supposed to be incurable!'

'Not true,' Garrett said. 'No disease is incurable. Medicine has long sought evidence of cures in the sick, but we took a leaf from scientists inspired to seek cures among the *healthy*. Resarchers from the Mount Sinai Hospital's Icahn School of Medicine studied the DNA of some six hundred thousand people, searching for genetic mutations that could damage them. But instead of studying the people who contracted illnesses, they focused in on people who carried the mutations but did not fall ill. Just thirteen individuals were found, but could not be contacted because of clauses in their contracts. We deliberately broke those laws in the interests of science and protecting mankind, and obtained their DNA directly with their consent.'

Martin Beauchamp stepped forward and spoke softly.

'We joined this information to specimens recovered from a drilling operation by the International Ocean Discovery Program in the Gulf of Mexico that penetrated into the heart of the Chicxulub crater, the remains of the impact site of the asteroid that killed the dinosaurs. The cores we extracted contained pressurized crystals formed in the impact, but also virgin rock from the heart of the asteroid, and in those specimens we found the virus itself.'

Garrett smiled to himself, apparently in scientific pride.

'For the first time, an independent investigation used multi–disciplinary science to match an alien virus with human super–DNA, as it's become known as, and the genetic material held by the Brazilian government of a species captured in Varginha that did not originate on this planet. Those combined resources acted as a sort of Rosetta Stone, enabling us to isolate the virus's weaknesses and a potential vaccine alike.'

Kruger stared aghast at Garrett. 'But Madagascar...'

'A confined outbreak, created on purpose for effect, to convince you of an oncoming apocalypse and bring you here,' Garrett replied. 'Had the Malagasy Air Force not intervened at our bequest, we would have easily shut the spread of the disease down with an inoculation program and a similar firebombing of the local area using private aircraft. Few species were lost, especially when compared to the daily loss of biodiversity at the hands of people like yourselves. *The needs of the many*, and all that. Of course, the disease evolves continuously when subject to treatment in isolation, and eventually defeats the medicine. We found one particularly virulent strain that we could not control, so we kept that one right here. It will be destroyed soon, but not before it's leaked into this control center.'

Kruger shook his head in bewilderment, stunned that he and his accomplices could have been so completely blind–sided by this man.

'So you will murder us,' he said finally, his fury restrained by the helplessness of his situation, 'cause us to suffer whatever horrible fate it is that your disease creates. But others will take our place and they will hunt you down.'

'No, they won't,' Garrett replied, 'it's all in hand. And I will murder nobody. The atmosphere in this room is already filling with the plague we've been studying, which was once brought here by an asteroid collision. The species of extra–terrestrial that were captured here in Varginha provided useful test subjects, despite Brazil's mistakes in allowing some of them to escape over the years. Cunning creatures they are really, although poorly adapted to life in our atmosphere. It also turned out that they're immune to the same plague that could destroy all life on earth, probably picked up due to exposure somewhere in their own evolutionary past on whatever planet they originated. That immunity, a study of human DNA and the growing of living dinosaur bones from stem cells eventually gave us the cure we needed.' Garrett smiled again, folded his hands before him. 'There are ten of you, and only three breathing masks with atmospheric filters suitable for protection against ingesting the plague. Those of you who fail to obtain a mask will die very, very slowly. Goodbye Samuel, gentlemen. Think of my father and all of your other victims as you die here in agony.'

An instant later, both Garrett's and Beauchamp's projections flickered out.

Samuel Kruger turned to his companions. A long, deep silence filled the control room as they stared at each other. Their two escorts likewise exchanged glances, and Kruger saw in them the sudden realization that they were on their own now and that only three people could possibly survive what was coming.

Kruger reached into his jacket and whipped out a pistol even as the two escorts moved to fire upon their employers. Kruger fired first, hitting one of the escorts square in the chest as he then ducked down to avoid the gunfire from the second, the shots clanging loudly off computer monitors nearby as the escort screamed and fired wildly into the men around him.

Kruger saw his fellow members of Majestic Twelve pile into the gunman and topple him to the floor as they fought for the gun. The screams and cries and growls of men fighting to the death soared in primal chorus through the room as Kruger staggered backward from his hiding place and looked about the room.

He saw a mask almost immediately, hanging from a post on the wall on the opposite side of the control room. He dashed across to it and hauled it onto his face, the mask smelling of plastic and dust as he tightened the straps around the back of his head.

The screams and grunts and strangled cries became more furious and several gunshots shattered the air around Kruger as one of his companions picked up the dead guard's pistol and began firing into the backs of his fellow MJ–12 members.

In the confusion and disarray, Kruger hunkered down behind a control console as he saw his former colleagues turn into a screaming frenzy of murderous apes. Some scratched at the faces of others as they fought over the remaining two masks, both of which were sitting in plain sight on a counter across the control room. Others kicked and punched, pulled hair and scrambled over each other in a desperate race to reach the masks.

One of the older members reached the counter and grabbed one of the masks, pulling it over his face. But then a younger man grabbed the mask and ripped it from him, drove his knee deep into the older man's groin and collapsing him in agony as he turned to pull the mask on.

A gunshot and the younger man stumbled sideways and fell, the mask falling from his hand and clattering onto the floor as the gunman stepped over his body and picked up the mask. He pulled it into his face, tightening it as he stepped back from his former friends, the gun pointing at them.

'Don't even think about it,' he growled.

Kruger gradually stood up, saw that a third member of MJ–12 had put on the final remaining mask and was wielding a fire axe he had lifted from the wall. Kruger looked around and realized that there was another axe hanging from the wall nearby, ostensibly for health and safety reasons but most likely put there by Garrett for his entertainment.

The unmasked members of MJ–12 looked at the axe, Kruger's pistol, and he saw them make their decision.

Kruger moved quickly as several of the unmasked MJ–12 members made a dash for the remaining axe. He fired once, dropping the nearest of his former comrades, and then whirled and made for the axe. Kruger ran on legs weak with fear and loathing, heard the scramble behind him as he reached up for the axe, footfalls bearing down on his position from behind as he lifted the axe from the wall and spun on his heel, swung the weapon as hard as he could.

The heavy steel blade sliced through the air and smacked into the temple of a Baltimore real estate mogul with a dull crunch that split his skull just above his ear. The steel swept through his brain as though it were of no more substance than butter before finally lodging half way into his skull, the man's left eyeball slithering from its shattered socket to dangle on glistening tendrils as he collapsed sideways into the wall and slid to the ground with the axe still embedded in his skull.

Kruger fired his pistol straight into the face of the next man, a shipping magnate from Buenos Aires. The bullet passed directly through the man's face and blasted out through the back of his skull in a cloud of crimson blood that splashed across the face of another, who promptly doubled over and vomited at the sight of the carnage before him.

Kruger stepped back, aiming the pistol at the four men remaining without masks in the control room. In seconds, they had killed three of their own with incomparable brutality, the fearsome rage of survival coursing through their bodies. Kruger felt weak and nauseous, blood thick on the sleeves of his expensive jacket, on his hands, the visor of his mask. He saw the faces of the four unprotected men staring at him in horror.

'We're going to die here,' one of them gasped, his face smeared with blood from the gunshot victim.

Then, Kruger realized, the blood wasn't splatter from another victim. The man coughed and a splash of blood spilled from his lips and stained the floor at his feet. The man stared in horror at the marks, and then his breath began to rattle in his chest as he looked up at Kruger with sheer terror in his voice.

'Help me!'

A slither of hair spilled from his scalp as the flesh on his face began to slide as though he were suffering from some kind of stroke. By his side, the other three men began to cough blood as their bodies began to disintegrate before their very eyes.

***

XLI

'What's the Extinction Code?' Lopez asked Mitchell, her eyes fixed upon the barrel of the assault rifle he held pointing at them.

Ethan could see that Mitchell had positioned himself to block their only escape route, and there was nothing in the corridors to either side that would allow them to escape before Mitchell pulled the trigger and perforated them both. At a range of less than ten feet, Mitchell could not possibly miss. The assassin looked at Ethan expectantly.

'I think it's what Garrett's had in mind all along,' Ethan replied to her. 'His plan isn't to make humanity extinct, just Majestic Twelve.'

'Very good,' Mitchell said. 'You know, for a pain in the ass you're a good detective, Warner. It's a shame that it's gotta end like this, with us all stuck down here.'

Ethan felt a pinch of alarm twist his guts.

'We can make it out,' he said. 'All of us.'

Mitchell smiled and shook his head. 'I doubt that, and even if it were possible I wouldn't let it happen, Ethan.'

It was the first time Ethan could recall Mitchell ever using his given name, as though somehow, now, in this final confrontation, Mitchell had finally recognized that Ethan was as much a victim of their war against Majestic Twelve as he had been. In the strangest of twists, they now stood on the same side of the war, and yet remained as opposed to each other as they had always been.

'We can't make them face justice if they're dead,' Ethan said to Mitchell. 'Majestic Twelve must be made to pay for all that they've done.'

'Pay?' Mitchell uttered, all pretence of friendliness gone again. 'Men like those don't pay for their crimes even when they're found guilty. How many senators and congressmen can you think of who have been found guilty of the most awful crimes and yet served meagre sentences before being released? Yet you or I, under the same charges, would spend half of our lives rotting in a prison cell?'

Ethan bit his lip. He knew that Mitchell was right, that the justice meted out to those in power was far less harsh than that delivered to the ordinary man in the street. That it should be so was an injustice in itself and yet few thought to cry out against it, to speak as one in their millions and demand the justice denied to those who possessed the money to avoid it.

'Killing MJ–12 won't get justice for anybody else,' Lopez said. 'They'll simply be replaced by more of their kind. They need to be tried, exposed, have their faces across every newspaper in the world showing people what they really are, who really controls what happens in our governments. You say that the people won't stand up to these kinds of injustices? How the hell can they if it's all swept under the rug out here and nobody learns of what they've done?'

Mitchell remained silent, but Ethan could see his mind working. It was true that MJ–12 would probably never suffer the indignities that other people would for the crimes that they had committed, but it was also equally true that an anonymous death out here would also be an insufficient punishment in Mitchell's eyes, that he wanted to see them suffer.

The sound of agonized cries broke the silence, and Ethan turned to peer into the observation windows. What he saw there chilled him to the bone. Dead bodies littered the floor of the control room. Three men were wearing masks, while four more were clawing at their faces and screaming in agony, the flesh falling from their skulls and their hair spilling from their scalps. Ethan saw their hands starting to come apart as whatever hellish infection Garrett had created tore through their bodies.

'They need to *suffer*,' Ethan pressed his point, 'but for a *long* time. Nothing else will do. This is a horrendous but short pain, and then nothing.'

Mitchell kept his rifle aimed at them, his finger on the trigger and conflict warring in his expression.

'You're defending the people you came here to kill,' Mitchell growled. 'You're defending Majestic Twelve!'

'I'm defending my right to see them locked up for decades,' Ethan shot back. 'To wake up every morning for the rest of my life knowing that their money is gone, their power is gone and that they're rotting in a federal prison someplace. Don't you want that?'

Mitchell hesitated a moment longer, and then slowly the rifle barrel fell and his big shoulders sagged.

'I don't like this,' he rumbled.

'We don't like it either,' Lopez replied. 'But this is the right thing to do, Mitchell. Isn't that what separates us from men like Majestic Twelve? The ability to do the right thing?'

'It's also what gets us killed more often,' Mitchell pointed out.

Ethan turned to the door mechanism and reached down for the release handles as Lopez grabbed a pair of breathing masks from hooks on the walls and tossed one to Mitchell and another to Ethan.

'We've gotta do this fast,' she said as she pulled a third mask over her head.

Ethan turned to Mitchell. 'You got enough explosives on you to blow the control room and vaporize whatever's in there?'

Mitchell slung his rifle over his shoulder and opened his bag to reveal a dense cluster of C4 explosives, all of them packaged for force rather than precision cutting. The assassin pulled his mask on and prepared to toss the explosives directly into the control room as Ethan grabbed the release handles once more.

'Remember, we let the masked ones out, okay? Then we throw in the charges.'

Mitchell nodded once in silence, and Ethan turned and then heaved the pressure release latches over and spun the pressure wheel. Ethan figured that Garrett had created a low pressure environment inside the control room once the doors had been closed so that if the doors were opened again, air would initially only flow *into* the room and not out, keeping the infection inside. The massive doors hissed as Lopez stepped back, her pistol ready in her grip as the doors rattled as the internal locks opened and then they swung open as Kruger and the surviving masked members of MJ–12 tumbled out of the control room.

Mitchell stepped to one side and tossed a handful of charges into the room as Lopez heaved against the door and it slammed shut. Ethan rammed the locks back into place and heard the seals hiss as the door sealed itself once again and the terrible keening cries of agony were shut off. A deep burst of explosives shuddered against the doors, muffled as Mitchell's charges detonated within.

Mitchell reached for his rifle once again and as Ethan turned he saw Kruger move suddenly toward the assassin.

'Gun!'

Ethan shouted the warning as Kruger aimed a small, black pistol at Mitchell. The assassin's rifle swung around, too slow, imprinted on Ethan's mind as moving in slow motion even as he saw the pistol's muzzle flare with bright flame and smoke, heard the gunshot echo through the corridor.

The bullet hit Mitchell high in the centre of his chest. The big man staggered backwards, the whites of his eyes stark against his ebony skin as he toppled over and slammed down onto his back in the corridor. The assault rifle fell from his grasp and clattered onto the ground beside him as his eyes closed.

Ethan hurled himself at Kruger as the tall, gaunt man stepped forward and aimed to put another bullet into Mitchell's skull. He slammed into

Kruger's side and the two of them sprawled onto the ground as he heard Lopez scream from behind him and a gunshot shatter the air once more.

Kruger growled and spat as Ethan wrestled the pistol from the cabal member's grip, twisted it viciously against his wrist until the older man cried out in pain and released the weapon. Ethan jumped up and away from Kruger as he whirled to see Lopez on her knees on the ground, one masked man pointing a pistol at her as the other recovered Lopez's weapon from her grip.

'Don't even think about it,' one of them snarled at Ethan.

Ethan looked down at Kruger, who hauled himself to his feet and glared with malevolent delight at Ethan.

'We just got you out of there,' Ethan uttered in disbelief.

'Worst thing you could have done,' Kruger shot back as he held out his hand.

'Don't give it to him,' Lopez shouted at Ethan. 'Kill him!'

Ethan looked at the two masked MJ–12 survivors, and the one with the pistol took aim at Lopez more carefully. Ethan turned to Kruger and handed him the pistol. The gaunt man took it from him and smiled, his black hawkish eyes glittering with malice.

'Did you really think that I or my companions would bend to the will of little people like you?' he asked. 'You're nothing, Warner, you and your pitiful little band will be eradicated from existence, starting here. We will annihilate you all along with Garrett and everybody else connected to you.'

Lopez shook her head. 'Go to hell, Kruger, it's where you're headed anyway!'

Kruger looked at her and grinned. 'Let her live,' he said to his companions.

In an unspoken gesture of deference they stepped back from Lopez and joined Kruger. The gaunt man surveyed their two captives, the heavy steel doors and the faint screams of terrible pain coming from within as the few members of MJ–12 who had survived the explosive charges died in horrific spasms inside.

'I think this a most fitting end to your project, don't you?' Kruger asked Ethan. 'Buried here, alone and with only this horrendous disease for company. You do know that the filters in these masks will only last a few hours, right, and that sooner or later those door seals will fail once we cut the power to this facility? If there is the slightest trace of the virus remaining…'

Ethan said nothing, not willing to dignify Kruger with a response.

'Come,' Kruger said to his companions as he turned away. 'We'll seal this place and leave them to die down here alone.'

The two other surviving members of MJ–12 turned with Kruger and moved away from the vault doors, careful to not allow Ethan the chance to pursue them. Moments later, they were hurrying away out of sight toward the main entrance.

***

XLII

Ethan whirled and dashed to Mitchell's side, looked down at the big man's shirt. The bullet had punched high in his chest, but then he reached down and ripped the shirt open to reveal a bullet proof vest, the silvery shell buried deep in the Kevlar.

Mitchell coughed and jerked awake, almost took a swing at Ethan on instinct. Ethan blocked the impulsive blow with his forearm and pinned it in place as Mitchell winced at a sudden pain ripping across his chest.

'The vest caught it,' Ethan said.

Mitchell glanced down at his vest, and then his brain re–engaged itself and he hauled himself to his feet.

'Where's Kruger?!' he demanded.

'They're gone,' Lopez replied, 'and we need to find a way out of here.'

'No way in or out except for the main entrance,' Mitchell growled as he reached down and yanked a small pistol from a holster buried in the small of his back.

Ethan saw the weapon and grinned. 'Shall we?'

Mitchell turned and lumbered along the corridor as Lopez and Ethan followed him away from the vault toward the entrance. Ethan could see movement ahead, bright light from outside flaring briefly in the darkness, and then the light vanished and he heard a loud crash as the door was slammed shut.

Ethan sprinted to the door controls and sought a way to open them as Lopez made for the side entrance. Instantly he could see that the wiring was fried, the smell of burning cables in the air and a faint haze of smoke lingering.

'Garrett must have triggered the circuitry to blow after he got MJ–12 inside the facility,' he said. 'There's no way we can open the main doors.'

He turned to Lopez, saw her try the door even as he heard a vehicle engine from outside and then a crash against the side door. Lopez jumped backwards in shock at the impact, and Mitchell pushed past her and tried to open the door with brute force. After a few attempts he gave up.

'They must have backed up one of the jeeps against it,' he roared in fury and kicked at the door.

Ethan turned to the control office and saw a series of screens inside. He hurried in and saw CCTV feeds showing him the outside of the compound. There, he could see Kruger and his two companions back away from the facility and pull the masks from their faces. They threw them down onto the dusty ground, and then Kruger looked up at the camera and waved.

'I suspect you're just the other side of those walls, Mister Warner!' he called, his voice reaching the interior of the facility through speakers inside the office. *'They're six feet thick and according to Garrett they would stand up to a direct hit from a thousand pound projectile, which doesn't bode well for your chances of escape!'*

Ethan heard the two men alongside Kruger chuckle as Lopez and Mitchell joined him inside the office.

'Son of a bitch,' Lopez growled through her mask.

Kruger's voice called out one last time as he and his companions turned to the jeeps parked in the compound.

'Don't worry though! Once we've killed Garrett and taken control of his corporation, we will return here and recover the virus before we ensure that nothing remains of you or this facility. You'll all become a dusty piece of history, Warner, one that nobody will ever know about because we both know that once those seals are blown you won't open the facility doors and risk letting the pandemic out to infect mankind! You're all just too damned nice! Your remains will never escape this place!'

Lopez seethed beside him. 'The asshole's right. If we don't get out of here before those seals fail, we'll never leave.'

Ethan felt futile rage surge through his veins as he watched Kruger turn for the jeeps as his companions climbed into each of them. He was about to search for a button to reply to the men outside, to plea for some sort of compromise as a last ditch attempt to save their lives, when a strange noise burst from the speakers.

Like a rush of waves crashing suddenly against a rocky shore it blazed noisily and then subsided almost immediately into silence. Kruger and his two companions looked up into the sky, and then both the jeeps suddenly accelerated for the gates and left Kruger standing alone in the dust.

Ethan saw terror rip across Kruger's face and he rushed back toward the facility's side entrance once more, his arms waving wide and his voice pitched with terror.

'Open the side door!'

Ethan backed away from the screen as though doing so could distance himself from what was about to happen, and then he saw Lopez's confused expression.

'What was that noise?' she asked.

It was Mitchell who answered, his experiences in Vietnam reminding him of the same noise.

'Fighter jets,' he said. 'The first one recons the target if no enemy fire is expected, and confirms its location.'

'And the second one?' Lopez asked.

Kruger's face appeared on the camera covering the side door, gaunt and filled with horror.

'Open the door! Please, open the door!'

Suddenly trapped outside the only safe place on the island, Kruger had nowhere to hide. His screams soared through the office as Ethan found the speaker button.

'The third jeep!' he shouted. 'Move the jeep!'

Kruger's face stared blankly at the camera for a fraction of a second, and then suddenly the screen went white. In a fragment of time Ethan saw the blast rip the gaunt man's body apart as though he had been constructed from nothing more than dried leaves that had been swept aside in a tremendous gale. A terrific blast hit the compound outside and the entire facility shuddered as it shouldered the explosion. Ethan saw the fences outside ripped from the ground and hurled across the forest, saw the two escaping jeeps hit the gates and then vanish in the fireball as they were lifted and thrown in flames onto their roofs.

The third jeep was lifted off the ground and hurled aside amid the roiling flames as the cameras suddenly switched off and the monitors went blank.

In an instant, Ethan turned and dashed for the side entrance with Mitchell and Lopez alongside him. They needed no words, no sharing of the knowledge that bigger bombs would follow in seconds to entirely destroy the facility. Whether called in by the Defense Intelligence Agency or by Garrett himself, the total destruction of the site was clearly required to prevent the virus contained within from ever reaching the world outside, and they would spare no expense in hitting it with everything they had.

Ethan hit the door head on and it burst open to reveal a terrific firestorm tearing through the jungle around the site, columns of flame and smoke twisting up into the air. Ethan kept the mask on as he dashed through the searing inferno, felt the pain of the heat searing his skin as he sprinted directly south toward where he knew the fences had once been.

Mitchell followed, Lopez alongside him as they ran through the terrible flames and smoke, plunged into the jungle undergrowth and plowed through the trees and the ferns as they attempted to get as far away from the site as possible.

Ethan ran a hundred paces into the jungle before he ripped off the face mask and hurled it aside, crashing through the foliage and hoping against hope that he didn't collect a venomous snake or spider bite as he plunged his way south.

'Incoming!'

Lopez cried the warning and he heard the roar of fighter engines just a moment later as an aircraft that he did not see thundered overhead somewhere above the jungle canopy and a terrific blast shook the ground beneath his feet.

Ethan tumbled onto the jungle floor and rolled alongside a large fallen tree trunk. Lopez crashed down on top of him as a shockwave blasted through the trees around them and a fearsome fireball lit up the site. Ethan squeezed his eyes shut and rolled protectively over Lopez, threw his arm over her head and huddled down behind the trunk as a blast of heat washed over them on the wings of a ferocious wind. Sharp pain pierced his ears as the infernal roar of high explosives, burrowed deep into the ground from the kinetic energy imparted them by the fighter's airspeed, exploded and churned the earth upward in a blaze of flame and shattered rock.

The trees of the jungle leaned away from the blast and sheets of flame tore through the canopy above, dense leaves shredded by supersonic debris scattering in clouds to fall all around them.

The tremendous noise and heat from the blast faded away, and Ethan lay with his arm across Lopez's head and his ears buzzing. His vision was blurred, his body ached and he could feel little stabs of pain from where tiny pieces of shrapnel had buried themselves in his flesh.

With a force of will he managed to drag himself to his feet, saw Lopez wearily crawling onto her knees, her arms trembling. He grabbed her hand, staggered unevenly away as she clambered to her feet and followed him clumsily through the jungle. They got another thirty yards when the third blast hit, bigger than the previous two, and they both collapsed into the jungle and covered their heads and prayed that they might survive the hellish onslaught.

Ethan's last conscious thought was that Mitchell was nowhere to be seen.

**

XLIII

DIA Headquarters,

Anacostia–Bolling Airbase,

Washington DC

A deep silence had enveloped the ARIES Watch Room for over four days, much of it spent sitting staring at monitors and display screens on the walls as investigative teams from the Central Intelligence Agency, DARPA, the Center for Disease Control and other major government agencies scoured the scorched jungle of Ilhabela.

Hellerman sat in a swivel chair and stared vacantly at them as staff hurried to collate information, some of them former field agents themselves who now liaised with teams on the ground as evidence was collected and data processed.

It had occurred to him that he was sitting in Nicola Lopez's chair, something that he had only consciously realized when he had detected the scent of her perfume. For one brief and joyous moment he had expected to turn around and see her walk into the watch room with Warner behind her, her gorgeous smile and playful bravado lighting up the room, and Hellerman's life, once again.

It had been with great dismay that he had realized the tantalizing scent was instead coming from a thin silk scarf that she had draped over the back of her chair. Hellerman, without conscious thought, had then picked up the scarf and held it to his face and closed his eyes, completely oblivious to the bemused stares of his colleagues.

There had been no word from either Warner or Lopez since the blasts that had struck Ilhabela, a series of no less than eight bunker–busting GBU–14 air to surface missiles delivered by FA/18E Super Hornets of the United States Navy having scoured the site of life in titanic blasts that had rendered the once lush tropical jungle a barren and scorched wasteland. Satellite photographs had revealed that there was, quite literally, nothing left of the facility that Garrett had built on the island. News media were already carrying the official report of a Brazilian Air Force jet that had supposedly crashed on the island after an engine failure, its fully armed weapons igniting on impact after the pilot had safely ejected. The reports claimed that there had been "no loss of life in the incident".

Transmissions intercepted from the island's sensors and NSA satellite imagery had revealed that Garrett, Warner, Lopez, Mitchell, most of the members of Majestic Twelve and a small number of private security guards had been present at the facility when the blasts had struck. The idea that any of those present could have survived such an assault seemed limited in the extreme, but both Warner and Lopez were professionals and they had escaped from equally perilous crisis numerous times in the past. At least, that was what Hellerman kept telling himself. There was just no way that…

'You okay?'

Hellerman blinked awake from his reverie, realized that his eyes were still closed and that he was still clutching Lopez's scarf as though it were an anchor to reality. He glanced up and saw General Nellis looking down at him with a strange expression. Hellerman coughed, sat up and tossed the scarf to one side as though it was a mere irritation.

'Sure, I'm fine. Any news?'

Nellis inhaled a deep breath and Hellerman sensed both the coming of great revelations and great disappointment.

'We just got word from the White House,' the general said, 'which confirms that no trace of whatever extra–terrestrial toxin may have been present at the facility has been found. Investigators have however detected small amounts of such things as sarin gas, anthrax, various acids and other nasty chemicals that might indicate some kind of manufactured and lethal aerosolized contaminant. You got any ideas on that?'

Hellerman's mind ticked over for a few moments.

'It's possible that you could mix together a few real evil concoctions and then spray it over people in a fine enough mix that they wouldn't notice it until their skin started falling off and their lungs began to burn, quite literally.' He swallowed, thickly. 'Have any bodies been found?'

Nellis nodded.

'Eight bodies have been located in and around the site,' he said. 'None have been identified as Warner or Lopez. Forensics are doing their work now, but there's not much left to see and dental records are mostly being used to confirm identities.'

Hellerman looked at the screens as a slim ray of hope appeared through the gloom of his depression.

'At least ten members of Majestic Twelve walked into that facility,' he said.

'Yes, and three of them walked out and were incinerated less than two minutes later,' Nellis agreed. 'They all were identified as members of Majestic Twelve and they appear to have escaped the facility in some way. But then one of them tried to get back inside the facility. He probably heard the jets coming and figured that indoors was the best place to be. It was, for all of sixty seconds.'

Hellerman closed his eyes as he replied.

'And we didn't get any coverage of the site after the initial strike?'

'No,' Nellis replied, almost apologetically. 'The first hits were designed to neutralize any defences and take out anybody in the compound who might have any weapons to take a pot–shot at the second wave. The debris blocked any view from our satellites, even in infra–red, because of the heat. Then two more jets hit the target with the bunker busters, followed by the rest. By the time that cloud had cleared and the fires had burned themselves out, the whole area had been flattened.'

Hellerman nodded and sank back into Lopez's chair.

'No survivors,' he whispered in reply, 'collateral damage.'

Nellis, his hands behind his back, replied as gently as he could.

'It wasn't our decision. The White House made the call. With Warner and Lopez underground there was no way to send a warning, and Garrett shut down the facility's communications suite before he was killed in the blast, so we couldn't have warned any of them even if we'd wanted to. With MJ–12 trapped so completely, it was decided by the president to end this for once and for all.'

Hellerman saw in his mind's eye an image of Jarvis and his fists slowly clenched by his sides.

'Jarvis,' he echoed, struggling to keep the rage from his voice. 'Where is he?'

Nellis sighed.

'He's in the wind. We can't worry about him right now, what do you have on MJ–12's assets?'

Hellerman shook his head slowly and reached for a folder that he handed to Nellis. The General opened the surprisingly slim file and scanned a meagre handful of sheets of paper inside.

'This is it?' he asked, amazed.

'That's all that's left,' Hellerman replied without looking up at Nellis. 'Jarvis was handling the whole thing. When he started I know damned well that we were chasing so many financial leads I figured it would take us at least five years to track everything down, to account for every contact and shell corporation that Majestic Twelve were using. Now, ninety five per cent of it has just disappeared.'

'Disappeared?' Nellis echoed.

'Gone,' Hellerman confirmed, 'moved, buried, hidden, whatever you want to call it. All of our collated data on the financial transactions of Majestic Twelve are gone. What we have left covers assets to a value of about three billions dollars, which is the amount I reported to the National Security Agency and the administration two days ago.'

Three billion dollars was a great deal of money, and Nellis had been able to walk into the White House and report on their work with a great deal of satisfaction, while the President had been able to tell the media that the American tax payer had saved a similar amount of money through the administration's ruthless hunting out of corruption in big business. A leaked document of data containing millions of files and dubbed *The Panama Papers* by the media had revealed the largest transactions routed through corrupt banking practices in the Cayman Islands, some of which belonged to Majestic Twelve. But both he and Hellerman also knew that three billions dollars had represented loose change to Majestic Twelve, merely the tip of their financial iceberg.

'He set this all up, y'know that, right?' Hellerman uttered, and then looked up at Nellis. 'Jarvis.'

Nellis nodded. 'Jarvis had made his mind up that Majestic Twelve could never be fully stopped unless they were eradicated completely. I tried to reason with him and I thought that he was aboard with us, but he had his own agenda. You know he was nearing retirement?'

Hellerman shook his head. 'I thought he'd serve until he was dead.'

'So did I, but privately I think he'd had enough of the game and wanted to do something to finish all of this before he threw in the towel.'

'Was killing Ethan and Nicola a part of his grand design?'

Nellis sighed again, shook his head. 'I just don't know. Go home, get some rest. Majestic Twelve may be gone but they have a huge corporate network that needs dismantling and I'll need you on top form to help us. ARIES isn't over just because our top people have disappeared in the field, Hellerman. You're number one now.'

Nellis turned and marched from the watch room, leaving Hellerman to wonder just what the hell he would do if he did go home. Nothing, other than think about what he could be doing at work.

Hellerman stood up and gave Lopez's desk one last glance, and then he trudged across the watch room to his office and stepped inside, quietly closing the door behind him. He sat down at his desk and stared blankly at his monitor for a moment, wondering whether he wanted to play this game anymore. After graduating from MIT in computer science he had been happily employed at a games company designing three dimensional worlds for virtual reality headsets, before he'd joined the DIA at their request, and had been enthralled at the way the new technology could change the way people lived and communicated as well as the advances in gaming. His former employers would welcome him back with open arms, the pay was better, he could even move back to San Diego.

Hellerman reached out for the phone on his desk, but before his hand touched the receiver his cell phone buzzed in his pocket. Hellerman reached down with a sigh and pulled it out to see a text. His heart skipped a beat as he saw an image of Lopez alongside it.

YOU IN THERE, GENIUS? :)

Hellerman bolted from his chair and yanked the door of his office open to see Lopez standing with her smile as wide and bright as it ever had been. Hellerman didn't even see that her left arm was in a sling as he threw himself at her and hugged her.

'Easy, Einstein,' Lopez gasped, managing to return the embrace with her good arm as she winced against the pain.

Hellerman stood back, barely able to contain himself. 'I thought you were… I mean we all saw what happened and… we figured you'd…'

'So did we,' Ethan said as he strolled up behind Lopez, one side of his face marked with scratches and patched with medical tape, 'but hey, another day, another dollar.'

Hellerman thrust his hand out and shook Ethan's vigorously.

'Nellis was just here,' he informed them. 'We got some of Majestic Twelve's assets but…'

'We know,' Lopez said. 'I always said Jarvis would do something like this, but nobody listened to me.'

'We don't know what he's done yet,' Ethan said cautiously. 'Right now, General Nellis tells us that you're making headway with that sphere we recovered from the Black Knight, *Die Glocke?*'

'It's a computer,' Hellerman nodded, 'and Die Glocke was a monitor of sorts, pre–programmed to descend at a given moment in time. Something made it come down, and whatever that something was is what Majestic Twelve was formed to figure out, before they became corrupted by power and money.'

'Jarvis wanted to know the answer to all of that just as much as we do. Let's figure out where he's gone and then we'll find out why. Are you in, Hellerman?'

Hellerman glanced at the phone on his desk. *Video games, video schmames.*

'Where do you want me to start?'

***

XLIV

Tortola, British Virgin Islands,

Caribbean

The white sands of the private beach stretched for what seemed like endless miles in both directions alongside a glassy, gin clear sea beneath a flawless blue sky. Palms lined the secluded cove, their broad leaves rustling in the warm breeze as Jarvis strolled near the water's edge.

For the first time in as long as he could remember he was not wearing a dark blue suit. Instead, beige slacks and a white shirt were all that he needed, along with the sunglasses that shielded his eyes from the brilliant beach before him.

They would come for him, he knew. Sooner or later, the DIA would set their agents in pursuit of him and he would once again have to look over his shoulder. The joy of his position now was that he had done no wrong. With the media focused entirely on The *Panama Papers* and the scandal causing such uproar in the press, Jarvis had been able to slip silently away and at this time was merely missing in action. Nellis, and Hellerman no doubt, would guess at what had happened but it would take them an age to figure out how he had achieved it: long enough that he would be forever beyond their reach.

He was tired, although the warmth of the beach and the freedom of his flight from the DIA had invigorated his soul. His advancing years had precluded him from ever seeing Majestic Twelve suffer the fate that they truly deserved, the years spent rotting in some cell somewhere, and so he had decided that this last act, this late in his life, would be committed to give him some sense of satisfaction, to know that he had completed what he had set out to do. However, he would never have expected to be doing what he was now doing. The irony of his path was not lost upon him.

At his insistence, the meeting was to take place on a tourist beach at a popular holiday island. Some had been appalled at his choice of location, but Jarvis had always been a firm fan of hiding in plain sight. The DIA and others would be searching for them in exclusive villas or private islands, in the most expensive and salubrious locations on earth, not in bars popular with retirees and vacationing families. Only moderate disguises were required, simple means to conceal one's true identity and avoid easy recognition, especially when most of them were entirely anonymous beyond their offices anyway.

Jarvis reached the small veranda of a bar nestled amid the swaying palms. This early in the morning it was mostly empty, a few vacationers and honeymoon couples sprawling in bliss beneath the sun as he walked onto the veranda and sat down at a table occupied by a small group of men and women.

All of them looked unremarkable, except perhaps for the physical size of the dark skinned man who looked at Jarvis.

'You're alive then,' Jarvis remarked as he sipped from the coffee awaiting him.

Aaron Mitchell raised an eyebrow. Beneath his loose shirt Jarvis could see fresh wounds concealed by medical tape and what was probably carefully applied make up, but Mitchell seemed otherwise intact.

'No thanks to you,' he growled.

'Ethan and Nicola?' Jarvis asked, genuine concern in his voice.

Mitchell leaned forward on the table between them. 'They got out just in front of me. They made it.'

Jarvis sighed and sank back into his chair as the coffee and warm sunshine suddenly seemed to take effect on him and the last tight knots of anxiety unwound somewhere deep inside his belly.

'So, we're all good then,' he smiled finally.

On the opposite side of the table, Rhys Garrett raised a glass of what looked like sparkling champagne in Jarvis's direction.

'Three billion down, but still standing.'

'Don't knock it,' Jarvis replied, 'you can't spend money when you're dead. How did the leak go?'

'I take it you've seen the news?' Garrett replied. 'I managed to warn most of my clients before the leak was made, and it'll probably sink *Mossack Fonseca* in the long run, but it covers the presence of Majestic Twelve's missing money for now.'

The Panama legal firm *Mossack Fonseca* had been the source of a massive data leak of clients who were subject to international sanctions. Dozens of individuals and companies under sanctions by the US Treasury had been exposed, with *Mossack Fonseca* registering companies as offshore entities operated under its own name to conceal the identities of the real owners. Although some clients were registered before international sanctions were imposed, *Mossack Fonseca* had continued to act as a proxy after they were blacklisted. No less than eleven million documents held by the Panama–based law firm were discreetly passed to the German newspaper *Sueddeutsche Zeitung*, which shared them with the International Consortium of Investigative Journalists and media organisations in over seventy countries to show how the firm had helped clients launder money, dodge sanctions and evade taxes.

'Majestic Twelve's assets will now be frozen to the tune of three billion dollars,' Garret said, 'and in fact they probably already have been. The rest…'

Garret shrugged and smiled as Jarvis sipped from his coffee as he turned to look at the other people around the table, and smiled at a young blonde woman whom he recognized instantly.

'Lucy, glad you could make it.'

'Grandpa,' Doctor Lucy Morgan replied with a slightly nervous smile. 'Why'd you bring me all the way down here from Chicago? I was working on a project for the museum. What do The Panama Papers have to do with you? And what's Majestic Twelve?'

'It's a long story, Lucy, but you know that Ethan Warner worked for me and has helped you too on occasion with sensitive investigations into your work.'

'He saved my life,' Lucy acknowledged, 'more than once. Is he involved in this?'

'He still works for the DIA,' Jarvis explained, 'but I don't. Majestic Twelve was a cabal that had infiltrated governments and corporations around the world and was manipulating politics and world markets for their own benefit. They maintained the boom–bust cycle of international banking, making appalling profits each time as ordinary people suffered. The Panama Papers are the result of their exposure and destruction.'

'What does that have to do with me being here?' Lucy asked.

'All will be revealed,' Jarvis replied, and then looked across the table. 'Rhys, would you do me the honor of introducing our guests?'

Garret gestured to a woman sitting alongside Jarvis, who might have been forty years old but glowed with health and vitality.

'This is Lillian Cruz,' he said. 'Lillian had business with Majestic Twelve some years ago after a series of events in New Mexico, with which I'm sure you are familiar?'

'I am,' Jarvis replied, 'but others here are not. Lillian, if you could explain why you're here?'

Lillian spoke clearly and with extraordinary confidence.

'My name is Lillian Cruz and I was born in Montrose, Colorado, in the year 1824. I am the last survivor of eight soldiers of the Union army who took sanctuary in a place called Misery Hole in New Mexico in 1862, just after the Battle of Glorietta Pass.'

A silence enveloped the table, and Lucy Morgan stared blankly at Cruz. 'That's ridiculous.'

'It's true,' Jarvis replied. 'Lillian?'

'I was hunted by Majestic Twelve,' Lillian went on, 'in particular by a man named Jeb Oppenheimer, who was intent on discovering the secret to immortality. I and my husband, along with a small troop of former soldiers, had hidden from enemy soldiers in a cave in New Mexico and drank water from a subterranean cave that slowed the ageing process via a bacteria present in the water known as *Bacillus permians*. Oppenheimer killed the other members of the group, my husband included, but I survived long enough to cut a deal with MJ–12 after Oppenheimer died. They got the elixir of life, I got my freedom from persecution. The deal was struck with a man named Gregory Hampton III, whom I now understand to be deceased, along with the rest of MJ–12.'

'He is,' Jarvis confirmed, and then looked at another young woman at the table, with long dark hair and intelligent eyes. 'And you, my dear?'

'My name is Amber Ryan, and my uncle was a man named Stanley Meyer. He invented a fusion device that could have powered the world for free, but was killed by Majestic Twelve before he could give the fusion cage he built away for nothing because it would have cost them profits from oil interests.'

Amber's introduction was almost spat across the table, enough so that nobody present could deny the contempt in which she held men of power. Jarvis looked across at Mitchell, and the big man hesitated in silence for a moment before his deep and melodious voice rumbled across the table.

'My name is Aaron Mitchell, and I am a Vietnam veteran and long service assassin for Majestic Twelve.'

Amber Ryan's eyes flew wide and she sucked in a deep breath as she stared in horror at Mitchell, who directed his dark gaze in her direction.

'I did not kill Stanley Meyer but I am directly responsible for his death.'

From nowhere Mitchell produced a pistol that he placed on the table and slid across to Amber Ryan. Jarvis almost backed up out of his seat as Garrett leaned forward, his eyes fixed on the weapon.

'This isn't why we're here,' he warned Mitchell.

Amber stared at the pistol and then at Mitchell. 'My uncle died because he wanted to do the right thing,' she snarled.

Mitchell said nothing, simply sat in silence and watched Amber. Jarvis took a breath as he watched the young woman who had lost so much.

'That's right,' Jarvis said. 'He did the right thing.'

Amber shot Jarvis a glance, and in a moment they shared an understanding. Amber Ryan was too sharp to miss Jarvis's point as she turned back to Mitchell. 'Why are you here?'

'To put right what was done wrong,' Mitchell replied. 'You can either help me, pick up that gun and kill me or walk away from this table and never come back.'

A silence enveloped the table as Amber Ryan looked from the pistol and back to Mitchell, bit her lip, her hands twitching as she fought with the demons that must be screaming through her mind, willing her to pick up the gun and kill the assassin who had caused so much pain to so many.

Amber flinched as though she were about to pick up the gun, and then she hissed her response.

'It's not what Stanley would have done,' she muttered as she pushed the weapon back toward Mitchell.

Another man who sat alongside Rhys Garrett, a bespectacled and bearded scientist by the name of Martin Beauchamp, spoke softly to Amber.

'I'm glad you think so. This is not a gathering built around vengeance, but one conceived by hope. We have all lost a great deal, but have far more to gain by working together now.'

Jarvis breathed a sigh of relief as he saw Garrett stand up and lift his champagne glass again.

'My name is Rhys Garrett, and my father was a scientist named Aubrey Channing who was murdered by Jeb Oppenheimer, the same man who hunted Lillian Cruz and former member of Majestic Twelve. It has been my life's work to hunt MJ–12 down and destroy them, which I have now done with Doug Jarvis's help and that of the Defense Intelligence Agency, although they don't know it.' He smiled. 'A scourge of humanity has been slain, and a new future awaits us all.'

Lucy Morgan, who had watched the exchange in amazement, shook her head in wonder.

'Will somebody tell me what the hell is going on here?'

'You have all been chosen because you have all suffered, in one way or another, at the hands of the cabal known as Majestic Twelve,' Garrett said. 'That cabal is no more, but I can tell you that their entire assets...' Garrett looked pointedly at Jarvis. '... minus three billion dollars, now sit in off shore accounts in my name, and all of yours.'

Lucy Morgan's eyes widened. 'Say what now?'

'Six account names, spread evenly with a hundred twelve accounts to each name,' Garrett said, 'totalling one point four trillion dollars in cash, assets and shares.'

Even Jarvis had not expected such a sum, and he forced himself not to cough on his coffee as Cruz, cool as ever, shrugged.

'What makes you think we'd want any of their blood money?'

'Speak for yourself honey,' Amber Ryan replied, 'but I could do a lot of good with that money, just like my uncle would have done.'

'That's the idea,' Jarvis said with an easy smile. 'There's a lot to be done and unless any of you have any objections, we'd like all of you to be working together to ensure that the future of our planet is not controlled by corporations.'

'You want us to be the next Majestic Twelve?' Lucy Morgan uttered in disbelief.

'Not the next Majestic Twelve,' Jarvis countered, 'more like the Reluctant Six. MJ–12's legacy is a lot of suffering across the globe. We can change that. It all depends on how much involvement you want? None of us would blame any of you for choosing to walk away from the table.'

Cruz frowned. 'And how would we be going about this new crusade of yours?'

Jarvis and Garret exchanged a glance, and Garrett willingly gestured for Jarvis to continue. 'This is your area of expertise, Doug.'

Jarvis set his coffee cup down before he spoke.

'Our politicians do not really control our countries,' he began. 'Big corporations do, and most are as corrupt as they come. Our leaders routinely sell arms to countries that defy international human rights laws if the money's right, allow millions to die in squalor while pharmaceutical companies profit from new medicines that those countries cannot afford. We cannot operate within those confines and thus beyond them we will be opposed, persecuted and even hunted down as criminals, often by our own countrymen. The only thing we have on our side is the financial power bequeathed us by Majestic Twelve and safely harboured by Rhys Garrett, and the corruption of the people we'll be hunting: they'll do *anything* to avoid exposure and loss of wealth or power, and I intend to grab every last one of them by the balls and squeeze real hard. Politics likes the *status quo*, of an elite controlling what happens and hoping the people won't notice, and we're going to blow that out of the water. The Panama Papers is just the first step.'

Jarvis stood up and looked at them all as the warm breeze gusted across the beach.

'We have a lot to do and it starts here. There are those who believe that our race faces extinction in the next few decades, an event that Majestic Twelve were keen to expedite. We're now here to do everything we can to prevent it. Who's in?'

***

ABOUT THE AUTHOR

Dean Crawford is the author of the internationally published series of thrillers featuring *Ethan Warner*, a former United States Marine now employed by a government agency tasked with investigating unusual scientific phenomena. The novels have been *Sunday Times* paperback best-sellers and have gained the interest of major Hollywood production studios. He is also the enthusiastic author of many independently published Science Fiction novels.

www.deancrawfordbooks.com

14191407R00168

Printed in Poland
by Amazon Fulfillment
Poland Sp. z o.o., Wrocław